The Greystone Chronicles

Book 5

World at War

By

Dave Willmarth

The story so far…

Alexander and his core group – Brick, Max, Sasha, Lainey, and Jules – have built up Dire Keep into the Kingdom of Elysia. In addition to the Dire Woods that originally made up the lands granted to Alexander and friends, they discovered and claimed an entire forest valley up on the plateau above the keep.

They battled an orc horde that invaded their lands from the north, driven by Molgo and his minotaur army. After defeating the orcs by killing their warlord, Alexander made allies of the minotaurs and the remaining orcs. They moved into the two vacant villages up on the plateau and are considering becoming Elysians.

King Alexander and his citizens also had to defend against on army of demons and undead that attacked both on the plateau above, and the keep below. They were eventually victorious, even though the demons sent an undead dragon slave against them. But the losses of npc citizens that he had promised to protect was wearing on Alexander's conscience.

The guild defeated the player-killer guild PWP, as well as its ally Chaos Nation, both of which were controlled by the mysterious 'Dark One' and were based in Antalia. They uncovered and thwarted a plot to kill Queen Margaret, destroying the presence of the drow and the Dark One's other minions in that city. In the process, they claimed both guild houses, created a compound, and establish an Elysian embassy in the city.

The Dark One, having lost Antalia to Alexander and company, has moved on to the Kingdom of Damerion where he kidnapped and tortured two of its princes in an attempt to gain knowledge of a secret entrance to the palace. Fitz has gone to investigate, taking Sophie with him. Meanwhile the strife between Alexander and Matt, also known as the Dark One, continues. Matt is determined to destroy Alexander, his family, Olympus, and Jupiter Tech using any means necessary, in and out of the game.

Fibble has been given the ability to control his stats and growth path, and named Champion by Hermes, god of thieves and travelers. This mischievous god has given the little goblin some extra skills, making it so that no cookie or pillow anywhere in the keep is safe.

And in the real world, doctors have expressed concern that Jules' brain has sync'd so completely with the game that she might not want to, or be able to, return to her own body. Her body has healed from the trauma she suffered, and they've determined she needs to be awakened…

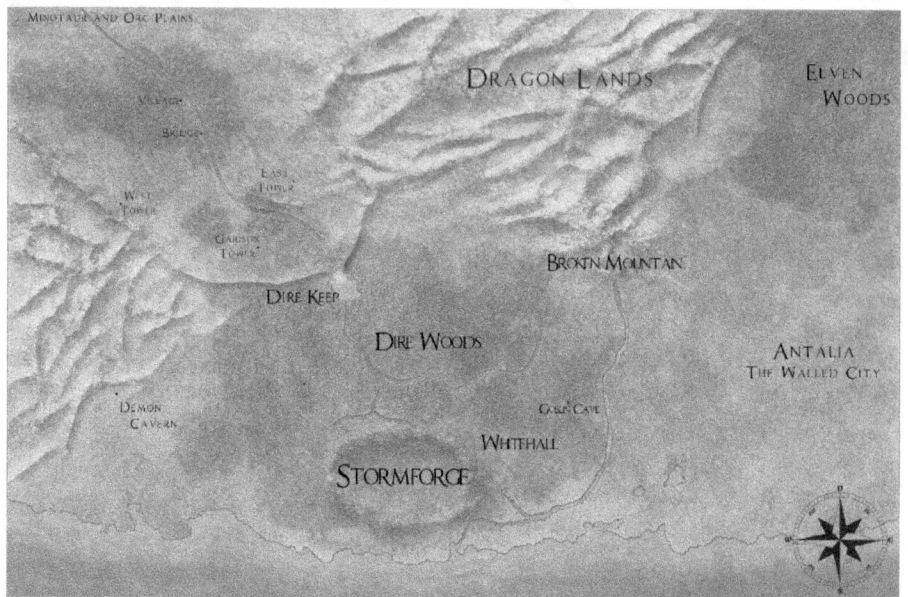

Chapter 1

Rebirth

Alexander woke in the morning with a thick head. The celebration had gone on until the early hours of the morning. He had no idea how much he'd had to drink, but he knew it was too much. He turned his head to look at Jules. Somehow she managed to be in her pink bunnymonster pajamas. She'd been just as drunk as he was, if not more. Right now, she was snoring softly and drooling on his shoulder.

From the angle of the light coming through the windows, it was nearly noon. Alexander didn't hear much activity outside. The entire keep participated in the night's festivities. And for the first time since they'd claimed this keep, Alexander didn't feel like an army might attack at any moment. It was good his people got a chance to rest and relax.

He carefully slid his arm out from under Jules' head. Though he needn't have bothered. He doubted he could wake her with a bass drum and a trumpet. She wasn't a morning person at the best of times. Hungover Jules would probably sleep until sunset.

He stepped into the shower and let cold water run over him. His heart rate jumped and the blood pumped oxygen through his system. Well, in the real world. His real-world heart rate was being elevated. He wasn't sure if his avatar really needed oxygen, or whether it was just a mechanic that kicked in for specific circumstances. Like when he was underwater.

Drying off, he equipped all his gear and headed down to the kitchen. First things first. He needed bacon and eggs and maybe a pitcher of water to get rid of this hangover. He tried a healing spell on himself, but the hangover within the game system was more of a debuff and not so easily cured. Besides, bacon and eggs were a tasty way to fix his head.

There were more people than he expected in the dining area outside the kitchen. It was the silence. Normally, a crowd this large would be chatting and laughing. Not today. Everyone ate in silence, some barely awake, others still drunk.

Alexander took a seat, smiling at citizens who couldn't have cared less at that moment. He was about to dig into his meal when everyone else froze. Everyone except Helga, who was a few tables away. She noticed the freeze and knew what it meant. "Uh oh. Daddy pissed at you for getting so drunk last night?"

Richard's avatar walked up to stand next to Alexander. He smiled at Helga. "Just a little family business to discuss. How's your head?"

Helga rolled her eyes, then let her head fall, forehead slamming into the table and making the dishes jump. Richard chuckled. "Go find the priest. He can cleanse the debuff from you."

Turning to Alexander, he said, "We need to talk." Before Alexander could even respond, the two of them appeared in the grey room referred to as limbo.

"What's wrong, Pop?" Alexander was instantly wary. His father wouldn't pull him out of the game unless it were for something important. Last time, it had been the death of their friend Dayle.

Richard waved a hand and two soft chairs appeared in the room. He motioned for Alexander to take a seat and took the other himself. "I need to talk to you about Jules."

Alexander tried to be funny. "Hey, umm… if this is about the birds and the bees, I'm good, Dad. Really."

Richard grinned at him. "No, son. It's about Jules' health. Her current status. She's now reached a sync level higher than yours. Higher than anyone's. At the same time, the pod has healed her body enough that she can re-inhabit it without pain. Well, not much pain. Her muscles haven't been used in a long time and the nanites in the pod can only stimulate them so much."

Alexander interrupted him. "She's like, really healed? As in, she could get up and walk around?"

Richard held up a hand. "Slow down, son. Yes, she's healed. But she won't just get up and walk around. She's been in her elf body nonstop for months. She'll have to re-learn how to operate her human body. It'll take a good bit of therapy, or so I'm told. But there's an issue."

Alexander's face tightened up. Here it was. The reason his father had pulled him out. His gut clenched and his heart rate sped up.

"We're not sure Jules is going to be willing to go back to her body. The game has been her world for so long. And her body, at least in her mind, represents pain and darkness. Her sync level is so high that she likely views the game as more real than the real world now. We're worried that if we try to revive her, her consciousness just won't make the connection."

Alexander shook his head. "She's told me lots of times that she can't wait to get into her real body so we can..." He paused and blushed a bit. "So we can meet face to face. Hold hands 'n stuff."

Richard chuckled despite the seriousness of the conversation. "Well, that's what I want to speak to you about. We need you to prepare her. Talk to her. Make sure she's anxious to wake up. Promise her lots of that… hand holding, if you have to." He winked as he said it. "Anything you can do to motivate her to jump back into her body when it wakes will help her."

Alexander nodded his head. "I can do that. When do you want to wake her up?"

"Ideally, as soon as possible. The longer we wait, the harder it may be. How about tonight?"

"Tonight can work. I'll go wake her up. Spend the day with her. Everything else around the keep can wait. Others can handle it. This is the most important thing right now."

Richard leaned forward and placed a hand on his son's shoulder. "I need to be sure you're prepared, too. This isn't going to be the handsome prince kissing the princess and she just wakes up and birds sing and everything is fine. First, you're just not that handsome."

Alexander rolled his eyes. "I get it, Pop. She's going to need time and therapy and... none of that matters. I'll be there for her. Just like you and Lainey and Sasha have been there for me."

Richard nodded. "Good. That's what I hoped to hear. Go wake her up. I'll see you tonight. We'll pull you out, too. Your pods are close by, so you'll be there when she wakes."

Another wave of his hand and Alexander was back in the dining area, the citizens around him eating and moving again. Well, not Helga. She appeared to have fallen asleep face down on the table.

Alexander quickly scarfed down his breakfast. He drank a couple mugs of water and got up to return his dishes to the kitchen. He found Sasha there, looking much like he'd imagined she felt. Her hair stuck up everywhere and her eyes were bloodshot.

He couldn't resist. Setting down his dishes, he ran up and grabbed her in a bear hug, spinning her around. "Good morning, sunshine! Did you have fun last night? I've got some BIG news!" he practically yelled, causing Sasha and everyone else in the kitchen to wince. He took pity on them and lowered his voice. "Come with me. You can eat later."

He grabbed her hand and pulled her toward her lab, which was near the kitchen.

"But... coffee," she protested weakly. She trotted along behind him, grumbling about morning people, until he closed the door behind them. Looking her in the eye, he said, "We're going to wake Jules up."

Sasha shook her head. "Look, I get that you're in a good mood for whatever reason. But Jules is drunk and you need to just let her be. And I'm certainly not gonna help you plan some ridiculous prank that'll just make her mad."

She stopped speaking because Alexander was grinning and shaking his head *no*. Finally, he said, "No, in the *real world*. Dad just pulled me into limbo. We're going to wake Jules up in her real body tonight."

Sasha didn't catch on for several more seconds. Her fuzzy brain put the words together, then her eyes got as big as saucers. "Oh my god!

She's ready? Like, fully cooked? I mean, she's fully healed 'n everything?"

Alexander nodded excitedly. "And we need to pull her out, cuz the science types are worried she's grown to prefer the game world and might not be willing to go back to her body."

"Pshaw!" Sasha slapped his chest. "Nothing she wants more. She has plans for you, my friend." She poked him in the gut. "You should probably hit the real-world gym. You'll wanna look good when she…" She stopped and giggled at the horrified look on her best friend's face. Then she realized what he was thinking.

"Oh my god. No, no, no! I didn't mean that. You're fine. I mean, she knows all about your problems and she's not expecting…" She slammed her hand across her face. A tear rolled down her cheek as she looked into his eyes. "Shit, I'm sorry, Alexander. I'm not thinking straight. Just know that she wants to wake up more than anything. To be with you."

Alexander's mind was reeling. He'd thought often about being with Jules in the real world. And he'd considered his body's limitations. But mostly around the fact that it wouldn't last for all that long, and that their time together would be short. He'd never considered the more… personal logistics.

Sasha could see his thoughts reflected across his face. She slapped his face lightly to get his attention. "Don't. Just don't. It'll be just fine. Trust me. Now go wake up your princess and let me get some coffee in me."

Alexander nodded and started for the door. "Uhm… I'm going to be offline tonight and maybe tomorrow. Could you and the others make sure this place doesn't burn down?"

Sasha snorted at him. "It's not like you actually do much to run this place. We'll barely notice you're gone."

He smirked at her as he opened the door and exited. He walked slowly on his way through the main keep and up the stairs to his quarters, mumbling to himself, "Sasha's right. Jules talks about being together in the real world all the time. She's ready for this. She has to be."

Entering the bedroom, he saw that Jules had rolled onto her back. Her pink furry arms and legs were sprawled wide across the oversized bed and she was snoring loudly. Smiling to himself, he reached down and tickled her nose. She made a face and snorted a few times. Then went back to snoring. One of her hands twitched a bit.

Rather than pulling a prank on his drunken bunnymonster, he leaned over and kissed her. The kiss was long and soft, and she responded initially without even waking up. He extended the kiss until she had to gasp for breath, opening her eyes. When she looked surprised to see him, he grinned.

"Just who did you think you were kissing?" he asked with mock indignation.

"Uhmmm… Brick? I was dreaming that I was Sleeping Beauty and he woke me. Just like he did you." She pushed his face away and tried to roll over.

"Oh no, you don't. I need you awake. C'mon. Get up. Really. We need to talk. Let's get you in the shower then down for some breakfast. In fact, you get in the shower and I'll run and fetch your breakfast back here. Today is just you and me, all day."

His tone caused her to frown, though she didn't open her eyes. She waved at him to go away and mumbled something inaudible.

"Okay, I tried. One last chance to get up before it's ticklefight time."

"Nooooo! No tickles. No. Sleep. Sleep is good. Big head. Go away."

Alexander grinned. He truly loved this woman, though they'd only known each other a short time. He decided to give her ten more minutes. "I'm going to get your breakfast. Some oatmeal and vegetables. Be back in ten."

"Pancakes!" she demanded. "You bring me vegetables and I'll hurt you."

Somehow a dagger appeared in her hand. Alexander just shook his head as he left the room.

When he reached the kitchen, he found Sasha there again. "How'd it go?"

He grimaced. "Round one goes to her. But I'm gathering more ammo and going back in." He grabbed a plate and started piling on pancakes. Sasha snorted, handing him a bottle of syrup. He nodded his thanks and grabbed a pitcher of water and an apple as he passed.

He took his time getting back upstairs. Setting down the food and drink on a side table, he hopped onto the bed, sprawling across Jules and rolling back and forth over top of her. "Up, up, up! I have pancakes!"

"Mmmph."

"No, no. Up you go. Shower time. Then breakfast. Yummy pancakes." He poked her ribs gently, indicating his willingness to escalate to the tickle phase. She pulled back and curled into a ball with her back to him.

"Jules not here now. Check back tomorrow."

With a sigh, he got up and walked around to her side of the bed. Sliding his arms underneath her, he lifted her pink, fuzzy body up and carried her into the bathroom. Setting her down in the tub, he turned on the cold water.

The moment the cold water seeped into her footed jammies she yanked them back and sprang out of the tub.

"Cold! That was *mean.* I don't like you." She stomped a squishy foot on the floor.

"Now that you're up, get out of those jammies and grab a shower. Hot or cold, your choice. Then come out and get your breakfast." He grabbed her and pulled her close, giving her a deep kiss and bending her backward. Then he gave her a slap on the rear and walked away.

He heard her mumble, "I definitely don't like you." Then he heard her bunny suit shuffle to the floor and her feet slap against the tile as she walked to the shower.

Ten minutes later, she emerged from the bathroom. Her hair was still wet, but she was dressed in her full black leather armor. Without a word, she took a seat at the table where he'd set up her breakfast. She ignored him as she poured syrup over the very tall stack of pancakes and then dug in. Alexander waited patiently, knowing the silent treatment was only partly about him not letting her sleep and partly about her voracious appetite.

When she slowed down a bit, he said, "I have something important I want to talk to you about. I thought we might take a walk? Or visit Stormforge? Maybe have lunch in that little garden at the Stallion?"

That got her attention. She looked up at him. "Is something wrong? Why are you being so... nice?" She made a face at him that was half playful, half suspicious. He grinned at her and did his best to look innocent.

"I can't be nice to the woman I love? Even after she threatened to stick me with a sharp knife in my own bed?"

Now it was her turn to grin. "You should know by now. Don't let the pink fur fool you. It's not safe to wake the sleeping bunny."

She finished eating and set down the fork. She eyed the apple sitting next to her plate, but her stomach now held something like ten pancakes. The apple went into her bag for later. "Okay, yes. I would love to spend the day with you. We can walk, and talk, and have a romantic lunch. But not with whatever you have to tell me hanging over our heads. So just tell me, then we can have our day."

Alexander took a deep breath. She was right. Better to just rip off the band-aid. "I got a visit from my father this morning. They want to wake you up. Tonight." He watched her face carefully, but couldn't tell what she was thinking. He quickly continued, "Your body has healed. It'll feel a little stiff, and you'll have to get used to it again. But you're healthy enough to come back to the real world. To hold my real hand." He reached out and took her hand in his. She gripped it tightly as tears flowed down her cheeks.

"I... didn't expect this so soon. I mean, how can I be healed already?" she whispered.

Alexander pulled his chair over and sat right next to her. He put an arm around her. "You've been in your pod for months. The structural damage to your bones has mended. Tissue damage, too. The nanites have been stimulating your muscles so they don't atrophy. At least, not too badly. There's just one concern."

She looked up at him, waiting for him to continue. He saw fear in her eyes and it was like a punch to his gut.

"The docs are worried about your brain. Your sync level is now higher than anyone's. Your mind has accepted Io as the real world just as much, if not more, than the actual real world. I tried to tell them all they have to do is put a stack of pancakes next to your pod and you'd break the glass trying to get out…"

She smiled softly and squeezed his hand at that. "I'd… will you be there?"

He nodded. "I'm going to log out the same time as you. It'll take me a few minutes to reach you, but they'll still be checking your vitals and helping you out of the pod. Don't worry, I'll wait outside 'til you're decent, so there won't be any peeking." She barked a small laugh at that.

"I'm… scared. My body hurt so much before…" She gulped. "Before the blackness. Even in the blackness I could feel some of the pain. My body gave up. It wanted to die. I'm not even sure why it didn't."

"Because you were waiting for me," he answered. "You held on long enough for us to find each other in here. Call it fate. Luck. Whatever you want. But now that I have you, I can't imagine life without you. So you WILL wake up in your body tonight, right?"

She nodded her head, unable to speak. He could feel her trembling and squeezed her tighter against himself. He rubbed her back and kissed the top of her head to reassure her.

After half an hour of just sitting and being close, she said, "I'll be there. I promise. When they wake me up. I'll be there. Nothing could stop me. I love you."

Alexander's heart soared. He believed her. The steel in her voice told him she'd do what it took to make sure she left immersion and re-inhabited her body.

For the rest of the day, the two of them just wandered around. They walked the keep hand in hand, talking to citizens and visiting with Rocky. They found Lugs in the stables, asleep on his back and hugging Fibble like a teddy bear. Alexander took a screen shot and made a note to ask someone to print T-shirts. The little goblin was snoring nearly as loudly as his ogre mount.

Alexander teleported them to Stormforge for lunch at the Stallion. He'd warned Taylor and his guards ahead of time, and they grudgingly stayed behind. After lunch, they visited briefly with Lydia, then stopped by the Greystone compound to check on the dwarven Master Smiths.

They sat in the lounge in the mansion, curled up on the sofa. Alexander told her about the Olympus compound and his quarters in the tower. She asked questions about the others. What they looked like in real life. Especially Sasha. Which got them on the topic of Alexander and Sasha growing up together. He told her stories of shenanigans they got into, mostly those that were embarrassing to Sasha.

When the sun grew lower in the sky and the air cooled a bit, they went out onto the balcony and he summoned Tigger. The two of them lounged against the giant white tiger's side as Jules scratched his ear, and he purred contentedly. This was how they'd spent their first evening together, and it seemed to put Jules at ease. The time was approaching quickly.

Finally just as it got dark, Richard appeared. Melanie was next to him, wearing the bunny ears that seemed to have become a sort of uniform for her. Jules got up and hugged them both, crying openly as she thanked them for all they'd done. When she was feeling ready, Melanie took her hand and the two of them disappeared.

Richard looked at his son, who was doing his best to look strong. He patted Alexander's shoulder and said, "She's going to be just fine. Let's go."

*****

Alexander cleared his pod in record time. The moment he woke, he removed his head gear and was pushing at the plexiglass to make it lift faster. He practically ran to the shower, pushing his body as far as he could, then threw on a robe. He was leaving the bathroom when his father knocked.

He handed Alexander a pair of jeans and a button-down shirt. "You want her to see you for the first time in a robe?"

Alexander facepalmed and grabbed the clothes. Thirty seconds later, he was dressed and moving at his best speed toward the door. Richard walked with him, saying Jules was just down the hall a bit. Several staff members passed by, all of them giving Alexander big smiles. They all knew what was happening. Everyone in the building did. Alexander was like their boy prince, and he was about to meet his princess.

Alexander fidgeted outside her door. Richard had gotten word that she was awake, and okay. They needed a few minutes to get her cleaned up and dressed. He'd held Alexander back from just bursting into the room.

When the door finally opened, Alexander's legs felt weak. His father lent him a shoulder to brace himself for a moment until he was steady again. He walked into the room and the staff members who were gathered around Jules parted to make way.

She looked beautiful. They'd brought her a green summer dress that highlighted the green of her eyes. Her hair was freshly washed and still damp, and her skin was pale after so long in the pod. She sat in a wheelchair near the center of the room. Alexander stepped forward as she looked up at him with a small smile that was both nervous and hopeful at the same time.

His voice cracked as he said, "Hi there, beautiful. What's your name?"

Her smile grew as one of the nurses sobbed somewhere behind him. Richard quickly began to clear the room of all non-essential personnel. Only he and Doc Feelgood remained. Alexander didn't trust his legs, so he looked around for a chair and dragged it over. He sat right in front of her, leaning forward. He reached for her hand, then hesitated. "Can I?"

She rolled her eyes at him. "Dork. I've waited all this time to meet you face-to-face and you have to ask if you can hold my hand?" Her voice was faint and a bit scratchy. The doc handed her a glass of water with a straw and guided her hand as she lifted it. After a few sips, she tried again. "Yes. Take my hand." She lifted her hand from her lap unsteadily and Alexander took hold.

"Look at us. Star-crossed lovers in bodies we can barely move. They should write a book about us!" he grinned. She laughed out loud, and he thought it might be the best sound he'd ever heard.

*****

Matt's phone buzzed to alert him of an incoming message. He was just preparing to leave the house with the view of the mountain. Checking his phone, he froze.

"Well, that is unexpected. I'll have to adjust my plans a bit. With Jules awake, Alexander will be out of the game for a while. Maybe several days. They might even leave Olympus," he muttered to himself.

Quickly dialing a number, he waited for an answer, then said, "I need an address."

When he finished that call, he resumed loading up his truck. He traveled light. Several laptops and secure satellite phones, a cooler full of ice and drinks, a couple days' worth of food, and two changes of clothes. Somebody would come into the house after he left and erase any evidence he was ever there. Fingerprints, DNA, all of it.

He'd already chosen his next safe house. It was a foreclosure only about a half-mile from his current location. The house was going up for auction in thirty days, so he could safely squat there for two weeks. Assuming Jupiter Tech's security forces didn't catch up to him before then. He knew they would, eventually. Richard was putting millions into tracking him down. And his people were good.

Matt just wanted to avoid them long enough to hurt the Greystones as much as possible. With his dad in prison, it was up to him to manage the group of people they'd gathered to help execute their plans. Some were simple mercenaries while others were true believers. Simple-minded fools who'd bought his storyline and committed themselves to the fake

16

cause he'd created for them. Ironically, he'd decided on the same ridiculous anti-technology blather preached by the man who'd set off the bomb that killed his mother. It gave the law enforcement people a rabbit to chase and used up Jupiter Tech resources.

Climbing into his truck, he took another look at the top of the tower up on the mountain. "Olympus will run with blood before I'm through. You can't stop my plans now. You're too late."

As he started the truck and pulled into the street, he used his phone to check his bank balance. His family had been wealthy after the death of his mother. His father was smart enough to use the payments from the insurance company and Jupiter Tech to invest. Those investments paid off, and he and his family could have lived comfortable lives without working ever again.

But in recent years, they'd burned through most of it. Some had been set aside for his siblings and would not be touched. Matt had a few million left to work with. Mainly because many of those they'd agreed to pay had been killed or arrested, and never collected. He should actually thank the Greystones for that. Their efforts, along with the FBI's, had kept him from being bankrupted. And he'd find a way to put his remaining funds to use. There was no planning for his future. He knew he didn't have one. He'd be arrested or killed shortly. Maybe both.

No, he had nothing to lose. And that made him dangerous.

*****

Chapter 2

A Normal Life

Alexander and Jules sat on a sofa in his office. They were snuggled close, holding hands as they listened to Richard speak.

"Jules, the nanites in your pod can continue your therapy regimen. They'll stimulate your muscles as you move about in the game, helping to strengthen them. But they're no substitute for actual exercise. It wouldn't hurt you to log out once a week or more and get some physical therapy. Even if that's only a walk through the grounds or a swim in the pool."

He looked at Alexander, who had his eyes closed and a beatific smile on his face. "Ahem. A little more physical therapy wouldn't hurt you either, son."

Alexander opened his eyes. After a second, he got a wicked look in his eyes. "So, what you're saying is that Jules and I need to get more physical." His eyes darted from Jules to the bedroom door behind his father's back. Richard caught the look and rolled his eyes.

"Keep your mind in the game, boy." He tried not to let any of his amusement leak through in his voice. "This is serious. You've shown more improvement than we could have hoped for since you started using the pod. Combined with the drugs, this could be the answer we've been looking for. Not a cure, but a definite step forward."

The hope in his father's voice sobered Alexander. "I'm sorry, Dad. Of course I'm happy to be getting stronger. And I'm grateful for all you've done." He squeezed Jules' hand. "More grateful than I can say. We will do as you say. In fact, we could wheel down to the pool right now and bob around a bit like jellyfish."

Jules smiled. "I'll need someone to help me with a swimsuit. I'm afraid I don't have any clothes except this dress. And I don't think I'm strong enough to change on my own."

Alexander opened his mouth to volunteer but Richard cut him off. "There will be a trainer and a nurse waiting for you. As well as a selection of swimsuits to choose from." He looked at the doctor sitting next to him.

"The doctor will escort you down to the pool while I have a few words with my son."

Jules rose unsteadily to her feet and then fell awkwardly into her wheelchair. The doc pushed her to the elevator and they were gone.

Richard looked at Alexander. "Stop it, boy," he said, in as harsh a voice as Alexander had ever heard him use.

Alexander recoiled. He leaned back on the sofa and the smile disappeared from his face. "What?"

"That girl has just emerged from a year-long coma after being beaten nearly to death by an abusive boyfriend. And you sit here making jokes about sex as exercise and were about to offer to help her change into her suit. That is *not* okay."

Alexander swallowed as the words sank in. He felt guilty and angry and horrified all at the same time. He was so used to in-game Jules that it hadn't occurred to him that real-world Jules would be any different.

"Oh my god. I'm... shit. I'm sorry, Dad. I didn't think. I mean, she has no problems with intimacy in the game and I just assumed... No, that's wrong. I didn't even consider. Damn it. This is going to take some getting used to." He ran his hand through his hair and noticed it was shaking.

Richard's face softened. "I know you love this girl. And that you're also a walking ball of hormones right now. Both of you. But take it easy for now, alright?"

Alexander nodded his head, lost in thought. He was reviewing everything he'd said to Jules since she woke up, trying to remember her face and gauge her reactions. He hadn't seen any sign that he'd hurt her or scared her. But then, he hadn't really been watching.

"Relax, boy. You haven't traumatized her that I've noticed. Just be careful with her. You've got time." He grimaced as he realized the implications of that statement. Alexander didn't have a full lifespan ahead of him. At least, not yet. 'Time' for his son was still something less than a decade at the moment. "Now, get yourself down to the pool. Are you going to stay out here in the real world tomorrow, or go back?"

Alexander shook his head. "I think stay out? Depends on what Jules wants."

"Then I'll leave you alone for the evening. I have some papers for you to review and approve. But it can wait 'til morning." Richard got up and walked with his son to the elevators. He pressed the down button for Alexander and the up button for himself. His quarters were upstairs. When the doors opened, he bid his son good night and stepped in.

Alexander emerged from the elevator on the ground level of the tower. The pool was a bit of a walk, and he was already feeling tired. So he took it slow. He waved at the security guard at the desk and made his way down a corridor that led to several of the recreation facilities. There were actually two pools. One indoors, enclosed in solar glass, and the other outdoors with a large deck area meant more for entertaining than for exercising.

He stopped at his locker in the men's locker room and changed into his swim trunks. They were an impulse purchase on a shopping trip with Sasha. There were dozens of little neon-colored sharks swimming back and forth across the fabric.

Grabbing a clean towel from a stack near the door, he took a deep breath and wandered out to the pool, trying to look casual. Jules was already in the water, as was the trainer. The woman was supporting Jules' back as she did a sort of awkward arm movement that propelled her slowly through the water. Both women smiled at Alexander as he stepped into the water, but continued what they were doing.

Leaving them to it, he moved to one side of the pool and dove under the water. He enjoyed swimming. It took much of the stress off of his body and allowed him more freedom of movement with less effort. He swam underwater to the edge of the pool and surfaced. Then he laid on his back and let the water support him as he copied Jules and stroked his way across to the other end. He didn't put much effort into it, just gave his muscles a small workout. He only used his arms, letting his feet trail behind him. After a half-dozen laps, he began to feel a little fatigued, and stood up at the shallow end.

The trainer brought Jules over and had her stand as well. "That was great. You've made amazing progress, Jules. I'm proud of you. But that's enough for tonight. You guys can stay in here for a few minutes, then I want you out. The cool water's not good for your muscles if you're not moving. Jules, I'll be in the locker room when you're ready. Can you walk that far?"

She nodded and said, "Thank you. If I have any trouble, Alexander will help me. Or we'll shout for you."

She reached out and took Alexander's hand as the trainer left the pool. Pulling him over toward the stairs, they both sat. He could see that she was a little flushed from the exertion of her training session. But she was smiling.

"This is so amazing!" she bubbled with excitement. "I never dreamed my life could be like this, even before my… well, you know. How did I get so lucky?"

He grinned at her, splashing a little water in her direction. "You mean, how did you get lucky enough to land a super-rich boyfriend with his own castle and medical teams and gourmet chefs and access to a whole virtual world where you can kill things with sharp knives?"

"Yep, that's exactly what I meant," she laughed.

His eyes unfocused as he thought about the earlier conversation with his dad. "You… you know that we may not have much time together. A few years. That's the big drawback to the lucky rich boyfriend castle life. It doesn't last."

She squeezed his hand. "It'll last forever." Standing up slowly, she added, "Stop being such a buzzkill! This is my first night back in the world. Walk me to my personal valet so that I may transform from my current mermaid incarnation back to supermodel. Then we can eat some pancakes. I assume a prince can make pancakes happen?"

He grinned at that. "You are more beautiful than any mermaid or supermodel, my lady. Allow your humble prince to escort you." He rose himself, his legs only slightly steadier than hers. He put an arm around her waist and offered his other hand to her. Together, they walked slowly but surely across the room to the locker room entrance. From there she used the wall to steady herself as she moved inside.

As soon as she was out of sight, Alexander turned and made his way to get himself changed. After being in the water, his body felt heavier and more awkward. But his heart was soaring.

*****

Lugs woke up to a foul smell that threatened to burn his nose hairs. "Ugh! What died?" A moment later his left arm vibrated and a loud fart echoed off the walls of the stables. He looked down to see Fibble curled in his arm. The smell emanated from his little friend. "What the hell did you eat last night?" he asked. He slowly moved his arm, lowering the goblin to the straw floor as he held his breath. As soon as Fibble was safely down, he rolled away and gasped for air. "Seriously. How does a stink that big come from such a tiny body?"

Fibble unconsciously raised his butt in the air like a sleeping infant before emitting yet another noxious bomb. Then he smiled and settled back into the straw.

Lugs fled the stables, feeling sorry for any of the livestock trapped in there. The moment he stepped outside, the bright sunlight assaulted his eyes. He closed his eyes and held his head between his massive ogre hands, trying to remain upright. His hangover defeated him and he fell backward onto his rump with a grunt. A few passersby cheered or applauded. He wasn't sure if it was for his fall, or some stunt he'd pulled the night before. He was getting used to that. A surprisingly small amount of alcohol in his big body would send him into drunken shenanigans that he mostly didn't remember. But his friends and neighbors were sure to remind him later.

His eyes finally adjusting, he looked around. Not many people were moving about for what looked like the middle of the day. He guessed the others had celebrated quite a bit too. Getting to his feet, he stumbled to the food place. The dining area. There, he found Helga face-down at a table. He pulled up a stump, which he used to sit at the end of the table, as his body was too big for the benches. Dropping himself onto the stump, he looked longingly toward the kitchen. As hungry as he was, he didn't think he had the energy to get up and fetch food. Then he noticed Helga's uneaten breakfast next to her head.

"Thanks," he mumbled, as he reached across and snagged her plate. The bacon and eggs were cold now, but he didn't care. He wolfed them down, along with a full pitcher of water. With his hunger at least partially abated, he decided to join Helga and put his head down. The table was cool and felt nice against his face.

He was just dozing off when a loud voice invaded his skull. "Mornin, ye lightweights!" Brick thumped Lugs on his back, then slammed his breakfast plate onto the table. "Good party last night." He took a long drink of ale from a mug, then looked at Lugs with a grin. "Yer robot moves were legendary! That'll be the most popular video on the nets today, fer sure!"

Lugs' eyes opened wide, horrified. "Did… you say robot moves?"

"BWAHAHA!" Brick's laughter startled Helga and she fell backward off the bench. "Ye don't remember? First ye thought ye killed Fibble and was cryin' like a girly what lost her dolly. Then when the lil fella came 'round, ye celebrated with some spirits. Next thing we know'd ye was robot'n all 'round the square!"

A few blistering curse words drifted up from where Helga lay on the ground. A hand appeared and latched onto the table as she pulled herself up. "Damned dwarf. Have the decency to be hungover like the rest of us." She looked around for her breakfast, but couldn't find it. Deciding she'd imagined it, she went to kitchen to get some food.

Seeing where she was headed, Lugs called out, "Would you bring me some, too? Please?" He sounded so pathetic she took pity on him and nodded her head.

Brick was happily shoveling scrambled eggs past his beard into his mouth. Lugs just held his head and prayed that Brick was done talking. His prayers were not to be answered.

The dwarf waited for Helga to come back and take a seat. As she handed a heaping plate of food to Lugs, Brick began, "So did ye hear? Jules be wakin' up tonight!"

It was a few seconds before the information registered with either the barbarian woman or the ogre. Helga was first. She dropped her fork and leaned across the table toward Brick. "Like, for real? They're bringing her out of her pod?" At this, Lugs paused mid-shovel with his fork above his plate.

"Yup!" The dwarf had to be purposely talking too loudly. "Alexander took her ta Stormforge fer some quality time. In case somethin' goes badly. Then tonight they'll be wakin' her up and she'll get to see just how ugly Alexander actually be!" He chuckled at his own joke.

Helga shot him a dirty look. "She loves him. And Alexander's not ugly! A little scrawny, maybe. But not ugly. You big musclebound lout!"

Lugs piled on, happy to get a little payback for all the noise. "And among the three of us here, you're the only one who's kissed him like he was Sleeping Beauty." Helga snorted and glared at Brick, who was laughing.

"Ye got me there. Alexander do be pretty enuff, I suppose. Fer a damned elf." He winked at Lugs. The three of them settled into silence as they ate their breakfasts and considered Jules' upcoming rebirth. Eventually Sasha joined them, then one by one the other players drifted in. A sort of impromptu officer's meeting happened with Warren, Lyra, Max, Lainey, Beatrix, Benny, Misty, Grumpy, and even Pollock taking seats at the table. Sasha shared the news with those who hadn't heard and they all took a few minutes to soak it in. The loss of Dayle was still fresh in their minds and hearts, and they were concerned for Jules.

Beatrix lightened the mood. "We'll need to have another party when she comes back!" The table collectively groaned, most of them still hungover from the last party. "No! I mean it! We don't have to go all crazy like last night. But we should show her we're glad she's better. Like, *really* better!"

Sasha and Lainey joined in. "Beatrix is right. We'll make it a small affair in the Great Hall. Just us players and a few of the leading citizens. The O'Malleys can cater it for us. I'm sure they'd be willing," Sasha said.

Lainey added, "We could make her something. A gift of some kind. I mean, what does she like besides knives and leather? And sexy dresses?"

Brick and Lugs spoke in unison: "Pancakes," getting a laugh from several at the table.

Brick continued with a gleam in his eye. "That might not be a bad idea. Serve the lass pancakes fer dinner." Several people up and down the table smiled and nodded at that. He added, "I'll spend a bit o' time at me forge today 'n make her a special knife. We'll say it be from all o' us."

Lainey said, "My leatherworking has taught me a bit about needlework. I'll try my hand at a dress."

Misty sighed. "No, let me. I learned the tailoring skill so I could make my own robes at low-level. It's not very high. And I mostly poke my own fingers with the needle. But maybe if you work on the design and I do the stitching…" Lainey nodded in agreement.

Beatrix looked at Brick. "I can make a gem that you could mount to the dagger. An emerald, do ya think?" The dwarf nodded his head.

When nobody else spoke up, Sasha took over again. "Right. So, Alexander's going to be gone all day and maybe tomorrow. So the rest of you, I need you to help us keep this place in order. Circulate around the keep. Talk to the citizens, see what you can help them with." She looked around. "Grumpy, can you go to the mine and check on them? And the quarry?" When he nodded, she pointed at Warren. "Can you and Lyra go up top? Check on the towers? Bodine and Regina?" Warren and Lyra both agreed. They liked the beastmasters and their zoo.

Turning to Pollock, she said, "I need someone to check in with the orcs at the northern village. If you're willing, I can ask Braxis if he'll fly you up there." When he started to nod, she added, "But no starting any fights. You're getting kinda famous for going berserk and launching yourself into suicidal charges. No beating on our new allies." She winked at him to ease the sting a bit. He blushed and bowed his head.

Lastly, she looked at Benny. "I'll need you here with me. We've got some cleanup to do after the battle. And we should check on all those who were wounded, just to make sure everyone's healed. Plus, Alexander wants to journey to meet the elves soon, so we should get started on those preparations. It'll be an overland trip, as we don't know if they have a portal or how to connect to it." Benny didn't argue.

"Okay then, everyone's got their assignments for the day. I appreciate you all being willing to help out. And hopefully, we'll have both Alexander and Jules back here with us soon." With that, everyone began to disperse to go about their days.

*****

Fitz and Sophie walked through a tunnel beneath the city of Demarion. Fitz had already killed several drow moving about down there and captured two that he had questioned. One had been turned over to King Arand's men and was being questioned. Fitz sincerely hoped the king would come to his senses and realize the threat to his city. In the meantime, Fitz would do what he could.

Rounding a corner, they faced a dead end in the tunnel. Sophie started to turn back but Fitz held out a hand. "There are secret ways in and out of this city that even the king or the thieves' guild don't know about. You must promise me you will never share what you see here."

Sophie grinned and made a 'cross-my-heart' motion with her hand. "I promise, old wizard. Secrets are one thing I'm very good at."

Fitz grunted and stepped toward the end wall. He spoke a few words and touched his staff to the wall. A moment later, an arched doorway appeared and the stone slid to one side. Fitz stepped through and motioned for Sophie to follow.

Once she was through, he turned and faced the tunnel. "Ignus!" he shouted. A wave of fire blasted from his staff at about waist height and spread through the tunnel behind them. Two drow appeared, the flames catching their armor on fire. A bolt of lightning shot from Fitz's staff and the two spies began to fry from the inside out. Blood ran from their eye sockets and one of them bit the tip of her tongue clean off as they convulsed from the channeled lightning.

Sophie dashed out and slit each of their throats as Fitz cancelled the spell, just to make sure they were dead. She looted their bodies and returned to Fitz, handing him a folded parchment. He pocketed it without looking and ushered her back through the door. The stone slid closed behind him and Sophie could see no evidence of its existence.

She was in a workshop of some kind. She only had a moment to take in the workbench covered in alchemical tools and the desk covered in papers and books before Fitz led her through a wooden door and into a tunnel. The floor of the tunnel sloped upward gradually. She noted several traps, which Fitz avoided seemingly without thinking. She followed him carefully so as not to set them off herself, grinning at the fact that he had not alerted her. She was flattered by his assumption that she'd be capable of seeing them. They were not beginner traps by any means.

At the end of the tunnel was another dead end wall. This one had a lever on the side wall, which Fitz pulled downward. Again, the stone moved toward them a bit then slid to one side. The sun shone into the tunnel as Fitz stepped through the door. Sophie followed him out to stand on a ledge overlooking the sea.

Damerion was a port city built on a cliff facing the sea. Down below her, the cliff wall curved around to a small, protected cove, where stone piers stretched out. Half a dozen ships were docked, with a few more at anchor waiting for space. From the docks, the city curled up the rise to the cliff top.

There were three high stone walls protecting the lower part of the city. One just inside the docks stretched around to connect with the cliff on the other side. The second wall was a quarter mile inside the city. This one was shorter, and also extended from cliff to cliff. The third wall protected the palace keep itself. It was only about a quarter-mile long and stood fifty feet high. Damerion was one of the best-defended cities on Io, second only to the dwarven cities that used the mountains themselves as protective barriers.

Fitz waved to the docks, which was the only part of the city Sophie could see from her current vantage. Most of the city was above her, atop the cliffs. "That is where the Dark One will attack if he cannot find his 'back entrance.' What he doesn't know is that there isn't one, other than this one. I helped build this city atop these cliffs a thousand years ago. Only you and I know this route." He paused to impress that last statement upon her. "The docks are vulnerable to attack by ship. The walls are lowest there, and less heavily manned. I need you to convince the king to prepare to defend the docks. Now."

"I'll do my best. What are you going to do?" she asked. She didn't expect an answer from the wizard. He kept his business to himself.

With a wave of his hand, he teleported her back to the palace courtyard. Then he began to climb down a steep, rocky path along the cliff face. Below him, on the north-facing cliff, was a cave. He knew of an old rockworm tunnel that led from that cave to his destination.

The drow who had perished during questioning had refused to tell him where they'd taken the missing princes. But the second drow, seeing how the first had died, told all. Fitz was going to end the Dark One here and now if he could.

A few more steps and he squeezed behind a rock shelf in front of him. The small opening led to a round tunnel that led steeply downward. The worm had been following a vein of some metal or other, and only stopped when it neared the surface and the sound of crashing waves. Fitz followed the tunnel for half a mile deep into the earth. It turned hard left, heading southward toward the forest that lay at the bottom of the sloped side of the mountain. There was an old ruin there that the people of Demarion avoided like the plague. It was infested with undead, a curse placed on the old city by the drow wizards after a battle eons ago.

The tunnel that Fitz followed led him below the old ruins. When his earth sense told him he was in the correct spot, he cast a spell that revealed a door in the side of the tunnel. A door he had placed there himself.

Opening the door, he advanced into a stone corridor carved by dwarves. This was the lowest level of a city even older than the one above occupied by the cursed human undead. Here, the halls were quiet. It had been a small city even in its prime. The dwarves had abandoned it as the humans spread across the land. But dwarves built to last, and other than a deep layer of dust, this city looked as if it could have been newly built.

Fitz followed the main road to a temple off the market square. Within the temple was a tower that rose up to the cavern ceiling above. Unlike Damerion, the dwarves had left themselves several escape routes in the event their city was overrun. This tower was one.

The stairway wound around and up past the top floor of the tower into the rock above. There it connected to another tunnel that rose into what was now the cursed city.

This was where the Dark One hid. Fitz used his earth sense again to check above him before opening the hidden trap door. After climbing the ladder up into the hall, he closed the door behind him. No point in giving the drow a way out.

The old dragon in wizard form closed his eyes and touched a ring on his right hand. A moment later, six more dragons in human form appeared next to him. A full wing of dragons who specialized in hunting drow wizards. And the drow who served them.

Fitz spoke quietly. "The Dark One may be here. Leave him to me. But find the princes if you can. And kill every drow you find. Be careful. Their blades are coated with the dark poison. You all carry antidotes?" When all six nodded, he said, "Go, then. Teams of two. Be careful. Remember Daginalistros."

With fury in their eyes, the six dragons moved off, weapons in hand. They began casting spells that disabled the drow's stealth ability. They spammed the powerful spell every few steps. It sent a bubble of magic forward to expose any hidden assassins. Unlike the other humanoid spell casters, these were creatures born of magic. Their mana was a part of them. And they were ancient creatures. They could cast this spell nonstop for weeks and not begin to drain their mana supply.

Fitz closed his eyes and recalled the words of the drow prisoner. The Dark One had a throne room where he conducted business. It was near the center of the cursed city. Most of his drow servants were stationed near the entrances. Their job was to keep out the wandering dead.

Fitz picked a direction and moved forward. He had no fear of drow assassins; his cousins would have cleared this tunnel already. As if in confirmation, he found a corpse stuffed into an alcove a moment later. Its face was missing, but the skin on its hands confirmed it was a drow. He continued on, turning this way and that until he approached the throne room. He found it seemingly empty. No Dark One sitting atop the dark stone throne, no servants evident.

Knowing better than to just walk into the room, he cast a scrying spell. Several traps revealed themselves. None that could kill him, though. There were poison traps and alarms, and one that released a flammable gas. He chuckled upon seeing that one. Dragons were immune to fire.

Next, he cast the same spell his brethren were using. A bubble of magic spread across the room and exposed four drow guardians standing around the throne. Fitz cast his chain lightning spell. The smell of ozone permeated the air as electricity arced through the four. They clenched their weapons involuntarily as they spasmed. Fitz's version of the spell was ten times more powerful than Alexander's. The drows' bodies were cooked inside their armor, but they didn't make a sound. That is until Fitz released the spell and their corpses clattered to the floor.

Three more drow charged through side doors with weapons drawn. Another, that had somehow approached Fitz from behind, stabbed at him with a poison dagger. The tip managed to penetrate his robe and scratch a narrow line into his skin. But that was enough to transfer the dragon-killing poison. Fitz roared, the mighty sound that came from his human body rattling the room. Answering roars echoed back to him from his cousins, who now had no more need to be quiet.

Fitz spun and drove the butt of his staff through the chest of the drow behind him. His superhuman strength allowed him to then lift the dying dark elf into the air and hurl him into the others as they approached. He took a moment to pull a flask from his belt and drink a mouthful of the antidote before returning the flask to its slot. Then he pointed the business end of his staff at the three living drow.

"Putredine!"

The three warriors slowed, then came to a halt as their skin began to bubble. Their hair fell from their heads in clumps and they began to scream as chunks of their skin sloughed off and fell to the floor. Blood ran from them in a hundred places as they literally rotted away where they stood. In twenty seconds, they were piles of putrefied flesh and brittle bone.

Fitz shook his head. That was a spell he and the others of his race had sworn never to use on humanoids. It was among the most painful ways to die. But the Dark One and the drow wizards had broken ancient covenants through their use of the dark poison. A substance that, while it would kill most living things quickly, was meant to kill dragonkind slowly and painfully.

Fitz stepped over the rotted bodies and moved toward the throne. Another scrying spell told him there was a hidden compartment in the back. There, he found three of the dark orbs used to open portals. He teleported each of them back to the laboratory that he'd just walked Sophie through beneath Damerion. He'd go back and secure them when he was done here.

Beneath the orbs was a container of the poison. Fitz carefully removed it and set it to one side. Below that was a chest, which he also removed. It was trapped, and he didn't have time to fool with it just then. He'd give it to Alexander so that Max or Jules could practice on it. The last thing in the cache was a communication ring. He put that in his bag. The ring likely connected to one of the drow wizards. He might be able to use it to find them later.

Closing the hidden door, he lifted the jar of poison. Moving to the side of the throne, he pulled a scrap of cloth from his robe. He carefully dipped the cloth into the poison and began to rub it along both of the throne's arms. The poison blended easily with the onyx of the chair. Then, for good measure, he coated the rest of the chair.

After that, he produced several needles. Using earth magic, he softened the seat of the throne enough to drive the blunt ends of a dozen needles into the stone until just the tips were visible. Then he coated each of them with the poison as well. As an afterthought, he planted more poison needles into the floor in random spots around the throne. These he left sticking up far enough to penetrate footwear.

As he finished his task, others began to join him in the room. He held up his hands, keeping them back from the throne and the traps around it. He explained about the needles and showed them the poison. They growled their agreement and set about creating traps of their own.

The last pair to arrive brought a human with them. Prince Elrid. Or what was left of him. Though the dragons had healed him when they found him in the dungeon, there was no way to replace his missing hand, or missing eye. They had spells to help him regrow those parts, but they were slow and required some components. This was not the time or place.

Fitz nodded his head. "Prince Elrid. I'm glad to see you alive. Your brother?"

The prince lowered his head. "Dead. Along with his bodyguard and mine. The man in the black leather…" he started, but Fitz cut him off.

"He calls himself the Dark One. An adventurer who serves the drow wizards. We've set traps for him here for when he returns. Hopefully, they will kill him more than once. At the very least, they will send a message. He sought war with the dragons and our allies. Now he has it."

Elrid's eyes widened. "Our allies? Fitz, you're a… dragon?"

One of his escorts laughed. "The eldest of dragons. Fitz was here when the world was new. He's technically our great-grandfather several times removed."

Elrid's head whipped around. "All of you? You're all dragons?" They each nodded. Elrid adjusted quickly. "Then I am at your service. Dragons have saved my life this day. And I pledge my loyalty to the dragon king." He dropped to one knee and bowed his head to Fitz.

"On your feet, boy. I'm no king. I leave that to my progeny. But we'll accept your loyalty. And hopefully your father's as well. I have tried to tell him of the Dark One and the drow infiltrating your city, but he will not listen. He is blinded by his love for you and your brother and thinks to buy back your lives. I will send you to him now. Tell him what you've seen here. Make him listen. And make him prepare to defend the docks. When the Dark One finds you gone and is killed by one or more of our traps, he will be angry. He has forces close by that might overwhelm your city if you do not prepare."

Elrid nodded gravely, put his fist to his chest, and said, "I will tell him. I will tell everyone. In every allied kingdom. We will prepare. You have my word."

Fitz waved a hand and the prince was gone. The other dragons gathered around Fitz and waited. He reached out with his earth sense and smiled. "I think, after we have our fun, we should deny this Dark One his little safe haven here. Two of you remain. Stay hidden and observe.

"The drow holding back the cursed ones are dead?" he asked. When his brethren confirmed, he said, "Good. After he's died a time or two, seal this room and open the earth there." He pointed to a spot on the high ceiling. "Push the opening until you reach the river that runs underground. Flood this place, then leave."

Two of the younger dragons volunteered. Fitz knew they were more than capable of completing their task. Especially with all the drow minions dead. The cursed undead would fill the halls and maybe even the throne room, distracting the Dark One. If they didn't kill him, the traps would. Then they would take away his stronghold. Since he could not be killed permanently, this would have to do.

Assuming he'd set his respawn point for this room, he would die a time or two from the traps, losing levels each time. Then Fitz's people would flood the room, so that each time he respawned, he would drown. As long as the water remained, the Dark One would die again and again without end. At least, that was Fitz's hope.

He and all but the two who would remain teleported away. Fitz appeared on the cliffside where he'd last spoken to Sophie. He took the jar of dark poison and flung it high into the air before incinerating it. The poisonous smoke dissipated quickly and harmlessly in the ocean breeze. Then he teleported himself back to his tower in Stormforge.

*****

Chapter 3

Insanity

The morning sun pierced the window of Alexander's bedroom high in the tower, the light and warmth waking him. Disoriented by the glass and steel around him for a moment, he began to sit up. But resistance on his arm held him down. Looking over, he smiled. There was Jules. Drooling on his shoulder, just as she did in the game.

He laughed to himself, remembering the night before. He had emerged from the locker room to find Melanie standing there waiting for him. She had a wide smile on her face and was practically hopping up and down with excitement. Jumping toward him, she gave him a big hug. "I'm so happy for you!"

He withstood the assault without falling, though he had to put a hand against the wall for balance. "Umm... thank you?"

"You've got your very own princess! And she's like, perfect for you. I mean, she's just what you need to kick your ass or hold your hand when you need it. We got together and made a little surprise for you as soon as we knew she'd be waking up tonight."

Alexander looked warily at the bubbly woman. He waited for her to hand him something. When she didn't, he stuck out a hand. "Okay, what is it?"

She looked down at his hand, realizing what he was thinking. "Oh! It's not something I can give you. I mean, not that I can like, put in your hand. Well, I suppose I could if I had it right here with me, but that would ruin the surprise!" This time she did hop up and down. "I can't wait for you to see!"

Alexander leaned his back against the wall. He hadn't spent this much time on his feet in a while. Melanie noticed and said, "It shouldn't be much longer. I promise. Then we'll get you upstairs for... well, we'll get you tucked in."

Alexander was now more suspicious than ever. He was about to press the woman for information when movement behind her caught his attention. His jaw dropped for a moment, then he couldn't keep from laughing.

The trainer was pushing Jules' chair toward them. His girlfriend held up a hand to stop her, then used her arms to help push herself upright. When she was steady enough, she raised her arms and turned in a slow circle. "What do you think?"

"I think you look amazing!" He walked forward to gather his pink bunnymonster into a hug. Melanie giggled with glee and clapped her hands together. The trainer just grinned.

"We made it kinda fast, so I hope it fits," Melanie said.

Alexander took a step back and held Jules at arm's length. She was covered from head to toe in a pink bunny costume almost identical to the one she wore in-game, from the feet with the padded soles to the ears that stuck up at odd angles. When he let her go, she slowly sat back in the chair. "I'm glad you like it," she grinned. "But I'm kinda tired. Wasn't easy to get into this thing. Though it's very comfortable." She smiled at Melanie. "Any chance we could call it a night?"

They had made their way to the elevator and up to Alexander's office. He pushed her directly to his bedroom and helped her crawl into bed. He was on his way to go sleep on the sofa when she took hold of his hand. "Please, just stay and snuggle with me? No funny business. I'm too sleepy."

And that was how he found himself where he was now. And he couldn't think of anywhere in the world he'd rather be.

He pulled himself free as gently as possible. Jules didn't stir. Apparently she slept as deeply in real life as she did in the game. He doubted she could eat as many pancakes. Which he was about to find out. Moving out to his office and closing the door quietly, he said, "Heimdall, can you connect me to the cafeteria, please?"

A moment later a voice said, "Hello?"

"Good morning. It's Alexander. I was hoping I could have some food brought up, if it's not too much trouble?"

He could hear background laughter as the woman he was speaking to replied, "Would that be... pancakes?" Rolling his eyes, he began to rethink the policy of letting employees watch his feeds.

"Yes, it seems you're way ahead of me. A couple of short stacks with a bottle of maple syrup. Maybe some fruit? And scrambled eggs with bacon. And some orange juice. Please."

"We'll be there in ten minutes, boss," came the short reply, before the line went dead. He imagined the kitchen was having a good laugh at his expense. Not that it mattered. They were laughing more with him than at him. And he appreciated that they seemed to like and accept Jules.

Heimdall's voice floated down from the ceiling. "Your father is on his way down. I alerted him that you were awake."

"Tattletale!" Alexander teased the security AI. Nothing could put him in a bad mood this morning. His father stepped off the elevator a moment later carrying a folder full of documents. He sat at Alexander's desk, formerly his mother's desk, and began to pull out documents. Alexander pulled up a chair opposite him and his father began.

"Nothing complicated here. Most of this is transfers of assets and approvals for additional security spending." He let his son peruse the documents for a few minutes. Finally, Alexander said, "I don't see anything important here. Am I missing something?"

Richard shook his head. "Nope. Michael and I are handling everything. These are just items that require signatures from all of us. You can see Michael and I have already signed off."

Alexander took up a pen and began signing the documents one by one. A minute later, he pushed them back toward his father.

"What else have you got? None of this was worth you making a trip down here to bring to me personally." He eyed his father.

Richard laughed. "Don't worry, this wasn't some kind of test." He reached into the folder and pulled out several more documents. "This is why I'm here. These are the contracts that will get things moving for your charity. The pod production, the staff allocation for application review, medical, legal, marketing, and logistics."

Alexander sat up straighter and took the documents from his father. He began to read carefully, amazed at the amount of work his father had already put into their plan while he was fooling around in the game. He noticed Michael's fingerprints on a lot of what he read as well. "This is incredible, Pop. Thank you. And please remind me to thank Michael too before I go back under. The scope of this… it's even bigger than we discussed."

Richard nodded his head. "I took a few liberties in increasing the budget. For one thing, you've made several million dollars of your own since you went into immersion. The 'See Ya' t-shirt sales have earned you quite a bit. But one of our enterprising staff floated the idea to stream your feed live for subscribers, with the fees collected to be funneled into the charity. It was a good way for us to leak rumors of your charitable work and help fund it. In the last month, the subscription fees have been over three million dollars. And we're only charging ten dollars per month per person." Richard let Alexander do the math.

"Three hundred thousand people are *paying* to watch me play the game?"

"Not just you. There's a subscription channel for most of you. The core four, Lainey, Jules, Grumpy, Lugs, Helga. Warren, Lyra, Benny and Beatrix have followers as well, though they are less popular." Richard paused and flashed a wicked grin at his son. "The most popular behind you and Jules is Fibble. We are, of course, funneling all his proceeds into the charity along with yours. The others are all receiving theirs through direct deposits into their accounts."

Alexander laughed. Fibble as a celebrity. The little fella must be getting into a lot more trouble than he'd noticed.

Richard added, "And that's just the subscription fees. We've been approached by major advertisers. A bidding war has started for ad space next to the feeds. Of course, Jupiter Tech and Io Online are both buying space. We're giving ourselves the family discount. One company has offered a million cash for the rights to market Fibble plushies. And they are currently the top advertising bidder. They want to make a whole line of stuffed Fibbles, Bacons, Tiggers, and so forth. We're going to let them do it, but make them pay more before we agree. And all of that money will go to the charity as well."

Just then, Jules emerged from the bedroom. When she saw Richard, she ducked back behind the door. After a moment, she said, "Screw it," and walked out, proudly displaying the bunnymonster outfit. "Good morning!"

Richard laughed. "I'd heard a rumor, but I thought they were joking. Let me guess. Melanie?"

Jules nodded. "Yep. This thing's pretty comfy, too. Though a little warm. I think I might save it for special occasions." She moved to take the chair next to Alexander.

Alexander took her hand and said, "Ya know how you were all happy about having a rich boyfriend?" Jules blushed and looked guiltily toward Richard, who just smiled warmly. She nodded her head. "Well, turns out… I have a rich girlfriend!"

Jules' face instantly clouded over. She frowned at Alexander, ready to demand to know who this other woman was and why he hadn't mentioned her before. Alexander immediately saw his mistake and said, "You! It's you!" He motioned to his father, who slid a piece of paper across the desk to Jules.

She took it and glanced at it. Then stared at it. "This is a bank statement. With my name on it. And a LOT of numbers."

Richard explained. "You've been earning a salary while you were in the pod. We've been paying you as a tester just like Sasha or Brick or any of the others. In addition, your live stream from the game now has…" He tapped some holo-buttons on the desk and checked her numbers. "Three hundred and forty-two thousand and change subscribers." He tapped a few more buttons and chuckled. "Which is now about ten thousand more than Alexander has. You're one of the most popular feeds in the game right now."

Jules looked confused. Alexander explained, "Dad and the others set up live feed accounts for all of us. People pay a monthly subscription fee to watch us play."

Richard added, "They can only see the 'public' feed. They see nothing that happens inside your living quarters, bathrooms, etc." He held up a hand. "If you'd rather not let them watch your feed, we can disconnect it. But they'll see much of what you do from the others' feeds anyway. I recommend you let them pay you for the privilege."

Jules took another look at the bank statement and sat up a bit straighter. "So I'm like… a celebrity?"

Alexander squeezed her fur-covered knee. "Yep! Apparently a bigger one than me. So from now on, YOU buy the pancakes!" She rolled her eyes at him. Just then, the elevator door dinged and one of the chefs from the cafeteria pushed a room service cart into the office. "Speaking of pancakes… you asked me last night if a prince could make pancakes happen. Ta-da!" He waved toward the oncoming breakfast.

Jules clapped her fuzz-covered mittens together and then leaned over to kiss him. "My hero!"

The chef began to place covered dishes on the small table between the two of them. Richard got up, stuffing all the papers back into his folder - except the charity docs. He cleared his throat to get his son's attention. Alexander quickly grabbed a pen and signed the remaining contracts. Handing them to his dad, he said, "Thank you again. This is all wonderful."

Richard just nodded, and he and the chef made their way to the elevator, leaving the two young people to their breakfast.

*****

Matt was set up in his new safehouse. The truck was unloaded in the dark hours of early morning while the neighbors were asleep. The windows were covered from the inside so that no light would shine through in the rooms he was using. He sat back in his recliner and slid on his old modified headset.

A moment later, he awoke in his avatar, sitting on his throne deep underground. Immediately, he felt several small pinpricks on the backs of his thighs and his butt. A debuff appeared on his UI showing that he was poisoned. His health bar began to tick down rapidly and he shouted for his guards. No one responded. He reached into his inventory, searching for a poison antidote, but didn't find one. "Traitors!" he shouted. "I'll skin you alive and send your faithless corpses back to the wizards!" He coughed out the last few words as his health bar ticked down to zero. A moment later, he was in limbo, watching his respawn timer tick down.

The two dragons in the room flashed each other feral smiles and sat back to wait for the next part of the show. They'd already sealed the room and moved the earth above so that just a minor shove of earth magic from either of them would unleash the river upon the room. One of them pulled out a stick of hard candy and broke it in half, offering a piece to his companion. Dragons had a wicked sweet tooth when in human form.

A few minutes later, the Dark One appeared, once again sitting on his throne. Once again, he was stuck by the poison needles, though he'd tried to leap up and avoid them. With a furious growl, he removed a sword from his back and hacked at the needles on the throne's seat. He managed to break them all before he died again.

"I forgot to look," one of the dragons whispered to the other. "Did he lose a level?" The second one shrugged as they sat back to wait again. Beings who were effectively immortal had a great deal of patience. And watching this adventurer rage was amusing.

Back in limbo, Matt raged. He stomped around and cursed. After a few minutes, he began to take deep breaths. "Okay. The drow betrayed you. Set a trap. They must be angry about the failure to capture Antalia. They have to know they can't really kill me, so this must be some kind of message. A reprimand." His rage boiled to the top again. "Goddamned NPCs think they can teach ME a lesson?! I'll…" He paused. There really wasn't much he could do. The drow wizards who'd granted him the power he had and the drow who followed him were beyond his reach. They were so high-level he couldn't even SEE their levels when he inspected them. Even the servants they sent to him with messages or gifts were at least a hundred levels above him.

"So I'll take this punishment. Eventually they'll get tired of it and I can get back to work. The prince will break soon and I'll have my way into Damerion." He looked at his timer counting down the last few seconds.

This time, the moment he appeared, he leapt up from the throne's seat, using his legs and hands for balance. He felt a few snags on his armor, but nothing penetrated. He quickly grabbed his sword again and hacked at the broken needles until they were flush with the seat. Sitting back down very carefully, he relaxed when no more poison debuffs appeared on his UI.

Once again, he shouted, "Guards!" but no one responded. He slipped into stealth mode, hoping to detect any drow standing nearby. If they'd been told to punish him, they might be loitering about watching him suffer. But most of the drow had higher-level stealth abilities than him as well. It was innate to their race, and they improved it throughout their entire lives. Which for some of them had been hundreds or even a thousand years. Dropping stealth, he reached into his bag for a snack. He removed an apple and took a big bite. Immediately, the poison debuff appeared on his UI again.

"Dammit! How much is enough? I've learned my lesson! I won't fail again!" His shouting became ragged as he once again fell dead. This time, he could swear he heard laughter as his vision faded.

The elder of the two dragons chided his companion. "Do not expose us by laughing. He will search for us when he returns."

The younger bowed his head in apology. "I am sorry. But he will not be looking for us. He thinks the drow are punishing him for losing Antalia. I could watch this all day." He grinned. The other dragon produced another hard candy and handed it over.

Matt threw off his headset and jumped up from his chair. "Aaaaaargh!" he screamed into the empty room. Immediately he clamped a hand over his mouth, remembering where he was. It wouldn't do for the neighbors to hear him and report a squatter to the police. Every cop in the city had his face memorized.

Pacing the room as his limbo time counted down, he grumbled to himself, "I've lost three full levels in twenty minutes. They've GOT to see that losing levels makes me less effective. They need me! And how the HELL did they get into my inventory to poison an apple?"

It never occurred to him that the poison might be on his glove after touching the throne. Matt wasn't the smartest among his siblings. Or his peers. His father had been the smart one, the planner. Matt was the driving force and the charismatic face. The two of them had made a good team. Without his father, he knew his time and his capabilities were limited.

When he'd calmed down enough, he sat back in the chair and donned the headset again. This time when he logged in, he didn't bother jumping up from the chair. He sat there thinking. He removed every item of food from his bag and dropped it on the floor. He did the same with his water bottle. He'd sniffed it first, but there were plenty of poisons that had no odor. So he tossed it aside.

Standing up, he began to pace back and forth. He thought better as he moved. "Maybe I'll just go up to the surface and change my bind point for now. I can always change it back when this is over." He turned to head for the door and felt a sharp spike of pain in his foot.

"Come ON!" he shouted, as the poisoned debuff appeared on his UI once again. He looked down to see a needle poking up from the floor. Removing his sword, he swiped at it, breaking off the needle point. He spotted a few others and did the same. Then he sat down on the throne again and died.

The younger of the two dragons unstealthed and carefully approached the throne, watching for any needles in the floor. "He pulled a lot of items from that bag. Let's see what else he has in there? Could be something shiny."

The other dragon nodded. Dragons loved shiny treasure, whether they were in human form or their natural form. Bag in hand, the first dragon returned to their hiding spot and the two of them peeked inside.

*****

Alexander and Jules spent most of the day just relaxing. They talked about things. Logged onto the computer at Alexander's desk and viewed some of their friend's feeds. Alexander was keen to see Fibble's feed, and they watched the little guy sneak into the kitchen and steal a handful of cookies from a jar. Alexander noticed one of the cooks noticing the little guy, but she just smiled slightly and pretended she hadn't. They watched him run so fast that his fuzzy green slippers were just a blur on the screen as he dashed back to his little room in the stables. He stashed the cookies in a bag buried under his many pillows. When they were secure, he put his eyes to the gap in the floorboards and threatened any bugs that might be down there who were tempted to take his cookies.

From there he went to find Bacon, who was lounging near the stables in his own private mud pit. Fibble gleefully leapt right in and began to wrestle with the pig. They were both quickly covered in mud. Alexander was tempted to message Lainey and get her to give the little goblin a bath, but decided he'd dunk the thief in the lake when he got back.

They took a short walk around the grounds, Alexander pushing Jules' wheelchair and leaning on it at the same time. They walked down to the dock that stuck out into the lake and watched as a couple of teenagers paddled around in the water. On the way back, Alexander was nearly run down by a four-year-old on a Big Wheel that zoomed past. He eyed the retreating kid with a grin as an idea struck him.

Back up in his office that afternoon, they simply sat and snuggled on the sofa. They joined the crowd down in the cafeteria for dinner, during which many people stopped by their table to introduce themselves to Jules and to give their congratulations. It seemed everybody knew her, and she began to get a little overwhelmed by the attention.

After dinner, they retired to Alexander's bedroom. Jules said, "I think we should get back in the game. Maybe first thing in the morning?"

Alexander hesitated. Then he said, "Heimdall, could you call Dr. Feelgood for me?"

"*Of course, Alexander. She is in her office. One moment.*"

"Hello, Alexander." The doc's voice came through a moment later. "How are things going?"

"Great, Doc! Jules and I were wondering if it would be okay to go back into the game tomorrow. Wanted to make sure you don't have any… concerns."

"Nope! Our main worry was that Jules wouldn't want to return to this world. I think that question's been answered. You two are just adorable together, by the way." Both of them rolled their eyes. "You can log back in whenever you're ready. We'll monitor Jules carefully, of course. But we anticipate no problems. And we still want you both to log out maybe once a week for a few physical therapy sessions."

"Thanks, Doc!" Jules answered. "We'll log back in first thing in the morning. Have a good night!"

They crawled into bed on their respective sides and Jules squirmed a bit as Alexander rolled to his side to spoon her. "This bed isn't as big as the one in-game," she commented.

Alexander immediately replied, "I can have a bigger one brought up by the time we log out again. Princes can make stuff like that happen."

She giggled at him. "Don't be silly. I want to be close to you. Who needs a big ol' bed?"

*****

The next morning, they woke up before sunrise and made their way down to their pods. The support staff was waiting, having been alerted by the doc the night before. In just a few minutes, they were stripped down and loaded up in the pods.

They awoke on Alexander's balcony at Greystone Manor, where they'd logged out. Tigger wasn't there, having been dismissed to the nether when Alexander left the game. They walked together down to the portal and Alexander activated it. Walking through hand in hand, they greeted the few Elysians who were awake before the sun.

Jules simply said, "Pancakes," before kissing his cheek and dashing off toward the kitchen. It felt good to run after a couple days of stumbling around on uncertain legs. Alexander waited only a few seconds before he chased after her.

Reaching the kitchen, Jules hugged all the cooks one by one, much to their surprise and delight. They handed her a plate piled high with pancakes and a bottle of syrup. Alexander was given a heaping pile of scrambled eggs and toast and a separate plate with just bacon. The cook who handed him the bacon said, "Ya know she's gonna steal some."

Laughing, the two of them walked out to the dining area and took seats at one of the long tables. A few of the farmers were there already and they exchanged pleasantries. Alexander got updates on how the crops and livestock were faring. The farmers were thrilled with the health and growth rate of the crops that were sprouting up in the blessed soil around the keep.

As the sky lightened, others began to join them. Both citizens and players. Brick appeared and grabbed Jules up in a big bear hug, lifting her right off her bench. Alexander warned him, "Careful. She's eaten like, twenty pancakes. If you squeeze her too hard it might get messy."

The dwarf laughed and set her down. "Good ta have ye back, Jules!"

She gave him a smile and then looked up as the sun cleared the wall. "So this is what a sunrise looks like. Huh." Which earned her a general laugh from the crowd. Just as everyone at Olympus seemed to know her, she was semi-famous here at the keep for not being a morning person.

When Sasha and the other officers had joined them, Alexander said, "I want to go visit the elves as soon as possible. I was thinking of leaving this afternoon. Who wants to come along?"

Sasha shook her head. "I'll go. You might do something stupid and need healing."

Brick, Lugs, Max, Helga and Lainey all shook their heads no.

"Kai will come with me as a representative of the dragons. The alliance was their idea, after all. And I'll bring Lorian, as he's a member of the royal family. Lola, would you like to come along in case there are any trade agreements in the offing?"

The dwarfess nodded her head. "Aye, I'll go with ye. Never been to the elven kingdom."

Alexander looked around. No other volunteers presented themselves. Alright.

Opening guild chat, he said, "*Lorian, please come to the keep. Time to go meet your parents. Kai, if you wouldn't mind joining us?*"

45

Lorian responded with a simple, *"On my way,"* and Kai's response was easy enough – he appeared in the courtyard. Walking to Alexander, he said, "If it's alright with you, Alexander, I will fly you to the elven lands. Lia is sure our offspring will hatch any day, and I don't wish to be away any longer than necessary."

Alexander held up a hand. "Of course I'm okay with flying. But we can postpone the trip until another dragon can join us. You can summon one of your people and we'll go when they arrive."

Kai shook his head. "No, it must be me. The elves are unlikely to be cooperative. It will take the full weight of the dragon kingdom behind you to make them listen to what you have to say." Alexander nodded, acceding to his wishes.

It didn't take long for Lorian to appear. He'd been in the forest up on the plateau and used the mirror in the garrison tower to return to the keep. Alexander filled him in on their plan and he retired to his quarters to prepare for the trip. Lola, Sasha, and Kai did the same. Jules just looked at Alexander and smiled. "Have daggers, will travel."

When it was time to leave, Kai asked them to meet him outside the walls. They all walked out through the main gate and down the road to the outer gatehouse. Rocky greeted them at the moat, swimming up and laying his head on the bridge. Alexander scratched his ears a bit, then poured a handful of sugar cubes into the water dragon's mouth. "Behave yourself, buddy! We'll be back."

Kai was already in his dragon form when they crossed the moat. His real dragon form, not the smaller version he'd used at Greystone Manor or in the keep. Just his head was larger than one of their cargo wagons. His massive serpentine body stretched hundreds of feet from nose to tail. He was larger than a real-world 747.

Laying on his belly, he spread his wing slightly and laid it flat. Alexander climbed up onto the wing, then helped the others up as well. Then they marched across the leathery membrane onto Kai's shoulder, finally settling on his back between his massive shoulders. There were twin rows of spikes down his back, with just enough room in between that one could sit and hold onto the spikes to one's left and right like handlebars.

When all were aboard, he called out, "Hold tight, here we go!" and took a few running steps before launching himself into the air while beating his massive wings. They skyrocketed upward, quickly clearing the trees. With another beat of his wings, they were hundreds of feet higher. He turned slightly to the east and caught an updraft, rising quickly above even the level of the plateau. Already the keep below them looked small and far away.

Alexander enjoyed the scenery as Kai headed toward the elven kingdom. What would have taken a couple of days on the ground, even with their mounts, was going to be a short trip of a couple of hours. The wind screamed past them as Kai picked up speed. It was too loud to speak to anyone, so he spent his time thinking about what might persuade the elves. He knew very little about them, other than that they were unfriendly, aloof, and thought other humanoid races were inferior.

It didn't take long for him to worry himself into doubting every argument he could conceive. To distract himself, he thought about allies that would probably be easier to deal with. He still needed to formalize the alliances with the orcs and the minotaurs up on the plateau. He'd take Silverbeard with him. The old dwarf could draft a treaty or trade agreement faster than Alexander could read through his own character sheet.

His musings were interrupted when Kai banked again, angling them toward the ground. Alexander looked below, but all he could see was an old growth forest of towering trees. "That makes sense," he muttered to himself. "Elves live in trees. Were you expecting skyscrapers and clear-cut squares?"

Kai circled for a moment, letting out a roar of greeting. Less than a minute later, a flaming arrow flew into the sky and Kai descended. He folded his wings to squeeze through an opening in the canopy, then flared them out to slow their descent just before they touched down. It seemed the elves didn't make it easy for even the dragons to visit.

One by one, Alexander and the others slid from Kai's neck to his wing and walked down to the forest floor. Kai then assumed his human form and moved to stand behind and the right of Alexander. A group of elves in formal attire exited a doorway molded into a wide tree onto a balcony just above them. Rather than come down to greet the visitors, one of them called down, "To what do we owe the pleasure of your company, Prince Kaibonostrum?"

Behind him, Lorian growled. "They insult us. Etiquette dictates they greet us down here and offer hospitality. My father is not even here."

Kai called out, "I hear a voice, but do not see a body to go with it!" as he made a point of keeping his gaze down and searching the forest floor in front of Alexander. Lola grunted her approval and Lorian actually chuckled. When there was no movement above, Kai added, "Have the elves learned the stealth of the drow? If so, show yourselves so I may congratulate you!"

There were a few angry mutterings from above and the elves moved down a sloping ramp to the forest floor. They marched slowly and sedately to stand before Alexander's group. The one who had spoken before said, "My apologies, Prince Kaibonostrum. We have neglected the rules of hospitality, much to our shame. Welcome. Who have you brought with you today?"

Kai stared for a moment, making it clear he believed not one bit of the apology. "Allow me to introduce King Alexander of Elysia. Friend and ally of Stormforge, Broken Mountain, Antalia, and the dragon kingdom. Favored of Odin, Champion of Light, and sworn enemy of the drow wizards." Alexander inclined his head slightly to acknowledge the titles.

The elf bowed his own head just as slightly, eliciting another growl from Lorian. "Greetings, King Alexander. And welcome to our lands. I am-"

Alexander cut him off. "I don't care who you are. You've shown yourself to be rude and disingenuous and I've only been here a few moments. Where is your king?"

The group of elves all reeled in shock. The one standing in front stepped forward, getting within inches of Alexander as he leaned in. "How dare you!"

Kai stepped forward and roared. The force of the sound drove back the elves and made them cower. When he was done, he shouted,

"Fetch your king, you vile worm, or I will declare a state of war between the dragons and the elves here and now!"

The branches of the tree behind the elves rattled and several of them fled in terror. All around them, elves emerged from trees to see what the commotion was.

A voice called down from the balcony, "Why do you scare my children, Kaibonostrum?"

Lorian whispered, "That's him. My father."

Kai spoke to the elf who was walking down from the balcony. "Your children need a lesson in manners, Majesty." The elf who'd spoken shrank back even further, staring at the ground. The look on his face promised retribution.

The elven king came to a stop in front of Alexander. "Ah, the new human king. Alexander, I believe. I have heard much about you. I am Dothvanielen, Lord of the Elven Kingdom. Welcome." The king bowed his head slightly.

Alexander decided to be gracious. "Thank you, Majesty. It seems you already know Prince Kaibonostrum. This is my future queen, Lady Jules." He waited while the king acknowledged her. "Also my treasurer, Lola of the Broken Mountain clan. Lady Sasha of Elysia and second of the Greystone Guild, our strategist and healer. And of course, you know our Chief Scout and General, Dothloriandal."

The king acknowledged each of them with a slight motion of his head, except Lorian. To him, he said, "I did not think to ever see your face again, Dothloriandal."

"Were there not a dire need, I would not have, Father. This is no longer my home. I came here out of respect for King Alexander."

"What dire need?" the king asked.

Kai growled in his chest. "Your petty games grow tiring, elven king. Do not pretend that our messengers have not spoken to you about the rise of the drow wizards. Or that you do not know of the battles fought in Antalia and Elysia in recent weeks. Your spies are as good as anyone's.

If you persist, I will nullify any agreements between the elven and dragon kingdoms and we will depart now. We haven't time for your posturing."

Kai's voice was hard steel and flames lit his eyes as he spoke. Even Alexander wanted to step away from his friend. Lola broke the mood by laughing. "Ha! I hear'd all me life about the terrible elves and their haughty ways. I thought me old da were just pullin' me leg. Turns out, yer exactly the stuck up, self-centered arses he said ye'd be!"

This time it was Lorian who laughed as the king looked enraged. "She's got you there, Father. I've never seen such lack of courtesy from our people. Even when your lackeys drove me from the forest for being a half-breed embarrassment. Have our people sunk so far?"

By this time, a large crowd of elves had gathered in the nearby trees and walkways that ran between them. At Lorian's words, many of them nodded and murmured in agreement. The king took note of this and his face grew red with rage. He looked down at Lola. "I expect as much from my bastard son. But you, a lowly dwarf, *dare* to speak to me so in my own kingdom?" He drew a dagger from his belt and took a step toward her. Alexander stepped to the side and placed a hand on the king's chest. "You'll not touch her, Majesty. Take a breath and calm yourself. It was your people who started the animosity here."

The king threw off Alexander's hand, a snarl on his face. He turned, as if to attack Alexander instead. Alexander threw up his magic shield without a thought. When the dagger bounced off the bubble, he leaned back and kicked the enraged king in the chest. There were gasps of surprise from the surrounding elves.

Three of the original group of elves who stood behind the rude one instantly drew bows and aimed them at Alexander. They never had a chance to fire. The moment the king stepped toward Lola, Kai had begun to assume his dragon form. As the arrows went up, he unleashed dragonfire. The flames engulfed the archers, the first elf who'd spoken, and the elven king. A moment later, they were nothing but ash.

Dead silence reigned in the forest. Thousands of elves had just witnessed the death of the king at the hands of a dragon. Kai turned his head left and right, looking for more threats. When none made themselves apparent, he called out, "You all saw Dothvanielan draw a weapon and attack the King of Elysia. Does anyone deny this?"

Thousands of heads shook in unison. So Kai continued, "Where is the heir to the throne?"

There were murmurs and more head shaking. Finally, an elven ranger stepped forward. He took a knee before Kai and said, "Prince Kaibonostrum. We all witnessed the happenings here this day and attest that you acted as you must to defend the human king. I regret to inform you that both the heirs to the throne have been murdered. The princess just last week and her brother the prince more than a month past. We believe the drow to be responsible for both murders."

Kai reverted back to human form and indicated that the ranger should rise. "What is your name?"

"I am former commander Ithaniel of the King's Guard. I was relieved of my post shortly before the prince's death. Myself and the entire guard were dismissed. The elves you… dealt with just now took our places as the king's protectors."

Kai looked thoughtful. "Not all of the heirs are dead, Commander Ithaniel. Before you stands Dothloriandal, son of Dothvanielan. And, apparently, your new king."

This time the reaction from the crowd was much larger. There were angry shouts and cries from every side. Kai roared again to get their attention. "IS THERE ANOTHER?" he shouted. "IS THERE AN HEIR WHO WISHES TO STEP FORWARD?"

He waited in silence for a solid minute. Then he called out, "Then Dothloriandal is the rightful king. Is there anyone out there who wishes to challenge him for the throne? From the look on his face, I don't think he wants the job. Maybe he'll just give it to you."

Again he waited, and again no response. Kai and Alexander both looked to Lorian, who looked sick to his stomach. But he stepped forward and addressed the elven ranger. "I remember you, Ithaniel. You were always kind to me as I underwent the ranger training. You pushed me harder than the others, I think. But not out of malice. Am I wrong?"

Ithaniel bowed his head, then raised it with a smile. "You were one of the best younglings that I'd ever seen. But you had a chip on your shoulder. I tried to beat it out of you, or make you so tired you'd forget about it."

Lorian laughed. "Well, I thank you for your efforts. And as my first official act, I restore you and the rest of the King's Guard." Ithaniel took a knee and let out a single shrill whistle. Within seconds, fifty elven rangers dropped from the tree and took a knee around their new king. Ithaniel looked up. "Though we were unwanted, we held to our oaths as best we could. We have never been far from our king."

Kai nodded. "I regret that I had to remove him in such a manner. Let us retire to the king's chamber and discuss the immediate future. Are any of the old king's advisors present?"

Ithaniel searched the trees and pointed to several elder elves, who began to step down to join them. As they moved, he said, "They too were dismissed. Two who objected too strenuously were executed as an example to the others."

When ten elders had joined their group, Lorian led them back up the ramp and into the tree. They walked from tree to tree for several minutes before approaching a massive old giant of a tree. Lorian took them inside. There was a long table with ten chairs on each side. Lorian took a seat at the head of the table and the others arranged themselves. Elders on one side, Alexander and party on the other. The rangers secured the door.

Kai said, "I did not want to say this in front of your people, as it might have caused a panic. The elves who first approached us were tainted. They smelled of drow magic. Which is likely why they did not want to greet us properly. They were afraid of exposure." A murmur went up among the elders. Ithaniel nodded as if that answered some questions for him. Kai continued, "In case you're wondering, no one here shares that taint. Though I'd be surprised if those I disposed of were the only ones here."

Alexander looked grim. "First things first. Elders. You are the leaders among your people. Do you accept Dothloriandal as your king? Half-blood and all?"

They looked to each other, then one near the center spoke. "We would do so. But I fear the people would not. They are afraid now because of what has transpired today. But the prejudice against the king's blood would fester."

Lorian spoke up. "I have no desire to be king. I will serve until a better choice can be found. Then I will step down. My place is in Elysia. My one condition for stepping down peacefully will be that the alliance and trade agreements I establish with Alexander and the dragon kingdom as well as the human and dwarven kingdoms will be upheld."

The elder cleared his throat. "It is clear that the drow have become a threat. To all of us. We would welcome an alliance. We remember the last war with the drow wizards. No kingdom can stand alone. As for a better choice, we already have one, Dothloriandal." His eyes, and the gaze of every elder in the room, fell upon Ithaniel.

"Ithaniel is of a royal line. Not your father's, but an older line. Deposed eons ago by your great-great grandfather for his part in an unnecessary war with the dwarven nations. A war that cost many hundreds of our people's lives."

Ithaniel bowed his head. "This is true. But I am no king. I was trained from birth to protect the king, not replace him."

Alexander looked at Kai, who shrugged. Then he looked to Lorian. "What do you think, Lorian?"

The half-elf clasped his hands together on the table in front of him. "As I said outside, Ithaniel was good to me when he didn't need to be. When, in fact, it would have been better for him to treat me as the others did. And when my father shunned him, he and his men stood their posts as best they could. That showed loyalty and honor. And his men follow him without question. So he is a leader, whether he admits it or not."

The elders were all nodding along. "Would our people accept him?"

The lead elder smiled. "He is of the blood, and already a hero among our people."

Lorian looked to Ithaniel. "Will you swear on your life that you will serve our people better than my father did? That you will honor the alliance we establish, and help to defeat the drow wizards and their armies?"

Ithaniel knelt. "I swear by the gods of Io that I will serve our people to the best of my ability. That I will serve honorably, and will uphold the alliances and agreements with the human, dwarven, and dragon kingdoms. We will fight together, and die together if need be."

A flash of white light engulfed Ithaniel and thunder rolled through the forest.

Kai nodded, as did Alexander. Lorian said, "I hereby abdicate the throne of the elven kingdom in favor of King Ithaniel. May he reign forever."

The elders echoed, "May he reign forever!"

Alexander said, "Then it is official. Lola here will work with you on trade agreements. Kaibonostrum already had a treaty drawn up, which has been signed by the dragon king, myself, Charles of Stormforge, Margaret of Antalia, and Thalgrin of Broken Mountain." Kai produced the treaty and handed it to Ithaniel. The elf nodded and began to read as Lola and the elders spoke quietly across the table. Alexander got the attention of one of the elders. "Do you have a portal here in the city?"

The elder nodded. "Not far from where you landed."

Alexander said, "We have established a network of portals between all of the kingdoms in the alliance, so that we may transfer troops quickly to support our allies when needed. Or supplies during a siege. If you will allow it, we will ask Fitzbindulum to come here and attune the portal."

Kai shook his head. "There is no need. I will see to it, with your permission?" The elders looked to their new king, who nodded his head.

"Of course."

The discussions continued as Kai left the table. One of the rangers was detailed to escort him. Kai stopped at the door. "If I come across more of the tainted?"

Ithaniel thought about it. "Point them out to your escort. We will make note of them and deal with them quietly tonight."

Kai and his escort disappeared. Ithaniel finished reading through the dragon's treaty and called for the attention of the elders. "I have read this document, and find no objections to any of its content. I hereby signify our entrance into the proposed alliance by signing this treaty." And he did just that.

Hidden Quest Completed: Cleanse the Realm

You and your allies have discovered and removed an influence that threatened the Elven Kingdom from within. You have further installed a new king who is uncorrupted and will rule the kingdom well. And the Elven Kingdom has been brought into the alliance. Quest Reward: 80,000XP. Reputation gain with the Elven Kingdom.

Your Reputation with the Elven Kingdom has increased to: Friendly

The notification of the hidden quest completion surprised Alexander. He supposed it was a necessary part of completing the larger *World at War* quest line. Regardless, experience was experience. The quest and the killing of the king and the other elves had already taken him halfway to level 71.

While the others chatted, he took a moment to review his character sheet. He'd gained several levels in recent days, mostly from the battle with the demon army. And he'd neglected to assign attribute points.

Mage: Alexander	Level 70	Build: Ranged Magic/Melee DPS	
Heath: 38,000	Experience:	448,000/900,000	Atrrib Pts Avail: 25
Mana: 34,000			Skill Pts Avail: 5
Stamina: 14 (27)	Dexterity: 6	Armor: 240	Heath Regen: 210
Strength: 12 (28)	Wisdom 80 (109)	Defense: 150	Mana Regen: 400
Agility: 12 (22)	Intelligence 80 (109)	Phys Attack: 65	Magic Attack: 180
Luck: 14 (22)	Charisma: 12	Stamina Regen: 28	Race: Elf

His glass cannon imbalance was getting out of hand. He decided to put four points each into Stamina and Strength and four into Dexterity to bring it up to ten. He added a point to Luck and two points to Charisma. As a leader, he figured he would need it. Then he put two points into Agility. The remaining eight points he decided to save.

With the additional levels, he'd hit 70. Which meant he needed to find Fitz and receive more training. A thought struck him. He hadn't seen Fitz in several days. Since before the demon battle. Granted, he'd been offline for a couple days, and he supposed the wizard could have stopped by while he was gone. Still, he would make a point of looking for him when they got back to the keep.

Alexander noticed Ithaniel looked as bored as he was with the trade talks. So he asked the king if he'd like to go for a walk. The two of them left the meeting room and strolled along a raised walkway, looking down at the forest floor. Alexander started, "Will there be a coronation celebration?"

Ithaniel grimaced. "I suppose there must be. We elves do like our formalities."

Alexander halted, pulling a bit of obsidian from his bag. First, he shaped it into a ring. Then he closed his eyes and imbued the ring with the same Undying and Heal spells that he put into his people's dragon pins. Only this time, he continued to channel the heal spell until the ring told him it was full. A king in a situation where he'd taken a fatal blow would need to be as close to full health afterward as possible. He handed the ring to the king. "An early coronation gift. May you reign forever."

Ring of the Eternal Reign
Quality: Unique
Should the wearer of this ring receive a fatal injury, the ring's magic will restore and hold them at a single health point. Any further damage taken will result in the wearer's death. In addition, use of the healing spell contained within the ring will restore 10,000HP. Each spell will only work once before having to be recharged.

Ithaniel looked at the ring and his eyes widened briefly. "This is a valuable gift indeed. Thank you, Alexander. I look forward to a long friendship between us."

The two kings walked and talked some more as Alexander brought Ithaniel up to speed on the conflict with the drow wizards and the Dark One so far. Eventually, they returned to the room where their people were gathered. Lola smiled at Alexander, saying, "It be done."

Servants appeared with elegantly carved wooden cups and pitchers of elven wine. Everyone received a glass, and Ithaniel raised his in the air. "To the new alliance!" The others echoed his toast and everyone drank.

The entire group walked back to where they'd started, then a bit farther to where Kai waited by the portal. The crowd of elves had not dispersed, seemingly fascinated by the dragon prince. Kai looked to Alexander and nodded. The portal was tuned to allow access to all the allied kingdoms, except, presumably, the dragons' home city. Kai's ranger escort went and whispered into Ithaniel's ear.

The lead elder raised his hands, seeing they still had an audience. "Let it be known this day that we recognized Dothloriandal as the legitimate heir and new king!" He paused as there was grumbling and shouting. "Let it further be known that in a demonstration of great honor and wisdom, King Dothloriandal abdicated the throne in favor of Ithaniel!"

The change was immediate. There were cheers and cries of joy. Flowers were tossed down from above as Ithaniel raised his hand in acknowledgement. The elder spoke again. "There will be a coronation one week from today. Prepare yourselves!" The cheering continued as the elders bowed their heads to Alexander, Kai, Lorian, and Ithaniel before departing.

Ithaniel hugged Lorian, then shook hands with Alexander. He bowed deeply to Kai. With the public formalities over, Alexander activated the portal to Elysia's keep.

Ithaniel said, "Please, I would like you all to attend the coronation."

Alexander smiled. "Lady Jules would literally kill me if I passed up a chance for her to get dressed up and attend a party. We'll be back in a week." He leaned in close to whisper, "If you need us before then to address your drow issue, send a message through the portal."

And with that, Alexander and his party stepped back into Elysia.

Chapter 4

Allies

Silverbeard appeared as they stepped through, having been notified that a portal was opened. "How'd ye do?"

Lola snorted. "Alexander 'n Kai scolded them snooty elves, killed the king. Lorian were king for about five minutes, then made a good lookin' ranger elf the new king instead. We got a treaty plus good trade agreements. There'll be plenty o' elven wine in the cellars soon!"

The rest of the group laughed at her interpretation. Silverbeard took it in stride, just nodding his head. "Well done, then!"

As everyone dispersed to go about their business, Silverbeard pulled Alexander aside. "We got business with the minotaurs when yer ready. And ye should talk with 'em about the orcs as well. Also, there be a private gathering in the Great Hall this evening. Ye'll need to be there." He looked around suspiciously and Alexander knew he was looking for Jules in stealth mode. "I canno' tell ye more right now."

Chuckling to himself, Alexander agreed to attend. Then he switched gears. "Let's go to your office and discuss the plateau." The two of them walked the short distance to the donjon entrance and down the main corridor to the old dwarf's office. Once inside, they took seats.

Alexander began by looking up at the ceiling. "Good day to you, Jeeves. Long time no talk."

"Good day, Majesty. I hope you have been well?"

"I have, thank you Jeeves. Please update me on the construction we discussed for the northern villages."

"Of course. The two longhouses you requested have been completed, as have the underground structures beneath each of them. Both longhouse structures have been occupied. At the request of Chancellor Silverbeard, I have been removing stone to create a wide cavern deep within the cliff for a market square. There is currently a tunnel two hundred feet in length, fifteen feet high and fifteen feet wide

that leads to the square. We now have a significant surplus of stone resources."

"Thank you, Jeeves. We'll spend some quality time on your status and resources soon."

"You are most welcome, Majesty. I am at your service, as always."

Alexander raised an eyebrow at the 'Majesty' title Jeeves was using now, but decided to let it go. He turned to Silverbeard. "Okay, what do you need from me before we go see the minotaurs?"

Silverbeard stroked his beard thoughtfully. "Ye need to decide what ye want from 'em. Ye already give'd 'em a home. Shelter, a place to farm, and ye killed the rogue orcs. So do ye just want farmers, or do ye need soldiers? What kind o' taxes do ye want to charge?"

Alexander knew these items were important. In his world, he would know exactly what to do. His father had trained him, prepared him to participate in the running of Jupiter Tech. But expectations and economy were different here. The minotaurs had chieftains, but didn't have a 'king.' And the orcs were just freed from a tyrant who forced them into war.

"I'm afraid I'm new to all this king stuff. What would you recommend, Chancellor?"

Silverbeard chuckled. "Good lad. Know when to admit ye don't know. Ye need soldiers. The minotaurs got plenty. I dunno 'bout the orcs. We killed a good number o' their warriors and sent the rest to Thalgrin. What they've got left will likely be farmers 'n crafters, the weak 'n the old, and children. But ye need farmers 'n crafters as badly as ye need soldiers."

Alexander ventured, "So, maybe I should offer them a deal similar to what I offered the volunteers here? A salary for the soldiers, plus room and board at the barracks. A place for the farmers and crafters to do their work, and access to the resources of the forest. No taxes for a year, to give them time to get on their feet? Then beyond that… ten percent for the kingdom?"

"Aye, lad. That be good. Maybe offer them access to the dragon forge fer the best smith from each o' their tribes. Have Jeeves build more o' what they need. Housing 'n such. And in return, they swear the oath and support the kingdom."

Alexander nodded. "Sounds right. Let's plan to visit them tomorrow. Oh!" He pulled out the signed treaty document. "Please put this somewhere safe. In case we need to add more kingdoms. Which seems likely. And if you could have copies made?"

Silverbeard took the document and nodded. "We chancellors have duplication magic fer that." He waved his hand over the scroll and muttered a few words. A moment later, he handed Alexander back what amounted to a photocopy of the treaty, complete with signatures.

"That's awesome! Can you do that with spell scrolls and books?"

Silverbeard nodded. "Simple scrolls and books, aye. Non-magical. I canno' copy magic scrolls or trainin' books unless it were me that wrote them. Or with the permission of them that wrote it."

Slightly disappointed, Alexander sat back in his seat. He'd been seeing free spell scrolls and training manuals for each of his people dance in front of his eyes. Still, it was a handy skill to have. "How about maps?"

"Aye, again, if they be non-magical," Silverbeard confirmed.

"Good enough. Thank you, Master Silverbeard. Now, do you have drawings for the new market square and interior spaces?"

The two of them dove into the planning and designing of the improvements at the keep. For the next two hours, Alexander lost himself in the kingdom-building details. He hadn't realized it before getting the quest to help rebuild Whitehall, but he really enjoyed building things. Not just with his bare hands or his magic. He enjoyed making things grow, meeting people's needs. The strategy of making sure his kingdom expanded in a workable way.

He thought back to when he was a kid and Olympus was being built. And the times, like now, when his father and Michael built expansions. Then the thoughts of Olympus reminded him of something.

He thanked Silverbeard and took a set of the drawings with him to study more thoroughly later.

Leaving the office, he headed straight for the smithy to find Brick. When he located the dwarf, Brick was standing over an anvil, hammer in one hand and a dagger in the other. He was zoned out, a look Alexander recognized. "He's doing that spooky shaping/engraving thing again, isn't he?" he asked one of the nearby smiths. The dwarf nodded his head, looking jealous.

Alexander sat on a nearby stool and waited. Brick normally wasn't in these trances too long. Crafting in the game wasn't like in real life. A smith, once they had the ingredients prepared and the necessary tools in hand, could craft an item in just a few minutes. Whereas in the real world it would take hours or days.

Since Alexander knew they'd be recruiting more fighters, he passed the time while he waited by pulling out bits of obsidian and enchanting them with the Undying and Light Heal spells. He left them as unshaped cubes as he set one after the other on the bench next to him. With his new levels, higher stats, and much larger mana pool, he wouldn't need to stop to rest anytime soon. He had maybe a dozen of them enchanted when Brick woke up.

The first thing Brick did upon seeing Alexander in front of him was to hide the dagger behind his back. "Shit. What're ye doin' snoopin' around me forge?" he demanded. He seemed almost to be blushing.

"Snooping? I came here to see you and you were all twilight zone, so I'm making some more dragon pins." Alexander poked at him. Now he was dying to know about the dagger. "Whatcha got there?"

"Where?" Brick pretended to look around in confusion. When he saw Alexander wasn't buying it, he said, "I got me a big ol' hunk o' none o' yer damned business!" He glared at his friend.

Alexander chuckled. "Okay. I'll cover my eyes while you put away the dagger you're not holding. Then can we talk about why I came here?"

Brick turned his back to Alexander for a moment and the dagger disappeared into his bag. "What'ye need?"

Alexander grinned and leaned in to whisper to the dwarf about his idea. A moment later, Brick laughed. "BWAHAHA! That be the best idea I hear'd all day. We can do it here, methinks. We'll need ta make a chain… difficult, but not impossible. The gears 'n such won't be a problem." Brick wandered off and began shouting at apprentices. He'd already forgotten Alexander was there.

*****

Matt sat back in his chair and donned his headset. He'd taken some time to cool down. Drink a few beers, get some rest. And he was reasonably sure he'd cleared the traps. At least, enough of them that he could make it out the door and find a new bind point. As a last resort, he had some teleport scrolls in his bag that would take him to other safe houses.

He hated giving up that bind point. But it wasn't like he could complain to the admins about it. His account was still under the radar, and so far undetectable. He needed to keep it that way. The minute Odin or the Jupiter Tech folks could spot him, he'd be done. The authorities would be on him before he could run. And he had no intention of going to jail.

Closing his eyes, he triggered the login. As before, he found himself on his throne. He sat there for a while, remaining still as he surveyed the floor in front of him while he strummed his fingers on the arm of the throne. Standing, he stepped carefully down and toward the doors. He managed to reach the doors without stepping on a needle.

"Yes!" He pushed on the doors to open them and head up to the surface. But the doors didn't budge. He slammed his shoulder into them a few times, but they didn't budge. With a rogue's build, he didn't have the bulk or the strength for something like that.

"Really?" he shouted at the ceiling. "How long are you going to keep me in here? This is just overkill!" He reached for his bag to grab a teleport scroll. "Come ON! You took my bag, too? Return it immediately!" He began to mutter to himself and pace, thinking of a way to escape. Being a rogue class, he decided to pick the locks. His lockpick tool case was in his bag, wherever that was. But he believed in being prepared. He pulled at the lining of his vest and loosened a thread. A moment later, he withdrew a lockpick. This was his last pick, and he needed to be careful.

Grabbing one of the fingers of his glove with his teeth, he pulled it off so that his sensitive fingers could better feel the pins of the lock. Immediately, the poisoned debuff appeared on his UI again as a foul taste filled his mouth. "Poison on the gloves? The chair! Dammit! This isn't funny!" He dropped the lockpick as he fell to the floor.

Back in the real world, he threw off his headset and walked stiffly to the back of the house and out the door. A few blocks away, he got into his truck. The moment the door was closed, he screamed and began to punch the roof, the door, the steering wheel. An accidental honk of the horn finally stopped him as he looked around in a panic. Starting the truck, he drove away. He needed to get more supplies anyway. It would be good to chill for a few.

The younger dragon was tempted to move forward and take the lockpick dropped by the adventurer who called himself the Dark One. Remove his last hope of escape. But he was amusing. More fun than they'd had in quite some time. He still insisted on blaming his drow masters. And his anger levels were only rising as his experience levels dropped. So the dragon left the pick where it was. The two of them began to wager on how long he would spend trying to unlock an already-unlocked but sealed door.

*****

That evening, Alexander and Jules joined Silverbeard in the Great Hall as requested. They found him with Lola and all of the player members of the Greystone Guild. Trying to remember if it was his birthday or something, Alexander called out, "What is this? A coup? Any one of you wants this throne it's all yours!"

There was some scattered laughter as Sasha stepped forward. "We just all wanted to say how happy we are that things went smoothly for Jules. That we love her and we can't wait to see her in the real world, too." There were cheers and applause as Jules blushed.

Alexander took her hand and led her to a spot at one of the tables near the center of the room. He picked up a mug of ale that had already been filled and raised it into the air. "To Jules!" The others answered the call with mugs of their own. "Jules!"

Everyone took seats and the meal began. There was plenty of laughter and lots of questions about how it felt to be back in the real world after so long. When everybody had eaten their fill, Lainey and Misty approached Jules with a package. Lainey said, "We're neither of us any good at sewing, but we wanted you to have this."

Jules opened the package and pulled out the bundle of fabric. It fell open to reveal a beautiful dress in the Greystone colors. She hugged it to herself as tears formed in her eyes. "It's... wonderful! Thank you!" She hugged both women tightly.

Brick cleared his throat and stepped forward next. "This be from all of us." He handed her a wooden box with a small silver clasp. She took the box and set it on the table. Reaching out to open it, she paused. Turning to Brick, she asked, "Is it going to explode?"

Everyone in the room laughed as she pulled out a lockpick and probe and pretended to check it for traps. A moment later, she set down her tools and opened the box. There were gasps from the others who hadn't seen the dagger yet. Jules' eyes sparkled as she reached for it.

"This is so *awesome!*" she cried. Lifting the weapon up and holding it in both hands, she showed it to everyone.

> **The Queen's Dagger**
> **Item Quality: Epic, Unique**
> **Stats: Agility +6, Dexterity +5**
> **Enchantment: Crit Chance +10%**
> *This dagger was crafted in a Dragon Forge blessed by the gods of Io specifically for the first queen of Elysia. Forged of mithril with an emerald stone, it is enchanted to increase the wielder's chance of a critical hit by 10%. Sneak attacks and attacks on a helpless target will have an extra 10% chance of critical hit damage bonus. This item is soulbound and cannot be lost, stolen, or traded.*

"Thank you so very much." Jules' voice was quiet as she gazed at the dagger. "I... wish I had something to give all of you." Tears rolled down her face as she placed the dagger back in its box and closed the lid carefully. She sat on one of the benches and tried to smile at everyone at once.

Alexander patted Brick on the shoulder. "Well done, my friend. Thank you."

The dwarf looked at him. "Bah! She be always threatenin' to stab ye. I just figger'd she should have a proper weapon when the time comes!" He grinned at Alexander.

After that, the celebration continued for a short while, with more toasts and lots of hugs for everyone. At one point, Alexander noticed a pair of big green ears poking out from behind one of the tables. They moved like twin shark fins toward the table where some treats were laid out. Alexander tapped Jules on the shoulder, then Sasha. As they turned, he pointed out the cookie thief moving in to strike. Others noticed and followed their gaze. Soon enough, nearly everyone in the room was watching Fibble creep toward his prize.

Jules went into stealth mode and dashed toward the table. She intercepted the little goblin, grabbing him and tossing him into the air as he squawked. Lugs caught him and flipped him over to Brick. The little guy's arms and legs waved furiously as he tried to get some traction and get away. When Brick caught him, he held Fibble up before Alexander.

"What do we have here? I believe we've caught a cookie thief!"

Fibble shook his head so hard his ears slapped Brick on both sides of his face, causing Lugs to bend over laughing. "No thief! Minister of Cookies! My job to test cookies, make sure they safe for 'Zander and rest of clan!"

Alexander grinned at the quick-thinking little thief. "That's true, I did give you that title, didn't I?" Fibble nodded his head furiously, grinning with his few remaining teeth. His feet were still wiggling, as if trying to run on air as Brick held him up.

"Well, I suppose we'll have to take back that title. Give you another one. Minister of Baths, maybe? You can test each of our baths before we get in. To make sure the water is just right."

"Nooooooo!" The pitiful wail that escaped Fibble instantly made Alexander feel bad. He patted Fibble's head. "Okay. We won't change it this time. But don't let me catch you stealing cookies in the keep again."

Fibble made a grumpy face and mumbled, "Not mean to let you catch me this time." Alexander did his best to keep a straight face as he nodded for Brick to set the goblin down. Fibble immediately stuck his tongue out at Jules, who he blamed for exposing him. Then he stomped over to the table of treats and deliberately reached up to grab several cookies. Turning, he showed them to everyone.

"Not steal. Testing!" He shoved the cookies in his bag and stomped grumpily out the door.

A short time later, the friends began to drift away. Some headed to their beds, others to work on their crafting or deal with other business. Alexander and Jules retired to their quarters and were quickly asleep.

The next morning, as usual, Jules was in her pink bunnymonster suit. Alexander had the urge to ask the devs how she was doing that, but remembered that they couldn't observe her in the bedroom. "It seems this will remain a mystery," he said to himself.

Jules nuzzled against him, saying, "Hmmmm?"

He kissed her forehead. "Never mind. Stay here and sleep. I'm going with Silverbeard to the northern villages to talk to the minotaurs and orcs."

She wrinkled her nose and replied, "Mmmhmm. Morcs. Fun."

Alexander got up and equipped his gear. Heading down to the kitchen, he grabbed some fruit and went to sit in the dining area to wait for Silverbeard. The sun was up and many of the citizens had already finished breakfast. The forge was already crowded and busy.

Noticing Blix at one of the tables, he went to sit with the gnome. "Blix! How goes the banking business?"

The gnome banker bowed his head in greeting. "Good morning, Alexander. Business is good. Many of the citizens have deposited funds with us, and there have been several more loan applicants. I have approved three more loans using your… unorthodox guidelines." The gnome sniffed as if offended by the inability to charge market interest rates.

Alexander chuckled. "Thank you, Blix. I promise, soon enough you'll be able to charge exorbitant interest on loans. Especially once we open this place to trade. And other adventurers. Feel free to take as much of their money as you can." He grinned as Blix perked up.

Silverbeard joined them, a plate of eggs and toast in hand. Alexander made small talk with the chancellor and banker as Silverbeard ate his meal. Alexander finished off an apple and looked at the core. "Where's Bacon when you need him?"

The oversized pig answered immediately. His snout rose up from behind another table, where he'd been lazing about waiting for scraps. When he got to his feet, his head was well above table level. He looked at Alexander and tilted his head.

Alexander laughed. "Here you go, you big pig." He tossed the apple core to Bacon, who caught it in his snout and made it disappear without even chewing. The pig started moving in Alexander's direction, hoping for more. But he held up his hands. "Oh no, you don't. We're out of here." He laid his hand on Silverbeard's shoulder and the two of them disappeared.

Their first stop was the garrison tower up on the plateau. Alexander could almost teleport them straight from the keep to the first of the villages, but his range hadn't increased quite that far. So, after a quick hello to Bodine and Regina, and Jake and Bobby - who chittered and made rude gestures at him when he denied having any fruit for them - they moved on to the first of the villages north of the river.

This one was inhabited mainly by orcs. There were a few minotaurs walking around, but the orcs outnumbered them twenty to one. Alexander and Silverbeard took a few minutes to speak with them, making sure they had what they needed. The orcs seemed reluctant to speak with the elf and the dwarf. Nervous, even. Alexander decided not to push them, and teleported Silverbeard and himself to the northernmost village.

There he found Molgo and Dawn. They had taken up residence in the largest of the single homes. Molgo was holding a meeting out in front, where they had placed a dozen or so sections of logs as seats in a half circle. He saw the two approaching and raised a hand in greeting. "Alexander! Silverbeard! It is good to see you. We were just talking about you."

He grunted something and a young minotaur grabbed a crude wooden bench and set it next to Molgo. "Please, sit. These are the elders of my clan. They have questions about being Elysians."

Alexander looked to each of them in turn as he moved to the bench. Silverbeard plopped himself down first without ceremony. As Alexander sat, he said, "Of course. I'm happy to answer questions."

The first of the elders, the one seated on the other side of Molgo, spoke first. "We will not be slaves."

Alexander nodded his head. "Not exactly a question, but I understand. No, you will not be slaves. You will be free citizens. You must take an oath of loyalty to remain here. But that only binds you if you attempt to betray the kingdom. Otherwise, you are free to go where you please. You can live here, or in another of the villages, or at one of the towers. Even the keep. Though we don't have much room there just now. You can craft, or farm, or be employed as a soldier of the realm."

Another spoke up. "When we hunt, you will take some of the food?"

Alexander said, "No, not now. For one year, you will pay no taxes. This is meant to allow you to use all the resources you gather to strengthen your people and your village. After one year, ten percent of all that you gather from hunts, farming, mining or other activities will be owed to Elysia as a tax. This will go to help build the whole kingdom. The rest you keep for yourselves."

Another elder asked, "The ones you accept as soldiers. They will be front-line troops, yes? First into the fight?"

Alexander considered his answer. "Very likely, yes. Your warriors are strong and experienced. Good shock troops. There will be situations where I ask them to go first into battle to scatter and frighten the enemy."

The elders all raised a fist and roared. The one who had asked the question nodded. "Good. You grant us honor and glory. As it should be."

The next elder, a giant of a minotaur with silver fur, stood up. Pointing to the two new longhouses, he said, "You give us strong shelter. Easy access to water and food. Do you think we are weaklings?" His eyes were full of challenge.

Alexander stood as well, shaking his head. "I saw the trail of orc bodies from the army you drove into my forest. I know you can more than take care of yourselves." He motioned to the village around them. "This village was already here. With no one to occupy it. Yes, I added the longhouses. For two reasons. I was unsure of how many of your people would come. And because we do not yet know what dangerous beasts might roam these woods. Molgo told you about the demon army?"

The elder nodded with a grunt. Alexander went on. "More demons could come at any time. Or drow. Or the monsters that serve them. The longhouses allow you to gather your people in a defensible position and hold out until help arrives. If you will follow me, I'll show you."

He walked toward the nearest longhouse, which happened to be the single-story version. He motioned for the others to follow him inside. As they did, he used his earth sense to find the stairway to the underground room. Once he located it, he said, "Each of the longhouses has a fallback position." Using his earth magic, he separated the stone that covered the stair, then levitated it up and over to one side. Setting it down, he cast a light globe down into the stair. "Go ahead, see for yourself."

Molgo went first, stepping down the wide stairway. When he reached the bottom and found the large circular room, he grunted in surprise. The others had similar reactions. Alexander and Silverbeard brought up the rear. Stepping into the room, he pointed to the back. "There are bathrooms back there. And a water supply. If you stock this place with provisions, you could survive down here for a very long time. I can send you dwarves to make it so that the doorway to these stairs is very hard to find once closed."

He stepped aside and let the minotaurs speak amongst themselves. After about five minutes, Molgo stepped forward. "We have all agreed. We will take the oath and become Elysians."

Alexander held out a hand and Molgo grasped his forearm. "Thank you. And welcome to Elysia. I'll come back soon with Prince Kai, who will accept your oath. It will be magically binding, so make sure your people know this. Those who do not wish to take it will not be harmed, but they will not be allowed to remain here." Molgo nodded in understanding.

Silverbeard spoke up. "What about the orcs?"

Dawn shook her head. "They are concerned. They too have questions. And the answers you have provided us may help. But they are also afraid. Most lost family in the battles against us. My people and yours. The warlord forced them into what amounted to slavery. Providing their males for the army, giving up their food to feed the army. They are hesitant to place themselves under any ruler again."

Alexander asked, "Can you help me speak to their leaders? And who are their leaders now? Do they go by strongest? Or do they honor their elders as you do?"

Dawn and Molgo both agreed. Dawn said, "They have a council of elders, just as we do."

Alexander was about to teleport them all when Silverbeard held up a hand. Looking to the elders, he asked, "What d'ye need? Have ye enough food?"

The silver-haired elder nodded. "We do. The forest provides plentiful game, as well as fruits and berries. We have already begun to plant crops. And we have brought our harvest from the fields the warlord did not destroy. There are fish in the river. We will thrive here."

Silverbeard added, "Ye have enough tools? I hear the forge workin'." He grinned at them.

"We have all that we need. Thank you, Master Silverbeard."

The elder dwarf nodded, then looked to Alexander. He teleported the four of them back to the orc village. Molgo and Dawn entered first, with Alexander and Silverbeard following. Dawn grabbed a female orc child who ran past and told her to fetch the elders. The four of them waited near the center of the village. There was a simple fountain with a short wall around it. The water bubbled up clear and cool into a pool from which water could be drawn. Alexander took a seat and reached a hand in to taste the water. He made a mental note to see about adding plumbing to the single homes. The longhouses already had it.

After a time, six orcs approached and were greeted by Dawn. There were three males and three females. Two of the males were battle-scarred. Obvious veterans who had earned much honor. The third was smaller by comparison, though still taller and bulkier than Alexander. He carried a staff and looked to be a shaman of some kind. The females were all tough-looking, with weathered skin and calloused hands.

Dawn introduced Alexander and Silverbeard, then named each of the elders. Alexander was busy watching their faces and did not catch all of their names. When none of them spoke, he started things off.

"I would like to begin by saying we regret having to kill so many of your warriors. Our lands were invaded and we had to defend ourselves. We too lost loved ones in that fight. We spared as many of yours as possible, and they will be returned to you after they serve their time at Broken Mountain. They are being treated well and no harm will come to them." Silverbeard nodded in confirmation.

"Next, I know that your people have lived in relative peace with the minotaurs for generations. And that the warlord pushed you into a war that most of you did not want. I hold no ill will against your people for his actions. As I mentioned, we have lost people in recent weeks. In both the battle with your warlord and defending against an invading demon army. Elysia is a large kingdom with a small population. I'm sure you saw that this village was empty when you arrived. I seek honorable people willing to work hard to help me build my kingdom into something great. I hope your people will join me."

He sat down on the ground with his back to the fountain wall. The others all joined him. Molgo shot him a wink and Dawn smiled. She began to speak. "Alexander speaks the truth. We witnessed the last battle with the demons. He and his people fought bravely. And he treats his people equally. All his people. Elves, humans, dwarves, gnomes, duergar, gryphons, dragons, even a tiny goblin. They have welcomed us and provided for us just as they have for you. Molgo's tribe has agreed this morning to become citizens of Elysia." Molgo nodded his head once to confirm.

The orcs whispered among themselves. One of the scarred males said, "We found a mine nearby. We have been pulling iron from it for two days." He pointed to a hut near the outer edge of the village. "The iron is there if you wish to take it."

Alexander shook his head. "No. It is yours to use if you need it. Or we will purchase it from you. The terms we offer you are as follows. For one year from today, the resources you gather are for you to use to build your village. Whether it be iron, or even gold, from the mine, meat or lumber from the forest, or stone from the earth. At the end of the year, you will begin to pay ten percent of the resources you gather or items you craft to Elysia. To help the rest of the kingdom grow. We will employ some of you as soldiers to help us defend ourselves or our allies. We'll offer you protection and assistance when needed."

The orc nodded, seeming satisfied. Another spoke up. One of the females. "You will take our young females for your pleasure?"

Silverbeard laughed and answered before Alexander could. "Alexander has his queen. She be a feisty one, too. If'n he were to lay hands on one o' yer lasses, the queen would stab him with her pretty daggers!" It was Alexander's turn to nod in agreement and blush slightly as the orcs laughed along with the dwarf.

The female nodded her head. "I would like to meet this queen."

Alexander sent a quick message in officer chat. "*Jules, you awake yet?*"

"*Pancakes. Leave me alone.*"

"*No can do. Need your help. The orcs want to meet their potential queen. Be there in a second.*" He thought for a second, then added, "*Kai, can you join us? The minotaurs are ready to take the oath, and the orcs might be as well. If Jules isn't too sleepy to charm them.*"

73

He looked at the orc. "I can fetch her right now. Will you wait a few moments?" When she nodded, he disappeared. He stopped briefly at the garrison tower, then popped into the keep. Walking from the teleport zone to the dining area, he saw that Kai had already joined Jules, who was shoveling pancakes into her delicate mouth like she was in an eating contest.

Kai grinned at Alexander. "Is Jules expecting? I've only ever seen a female eat that way when Lia was first fertilized."

Jules coughed and spit out a mouthful of pancakes as Alexander guffawed. "Nobody has impregnated anybody here, you big dragon oaf!" she growled at him.

Kai simply raised an eyebrow. "Testy, too. Just as Lia was."

Alexander got himself under control and said, "We really need to go. Are you two ready?" When they both stood and moved closer, Kai took the liberty of transporting them. His range was more than enough to take them straight to the orc village. They walked back to the fountain and Alexander introduced them.

"This is Prince Kaibonostrum of the dragon kingdom. He will be the one to administer your oaths should you decide to join us. We have a treaty with the dragon kingdom, the elven kingdom, and two human kingdoms, as well as the dwarves at Broken Mountain." Kai nodded to the gathered elders and smiled reassuringly. The orcs were a bit taken aback to suddenly have a dragon in their midst.

"And the most dangerous of your guests today is Lady Jules, my beloved, and queen of Elysia." Jules smiled prettily and waved at Dawn. She looked impressive in her head-to-toe black leather armor and emerald choker. Daggers were strapped to each thigh and throwing knives lined a thin bandolier across her chest.

"Good morning to all of you," she said.

Alexander indicated the female who had asked the question. "The elders wished to meet you. They had a concern about me taking their young females for my amusement."

Jules snorted. "Don't worry about your young ladies. If I even catch him looking at them, I'll cut off parts of him that he'd rather keep." To which the females grinned and grunted their approval. Jules shot him a dirty look as if she thought he was already guilty. One hand fingered the hilt of a dagger. This earned more laughter from the female orcs. She turned so that only he could see her face and gave him a wink.

"Yes, well. Now you've met my queen. Who scares me more than a little most of the time. Any other questions?"

Another female stood up. "Borag forced us to breed quickly. To make more warriors for his army."

Jules growled and actually drew a dagger. She waved it around as she spoke. "There will be none of that here. Ever. You will have as many or as few children as you wish. If Borag were not already dead, I'd slit his throat for you. Let me be clear. You are free. Free to do as you choose, when you choose. You may become citizens and remain here. Or you may reject our offer and leave in peace. Go back to the plains. If you choose to stay with us and take the oath, you will be subject to our laws. Thieves will be jailed. Murderers will be executed. I'm afraid I do not know the laws of your people, but I imagine ours are much the same."

Alexander added, "We will not force anyone to fight. Those warriors who wish it can join our army. Or, some of them can. They will be paid, and housed, and fed. The rest of you can farm, or mine, or hunt and fish, or craft. You can teach others. We have a desperate need for farmers and crafters, and yes, warriors. But it will be up to you which path you choose."

The smaller of the males, the shaman, asked, "We will have to worship your god?"

Silverbeard took that one. "We do no' worship any one god. Each of us be free to worship who we choose. I be a paladin o' Durin. Alexander there be a Champion O' Light, favored by Odin and the god's o'light. There be a wee goblin at the keep who be a chosen o' Hermes, god o' thieves 'n travelers. We have a dragon forge created by Prince Kai here that were blessed by many gods. And there be a temple with a priest o' Asclepius the healer god."

The shaman nodded. "And if our god is a dark god?"

Alexander thought for a moment. "Do you all worship the same god? And who would that be?"

One of the females cut off the shaman before he answered. "Some of us worship more fervently than others. Grang there is a shaman of Gromish, God of War. I worship Laktar, Goddess of the Hearth and Protector of Children."

Alexander looked to Kai. The dragon said, "They are indeed dark gods. But not evil. And not tied to the drow wizards that I'm aware of."

Alexander looked back to the shaman. "Does Gromish require you to sacrifice people?"

The shaman spat on the ground at the idea. "Gromish requires an honorable death in battle. He is a god of war, not blood. We rejected the blood god long ago."

"Then I see no problem with you worshipping your dark gods. As long as they do not require you to break any of our laws. If you like, we will even help you construct a temple. You can request the blessings of your gods and they may provide boons to your village. We have done the same at our keep and a village called Whitehall. Crops grow faster, people heal faster. Though I don't know if the dark gods would be so beneficent."

Alexander waited for more questions, but no one else spoke. The elders whispered among themselves. With their elven and dragon hearing, Alexander, Jules, and Kai could hear every word if they chose to. But Alexander let them have their privacy.

Eventually, they stood and faced Alexander. "We will accept you as our king. And take the oath." Jules clapped her hands in excitement. Alexander shook hands with each of the elders in turn.

"Please, call your people together. Make sure they're all here and we'll administer the oath." Several runners were sent off in various directions. "While we wait, I would ask that two of you be designated as representatives of your people on my council." He looked at Molgo and Dawn. "Will you two be serving as the representatives of the minotaurs?"

Molgo said, "I am not one for meetings and talking. I know war. So I will not have much to say in your councils."

Alexander laughed. "Elysia has been a kingdom only a few weeks and this is one of very few days that we have not been under attack. We've had to defend against the drow and their minions, other adventurers, the warlord's orcs, the undead army, and the demon army. We fought battles in Stormforge and Antalia. And we're part of an alliance that's at war with the drow wizards. I think your expertise in war will be much needed."

Molgo and Dawn, along with several of the orc elders, grinned at this. Dawn said, "Maybe we should reconsider becoming Elysians. It seems to be dangerous to be near you."

Alexander thought of Dayle and the citizens who'd been lost in the various battles. "That is true," he answered solemnly. "I have enemies. And Elysia as a nation has enemies. And you *should* consider that seriously."

He looked up to find that several hundred orcs were gathered around in the open spaces and streets. All of them were looking on curiously as they mumbled questions. Several minotaurs were mixed in here and there.

The shaman hopped up on the low fountain wall and raised his staff. The crowd instantly grew quiet. Alexander didn't blame them. He'd seen what a shaman could do in the battle on the bridge. "We elders have spoken with King Alexander and Queen Jules of Elysia. This is their land, their forest. They have invited us to become Elysians. They offer a good life, one of freedom and honor. And resources. And the opportunity to fight alongside them to earn glory!"

He waited while the crowd reacted. Some with shouts of support, others more angrily. "We have decided to accept their offer! Those who wish to follow our advice and do the same may take an oath and remain. All those who do not wish to follow us must leave the forest and return to the plains. Or take your own path elsewhere."

A voice shouted out from the crowd, "Do all the elders agree?" One by one, the elders stepped up next to the shaman and confirmed their agreement. Then they all stepped down and moved through the crowd, answering questions or, in a few cases, cuffing objectors on the head. Five minutes later, they had all returned to the fountain. Some twenty orcs could be seen gathering belongings, and within a few minutes they were headed north out of the village.

Alexander called out to them, "Beware the beasts in the forests! Do you have weapons to defend yourselves?" When they ignored him and kept walking, he added, "If you change your minds, you will be welcome here."

Kai stepped up onto the wall, raised his hands, and in a deep, ground-rumbling voice, said, "Your oaths shall be sworn on your lives. Bound to your souls. Violation of your oaths will cause you to be incapacitated until you can be judged for your violation. A judgement of guilt means death. One last time, any who do not wish to utter the oaths, stand aside now."

None of the remaining orcs moved.

"Very well. Repeat this oath: 'On my life, I swear my loyalty to the kingdom of Elysia, and my obedience to its king and queen."

He made some simple hand gestures as he spoke and a blue aura extended from him, encompassing all those who stood in the crowds. As one, they spoke the oath. A few fumbled with the words but managed to follow the lead of the others. Dawn and Molgo held their tongues, as they would take the oath with their people.

Then Kai instructed the orcs to approach in a line, beginning with the elders, touching each of them on the shoulder and speaking a word. As he did, a black dragon icon appeared above the head of each one, then faded away. It took a while, but eventually all had passed by and been accepted. And just like that, Elysia had over two hundred new citizens.

As Kai was accepting the long line of oath-takers, Silverbeard began to quietly discuss logistics with the elders. He made a list of items they needed and resources or craft items they wanted to sell. By the time Kai was finished, the dwarf looked satisfied and the elders looked hopeful. The shaman stood in front of Alexander and Jules and took a knee before bowing his head. Immediately, all the others did the same. "Thank you, King Alexander. For giving us a new start."

Alexander nodded gravely. "Please, stand. You are most welcome. I need all of you just as much as you needed me. And please…" He changed his voice to a loud whisper that many of the nearby orcs could hear. "Unless there are other kings or queens around, it's just Alexander."

The shaman smiled. "Fair enough, Alexander."

Silverbeard called out, "Fer those of ye who wish to serve as soldiers. We'll be needin' about forty to start. Make yer way down to the garrison tower on the other side o' the bridge tomorrow. If there be less than forty of ye, that be fine. We'll make other arrangements. If there be more than forty, decide among yerselfs who be first."

The silver-haired elder asked, "Can those who stay serve as guards to protect the village?"

Silverbeard said, "O'course. We'll assign ye a few o' the paid soldiers, orc or otherwise, ta guard the village. If ye feel ye need more, then ye can pay them yerselves or petition us fer more. And if an attack be comin', ye'll have a way to reach us to call fer help."

Alexander added, "There is a bank and an auction house at the keep. You now have access to both. You can sell your goods to us at a fair price, or sell them through the auction house. And for those of you wishing to protect your gold, you can deposit it at the bank where it will be safe." Looking at some of the battle scars on the orcs around him, he added, "We also have a temple and healers. I don't know if you have healers among you, but they are there if you need them."

When it seemed there was nothing more that needed their immediate attention, Kai teleported them to the minotaur village. Molgo and Dawn led them into the village center and the process repeated itself. Only more quickly, to start with. The minotaurs already knew the deal, and when Molgo called for any who didn't wish to become citizens to leave, not one minotaur moved. Kai administered their oaths and that part took longer, as there were something close to five hundred minotaurs.

As Kai was doing his thing and Silverbeard was talking over logistics with Molgo, Dawn, and the elders, Alexander stepped to one side and said, "Jeeves, are you there?"

"Of course, Majesty. You are in the center of one of our villages. How may I serve?"

"There are more minotaurs here than I expected. I don't know that the housing here is sufficient, even with the longhouses. I know you are pulling stone from inside the cliff to create the market square. Can you build more here as you do that?"

"I can, Majesty. Removing the stone is not technically constructing anything. It is resource gathering. So I may add more structures while I gather stone."

Alexander waved at Dawn, then motioned for her to join him. When she did, he said, "Dawn, meet Jeeves. He is the spirit of Elysia, and controls the physical kingdom development. Jeeves, this is Lady Dawn of the minotaurs. She will serve on my council and may have requests from time to time. Please relay those requests to me for approval."

"Pleased to meet you, Councilor Dawn."

Dawn's eyes flicked around as she tried to locate the source of the voice as she said, "Pleased to meet you as well, Jeeves."

Alexander clarified, "Jeeves communicates through the structures around us. He can hear you and speak to you as long as you are close by any building, mine, or on the bridge. You can use him to call for help if needed, and send along any important information. Or if you'd like a meeting." When Dawn nodded in understanding, he said, "We were just talking about housing. It looks to me like you don't have enough."

Dawn said, "We are managing. Our people will cut timber and build more homes in time. It is still warm enough to sleep outside in tents for now. We should have shelter for everyone before the snows come."

Alexander shook his head. "Not good enough. I want your people to have proper stone structures that won't catch fire if the village is attacked. Would you prefer more longhouses? Or more single stone homes?"

Dawn scratched her head. "The longhouses are useful. Many can sleep there, and after we build more homes they can be used for storage. Maybe one more longhouse? Then a few dozen of the homes?"

"Jeeves, start on another two-story longhouse. If I remember, that takes a full day, correct?"

"Yes, Majesty. That is correct." Alexander noticed Dawn's eyes still darting about and smiled.

"And how long will it take you to construct each house?"

"That will depend on the type of structure you wish? The standard huts here are simple structures with one great room that includes a fireplace and a bedroom. More advanced housing with extra rooms, kitchens, bathrooms and such take longer."

Alexander looked at Dawn. "I have not seen many children. Did you bring families with you?"

Dawn nodded. "Twenty of our families have children. One or two per family."

Alexander said, "Jeeves, Dawn will give you a list. For individuals or couples without children, build a simple hut with a bathroom and kitchen added. For families, add a bedroom for each child. Start with the twenty families and let me know when that is done."

"Of course, Majesty. Each of the houses will take half a day at most. Would you like me to construct a central water supply and sanitary system and connect them?"

"Yes! Please, Jeeves. I didn't know you could do that." Alexander grew excited.

"I could not, before I reached my current level. The longhouse, the twenty family houses, and the plumbing system will require twelve days in total and approximately one thousand two hundred stone units. I can gather some of those units by forming the underground chamber below the longhouse. The rest will come from stone gathered at the keep. Upon

completion, I estimate you will have a surplus of nearly two thousand units of stone."

"Thank you, Jeeves," Alexander said as he turned to a wide-eyed Dawn. "You'll make up the list for him?"

She nodded her head, not speaking. Alexander took her arm and led her back toward the group. She immediately began to whisper to Molgo, likely about the disembodied AI that was going to magically nearly double the size of their village. Molgo approached Alexander. "Thank you again, Alexander. For all you are doing for our people. I would make one more request about the building. Would it be possible to add a lookout tower for guards and archers?"

"Of course. I should have thought of that. Let's take care of the housing first. It will take almost two weeks. After that, we'll work on defenses." Molgo agreed.

Kai finally completed the oaths for the roughly five hundred minotaurs in attendance. Silverbeard had finished his logistics discussions with the elders and Jules was pulled away from playing 'sneak up on the minotaur children.' With a last round of thanks and goodbyes, Kai teleported himself, Alexander, Silverbeard, and Jules back to the keep. He immediately took his leave and disappeared back to his roost to check on Lia.

Chapter 5

Death & New Life

Alexander and the others went to find Lola, then he teleported all four of them up to the keep's control room.

"Hello again, Jeeves. Please display the kingdom's status sheet," Alexander asked.

"Of course, Majesty." The familiar blue hologram appeared above the control desk.

Elysian Keep: Level 22/50	
Physical Status: 4,100/5,300 See Infrastructure tab for details	**Resources: 234,000 units** See Resources tab for details
Current Population: 1,201 Citizens: 1,197 Guests: 4	**Defensive Capabilities: 100%** See Defense tab for details
Ancillary Structures: 30 See Ancillary Structures tab for details	**Production Rate: 56%** Production will increase with population and use of ancillary structures

"Thank you, Jeeves. I should have asked. Do you have new abilities available since you gained level 22?"

"I have unlocked several new blueprints for structures and other keep systems. Including defensive weapons. And you have the option of upgrading my current abilities. No new abilities were unlocked."

Alexander looked at Jules and the dwarves. "Last time, we discussed upgrading the stone golems. Or upping Jeeves' interface to level three."

Silverbeard spoke first. "With nearly eight hundred new citizens, we've less need o' the golems fer battle. They still be handy for daily work. They do no' sleep and can do nearly any simple job ye give 'em."

Jules asked, "Jeeves, what would Improved Interface III give you?"

"Several improvements, Lady Jules. My area of detection will increase by twenty-five percent. I will be able to anticipate the needs of the kingdom more easily and with more detail. This holographic status can be displayed anywhere within the keep or an ancillary structure upon demand by authorized individuals. I can maintain a detailed roster of every citizen and their status, including skills and abilities. I can also communicate directly with allied keeps to relay messages on your behalf. As long as they also have Improved Interface III or higher."

Jules' eyes moved from Lola to Silverbeard to Alexander, gauging their thoughts. "Sounds to me like we're going with Improved Interface III. Anyone disagree?"

Alexander didn't answer. He was off in space imagining all the ways he could make use of the new interface. By the time he blinked and came back to the present, the others were staring at him. His brain had half-registered their conversation and he realized they were waiting for him to give the order.

"Jeeves, please execute Improved Interface III."

"Thank you, Majesty." There was a short pause as the upgrade took effect. *"That feels much better. Now, I can inform you that the elves and dwarves have both upgraded their interfaces sufficiently to allow us to communicate. I have already established connections. Stormforge and Antalia are both at level 2, unfortunately. Also, with my extended detection range, I have discovered a natural chamber in the stone below, not far from the area I am hollowing out for the market square. It is located approximately five hundred yards north and twenty yards below the back wall of the current opening."*

"Thank you, Jeeves, we'll look into it later. Please relay my greetings and best wishes to Thalgrin at Broken Mountain and Ithaniel in the elven kingdom to let them know of your new ability."

"Of course, Majesty."

*****

Matt picked up his groceries and managed to calm himself as he walked through the aisles of the store. Back in his truck, he drove carefully back to the neighborhood of his current safe house and parked.

A shortcut through a back alley, and five minutes later he was back in the house. He put away the groceries, then stared at his headset.

"Are you done with your petty punishment?" He spoke to the drow as if they were standing there with him. "You need me to capture Damerion for you. I can't do that if you kill me every time I log in."

Taking a deep breath, he took a seat and placed the gear on his head. A moment later, he was in the game. Once again, he sat on his throne. He quickly lifted his arms and inspected the arms of the chair. Sure enough, there was poison smeared there. So the apple he'd eaten, it wasn't the fruit that was poisoned, it was his glove. And then he'd stuck it in his mouth like a fool. "I bet you're getting quite a laugh from this, you sick bastards."

As he uttered those words, both dragon observers froze. For a moment, they'd thought he had discovered them.

"If you're done punishing me now, I'd like to go about the business of torturing the prince and gaining access to the city." He stood and moved toward the doors. His lock pick was sitting right where he'd dropped it. Now that he knew it might be poisoned from previous contact, he left his gloves on as he picked it up. He worked slowly, using the pick to probe the lock. Only, the probe was telling him that the door was already unlocked.

To make sure, he reversed his work and locked the door. Then he unlocked it. When he shoved on the doors, they didn't budge. "Oh, come ON!" he shouted, pounding on the door. "Since when do drow have earth magic? Why seal me in here? Even if I starve to death, I'll just come back again! And every time you kill me it makes me weaker when I need to be getting stronger!"

He kicked the doors in frustration. On instinct, he reached for his inventory bag, forgetting it had been taken. "No teleport, then. No way out. Unless…" He jumped up and moved the secret panel at the back of the throne. When he opened it and found the portal orbs missing, he howled in anger.

The two dragons shared a look and the elder closed his eyes. A moment later, the ceiling shattered and tons of water from the underground river poured in. The last thing the dragons saw as they teleported away was the Dark One's body being crushed by tons of water slamming him into the sealed doors.

Matt didn't even see what killed him. He heard a cracking sound and a roar, and began to turn to look. But he was slammed into something hard and died. He'd had a vague feeling of cold and wet. He stomped around in limbo, waiting for his timer to run out. As he waited, he looked at his stats. He'd been level 75 when last he'd seen the prince. He was already down to level 69.

When the countdown ended and he re-entered his body, he found himself underwater. He instinctively began to hold his breath and stroke upward. The water was dark, all the torches in the room had been extinguished. By the time he approached the high ceiling, his lungs were complaining. When he bumped his head on the ceiling without finding air, he began to panic. He pounded on the stone above in frustration. Ahead of him, he could feel a current. The water still rushing in from the ceiling. He tried to swim out through the opening when he found it but the current was too strong. He had just managed to latch onto a jagged edge of the opening to pull himself through when his oxygen ran out and he drowned.

Back in limbo and down to level 68, Matt was frustrated but in a better mood. "Now I have a way out. I just have to survive long enough. The pressure from the current tells me the room was either still filling, or the water is exiting somewhere. If I wait a few minutes, it should be full. Then the current won't be as strong and I can swim out of the ceiling. If the water is escaping somewhere, I'll find it. And follow it out."

Ten minutes later when his timer ran out he respawned in his throne again. Holding his breath, he swam upward. Quickly locating the opening in the ceiling, he pushed against the current, which seemed weaker but was still difficult to overcome. He pulled himself up through the hold by grabbing its edge. Then he moved with the current of the underground river as he pushed upward, trying to reach the surface and fresh air.

He didn't make it. Either the river was deep, or his sense of direction was off. Either way, he'd try again.

Six deaths and more than an hour later, he changed his tactics. There had remained a slight incoming current at the ceiling opening, so he began to search with his hands along the floor and walls for the spot where the water was draining out. He drowned four more times before he realized it was exiting beneath a door behind a tapestry that now fluttered in the small current.

Hope exploded within him as he braced a hand against the wall next to the door and pulled it open as his oxygen bar dipped close to empty. Without any light, he fumbled around inside the room until his hands found stone. The water was flowing into a stone bowl. As he reached inside, he screamed out the remainder of his oxygen.

Back in limbo and now down to level 56, he shouted, "A goddamned toilet! The water's draining into a stone toilet in the privy!"

All hope of escape that direction fled. There was no way he could squeeze through such a small opening. His only chance was to find a way to swim out. But he was in no hurry to try again. Maybe if he waited offline, the drow would cease to be amused by his suffering and open the doors.

So he logged out, removed the headset, and got to work on his first beer of the evening.

*****

That afternoon, King Arand sat in his study with his wife and two remaining sons. He listened as Elrid told him of the Dark One, as Sophie had called him. He listened to the tale of the torture and death of Bain, the trusted companion and bodyguard he had assigned his son at a young age. He heard about the beatings and torture his son had endured. And the man in black leather's desperation to find a back way into the city. He listened while Elrid told him what the man had said about killing his youngest brother. His wife cried into his shoulder as he held her while Elrid spoke. The prince, to his credit, kept his composure.

"Fitz tried to warn me and I did not listen." The king's voice was barely a whisper. "We must do as he asked and fortify the docks. The drow and whatever army he has could attack at any time. Increase the watch on all the walls. Four-man patrols. Drow use stealth and we cannot have them eliminating our guards by surprise. The gates will be sealed at sunset. No one through without specific authorization from me. Every wagon checked, every barrel and crate opened before they come inside the city."

Elrid made a suggestion of his own. "They could be in the sewers already, Father. Let us seal all the exit grates and post a guard near each one. We can use untrained militia, as they will only be there to raise an alarm. Have the mages set some alarms within the tunnels as well."

King Arand nodded his head and sighed. "We have become a city under siege. And I must mourn a son without even a body to bury."

"More than just a son," Elrid corrected.

Arand looked at his son's face. He was closer to breaking now than when he'd spoken of his own torture. "I'm sorry about Bain."

"He was my brother. Blood or not. For ten years, we've been together every day. He died horribly, Father. But even after they'd cut more of him away than there was left of him, he stayed strong. He taunted the man in black into killing him. Spat in his face before he died."

The king placed a hand on his son's shoulder. "We will honor him along with your brother and his bodyguard. A small family affair. No reason to waste resources on a lavish funeral if we're about to be under siege."

He comforted his queen for a few moments longer, letting her cry herself out. She'd been weeping nonstop since Elrid appeared with the news of his brother's demise. When she quieted down, he motioned to his eldest son Apollos to open the doors. Two guards waiting outside saluted.

Apollos whispered, "Fetch my mother's ladies. And bring Sophie of Stormforge." A moment later, three women bustled into the room and gathered up the queen. Her husband let her go reluctantly, gently releasing her hand as they led her from the room. She would prepare the funeral ceremony.

Sophie walked in as the queen departed. She bowed at the waist to the king. "Your Majesty wished to see me?"

The king was distracted, and Apollos answered for him. "The drow you brought us speaks of two armies. One undead, the other demons. They are poised to attack the city. Yet none of our scouts or hunters, nor any of the adventurers who are always flitting about the forest nearby, have seen any trace of them."

Sophie pulled out a scroll. "A messenger came through the portal not an hour ago. He brought this message for the king. And one for me. Mine spoke of a battle involving two armies that match that description. They attacked Elysia a few days ago. They did so using a portal orb, transporting from some base of operations that may be far from here."

The king opened his message and began to read. Apollos looked over his shoulder as Elrid waited patiently.

Arand confirmed, "My letter says much the same. It seems Alexander defeated both armies. One of which included an undead dragon. Impressive for a brand new king. Let us hope the armies the drow prisoner spoke of were the same two. Otherwise we may be vastly outnumbered." He continued to read.

"It says an alliance is forming. Initiated by the dragon king to gather a force capable of resisting the drow wizards. I remember childhood tales of the drow wizards, but I confess I believed them to be just that. Stories to scare children into behaving."

Sophie shook her head. "They are very real. They attempted to murder the queen and take over the city of Antalia. Alexander and his people thwarted the attempt and drove them from the city. They have attacked Stormforge as well, using drow assassins and adventurers who served the Dark One. And of course, you've just read about the all-out assault on Elysia. The Dark One has a special hatred of Alexander and his companions. They have borne the brunt of the aggression."

Arand asked, "Charles recommends a meeting with this Alexander. If I send my eldest son with you, can you arrange such a meeting? If there are armies of the dark waiting to sack Damerion, I am not too proud to accept help."

Sophie produced a teleport scroll. "This will take us to the palace at Stormforge. From there, I can either take Apollos to Elysia or arrange for Alexander to meet us in Stormforge. We can leave right now. Or if you two need time to discuss acceptable terms of the treaty, I can wait outside."

The king shook his head. "My son has been groomed to take my place since the age of ten. He knows well enough how to protect the interests of Damerion. He has full authority to act on my behalf."

Apollos looked at Sophie. "I'm ready. Let us get this done quickly. I fear an attack is imminent." He stepped closer and Sophie placed a hand on his shoulder before triggering the scroll. The two of them appeared in the courtyard of Stormforge Palace. Two guards approached with weapons drawn until they recognized Sophie. Their weapons dropped and they saluted. She ordered, "Please inform the king and captain that Prince Apollos of Damerion has arrived. I believe we are expected."

One of the guards walked with them toward the palace entry as the other sent a runner ahead. Two more guards appeared as if out of nowhere to watch over the teleport zone.

Captain Redmond met them at the doors. He bowed slightly and smiled at Apollos. "Prince Apollos, welcome to Stormforge. I have not seen you since my wedding, and you were about half as tall as you are now."

Apollos chuckled. "And you do not seem nearly as tall now as you did then!" He reached out a hand and the captain shook it. Sophie had already disappeared.

The captain led the prince to the king's study, where both the king and queen were having tea. They rose and welcomed the prince, the queen giving him a hug. "I'm sorry to hear about your brother, child. Please give my love to your mother. She is a good woman and it has been much too long since we've spoken."

"Thank you, Majesty. I will pass along your message. I know she feels the same."

Charles shook the prince's hand and motioned for him to sit. "I've just sent a message to Alexander, and expect he'll be here shortly. He has a portal of his own, but the boy has teleportation magic and tends to pop up – ahhh... see what I mean?"

The king pointed his chin toward the door, where Alexander had just appeared. The young king bowed his head to the king and queen before shaking the captain's hand. Turning to Apollos, he offered his hand to the prince. "I am Alexander. Pleased to meet you."

Apollos bobbed his head quickly before accepting the handshake. "Majesty. Thank you for coming so quickly." He shot a glance at King Charles, who laughed.

Charles said, "I was just telling Apollos that you have a habit of just popping up here and there. Usually to cause some kind of trouble."

Alexander looked sheepish. "I'm afraid I learned it from Fitz. The wizard has some bad habits." Everyone in the room made noises of agreement. Turning back to the prince, Alexander said, "I'm afraid I've had a hectic week and have not heard much news of the world outside of Elysia. And I'm only slightly familiar with Damerion. I'm an adventurer who got suckered into becoming king, and I'm afraid I've not had the training a prince like you would receive."

Apollos quickly brought him up to speed on Elrid's capture and torture, and that of his other brother. And the Dark One's plan to seize the capital city of Damerion. Then he gave a little background on Damerion. "We are a port city, built atop a cliff above the cove. Our walls are high and strong, but we have little defense against an army that could just appear within our city using one of these portals Sophie mentioned. We have mages and a standing army, as well as a city guard. But they are not strong enough to take on an army of demons."

Alexander replied, "The first thing you should do is give the adventurers in the city a quest to defend it against the attack if it comes. They'll throw themselves into the battle again and again and should greatly reduce enemy numbers." Apollos nodded, having already discussed that with his father.

Alexander continued. "Have you read the terms of the alliance proposed by the dragons?"

When the prince shook his head, Charles produced a copy from his desk. The prince took some time to read it. It wasn't a complicated document. Mutual protection and support. The opportunity for trade, eventually. The fact that the document was created by dragons made Apollos' hand tremble as he held it. He'd never met a dragon, though he dreamed of flying on one as a child.

He said, "These terms are acceptable to Damerion."

Alexander grinned. "Great! If you'd like to come back to Elysia with me, Kai can get you an original copy to sign and answer any questions you may have. In addition, I will create a few weapons that will help you in battling drow. You can take them home with you." He glanced at the king and queen. "All of you are welcome to join us. Lydia too, of course. The place has grown a bit. We have our own Ogre and the food is just as good!"

The queen laughed. "We would love to see the keep. But another time. You have more urgent matters to address. And bring Apollos back here when you're done with him. We will send Edward to Damerion with him to train his men how to play with your light sticks."

Alexander bowed deeply. "As you wish, Majesty. But please visit soon. Jules always enjoys an excuse to dress up."

A moment later, Alexander and Apollos stood in the teleport zone at his keep. The prince looked around, his eyes appraising. "I'm sure this doesn't compare to your family's palace. But a month ago, this was an old ruin filled with undead. We're growing as quickly as we can."

Apollos eyed the massive walls and the gatehouse with its heavy portcullis and murder holes. "I believe you could easily drive away an invading army here."

Alexander chuckled. "The secret is not to let them get this far. We fought off the orc and undead armies up on the plateau," he pointed up and watched the prince's eyes go up and up, "then we fought the demons outside our outer wall. Oh! Something else you should do. We asked the gods to bless our temple here. The blessing they gave us makes the land itself damaging to the forces of the dark. Rogues and drow get knocked out of stealth as soon as they set foot here. And demons burn like someone threw acid on them."

Alexander walked Apollos around as he sent a message to Kai in guild chat. *"A prince of Damerion is here to sign the treaty and join the alliance."*

"Lia's eggs are about to hatch. Would you mind terribly bringing him up here? I don't wish to miss this. Lia would be... angry." Kai's voice was excited and scared at the same time.

"WHAT??" Alexander shouted, forgetting guild chat even as sounds of exclamation erupted from the other guild members, both in-chat and out loud. Without explanation, he teleported himself and a suddenly-confused prince up to Kai's roost.

The prince's eyes grew wide as he took in the sight of two dragons curled around an indentation in the center of the large chamber. Lia's head hovered over the eggs and she was half-humming, half-growling what sounded like a lullaby. Kai raised his head and moved so that he was a few feet in front of them.

"Prince Kaibonostrum and Lady Lia of the dragon kingdom, may I present Prince Apollos, heir to the throne of Damerion."

Apollos stuttered something and bowed deeply at the waist. Kai chuckled in his dragon voice, startling the young man. "Welcome, Apollos. You are just in time to witness the hatching of our dragonlings." He looked at Alexander. "Pay attention to guild chat, Alexander. Your mate and several others are demanding to be brought up here. They are, of course, welcome. This is an event one should share with friends."

Alexander popped back down to the courtyard, where most of the players - as well as Silverbeard, Lola, Mattie and Taylor, Thea, and Fibble - were gathering. A moment later, Regina came sprinting across the courtyard with Bodine right behind her. She huffed a bit when she reached them.

"No way we are going to miss this!" she gasped. They had run through the mirror from the garrison tower.

Alexander waited for Bodine to arrive, then teleported the whole group. There were lots of ooh's and ah's as they all took in the roost for the first time. Kai welcomed them and gave them a warning. "When the hatchlings first emerge, they might be dangerous to humanoids. Their mother has been teaching them manners, but the excitement of the hatching combined with the need to feed sometimes makes young ones a bit… bitey."

Sasha snorted. "A bit bitey, says the giant dragon guy. Is it too late to go back downstairs?"

Alexander looked around. "Okay, who's got meat in their bags? Cough it up. These are going to be the best-fed hatchlings ever to be born in Elysia."

Lainey rolled her eyes as she pulled several boar carcasses from her bag. "Lorian and I were hunting this morning." Sasha pulled some meat from her bags, as did Regina and Bodine.

Fibble, not wanting to be left out, produced a couple of cookies. "Do… do baby dragons like cookies?"

Lia spoke from behind Kai. "Baby dragons *love* cookies, little one. But do not give them more than one each. We do not want to spoil them."

Fibble looked at the two cookies he held, and then looked at the fingers on his other hand. "How many babies is there?" Alexander could see him fighting the urge to hoard his stash.

"There are seven eggs, little one. Let us hope that means seven baby dragons. Sometimes they are not strong enough to emerge from their shells. Though I am sure any progeny of Kaibonostrum will be more than strong enough."

"P…p-proggy?" Fibble fumbled over the word. He reached into his bag for more cookies.

Sasha leaned down and whispered, "Babies," as Fibble pulled out six more cookies. He looked up at Sasha with a question on his face. She took one of the cookies and put it back in his bag.

"This is seven. One for each baby dragon." The little goblin nodded his head so hard his ears slapped his face.

He turned to face the dragons. Standing on his tiptoes, he strained to see over Lia's tail. Lugs snatched him up and placed him atop a shoulder, and Fibble grinned. "I see the babies. I mean, eggs. Babies come soon?"

Lia nodded. "Any moment now. They are straining against their shells."

The group stood patiently, all eyes on the dragon eggs. A moment later, there was a tiny pop, followed by a cracking sound. A small piece of one egg separated itself and fell to the floor. A nose pushed outward, causing more cracks and widening the gap. Soon there were more pops and crackings, and the other dragonlings pushed to free themselves.

As the first tiny head emerged, Jules squealed and took a few steps forward. Kai cleared his throat to remind her to stay back. Sasha looked like she was going to need to be restrained as well. "Look! Sooo cute!"

When the baby dragon heard her voice and turned to look at her with the tip of its tongue sticking out to one side, she gasped, "Ohmygodineedtohugher!" She physically leaned toward the little hatchling. "Come on! Push! You can do it!"

The others began to encourage the dragonlings as well and the chamber began to sound like a VIP box at a dog track. Everyone was urging their favorite to push harder. Fibble dropped a cookie in the excitement, but Lugs caught it and handed it back to him.

After a few more minutes of struggle, all seven of the hatchlings had emerged. They flopped about a bit, their legs not yet working properly. They flapped tiny wings and took in their surroundings. Lia lowered her head and softly grumbled at them, and they formed into a rough line across the nest, stumbling over chunks of shell as they moved.

The first were twins as green as freshly-grown grass. A blue very similar to Lia's own hue stood next to them, followed by a silver with sparkling scales and a red that almost glowed. A black dragonling was larger than the others and seemed to possess more poise. The last and smallest was a white dragon with scales that looked as if they were made of cream and honey.

Fibble leapt off of Lug's shoulder without warning. He dashed forward and offered a cookie to the first of the greens, which was closest. Lia nudged the dragonling with her nose and it opened its mouth politely. Fibble reached forward, suddenly nervous about losing a hand, and placed a cookie in its mouth. As it chomped down on the treat and made happy-sounding noises, Fibble grinned and moved on to the next. One by one, he placed a cookie in an open mouth. When he reached the white dragon, it didn't open up. Instead, it leaned forward and nuzzled the goblin's chest.

Unsure what to do, Fibble looked up at Lia. The dragoness spoke to her hatchling. "Fibble has brought you a gift, little one. It would be rude not to accept."

The little white dragon, barely as tall as Fibble, rubbed her face against him once more before a tiny sneeze burst forth. The others laughed as Lainey said, "Yeah, he needs a bath."

Horrified, Fibble turned to give her a dirty look. As he did, the sneaky little white dragon snatched the cookie from his outstretched hand and gulped it down. Then she poked her snout into his chest hard enough to cause him to take a step back. As he steadied himself, she burped at him. He happily returned the burp-greeting and stepped forward to wrap his arms around her neck in a hug.

Sasha had tears running down her face. "This could not be any cuter. I might melt."

Lugs called Fibble back and he left the little dragon reluctantly. She didn't seem any happier to see him go. She tried to follow, but her coordination wasn't up to the task.

Lia said softly, "Lainey?" and immediately the valkyrie and a few of the others moved forward to deposit meat in front of the hatchlings. They sniffed and poked at it for a bit, then tore into the meals with gusto. Both Kai and Lia rumbled happily like purring cats.

Fitz appeared out of nowhere. "Ah, the next generation." He smiled warmly at the little dragonlings as they ripped into their meals. "And they have proper appetites!" Turning to face Alexander, he said, "They will need to sleep after they feed. Breaking free of the egg is taxing. Alexander, we will speak later."

Lia nodded and added, "Thank you all for joining us, and for your kind gifts."

Alexander recognized a dismissal when he heard one. He bowed to the new mother and gathered the group together before teleporting them back down to the keep.

*****

The moment Alexander and crew were gone, Fitz sat down on the floor and said, "Come to me, little ones!" The seven dragonlings hopped and waddled their way over and mobbed the old wizard. He laughed long and hard as he wrassled with them like a kid playing with a litter of puppies. They licked his face and chewed on his hands, tugged on his feet. Lia and Kai watched on, the proud parents smiling as their oldest living ancestor rolled around on the floor with the newest of the dragons.

Eventually, their bellies full and their energy spent, the little ones trotted back to the warmth of the nest to curl up and sleep. Lia watched over them as Kai and Fitz moved outside to talk.

"Catch me up," Fitz commanded. Kai quickly told him about the trip to the elven kingdom, the death of the corrupted king, and Lorian's passing of the throne to Ithaniel. And about the drow infiltration that Kai had reported. There were more than a few corrupted elves just amongst those he had encountered during his walk through the city. Fitz scratched his beard absently. "A good choice. Ithaniel will do well. Assuming he lives."

Kai changed topics and caught Fitz up on the minotaurs and orcs becoming citizens. And the addition of Damerion to the alliance. Fitz grunted at that. He'd had faith that the boy prince would convince his father of the threat.

In turn, Fitz filled Kai in on his trip to the Dark One's lair and the traps he laid. "I figure he'll die at least ten times before someone realizes something's wrong and goes looking for him. We cleared their entire stronghold of drow, so the cursed undead will have permeated the halls by now. Whoever the drow send to check on him will have to fight their way through."

Kai shook his head. "I wish I could have been there to see his first few deaths. Would have been quite satisfying."

Fitz looked fondly over at the sleeping hatchlings. "Take good care of those little ones. Make them strong and teach them well. If things go badly, they may be all that's left of our people at the end of this." He placed a hand on Kai's head briefly, then disappeared.

Back down in the keep, he sought out Alexander, who was just sitting down to dinner in the dining area. Never one to turn down a meal, Fitz sat next to him and stole his plate.

"Haven't eaten in six hours. Feeling weak," he mumbled as he chewed the meat off a roasted rib.

Alexander just sighed and went to get another plate. It never paid to get between the old wizard and food. When he got back, Rufus was sitting on the brim of the old man's hat, nibbling on a small riblet of his own. He took a moment to wipe one greasy hand on the hat before waving to Alexander.

Fitz informed Alexander and those at the table with him of his adventure in the Dark One's lair. When he got to the part about setting traps with needles using their own poison, Brick couldn't contain himself.

"BWAHAHA! He's gonna think yer a real pain in the arse!" He bent over laughing at the image. "It be alright, though. Everything will work out in tha end!"

Alexander couldn't help but crack a smile himself. Less because of Brick's jokes and more about the rage he imagined Matt would fly into after dying repeatedly and being trapped. He was sure the psychopath got off on the power of being the 'Dark One,' and an NPC had just screwed up his plans big time. Maybe he'd make a mistake and expose himself. Alexander knew a lot of folks at Olympus were anxious to go back to their homes and live a normal life.

*****

Chapter 6

Friends In Low Places

Arc'men the drow wizard put down the communication stone and slammed his fist onto the table in front of him. "Where is that damned adventurer? He has not answered a summons in days. Who did we assign to watch over him?"

One of his lieutenants answered, "Kral'ven is with him. They were at the stronghold outside of Demarion at last report. But she too has been unreachable. Should we send someone to investigate?"

The wizard nodded and waved a hand. A portal orb floated up from a stand nearby and settled on the ground in the center of the room. Another wave of the hand and a portal opened. They could see little, the room on the other side was dark.

The lieutenant pointed to a drow guard standing nearby. The guard went into stealth mode and moved to the portal. The moment he stepped through, he began to float up and away. There was a moment of confusion on both sides of the portal before the wizard saw a string of bubbles escape from the drow's mouth as it drifted upward.

The guard realized the room was flooded. The purplish light of the portal revealed his face as he turned and began to swim back toward the portal. The wizard quickly clenched a hand and the portal closed. The lieutenant dashed forward as if to save the guard, then turned to the wizard. "Why? He would have made it back easily."

The wizard looked at him with contempt. He made a fist and the lieutenant began to gasp for breath. He fell to his knees, clutching his chest as if in prayer. "Do not EVER question me, youngling. I am older than the stone and wiser than you can even comprehend! That room was flooded. The moment your guard broke the plane, tons of water would have burst through with him to drown us all. Well, all of you." He smirked. Releasing his hold on his servant, he said, "Send someone to the stronghold to find out what that idiot has done. Bring him back here to answer for his actions."

The chastised drow rose to his feet and bowed. "My apologies, Master. It will be done immediately." He made several hand motions behind his back and three drow departed the room to relay his orders.

The wizard sniffed and looked disinterested. He quickly changed the topic. "Where are we with our plan for the elves? Has the king been replaced?"

The lieutenant bowed his head. "The king was to be removed last night. We are awaiting word from our spies. Their report is overdue as well."

"Incompetents! I'm surrounded by incompetent fools! Find out what is going on, or I will feed you to the next demon I summon!"

The drow bobbed his head and fled the room, several others following behind. When the wizard was in a bad mood, it wasn't safe to be near him.

*****

When Apollos had recovered a bit from the surprise of the dragons hatching, Alexander escorted him around the keep, making small talk as they went. The prince was particularly interested in the dragon forge, as was nearly everyone else who saw it. Alexander teleported him up to the top of the garrison tower on the plateau to give him an idea of the scope of Elysia's lands. Apollos was duly impressed.

"It seems your kingdom is larger than Damerion. Indeed, it may be one of the largest anywhere. The resources you have at your disposal will make you wealthy indeed."

Alexander grimaced. "Wealth isn't what interests me. Money is simply something we need to make sure that our citizens have what they need: food, weapons, shelter. Our strength will be in our people."

Apollos nodded. "My father has often said something similar. I think you two might get along well. And speaking of food… did I smell bacon back there at the keep?"

Alexander grinned at him. "You bet! I'll introduce you to him!" He teleported a confused-looking prince back to the keep. From the teleport zone he led the prince to the stables, where Bacon was lounging on a pile of hay, snoring away. Alexander produced an apple from his bag and placed it near the giant war pig's snout. A moment later, Bacon opened a lazy eye, moved his snout just enough that his tongue could reach the apple, and scarfed it down. He snorted once in appreciation and closed his eyes again. "Apollos, meet Bacon! Brick's glorious mount. Yes, he smells bad. But you get used it." Bacon made an offended snort, then farted in response. The thunderous explosion had both men stepping back to avoid the smell. They retreated back to the courtyard.

Apollos laughed. "That wasn't the bacon I was hoping for," he said, as he waved his hand in front of his face in mock disgust.

Alexander replied, "Sorry, I just couldn't resist. Let's go to the dining area and we'll get you some food while I work on your weapons." And they did just that. Hitting the kitchen first, Apollos stacked a plate with bacon, eggs, fruit, and fresh-baked rolls. Taking seats at one of the long tables, the prince began to eat as Alexander took out a couple of pieces of obsidian and began to shape them. A few minutes later, he was through, having created two light cannons. He no longer got any skill points for crafting these, as they were well below his ability level now. He'd have to come up with something new soon.

Walking to the smithy, Alexander handed the two new cannons to Brick so he could shape the triggers. While Brick worked, Alexander said, "You'll need a trigger word to call out as you depress the trigger. You have to do both at once or it will not fire. It's sort of a safety precaution."

Apollos didn't hesitate. "Elrid," he said, a mournful look on his face. "It seems fitting to me that our men should have his name on their lips as they kill those who tortured him and murdered our brother. Plus, it will make Elrid blush."

Alexander grinned at the prince as he took the weapons back from Brick and added in the trigger word. Then the three of them walked together out the main gate and down to the outer wall. Crossing the drawbridge, Alexander paused. "Steady, prince. You're about to meet another dragon. This one is our heroic moat monster, Rocky."

He whistled a few times, as if calling a dog home, and Rocky's head burst forth from the water. The spray reached all three of them up on the bridge, but Apollos didn't seem to mind. Rocky floated there, mouth open and tongue out. Alexander obliged by removing a handful of sugar cubes from his bag and tossing them into the water dragon's mouth. Rocky made a hooting sound of thanks before disappearing under the surface.

"Just how many dragons do you keep around here?" Apollos chuckled. "Any other surprises I should prepare for?"

Brick answered, "Well, let me see. There be a roost full o' gryphons up on the wall. And a bunch o' duergar livin' under us. There be villages full o' orcs and minotaurs up top, as well as giant kitties that could swallow yer head whole. We got a tribe o' rock trolls livin' in the mine…" His voice trailed off as he thought. Alexander willed him not to mention the Guardian deep in the mine above. "Yep, I think that be all."

Apollos shook his head. "In Damerion it's unusual to see any non-humans. Elves and dwarves visit occasionally for trade. And a few have made Damerion home. But I've never actually seen an orc. And I'm not sure anyone in Damerion has seen a minotaur."

Alexander nodded. "Until recently, I'd never seen a minotaur either. I'll take you to meet them if you like. In the meantime, let's talk about that cannon in your hand."

They spent the next several minutes teaching Apollos how to fire the light cannon. He used it to cut down a few trees and quickly became confident enough in its use. "I think I can show our weaponsmaster how these work. He can take it from there. I'll be sure Elrid's present for the training too."

Finished with that task, Brick returned to the smithy with a wink at Alexander. He'd been working on their special project. Alexander teleported himself and the prince up to the plateau. They stopped first at the garrison tower, where he was introduced to Regina and Bodine's menagerie. After a short visit, Alexander teleported them to the orc village.

The orcs greeted them with friendly waves and smiles that bared sharp teeth. Apollos had never met friendly orcs and it took some getting used to. Alexander led him to where the newest longhouse was located,

102

telling him the story of the battle at the bridge and how the orcs had come to occupy the village. After a formal introduction to some of the elders who were close by and a check to see that they were getting what they needed, they said their goodbyes and moved on.

Alexander teleported them to the minotaur village next. It looked much the same as the orc village, only another longhouse seemed to be building itself next to the first two. Both men watched this phenomenon for a few minutes as blocks of stone seemed to simply grow along the walls as the structure took form. Dawn joined them and was introduced to the prince. "Molgo is out exploring. He is like a child with a new toy. This forest already feels like home to us. Thank you, Alexander."

"No need for thanks, Dawn. You and your people are a welcome addition to Elysia. We needed you much more than you needed us!" He smiled at her. "You wouldn't happen to have any of that goat's milk drink, would you? I think the prince deserves a taste. This is a day of firsts for him. Lia's eggs hatched a few hours ago!"

Dawn grinned and led them back to her home. She fetched three mugs of the fermented goat's milk and brought them to the dining table. Alexander took a quick swig to reassure the prince, but didn't swallow right away. He watched as the prince took a deep draught and swallowed it down. He immediately began to cough and pound on his chest. He wheezed, "By the gods! What is in this?"

Dawn laughed, her deep voice booming through the room. "Ha! That's a secret, Prince Apollos."

Alexander swallowed his mouthful, then another as Apollos did the same. A pleasant burning spread through his chest and belly. He prudently set the mug down and said, "If you could produce this in large quantities, you could sell it to the dwarves for sure. Probably in the human cities as well. We can help you obtain more goats if you like. It could be a significant source of income. Especially from the dwarves." He pictured the village being mobbed by drunken dwarves demanding the drink.

Dawn nodded sadly. "We once had vast herds of goats out on the plains. But the warlord stole and slaughtered many for his army. We have enough to feed our people and provide milk for the children and for this."

She held up her mug. "But any additional stock you could provide would be welcomed."

Alexander allowed Apollos another drink before suggesting they move along. He didn't want the young man plastered when he got home. The prince was a little unsteady as he got to his feet as it was. They thanked Dawn and Alexander promised to look into the goats for her. When they'd exited the house and teleported back to the garrison tower, Apollos spoke up. "We have livestock. And not all of it can be brought into the city during the siege. I'm sure the farmers would rather sell it than lose it to the enemy or the wolves." His statement was slightly slurred and followed by a hiccup.

"We'll make that happen, then. We'll bring Silverbeard with us when we portal you back to Damerion. He can negotiate. But we'll need to sober you up before then. Have you ever met a rock troll?"

Alexander continued to ferry the prince around, introducing him to the various citizens of Elysia, including the rock trolls, gryphons, and duergar. They visited the memorial to those fallen in battle and took a walk through the keep. Alexander got directions from Jeeves and they followed the newly-made tunnel to the expanding market square deep in the mountain. Alexander hadn't been there himself, and was truly impressed with what he saw.

Apollos commented, "This is genius. I mean, it's not a new idea. The dwarves have built underground for eons. But the only things we've built underground in Damerion are sewer tunnels."

"Yes, this is much more than I expected." Alexander spun around, taking in the space. The open part of the square was a hundred yards across. Along its edges, the rough shapes of buildings were beginning to take form. These would become shops and housing and warehouses eventually. No wonder Jeeves had plenty of stone units to build the additions to the villages.

Jeeves' voice rang out. *"If you wish, I can scale back the plans, Majesty."*

Alexander shook his head. "No. No, Jeeves, thank you. This is wonderful. You've done very well here. Please continue as you have been."

"Of course, Majesty. In a month's time, barring any more additions to the villages or other projects, this zone will be able to house one thousand citizens, crafters, merchants, and guests, as well as store food supplies for approximately two months within the warehouses. Should the keep fall, you could retreat here and collapse the tunnel. There is a safe supply of water, and the two month period could be extended if you managed to bring livestock as well."

Apollos whistled. "That's... incredible." Alexander agreed.

"Jeeves, when this is completed, remind me to figure out a back exit. We'll discuss it with the group and pick a path."

"Of course, Majesty. That is a wise decision."

They left the new zone behind and returned to the keep's courtyard. The evening meal was being served, and Apollos met most of the other player guild members as they ate. Alexander explained to Silverbeard about the minotaurs' need for livestock and the dwarf confirmed that the coffers held more than enough gold to purchase whatever Damerion was willing to sell.

All through dinner, Fibble kept tugging on sleeves, asking everyone who might know when he could go visit the dragons again. Sasha finally lifted him up and set him on the bench next to her. "Lia will let us know when the dragons can play. I'm sure they're just as anxious to see you again. You're the perfect size for a snack!" She grinned at the horrified look that crossed his face. A moment later, he figured out she was teasing and his eyes narrowed. "Sasha big meanie! White dragon Fibble's friend. Not eat Fibble!"

She hugged him as she replied, "No, Fibble. The dragons won't eat you. But they are young and have not learned how to be gentle yet. So you must be careful not to get hurt while playing with them."

Fibble nodded, accepting the hug and the advice. He stood up on the bench and announced, "Fibble going to get more cookies. For the *dragon babies.* Not for Fibble. Well, maybe one or two for Fibble. And one for Bacon. And Tigger." He hopped off the bench and disappeared into the kitchen.

Sasha smiled fondly at the retreating goblin. "Five bucks says Bacon and Tigger never see their cookies." No one took that bet.

Lorian was sitting nearby. "I detailed a couple of hunters to procure some meat for the dragonlings. We haven't culled the direwolves in the lower forest for a while. Most of our people are too high-level to get any experience from it."

"Thank you, Lorian," Alexander answered. "I would think two hunters would be enough. If more are needed, I'm sure Kai can provide. If your hunters can't get experience from the direwolves, check with the minotaurs and orcs. Maybe a few of their people could benefit from the hunt." Lorian nodded and resumed his meal.

After dinner was eaten and Apollos was fully sober, Alexander took him and Silverbeard through the portal to Damerion. He'd wanted to take Jules along to introduce her, but she was nowhere to be found. He half expected her to be in stealth mode behind him as they stepped through the portal, but was disappointed. Taylor and his guard detail did appear, though. Alexander was going to have to pay more attention and see if he could figure out where they appeared from.

The portal opened onto a small courtyard within the innermost walls of the city. There were guards along the top of each wall, crossbows aimed at Alexander and party as they stepped through. When they saw the prince raise a hand, their weapons were lowered.

An escort appeared and Apollos led them into the palace. Taylor and the guards remained outside. He went straight to the king's study, where his parents and brother were finishing their own meal. They rose from their chairs to greet their new guests.

"Father, Mother, Elrid, this is King Alexander of Elysia and his chancellor Master Silverbeard." Both Alexander and Silverbeard bowed to the king and queen.

"Alexander! A pleasure to meet you." King Arand stepped forward and offered a hand. "We don't stand on much formality here. Please, call me Arand."

The group all took seats on chairs and sofas in a small sitting area near the fireplace. Servants entered and left, clearing away the remains of the meal and bringing refreshments. Alexander chose an ice wine that was crisp and sweet and quite tasty. He sipped at it as Apollos first handed over his copy of the signed treaty, then relayed the discussions in the various meetings as well as his day's adventures. He showed his father and brother the two light cannons as Alexander explained their uses.

The queen spoke up. "While my boys play with their new toys, I would like to thank you for taking such good care of Apollos today. I believe you've made yourself a lifelong friend." She smiled at her son as he nodded his head.

Alexander smiled back. "One can never have too many friends. And we'll need each other to defeat the drow wizards. As an alliance member, you'll benefit from increased trade, as well as mutual defense. And you will share in whatever intelligence we gain. If attacked, we can bring troops here through the portals within an hour of receiving your message. Humans, dwarves, elves, orcs, minotaurs, rock trolls, even dragons will come to your aid. I believe the dragon king will assign a flight of his dragons to you. They are very good at detecting and hunting drow, and can relay messages quickly to the rest of us if needed."

Apollos added, "Speaking of trade, Father. Alexander's minotaurs need livestock. Specifically, goats. I told him the farmers might sell whatever stock can't be brought into the city ahead of the attack."

"We actually would be willing to purchase whatever you have available. Goats, pigs, cows. We've just added roughly eight hundred citizens in the last few days and I want to be able to feed them," Alexander replied.

The king nodded his head. "I'm sure our farmers would give you a fair price. We have limited space inside our walls, and therefore have limited the amount of stock the farmers could shelter here. Some of their stock they'll butcher and sell to us to feed our army and our people. But some would have been left to roam free and probably gone to feed our enemies. Better you should have them."

Elrid volunteered, getting up from his chair. "I'll go see to it now. We'll send word out and have them gather what stock they wish to sell in the stockyards just inside the outer gate. Will tomorrow noon be alright?"

Alexander replied, "Perfect. If it's alright with you, I'll leave Silverbeard here for the night. He can negotiate for the purchases and talk with you about any other trade agreements that might interest you. He has my complete faith and authority. I'll return at noon tomorrow to pick up the livestock and bring you a couple more light cannons for your walls."

Elrid left and the group continued with talk of trade and defense for a short while. Alexander eventually got to his feet. "I must return home and take care of some business. Being a king seems to mean that you never have much time to just sit and chat." Arand nodded in understanding. "I'll return tomorrow. It has been a pleasure." He bowed his head slightly to the king and queen.

"The pleasure is ours," the queen replied. "And thank you again. A day ago, our kingdom was floundering. Now we have new friends and a real hope of surviving."

Apollos led Alexander back to the portal, and he traveled back to his keep.

*****

Jules was in their quarters when he got there. She was curled up on the sofa, spinning one of her daggers in her fingers. Alexander was rewarded with a big smile as he stepped through the door. "Those dragon babies are SO cute," she said.

He sat down next to her, pulling her toward him so that her head rested on his chest. "They sure are. And we're going to spoil them like crazy. Fibble's already stealing more cookies in their name. And the hunters are stockpiling meat." He kissed the top of her head. "I'm sure we'll get to see them again tomorrow. Won't be long before they're rampaging through the keep."

Jules tilted her head up to kiss him. "I'm sorry I didn't answer today. I went into the dungeon to test my stealth skill. I made it all the way down to the third level! There are some higher-level mobs down there and I didn't want to push it."

"How high were their levels?"

"Well, like Silverbeard said, level one was gremlins. Level 35 to 40-ish. I walked right past them. The second level was full of the badger dudes. A few of them could smell me, but not well enough to find me. They were all between levels 40 and 50. Level three was felines. Giant night prowlers like the ones we found at the tower. Lowest I saw was level 50. Speaking of which, I need to go back to the tower to see my favorite kitten soon." She paused for a moment. "And I heard barking. I don't know if the dogs or wolves or whatever are on level three or four. The cats didn't seem worried."

Alexander shook his head. "Dogs and cats living together, mass hysteria." He grinned at the classic movie reference as Jules rolled her eyes. "Let's go tomorrow. We can take Tigger. Then we can check on the orcs and minotaurs. Maybe even take Pollock and his guys and go back to see the wolves by the east tower."

The two of them crawled into bed a while later and were quickly asleep.

*****

Heimdall's voice rang through Richard's office, surprising him and making him flinch as he read through some security reports. *"I have found an interesting anomaly in the communications monitoring logs, Richard."*

As the sentence ended, Morris Talbott, the head of security of Olympus, entered the room. He took over for Heimdall. "A few minutes after you brought Jules out of immersion, a text went out from a burner phone. The text simply said, 'Jules is awake.'

Richard's brow furrowed and he began to tap his desk. "Can you identify who sent it? Or who it went to?"

"This is ten minutes old. Heimdall's been going through the incoming and outgoing calls for us, as he can do it a thousand times faster than my team. We've asked our people to limit outside communication, so the volume of traffic to sort through is smaller. But there are still thousands a day, between calls and texts. We've forwarded both numbers to the FBI as well. But clearly someone inside Olympus is acting as a mole. Whether they work for our enemies or are just trying to make a buck with a news outlet or something, we just don't know yet."

Richard slammed his hand on the desk. "Damn it! Olympus has its own communication tower because we're too far from other towers for decent service. Which means we also can't use other towers to triangulate the signal and pinpoint their location."

Talbott cleared his throat. "Actually, we might be able to. Not on the previous text. But if there's another one. We've got repeaters up around the compound to make sure our comms work. One of my guys can modify them, tune them to the frequency of the burner that was used, and next time a signal happens we should be able to pinpoint it to within about a twenty-meter radius. Then we can use the cameras to determine who was within that space at that time. It'll narrow down our suspect list."

"So then we just have to wait for another message. But who knows when that will be?"

Talbott grinned. "I have an idea about that, too. We have the number of the burner phone that the message went to. We already checked, and it's not turned on. My guy thinks he can ping the phone to make it think it has a message, without there actually being a message or any caller ID signal. When the recipient turns the phone back on, they'll see a blank message. Hopefully, they'll reach out to whomever is here in the compound. The FBI will try to trace the outside number and we'll track down the traitor here."

Richard looked skeptical. "If the blank message spooks him? If he tosses that phone and doesn't reach out?"

Talbott nodded. "That is a risk. Though I believe it's a small one. Worst case, he does exactly that and we have to track down the mole another way. My guys are already going through the HR files again with a fine-toothed comb. We're starting with medical staff, because the message went out before Jules had even left her pod room. Word spreads quickly around here, but not that quickly." He gave Richard a look that spoke volumes about what might be required. "We'll interview each of them. Extensively."

110

"I don't want anybody hurt," Richard ordered. "Scare them if you must. Threaten them with life in prison, conspiracy to commit murder charges and the corresponding death penalty, whatever might work. But no physical injuries of any kind."

Talbott nodded again. "I expected as much. We'll find a way. If he's got somebody on the inside who is willing to help him get back in, or even to place a bomb themselves, we need to know right now."

Richard wasn't taking any chances. "Get the bomb-sniffing dogs to make another round of the entire compound. Start with the pods. Prioritize the server levels and areas with high concentrations of people. The cafeteria, the living quarters, etc."

"Already underway. I made the call right before I came here."

"I need to talk to Michael. If our enemy does dump his burner, we may need to just jam all cell communication at the compound. Everything but our internal radios. Maybe we can cut off his access that way. It won't be popular with the staff, but if it means no more bombs…"

Talbott said, "Everybody's behind you on this, boss. They'll grumble some, sure. But they'll understand." He got up and headed for the elevator. "I'll update you as soon as I have any news at all."

*****

Matt sat back in his recliner and put on the headset. He was calmer now and ready to take another shot at escaping from his flooded stronghold. Following the draining water through the commode obviously wasn't possible. So he would try again to swim up and out.

The moment he logged in, he put his feet on the seat of the throne and pushed with all his might. His body soared up through the water to impact the ceiling. Feeling his way quickly across to where the weak current was still flowing into the hole, he pulled himself through and used his feet to push off once again. Frog-stroking with all his might, he burned through his stored oxygen as he tried to reach the surface. The sound of the water changed as he got closer, from the dull roar of the current to the splashing of surface water just above. He reached upward, hoping to feel his hand break the surface.

All he found was stone. He'd reached the ceiling of the river's path through the stone, but there was no open space for him to get air. His UI began blinking red as his oxygen ran out and his health bar started ticking down. He followed the ceiling, letting the current push him as he prayed for an opening with air.

A moment later, he was in limbo again and had lost another level. "So close! There has GOT to be a way. I mean, the game can't have a place where a player is stuck forever." As soon as he said it, he knew better. There were plenty of places where players got stuck. And a quick message to a game master would get them un-stuck. A message he could not send without alerting Odin to his presence.

The frustration ate at him. He spent the rest of his time in limbo plotting ways to murder the drow wizard he reported to. Even if it cost him a life, he was going to try it. Nothing could be worse than the place he was stuck in now.

His timer ticked down and he tried again. And again. After his fifth death, he managed at the last moment to find an open space! He gasped in a breath as the current pushed him along in the darkness. Just as his lungs filled with the dank air of the underground passage, his face struck a low-hanging stone. The impact nearly knocked him unconscious, his breath exiting in a cry of pain. The current pushed him down again and a few moments later he was back in limbo.

Furious, he yanked off his headset without even logging out of the game first. His mind reeled as it tried to make sense of the rapid transition from one reality to the other. The headset beeped angrily at him as he dropped it and jumped to his feet. Wobbling slightly, he reached out and used the wall to steady himself. Then he began to pace. "Damn it! So close! But now I know there's air there. I just have to keep trying."

He went to the kitchen and grabbed himself a beer, as well as the makings for a sandwich. When he sat down to eat, he took a moment to check his burner phone for any updates. His person inside had told him Jules was awake and he was hoping for an update on when both Jules and Alexander would be walking around the compound again. He'd take them out himself this time.

The moment he powered up the burner phone, it beeped and showed a 'missed call' message. No message was attached and there was no record of the number. He shook the phone a couple times, as if that might change the available information. His still-slightly-befuddled mind blamed the phone.

"Damned cheap burner phones. Never work right." He tapped the screen a few times and sent a message to his mole with just a '?' then stared at the phone for a minute or so, awaiting an answer. After the third sip of his beer, he remembered that his mole probably had their phone turned off. They would turn it on twice a day to check or send messages. And this wasn't one of those times.

He quickly shut off his burner and put it back in his pocket. Finishing his sandwich and gulping the last of his beer, he sat back in his recliner and grabbed his headset.

*****

Chapter 7

A Day Off

The following morning, Alexander and Jules were both up early. Jules rose from bed without complaint, showered and dressed shortly after sunrise. They grabbed a quick breakfast of oatmeal with honey and apple slices. As they sat in the dining area, Fibble appeared. He hopped up on the bench next to Jules and asked, "Play with baby dragons now?"

Jules patted the little guy on the back. "Not yet, Fibble sweetie. Lia will let us know. But we're taking Tigger to see the big kitties in the west tower. You liked the kittens. Want to come with us?"

Fibble looked sideways at her as he thought it over. After a moment, he nodded his head. Jules gave him the unsliced portion of her apple, which he immediately bit into. When all three had finished their breakfast, Alexander teleported the three of them up to the garrison tower. There was no sign of Regina or Bodine, but a few farmers were out and about. Alexander summoned Tigger. As soon as the giant white tiger appeared, Fibble leapt up onto his back. He walked forward and curled up between the cat's shoulder blades. "Soft," Fibble yawned and closed his eyes.

Alexander mounted the cat next, sitting on his back behind his shoulders. Jules gave Tigger a scratch behind the ears and stared into his eyes for a moment. Laughing, she stepped back and leapt aboard behind Alexander. "Tigger says we should go slow so as not to disturb the little smelly one's nap."

Following his own suggestion, Tigger turned and headed out the southern gate. He immediately turned right and began to trot at a sedate pace to the west. Fibble, snoring softly while nestled in the tiger's thick fur, unconsciously gripped a handful and pushed his face deeper between Tigger's shoulders.

It wasn't far to the western tower and the big cat's loping pace got them there in half an hour. As they approached, a shadowy blur flew at them from a nearby cluster of shrubs. All three passengers were knocked off of Tigger's back as Jules called out, "Nooo, wait!"

Fibble screamed as he was rudely awakened after hitting the ground and having a giant cat grab him gently in its jaws and toss him in the air. Arms and legs flailing, he shouted for help. "Help! 'Zander! Jules!"

Jules scolded the kitten as it caught the little goblin between its paws. It set him on the ground, then lowered itself onto its belly, butt wiggling as if about to pounce. Fibble spluttered and scrambled to his feet. His wand was out and pointing toward the kitten when Alexander called out, "Fibble! It's one of the kittens. He is just playing with you."

Fibble fired his wand at the kitten. "Pew!" He then stomped toward it, his underbite jutting out more than usual. "Kitty sneak attack? Fibble sneak attack!" He leapt toward the kitten's head, grabbing hold of its face with both arms and legs as it sprang into the air in alarm. When it shook the little goblin loose, the two of them rolled around on the forest floor for a minute or two before Jules called them to her.

"Come here, both of you!" she mock scolded the combatants. Fibble got to his feet and watched the kitten over his shoulder as he walked toward Jules. The kitten lay on its back for a while, paws waving in the air as if still fighting the goblin. Then it abruptly rolled over and joined Jules in a single leap. She scratched under its chin and whispered in its ear for a bit and it calmed down. A rumbling purr erupted from its chest.

She pulled a rabbit carcass from her bag and handed it over to the kitten, who made it disappear in two large bites. "We came to visit your family. Are they at the tower?" she asked the kitten, gazing into its eyes. It gave a sort of half-growl and moved behind her. It jammed its head between her knees, then lifted, causing her to fall backward onto its shoulders. A quick adjustment and she was riding it just as she would Tigger. It bounded off into the woods. Alexander grabbed Fibble just as Tigger jumped into the brush in pursuit. He let out a mighty roar to announce their approach as he followed the kitten towards its home.

The matriarch greeted them near the door of the tower. Jules hopped down off the kitten's back and ran to hug the giant black cat. Two seconds later, she let go of the matriarch's neck and gasped, "You're pregnant again!"

The mother rubbed her head against Jules' belly and stared into her eyes. Jules blushed, then laughed. "No, I won't be having my own litter soon." Alexander chuckled at her embarrassment.

He called out, "I keep trying, Your Highness. But Jules just won't have me. I'm not a good enough mate, it seems." Then he ducked as a dagger flew past his head.

The matriarch seemed to be laughing, her mouth open and teeth bared as she made a coughing sound. Jules pouted for a moment, then caved and hugged the big cat again. The kitten approached, nudging Jules from behind. It let out an inquisitive, "mrowr?" and headbutted her gently. She turned and froze as she met his eyes.

A moment later, she looked at Alexander. "He… just bonded with me!" she called out as she absently scratched his face. Tigger moved closer and chuffed at the three of them, giving the young one a slight swat on the head. Jules laughed. "Tigger just told my kitten that I will always have tasty bacon in the mornings."

"He's right about that. But I wish him good luck getting any of it away from you."

They stayed and visited for a few more minutes. Jules inquired about the other kittens and was told they were off hunting with their father. When it came time to leave, the matriarch growled at her offspring and gently bumped his head with her own. Then she pushed him toward Jules and turned to walk back into the tower.

Jules hopped aboard the kitten and Tigger led the way with Alexander and Fibble on his own back. When they reached the garrison tower, they checked in with Bodine and Regina. They agreed to hold off a day to gather some meat and get together a group to go see the eastern wolf pack. Regina wanted to head down to the keep in hopes of spending time with the dragonlings. When Fibble heard that, he leapt off of Tigger's back and straight into the surprised woman's arms.

Pollock and his guys wanted to try to bond with wolves, and they were off hunting and leveling. So, Alexander told them to bring back extra meat to give the wolves the following day. With that accomplished, Alexander teleported himself, Jules, and their two cats to the orc village.

Upon arrival, the two cats caused quite a stir as orcs nervously reached for weapons. Alexander raised his hands to show he meant no harm and they walked with the cats into the center of the village. A brief chat with the elders to make sure things were going smoothly and that the warriors who wished to serve as soldiers were already on their way to the tower. A few quick goodbyes, and they moved on to the minotaur village.

They spent a little time there, the cats exploring the nearby buildings and forest as Alexander and Jules spent time with Molgo and Dawn. The third longhouse was completed and new single homes were beginning to sprout up. The minotaurs were well fed and happy, and had already started clearing ground for crops. Their carpenters were using the lumber to make sturdy furniture for the homes. Molgo confirmed that a contingent of his warriors had headed south before dawn to join the Elysian military as well.

Alexander sent a message to Lola. *"The troops from the orc and minotaur villages are on their way to the garrison tower. Have the captains meet us there, please."*

"Already there, Alexander. Ye can join us if ye like, but it no' be necessary. Yer captains be knowin' what ta do with new recruits."

"Thank you, Lola. We'll stop by on our way back, just to observe."

Reassured that his new troops were taken care of, he grinned at Molgo. "If you have a supply of that special goat's milk I can take back with me, I think I can have quite a few dwarven customers for you by morning."

Molgo chuckled and handed him two large skins that each contained a couple gallons of the drink. "Dawn mentioned your interest. Do you truly think we can make money from this?"

Alexander took the skins, depositing them in his bag. "We'll need to get you some kegs to store it in. Maybe figure out some refrigeration to keep it fresher longer. But yes. I think a small keg of this could make you several gold."

After some more small talk with the minotaurs, Alexander teleported his group back to the garrison tower. He found the captains and sergeants yelling at groups of new recruits. They'd mixed the orcs and minotaurs together, for the most part. Though there were a few small groups of minotaur-only shock units that had been cut out of the larger force. All the soldiers were being handed weapons and directed to areas where they could practice formation drills.

Alexander checked with Taylor and the others, who were all quite busy. Once he was reassured that things were going smoothly, he returned to the keep.

There he found several people grouped in the courtyard, staring up at the dragon roost. Regina and Fibble were there, along with Thea, Lorian, Brick, and a few others. Alexander smiled at the look on Regina's face. Almost as if she were willing Lia to summon them. When Jules moved to join the crowd, Alexander decided to take pity on them. He teleported himself up to the ledge outside the roost. The waterfall ran past his shoulder as he stood quietly, waiting for Kai to acknowledge him. An intrusion near a dragon's roost would immediately be sensed by its occupant. A moment later, Kai's enormous dragon head snaked out and lowered itself to Alexander's height. "Good day, Alexander," Kai's voice rumbled.

"Good day, Kai. I was wondering if the little ones are up for some company. There's a whole crowd down in the keep standing on their tippy-toes and trying to will themselves to fly up here."

Kai stuck his head through the waterfall and looked down at the keep. A moment later, he chuckled. "It seems my little troublemakers have no shortage of volunteers to babysit. Bring them up, please."

Alexander popped back down to the keep and gathered everyone up. "Kai says you can play with the babies. Remember, they are still young and might be a bit bitey." He teleported them up to the main chamber, as there were too many to fit on the ledge.

The baby dragons hooted and dashed for the adoring spectators. They were still a bit unsteady on their feet, so their wobbling gaits caused some giggles. Fibble stepped forward and greeted his white dragon buddy with open arms. The little hatchling seemed pleased to see him and ran straight to him, bowling him over. As soon as he hit the ground, the dragonling started nosing at his bag, looking for cookies. Fibble snatched the bag away and growled at his new little buddy and pushed at its snout. "No! Ask nice. Lady Lia say dragon baby only gets one cookie!"

The push was enough to put the little white dragon off balance, causing it to fall on its rump with a squeal of indignation. Fibble immediately felt bad and produced a cookie from his bag. As he held it out with an apologetic look, the other dragonlings charged. The white hatchling quickly snatched the cookie in its jaws as Fibble was mobbed by cookie-seeking baby dragons.

Concerned for his safety, Lia moved her head over and gently captured the little goblin in her jaws and lifted him to safety. Fibble, understandably assuming that he was being eaten for pushing the dragonling, squealed in terror and passed out cold. Lia deposited him next to Alexander before turning back to reprimand her younglings.

"What is this?" she growled at them. The hatchlings instantly lowered their bellies to the ground, along with their snouts. "You would attack a small one who gifted you with treats?!"

The dragonlings mewled apologetically, their tails thumping slowly against the floor. Kai let out a remonstrative grumble of his own. "How would you feel now if you had damaged Fibble? Or killed him? Just for a cookie?"

The white dragon rose and hopped over to where Fibble lay still unconscious. On the way, it scooped up the bag full of cookies that Fibble had dropped in the excitement. When it reached Fibble, it dropped the bag on his belly, then gently licked his face. Sitting back to watch for a moment, it trumpeted a little cry of distress, then nudged Fibble's head with its snout.

Fibble coughed and opened his eyes. Looking around and remembering what had happened, he sprang to his feet and was about to flee the roost when Sasha grabbed him. "It's okay, Fibble. You're not hurt. The little ones wanted cookies and got carried away. Lia protected you."

The little dragon next to him whimpered and poked at his chest with its snout. Fibble, still shaking, reached out to pat its head awkwardly.

The sad whimper turned into a purring sound as the dragonling scooted closer to the goblin protector and sat at his feet.

Lia laughed. "It seems Fibble has been adopted. I've never seen a youngling bind so quickly."

"Bind?" Regina asked, hope in her voice. "As in a permanent bond?"

Lia nodded her great head at the beastmaster. "Yes. It is rare, as dragons don't spend much time around non-dragons anymore. Especially not our hatchlings. Since adventurers began seizing our eggs to hatch for dragon mounts, we have withdrawn and hidden our clutches from them. But a hatchling may choose to bind with a humanoid that they feel a special affection for. Snabb here has chosen to bind her life to Fibble's."

"Smart lass!" Brick interjected. "She'll never be short o' cookies that way." His smile faded as Lia stared at him, unamused.

"We will have to teach Fibble the proper way to care for Snabb until she is strong enough to fend for herself. He'll need to stay here at the roost for now. She won't tolerate being separated from him."

As Lia spoke, Fibble's eyes had grown wide and his mouth dropped open. "Dragon baby choose Fibble?" he asked, his voice trembling. "Forevers?"

Kai nodded his head at the tiny goblin, who wasn't much larger than the dragon at his feet. "Yes, Fibble. Forever. You are part of our family now."

The goblin's eyes began to water. "Fibble not have real family. Ever. Have clan. Goblin clan. And Greystone clan. Nice clan." He hugged Sasha's leg. "But Fibble can be family with dragon babies?"

Both dragons nodded their heads and smiled at him. The wide array of sharp teeth caused him to step back, tripping over Snabb and causing her to squeal. He immediately got back up and patted her neck. "S'okay Snabby. I protect you."

Tears were streaming down Sasha's cheeks and more than a few of the others looked choked up. Brick sniffed and pretended to have something in his eye. Even Lia looked touched, in a dragonish sort of way.

Fibble lifted his bag and started withdrawing cookies. He handed them one at a time to Sasha and the others. "You give cookies to babies. Fibble too small to wrassle them."

Sasha sob-laughed as she accepted her cookie. She stepped forward and offered it to the nearest hatchling, the red one. It looked up at Lia to ask permission, still cowering from her reprimand. She nodded her head and the dragonling gingerly reached out and took the treat from Sasha's hand. Brick, Alexander, Regina, Jules, and the others all stepped forward with cookies in hand. A few of them tentatively patted the heads or necks of their chosen hatchling. When the cookies were gone, they stepped back to join the group.

The black dragonling honked in excitement, then danced in a little circle while flapping its wings. When it came back around to face them, it tilted its head and snorted. Kai snorted back. "He believes, as he is my heir, he should receive an extra cookie." Kai paused. "He wished you to view him in all his majesty." The deadpan tone of Kai's voice wasn't lost on the dragonling. He settled back onto his belly and eyed his father. "Needless to say, we will teach him the meaning of humility."

Lia looked at Alexander. "We will take good care of Fibble. He will need to remain here at least a week until the little ones are grown enough to leave the roost."

Alexander nodded in understanding. Turning to the group he said, "Off we go. The little ones have had enough excitement for one day, I think." He bowed his head to Kai, then Lia. Then with a grin, he bowed deeply to the imperious little black dragonling. "Your Majesty," earning him a snort from Lia.

When the others had said goodbye, he gathered them together and teleported all but Fibble back to the keep. As they dispersed, Alexander noticed Regina was just standing still in the middle of the courtyard, looking thoughtful. "Regina?"

"Alexander. I'm sorry. Were you saying something? I was thinking about trying to bond with a dragon."

"I could see that. Your brain was practically humming. But I think it's mostly up to the dragon, from what Lia said."

"What? Oh, yes. Yes. But one might try to persuade a hatchling to choose them. Bring gifts, talk to them, scratch their bellies. Oh, I can think of a hundred things that might help."

Alexander, not seeing anything wrong with giving the baby dragons bribes or bellyscratchings, decided not to argue the point. "Well, good luck to you," he said, as he patted her shoulder and left her to her thoughts.

Just then, he remembered he was supposed to return to Damerion to retrieve Silverbeard and the livestock. He sat where he was and quickly fashioned two more light cannons. When they were done, he jogged over to the smithy and had Brick form the triggers. Adding the trigger word as he walked, he returned to the courtyard and opened the portal. As usual, Taylor and his men showed up out of nowhere to escort him.

Sure enough, Silverbeard stood there with Elrid and Apollos. As Alexander stepped through, Silverbeard chastised him. "I thought ye fergot 'bout us."

Alexander apologized. "I'm very sorry, Master Silverbeard, Elrid, Apollos. We had another little episode with the dragonlings. It seems the white one has decided to bond with Fibble."

The eyes of all three widened, and Apollos said, "No apology necessary. I wouldn't miss that for anything. I wish I had been there."

In short order, Alexander was led from the portal courtyard out of the palace and into a larger courtyard, where his guards spread out and formed a perimeter. Gathered there were more than a hundred goats, a few dozen pigs, sixteen cows, and crates and crates of chickens. There was also a small herd of sheep packed so tightly together Alexander couldn't count them accurately. He guessed twenty. Several farmers stood nearby in different areas of the courtyard, keeping the animals calm and under control.

"I gived them a fair price, plus a bit extra fer bringing them up here ta the portal. There be more outside, but I weren't sure if ye wanted to spend so much o' the kingdom's gold."

Alexander asked, "How many more?"

Apollos laughed. "About twice this number. Master Silverbeard is being modest. His prices are more than fair, and every farmer in the area is looking to sell excess stock."

"Can they be brought through today?"

"Aye," Silverbeard answered. "They be gathered just outside that there wall. I tried ta tell em' they be wastin' their time. And fillin' the streets with dung fer no reason."

"How much more gold would it take to purchase all the livestock being offered?"

"I dunno, exactly. The crowd out there be growin'. But methinks maybe three thousand gold." Silverbeard looked to Elrid and Apollos, who nodded.

Alexander pulled three thousand gold from his bag and handed it to Silverbeard in a bulging pouch. "Let's do this. We'll purchase them all now. We have the space to keep them safe, you don't." He looked at the two princes. "If your city has a need, we will sell them back to you at the same price."

Silverbeard wasted no time, jogging out the nearby gate and hollering to the gathered farmers. There was a cheer from the farmers and much excitement as animals were moved toward the gate. Several guards and stablehands moved to assist in managing the chaos.

Alexander remembered the light cannons. "Oh! Here, these are for you as well." He handed each of the princes a weapon.

"You are a generous friend, Alexander," Apollos said, putting the weapon over his shoulder like a spear shaft. "Thank you, for all of this."

Alexander just shrugged and walked back toward the portal. Already, the livestock was moving in that direction. "That's what friends do. We help each other."

He opened the portal and the animals were herded through. It took nearly an hour to push them all through and Alexander saw his people on the other side of the portal desperately trying to herd them out of the courtyard through the main gate. He imagined they were having difficulty protecting the crops growing between the inner and outer gates. He quickly sent a message to Brick.

"I screwed up. Just emptied a whole zoo's worth of critters into the courtyard. Get some folks together to help the farmers keep them under control. I'll be there in a minute to start teleporting them."

"BWAHAHAHA!" was the only answer he got.

When he stepped through the portal himself, he quickly discovered that they had obtained not only a large population of livestock, but a corresponding quantity of fertilizer. Some of which was now all over his boot. He looked up to see Brick grinning at him. "Watch yer step!"

Ignoring his friend's glee, he scraped his boot as best he could, then dashed out the gate. The livestock were crowded onto the path leading down to the drawbridge. As expected, several animals had left the path and were trampling crops on either side, or munching on them. He went to work.

First, he called out to Jeeves, "Loudspeaker please, Jeeves!" Then a moment later, he said, *"My apologies, folks. I just bought us a large herd of livestock and didn't think to make the proper arrangements for when they got here. I'm about to teleport them up to the garrison tower. They'll appear inside the walls by the south gate. All available hands who can help us direct them to the proper corrals and pens, please report to the tower. Regina and Bodine, please secure your more predatory critters inside for now. I'm about to march a smorgasbord past you."*

He waited a few minutes while folks dashed for the mirror that would teleport them up to the tower. When he figured there were enough people, he said, "Jeeves, please close the south gate of the garrison tower."

"It is already done, Majesty."

Alexander chose a group of cattle that were actively grazing on the green sprouts next to the road. With a wave of his hand, he sent them up to the plateau. He waited a minute or so for someone to move them, then did the same with a flock of sheep. He kept it up, sending a new group every minute or two so as not to drop them on top of each other. One of the farmers came to him after half an hour and said, "That'll be enough.

We can handle what's left down here. We've got the corrals over by the quarry and the stables here."

Alexander nodded and apologized again. "My bad. I'll do better next time."

The farmer laughed. "Don't think you'll need a next time. You've brought us enough stock to breed herds that'll feed the kingdom for years. A good number of them sheep 'n pigs are already pregnant."

Alexander shook his head. "Breed them quickly. Damerion may need to purchase these back from us if their city is put under siege." The farmer nodded in understanding and moved off to help with the last of the animals being driven across the drawbridge.

As he walked back into the keep, he saw unhappy citizens with shovels and brooms cleaning up the considerable quantity of poo left behind by the stampede. Alexander tried to sneak past unnoticed but received several glares as he passed.

Ducking into the donjon's main doors, he headed for Silverbeard's office. The old dwarf was behind his desk, buried in paper as usual. "So, I screwed that up, didn't I?"

Silverbeard chuckled. "Nay, lad. That be on me. I shoulda warned ye to get ready on this side. And I dinna' expect ye to take every critter they offered."

"I shouldn't have?" Alexander queried.

"It be alright, lad. I'd have said no, meself. Ye don't want to leave them short o' food because them farmers smelled a profit. But yer promise to sell the stock back if need be, and at no profit, were a good idea. Them animals will be well fed up on the plateau, and when their wee ones are born, we'll increase the size o' our herds even if we need to return the ones ye bought."

Alexander nodded as he thought about the mass of goats. "Oh! There's another benefit to those goats." He pulled out one of the skins full of goat's milk and poured some into a glass on the dwarf's desk. The old chancellor looked at it suspiciously and took a sniff.

"Bah! What'd ye give me?" He gave his king a dirty look. "Do this be some kind o' test o' me loyalty?"

Laughing, Alexander said, "Just drink it. Trust me."

Still looking skeptical, the dwarf picked up the glass and downed the drink quickly. He coughed once and slapped a hand on the desk. As the drink made its way down his gullet and into his gut, his eyes widened. "That be good stuff!"

"That's the fermented goat's milk the minotaurs make. The reason for the extra goats. I figure your fellow dwarves will snatch up every keg that Molgo can produce. Earn some gold for his village."

"Well, it ain't good ol' dwarven spirits! But it'll do in a pinch, that's fer sure." Silverbeard burped and then frowned at the fermented milk odor. "Ach. Not so good comin' back up!"

"I was planning on taking these two skins to the Ogre here and the one in Stormforge. Letting them give out free samples to generate business."

"Aye, lad. That'll do it. Ye'll need to put a steep price on it. If it be cheap as ale, them minotaurs'll never be able to keep up with demand. Sell to the taverns fer… a hunnert gold a small keg."

Alexander was surprised at the suggestion, but accepted it. Molgo and Dawn would be very happy with that number. Thanking Silverbeard, and refilling his glass before he left, he headed over to the Ogre II. Finding Mattie inside, he handed her the skin. "This is a new drink from the minotaurs. Fermented goat's milk. I think your customers are going to love it. Use this to give out some samples tonight. More will be available at one hundred gold per small keg."

Mattie's eyes widened. "So much?" She uncorked the skin and took a sniff. Her nose wrinkled and she quickly moved her face away. "Smells like something died in there."

Alexander grinned. "Yup! Hold on a second." He looked around the tavern that took up most of the ground floor of the inn. Spotting a dwarven guard eating a meal, he called out, "How'd you like to test a new drink for us?"

The dwarf didn't hesitate. He was on his feet and standing next to them in seconds. "What'ye got?"

Mattie put a mug on the bar and Alexander poured a shot of the goat's milk. "Fermented goat's milk. Drink of choice for minotaur warriors. They seem to think us smaller races can't handle it."

"Bah!" The dwarf took the mug and swallowed its contents all at once. He pounded his chest once as his eyes rolled up for a moment. Then a wide grin appeared on his face. "It be good! Better than it smells!"

"Spread the word," Alexander said. "Tell your friends to come get a sample while they last. The minotaurs will be sending more. But the supply is limited and it will be expensive."

"Aye, me mates will want ta try this. And what else would I be usin' me gold fer?" He chuckled as he went back to his meal.

Alexander left Mattie to her business and went to find a quiet spot to do some crafting of his own. He hadn't leveled up his enchanting in several days and felt like a slacker.

He was just sitting down to contemplate what he might try next when there was a scream from the wall. He leapt to his feet as a notification appeared on his UI.

> **Kingdom Alert! Your kingdom is under attack!**
> **Quest Activated: Defending Elysia**
> *Your kingdom has been attacked by an enemy force. Defend your land and your people!*
> *Experience: Variable*
> *Bonus Experience: Defeat your enemy without the loss of Elysian lives.*
> *Bonus Experience: Completely destroy the enemy force.*
> *Do you wish to share this quest with the citizens of Elysia? Y/N*

Alexander mentally hit the 'Yes' button as he ran across the courtyard toward the stairs that led up the interior of the keep's wall. A fast-moving shadow to his right warned him of approaching danger and he went into a slide as talons grasped the air where his body had been. Looking up as he slid, he saw a large, winged creature with skin that looked to be made of stone.

Gargoyle Scout
Level 55
Health: 28,000/28,000

As he was getting to his feet, Jeeves was sounding the alarm for every citizen to hear. Alexander ignored the stairs and teleported himself to the top of the wall. Already, the light cannons mounted there were being put to use. Beams of light shot into the sky in multiple locations as crossbows sent bolts aloft as well.

Looking up, Alexander saw three of the creatures swooping toward the wall or dodging defensive fire. One gargoyle was holding a human guard by the shoulders and climbing steadily. A moment later, a golden blur shot past beneath the gargoyle and Braxis began to dive back toward the keep with the guard in tow. He'd stolen the man right from the monster's claws. Two more gryphons attacked the gargoyle as it tried to dive after Braxis. Blood flew as beaks and talons raked at flesh in an airborne melee.

One of the guards with a light cannon managed to hit another of the monsters as it paused in the air before diving. The thing screamed in rage as the light magic burned into its wing. Another light beam joined it half a second later and the damaged creature began to drop slowly in a spiral pattern. Its burned wing was no longer able to keep it aloft. Guards rushed in the direction it was falling, determined to finish it when it hit the ground.

Alexander searched the sky. The third gargoyle was nowhere to be seen, until it popped up over the wall and snatched Alexander with its rear claws. Flapping its wings, it pulled him over the edge of the wall and began to climb. The guards nearby along the wall aimed their crossbows, but hesitated, not wanting to kill Alexander by mistake. Alexander looked up at the creature holding him and cast Wizard's Fire on it. The flames engulfed the creature immediately, causing it to scream. Still, it continued to beat its wings.

"If I die, elf, you will die with me!" it growled at him. Pushing through the pain of the flames, it lifted Alexander ever higher.

Gargoyle Scout
Level 60
Health: 27,000/31,000

Alexander shot it with several Magic Bolts, whittling away at its health as the thing dragged him through the sky. It was awkward with his body in tow and was moving slowly, more vertically than horizontally. As a result, Alexander could see when the gargoyle fighting the gryphons dropped from the sky. The two gryphons and Braxis were all headed in his direction. He could see that the two who had been in combat were badly hurt. The gargoyle hadn't died easily.

Alexander stopped his offensive casting to cast his biggest Healing Light spell on each of the gryphons, then shouted to Braxis, "Keep back! I have this!"

Braxis nodded and squawked at his companions, who altered their courses so that they surrounded the gargoyle as it continued to gain altitude. Alexander looked up and began to build up a charge of Ray of Light. He allowed the spell to build and build until he had accumulated nearly a thousand mana. Lifting his arm up toward the monster above him, he shouted, "Hey, ugly!"

The gargoyle looked down at him and he released the spell straight into its face. The compressed burst of light magic put a hole the size of a plum right through the monster's face, exiting out the back of its head. The thing died instantly, its claws still holding a death grip on Alexander as its burning corpse began to fall. Alexander cast a heal on himself to recover the health points burned away by his own Wizard's Fire.

Braxis and the other gryphons rushed in, intent on freeing Alexander. He shouted, "No!" and waved them back. The last thing he needed was fur and feather-covered gryphons catching fire mid-air. They backed off, but followed him as he fell. Looking down, he saw they were over the waterfall and dropping rapidly toward the rocks.

He took out his sword and hacked at the gargoyle's left leg. The blade cut cleanly through flesh and bone and he was free of one leg, though the talon still gripped his shoulder. And now he and the dead monster were spiraling badly, the force of the spin nearly making him lose his grip on the sword. His elven body didn't have the strength to overcome inertia and raise the sword.

A moment later, they bounced. The gargoyle's body struck an outcropping of stone not far from Kai's roost and acted like an anchor. It stopped their spinning and slowed their fall, but caused Alexander's body to swing toward the cliff face and slam into the rock. He felt his left arm break, and several ribs as well. He barely had time to register what happened when his weight and the momentum of their fall pulled the monster's corpse off the rock above him and they were once again dropping.

Alexander's mind was fuzzy from the pain of the impact but he managed to activate his teleport ability, moving his body and the gargoyle's out over the open water of the lake. They picked up speed as they continued to fall, and he realized as he looked down that he would hit the water first. If he survived the impact, he would be crushed a moment later by the monster above him.

Waving his sword arm in a panic, he managed to hack off the remaining leg that attached him to the gargoyle. He pushed the corpse away with a leg and closed his eyes to await the impact.

But it never came. He heard the splash of the monster hitting the water and felt a wet spray on his face. But his body was being lifted away from the surface. Opening his eyes, he saw that Braxis and his mate each held one of his legs and were pumping their wings to lift him into the air. The water was just feet below his head.

They carried him up onto the wall and unceremoniously dropped him the last couple feet. He managed to curl up enough that he didn't land on his head, letting his shoulders and back absorb the impact. With a groan of pain from his broken bones, he rolled over and used the wall to pull himself to his feet. He felt heals from Sasha wash over him. Once he was steady, he turned and bowed to the gryphons. "Thank you. I would not have enjoyed that bath."

Both gryphons squawked and Alexander thought Braxis might be laughing at him. They turned and trotted back into their roost.

Kai appeared next to Alexander a moment later in human form. "I smell dark magic!" he growled.

Alexander pointed to the gargoyle corpse that the gryphons had mauled and dropped into the courtyard. "Gargoyles."

The dragon prince's voice was filled with barely contained rage. "Servants of the drow wizards. These are scouts. They would only be here for one of two reasons. They were sent to observe our defenses ahead of an attack, or they were sent to capture someone to take back to their masters."

Alexander nodded. "That figures. One of them targeted me and was taking me away. It had plenty of time to kill me. It could have just dropped me and saved itself. But it didn't."

"Its masters don't react well to failure. If it was sent to fetch you and returned without you, it would have suffered a much more painful death."

Alexander looked at the dead mob as Beatrix bent to loot it. He smiled at the little gnome. She was even faster to loot than Max or Brick. "What I don't understand is why the guards didn't see them coming? The first warning I heard was when they actually grabbed one of our guards." He nodded toward the man that Braxis had saved. Sasha had healed him and he was recovering from the scare.

"Gargoyles have a stealth ability. They are nearly invisible until they attack. I might have smelled them if I were paying more attention. The gryphons should be able to smell them too, now that they have the scent. We will be more vigilant from now on. I would also like to summon a wing of my cousins here for added protection." Kai's tone made it clear that wasn't really a request.

"Of course, Kai. You know that your people are always welcome here. And we appreciate the added security. I will have Silverbeard prepare the nicest guest quarters we have."

Kai shook his head. "If it is acceptable, they will occupy the tower. The room at the top gives a good view of the area and a quick exit should they need to attack."

"The tower is all theirs. Please tell them to feel free to modify it in whatever way makes them most comfortable." Alexander smiled at his friend and ally.

Kai nodded and disappeared, presumably back to his roost to catch Lia up on events. His suspicion was confirmed a moment later when an enraged roar echoed out from the cliffs above. Alexander felt sorry for Fibble. The little goblin had big ears and was trapped inside a stone chamber with that thunderous sound.

After quickly checking on the still-shaken guard, Alexander made his way down to the courtyard. Sasha was waiting impatiently for Lainey to skin the gargoyle. As soon as the Valkyrie was finished, Sasha began harvesting parts from the monster. She took claws, teeth, its heart, and several internal organs. When she saw a small group observing her, she shrugged. "My alchemy skill is telling me this thing has all kinds of usable ingredients. We need to find the other two. This thing's heart is a rare purple ingredient."

Alexander nodded and teleported himself to the dock where the fishing boat was tied up. Untying the mooring line, he hopped in and pushed himself off. He let the boat drift in the general direction of the center of the lake as he gazed down into the water. Eventually, he spotted what he thought might be the gargoyle's corpse. Casting Levitate, he lifted it up out of the water and into the boat. Then he rowed himself and the monster back to the dock. Once he had the boat tied up again, he teleported himself and the gargoyle back to the keep where Lainey and Sasha looted, skinned, and harvested it.

Alexander noted several small celebrations as the experience from the dead monsters and the completion of the defense quest and both bonus rewards caused many of the lower-level citizens to level up.

Chapter 8

The Terrible Cost of War

The dragon wing arrived just before dark, causing quite a stir among the citizens. Six full-sized adult dragons appeared above them as they cleared the plateau and began a lazy downward spiral. Any one of them could have blacked out the noonday sun over the entire keep. They remained aloft as one of them ducked into Kai's roost. A few minutes later, Kai and another dragon in human form appeared in the courtyard. Alexander walked forward to meet them halfway.

"King Alexander, I present my cousin Delbalistros. Wing leader and friend. Don't let him near your supply of dwarven spirits." Kai grinned as the dragon bowed his head to Alexander.

"Welcome to Elysia, Delbalistros. And thank you for coming to help me protect my people. If Kai hasn't already informed you, the tower is yours for the duration of your stay." He motioned with one hand at the tower that rose above them on the opposite side of the keep from Fitz's tower. "If you need anything at all, please let me know. If I'm not nearby, Silverbeard or Lola can assist you." He gave the dragon a wink as he added, "And I'll ask Brick to send up a keg of spirits."

Kai groaned and rolled his eyes, elbowing his cousin good naturedly. "Thank you, Majesty." Delbalistros bowed his head.

"Please, just call me Alexander. If I can call you Del?" The dragon nodded his head. He looked up for a moment and the other dragons who'd been circling all made their way down to the upper room of the tower. Each of them began to transform, their bodies shrinking into human form just as they crossed the threshold of the upper windows.

With another nod of their heads toward Alexander, both Kai and Del disappeared.

Alexander opened guild chat. *"Okay, folks. In case you missed the excitement, we were attacked by gargoyle scouts serving the drow wizards. Looks like they were sent to capture me. Just FYI, they can friggin' stealth. And we have a new wing of dragons living in the tower now. They'll be on guard duty. Silverbeard or Lola, please make sure they're given a nice dinner. They just flew all the way here from the dragon kingdom. And Brick, their leader Del has a fondness for dwarven spirits. Mind parting with a keg or two?"*

He received messages of agreement from Silverbeard and Lola and smiled at the grumpy tone of Brick's reply. *"Bah! Ye keep givin' away me stash like it be water from the well. But o' course I'll be providin' decent drink fer our dragon friends."*

With that taken care of, Alexander spoke to Jeeves. "Jeeves, please activate loudspeaker. And will the northern villages hear me as well?"

"Your voice will be heard near every structure in the kingdom, Majesty. Go ahead when you are ready."

"Good evening, citizens of Elysia. I wanted to update all of you on the day's happenings. The keep was attacked a short time ago by gargoyles in service to the drow wizards. They were destroyed without any loss of Elysian life. But we fully expect that they will return. They have the ability to attack from stealth, so be prepared. Don't go anywhere alone. Stay in groups if you can.

"We have the honor of hosting a wing of dragon warriors who have come to guard against this new threat. So do not be alarmed if a dragon appears above you. They are friends and allies, and will not harm you. For those of you tending livestock, the dragons may help themselves to a cow or sheep from time to time. Do not worry. You'll be reimbursed for any losses.

"If you notice any suspicious activity near you, please report it immediately. The dark forces have many different servants at their disposal and this may be an indication of an upcoming attack. As always, we will work together to defend each other and our lands against any forces foolish enough to come against us! Thank you all for your loyalty and service. And have a good evening."

Alexander moved to the dining area, where some of the citizens were still gathered. Jules appeared out of stealth and took a seat next to him. He shook his head. "Remind me that if we ever break up, I need to move to a different continent."

She gave him her sweetest supermodel smile. "Wouldn't help. I'd find you." Her tone was so matter-of-fact that he wasn't sure how to take it for a moment. He decided it was a declaration of undying love and relaxed. Sasha, who had been standing behind them with a plate of food, snort-laughed.

As she sat down across from Alexander, she said, "I was going to go find Silverbeard, but since you're here, can you open the portal to Antalia for me?"

Alexander was immediately curious. "Antalia? This time of night? Planning an evening with your... what was he? A longbowman?" He grinned at her. Jules elbowed him gently in the ribs.

"No!" Sasha exclaimed, a bit too enthusiastically. "I mean, yes, he was a longbowman. But I don't even know his name, let alone how to find him. Even if I wanted to." She paused and growled at her best friend, "Shut up! I want to go to Antalia because there's an alchemist there who might be able to help me do something with these gargoyle bits."

Jules giggled when she said 'Gargoyle bits,' causing Sasha to blush slightly and Alexander to chuckle.

"What are you, twelve?" Sasha complained. Alexander and Jules nodded in unison.

"Of course I'll open the portal for you. I'll even go with you if you'd like, so I can open it for you to come back. Unless you were planning to spend the night?" Alexander carefully kept any hint of suggestion or humor from his voice and face. Still, Sasha eyed him suspiciously.

"Fine. You should pay a little attention to our guildies there, anyway, Mister Big 'n Mighty King." She stuck her tongue out at him and crossed her eyes, a face that had made him laugh since they were small children. "We should bring Brick, too. I know Princess Kimberly would be happy to see him."

"Ha! Good idea." Alexander turned toward the smithy and shouted, "HEY, BRICK!"

Their dwarf friend raised a hand to show he heard as he finished what he was working on. A moment later, he detoured into the kitchen for some food, then joined them at the table. "What's up?"

Jules answered first. "Sasha's going to Antalia for a hookup and we figured you'd want to come too. Princess Kimberly has been anxious to see you again."

The gruff and burly dwarf blushed slightly over top of his red beard. "Ssssh! Don't be spreadin' no rumors about!" he whispered loudly, looking over his shoulder as if Thea might be standing there. Reassuring himself that he was safe, he said, "Aye, I'll go with ye," and left it at that.

Brick was conflicted. Though he wore a dwarf body in the game and dedicated himself to role-playing a dwarf, he was still human in real life. And the human princess in her plate armor made his heart beat a little faster when she flirted with him. But Thea, the dwarven princess who'd also taken a liking to him, was attractive as well, if less in a physical sense. And both were NPCs, which had its own implications.

Alexander patted his friend on the back. "Your secret is safe with us. Finish your meal. I'll go find Silverbeard and see if there's any business we need to take care of in Antalia. Jules, could you let Taylor know we're going so he can send along one of the guard units?"

Getting to his feet, he went to Silverbeard's office. The old chancellor didn't have anything specific, but reminded him to stay at the guild compound. "It ain't polite to go roamin' around another ruler's city without bein' invited, or at least lettin' 'em know yer comin' first."

Alexander smacked his forehead. "I didn't even think of that. This whole king business takes a lot of getting used to."

Taking his leave of Silverbeard, he headed out to the courtyard. The others were gathered at the portal and Brick triggered it as Alexander approached. They all stepped through into the embassy compound, Taylor taking the lead and his team bringing up the rear.

The compound was basically two former guild houses joined together back to back. A gate had been built where the wall had separated their rear yards before Alexander and company had conquered the PWP and Chaos Nation houses. The former PWP house was where most kingdom business was conducted, while the other house was being used as residential space for guild members, training, and crafting rooms. There were a few small structures under construction that Alexander knew nothing about.

As they approached the back door to the main house, Michael emerged to greet them. "Well, this is a surprise. Welcome, Majesty." He bowed his head, a smirk on his face.

"Cut that shit out, Michael. There's nobody here but us chickens." Alexander frowned at him. "What's with all this construction?"

Michael cleared his throat. "Yes, well, Martin and I have been working on making the combined compound more efficient. We're adding a small stable with a smithy in the corner for our members who want to follow blacksmithing but don't yet have access to the dragon forges." He pointed to a wooden structure that was about half-completed to their right. "On the other side is going to be a building with crafting and market stalls. So, our people can make their potions or robes or armor and such, then display them for sale. Assuming they don't want to use the auction house. The second floor will be more residential spaces. Just simple rooms with a bed, dresser, table, and chest."

He pointed toward the gate between houses and added, "On the other side of the wall is a garden for the herbalists and alchemists, and some open space for gatherings and such."

Alexander was impressed. "Very good, Michael. Please give my compliments to Martin as well. That's solid planning, and I appreciate you taking the initiative to make it happen. Do you need anything? Gold? Supplies?"

Michael hesitated, looking a bit embarrassed. "Um. Silverbeard gave me limited access to guild funds to be used at my discretion. I thought you knew. My apologies if…"

Alexander cut him off with a raised hand. "No need to apologize. I can't be involved in every detail of the kingdom's day-to-day operations. You are a trusted member of our family now. Continue to do as you see fit. You only need to come to me or one of the others if you have doubts about something. You're doing a great job here, my friend."

He turned and walked toward the house, the others falling in behind. Michael matched his stride and walked next to him. Alexander asked, "So, what other needs do our people have that we haven't been meeting?"

Michael was silent for a while, thinking about his answer as they stepped into the house and moved through to the sitting room at the front. Tiny Sam waved at them as she descended the stairs to join them. Jules and Sasha took a moment to hug the girl.

"The crafting spaces will take care of many of our needs. Though the blacksmiths would obviously like more access to one of the dragon forges. And it would be helpful to have a daily portal schedule between here and the keep, so folks aren't sitting around waiting for the portal to open at random times." He paused to wait for a reaction from Alexander, who nodded.

"We can make that happen. What else?"

"Well, a lot of the crafters aren't the type to run dungeons or take the more lucrative quests. They've leveled up some because of the battles we've fought. And they actually gain some experience as they level their crafting. But they aren't earning money from loot like you lot." He nodded his head at Brick and the others. "So gold is a little hard to come by. As is experience. Many of them are healers. They could find groups to adventure with, but…" His voice trailed off as he saw the others get his point.

Brick spoke first. "As fer me forges, ye can tell 'em if they reach Journeyman level in smithing, we'll make some room for 'em at one or th'other. And we can provide iron 'n such at a discount. We've got the mines workin' now."

"Thank you, Brick. That will make them very happy." Michael bowed his head slightly.

Sasha was next. "We'll bring some of the rare herbs here for the garden. That'll help both the herbalists and alchemists level their skills. Though we'll need to put up a small greenhouse for some of them. And we can set up the crafting stations with whatever equipment is needed for each trade, as well as provide supplies like vials and bottles and needles at no cost."

Alexander added, "We could work out an arrangement where the guild purchases any items that they can't or don't want to sell at the auction house or here in the stalls. We'll pay a fair market price in gold and silver, or allow them to trade for more materials."

Michael grinned at them. "Exactly what we had in mind. Thank you."

Sasha coughed and said, "I'm off to find the alchemy trainer. I shouldn't be more than a couple of hours," as she headed for the front door. Brick followed after.

Jules waited until he was nearly out the door before shouting, "Say hi to the princess for us!" causing him to flinch as he stepped outside.

Alexander looked to Michael. "I have something to offer one lucky tavern owner here in the city. Fermented goat's milk made by the minotaurs who just became Elysians." He removed the second skin from his bag and poured a small amount into a teacup that sat on a nearby table. Handing it to Michael, he kept a neutral face as the man downed it in one gulp. As Michael's eyes bulged and he began to cough, Alexander continued, "At least for now, the supply will be limited. And it will be expensive. I expect the dwarves at the keep will grab up most of what the minotaurs can brew. But I thought we'd give the folks here in Antalia a chance to enjoy this too."

Michael got himself together and answered, "So you want an upper-end tavern, but not too fancy. One with customers who have gold to spend." He considered for a moment. "There's the Scarlet Corset. Offers gambling and… companionship. Lots of gold changes hands there, and-" he was going to say more, but caught the glare that Jules was sending his way.

Taking a chance that it was the companionship that she took exception to, he suggested, "Or there's Twirk's over near the barracks. The lads from the city guard and some of the knights go there to play cards and dice. Good food that's not too expensive."

Alexander looked sideways at Jules, waiting for a reaction. Seeing a brief nod of approval, he said, "Lead on, my friend. Take us to Twirk's." He held out an arm for Jules to take as they headed for the door.

She grabbed the arm and pulled him backward. "You can't just go traipsing around the city, *Your Majesty*."

He facepalmed. "Damn. Silverbeard JUST told me the same thing half an hour ago." Embarrassed, he looked to Michael. "If I leave this with you, do you think you can make a deal with Twirk? The minotaurs will want one hundred gold per small keg."

Michael whistled at the price. "Aye, that's steep. But I'm half-drunk from half a teacup. I don't think Twirk'll have any trouble selling the stuff. At a solid profit, if I know her." He grinned as he took the skin. "If you don't need me, I'll head over there now. It's not far."

Alexander nodded and took a seat on one of the sofas. Jules curled up next to him, tucking her feet up like a cat as she leaned against him. She waved at Michael as he walked out the door.

"So, who do you think Brick will choose?" she asked, already sounding sleepy.

"I think he's already chosen Kimberly. Unfortunately, that could make things uncomfortable with Thea. I don't want to lose her. You think you could fix her up with somebody? One of the dwarves at the keep, maybe?"

Jules shook her head. "Most of the NPC dwarves there see her as a princess, and out of their league. Except maybe Grumpy. I caught him staring at her butt once, so maybe he'd be interested. But I have no idea if Thea will accept anyone other than Brick. She's set her sights on him since day one."

Alexander's voice was contemplative as he answered. "I see this as being a potential issue with the new pods. More specifically, with the long-term immersion. It all seems so much more real and we spend so much more time interacting with the NPCs. Eventually, a player is going to fall in love with an NPC and vice versa. Then what happens if they leave the game?"

Jules chuckled and poked his rib gently. "Silly man. The NPCs here think and feel just like real people. They fall in love and get dumped. They lose family and friends. They grieve or get angry just like we do. Don't waste time worrying about it. You can't protect everyone from everything."

Alexander sighed and pulled her closer. "Such a wise queen I have. If only she weren't so ready to stab me all the time…"

Jules' answer was another poke in the ribs as she wiggled a bit to get more comfortable. The two of them sat there for a while in silence, just enjoying each other's company. Eventually Tiny Sam walked in with a tray of tea and cookies.

"I thought you might want a snack while you wait?" she offered with a shy smile.

"Thank you, Samantha!" Jules beamed at the girl. She helped herself to several cookies and began to munch on the first with small, delicate bites. Alexander took one too and it was gone in one bite.

Tiny Sam left them to return to the kitchen. "If you'd like something more, just shout. The chef is itching to make you something special."

Alexander winced. The last time he'd seen the chef was when they'd taken the house from PWP. They had tied the poor chef up along with Michael and Tiny Sam and interrogated them. He felt bad about the encounter now. "Please tell the chef we'd be honored to try something from his kitchen."

Jules growled in agreement, putting all but one of the cookies into her bag for later. Alexander added, "We'll take a quick tour through the other house before we eat."

Tiny Sam smiled. "That should be perfect. I'll let the chef know." She disappeared in a rush. Alexander and Jules got to their feet and headed outside. Rather than cut through the kitchen to go out the back door, they exited the front and strolled around the side arm in arm. They paused to examine the stable building's progress a bit more closely, then walked through the new gate into the other yard.

There were two druid healers already working at planting the garden there. Both bowed their heads to the king and guild leader, being already on their knees. He said, "Please, no bowing. And don't let us interrupt you. When you see Sasha come back through, flag her down. She has some rare herbs to add to your garden."

Moving into the house, the two of them greeted any guild members or Elysian citizens they encountered. Alexander noted as they moved down the first floor hallway that the round room that had been designated as the teleport and respawn point by the Chaos Nation folks was still filled with the spikes that Fitz had placed there during the battle. With the portal in place, there was no need for the room, and no point in allowing any of the drow or defeated guild members to teleport in if they were still carrying any scrolls targeted to that spot. At least, not without being shredded.

One of the healers saw Alexander pause to look inside and offered, "Not much activity anymore. But for the first week or so, random people would show up dead in there. We looted their corpses and added what they had to the guild vault." She grinned at them. Jules snorted.

"Sounds good to me!" Alexander returned the smile. "Have you guys had any trouble with Chaos Nation or former PWP folks attacking? Here or elsewhere in the city?"

The priest shook her head. "None. The drow can't stealth around since the city was blessed. And the few members of those guilds who dared show their faces since the battle have either been killed on the street or arrested as enemies of Antalia. Two made it as far as the street outside before the guards caught them. You should have heard them screaming about how we stole all their gear." The grin appeared on her face again.

"Well, since Henry looted most of the PWP vault, it only seems right you folks inherit whatever was in the Chaos Nation vault. I hope you can put it to good use." Alexander nodded to the woman before moving on.

He and Jules spent a few more minutes visiting with folks in the house before returning to find Tiny Sam and the chef already placing food on the dining room table. Alexander seated Jules before taking the chair next to her.

"It smells delicious!" Jules practically drooled as she complimented the chef. "What is it?"

"Thank you, Lady Jules." The chef bobbed his head quickly. "I'm afraid it's simple fare, as we did not expect you today. Roast boar with my own special-recipe gravy. Red potatoes roasted with butter and herbs. Fresh salad with buttermilk dressing. And for dessert, double chocolate cake with coconut frosting."

Jules got up from her chair and actually hugged the startled man. "This is wonderful! Thank you." She beamed at him and gave him a little peck on the cheek. "Now. Please take a seat, both of you, and join us. We insist."

The chef and Tiny Sam both hesitated until Jules pulled out one of the chairs and gently shoved Samantha into it. The chef joined her as Jules moved back to her own seat. She grabbed a knife and cut into the cake as she sat down. "I think I'll start with dessert!"

Tiny Sam giggled, then covered her mouth in embarrassment. Jules raised an eyebrow at her. "You've never started with dessert first?" When the young woman shook her head, Jules plopped a heaping slice of cake onto her plate. "Well, now you have!"

They passed the next half hour or so eating the meal and talking about Antalia. Jules asked the chef if he was happy that he'd stayed in the house and become an Elysian. He assured her that he'd never been happier.

Brick returned a short while after the meal was completed. Tiny Sam gave him a plate of leftovers, which he declared to be, "A meal fit fer a king!" making her giggle.

Michael was next to arrive back at the house. His face was slightly flushed and he spoke very carefully. "Twirk will take all you've got to sell her, and at one hundred gold per keg."

Brick laughed at the old knight. "Ye had to sample a bit more, didn't ye?"

Michael hiccupped. "It was the gentlemanly thing to do. One should never let a lady drink alone." He took a seat in one of the chairs and seemed ready for a nap.

Sasha returned less than thirty minutes later. She was smiling from ear to ear and nearly floating as she walked. "I've learned SO much! And we need to kill about a hundred more of those gargoyles. The ingredients they drop make the most amazing things!"

Alexander shook his head. "Three was bad enough. Let's hope we never see a hundred of those things."

After a few more minutes of chatting - mostly with Tiny Sam, as Michael was fading fast - the group headed back out to the portal. Alexander told the young woman, "When Michael wakes up, tell him we'll have someone open a portal twice daily. Mid-morning and sunset."

With that, he turned and opened the portal and they stepped through to the keep, Alexander's personal guard once again bringing up the rear.

*****

Matt put on his headgear and once again logged into the game. He was prepared for yet another session of swimming for his life. All told, he had died thirty-eight times in that accursed place, but he was determined to get out. He'd lost so many levels by this time that it barely even registered anymore. His only thought was to find a way to swim up to breathable air and escape.

This time, however, was different.

He found himself on his throne as usual, but as he went to raise his feet to push off and swim upward, he realized he could breathe. The water was gone. The room was still wet, water dripping from the tapestries along the walls. A steady stream still poured from the mostly-closed hole in the room's ceiling. And the stone doors that had sealed him in were shattered, the water running out through the opening. He could see the bodies of cursed undead and drow soldiers in the long chamber beyond.

A pair of drow emerged from stealth in front of him. The taller of the two stepped forward. "We were wondering if you would return. It seems you have fallen into quite the trap here." The drow took a moment, inspecting him carefully. "And you have died many times. You are weak now."

Matt growled in his Dark One avatar. He instinctively reached for his daggers before realizing he no longer had them. Or his bag. Shaking with rage, he spat at the drow. "Watch your tongue, worm! Yes, I died. Many times. But soon I will regain my lost strength. And I shall remember your words."

The smaller drow sneered at him. "What makes you think we'll let you live long enough to regain what little strength you had? You have failed our masters again and again. Failure is punished, not rewarded."

"Ha! You mean this was not punishment enough? The wizards sealed me in here, poisoned my throne, and drowned me over and over. How much more punishment will they need before they're satisfied?" He was nearly screaming at them by the time he finished.

The smaller drow stepped forward. "This was not the master's doing. We were sent here after he discovered the flooded room while searching you out. So watch your tongue, weakling! 'Dark One,' indeed. I do not understand what the masters see in you."

The Dark One had been looking past the drow as he spoke. Now he stepped down from the throne and turned to face the dark elf. Making sure he aligned himself properly, he growled, "I will show you who is weak!"

With a sudden exhalation of breath, he ducked his shoulder and tackled the drow, driving its body backward and to the ground, where one of the poison thorns he had not cleared slammed into the dark elf's back. There was a short scream of pain, followed by some thrashing as he tried to push the Dark One off of him. Then his eyes went blank and he stopped moving.

The Dark One got to his feet and delivered a brutal kick to the drow's head. Then he bent and looted the body. He placed looted daggers in sheaths on either thigh, then claimed the dark elf's inventory bag as his own. For good measure, he took the leather armor and equipped that as well. His old armor was in tatters.

Turning to the remaining drow, he said, "I assume since they sent you here, the wizards wish to speak with me?"

The drow nodded respectfully. "They do. Rather, one does. The Grand Master. He sent this." Producing one of the dark portal orbs, he set it down and on the ground and activated it. A moment later, a purple-tinged hole opened in the air in front of them. The Dark One stepped through first, the drow following. As the portal closed behind them, the moans of the cursed dead that inhabited the city above could be heard growing closer.

The Dark One found himself in a room he'd never seen before. One of the drow wizards, the Grand Master himself, sat on a raised chair in the center of the room. Surrounding him were kneeling servants; lesser wizards, guards, scouts, and assassins. The Dark One could sense several more drow standing around them in stealth mode. Some in the open, some behind the stone pillars that ringed the room.

As he took in the room, the old wizard spoke. "Welcome to my home, oh Dark One." His tone was mocking, and several of those on their knees chuckled. A few even raised their heads enough to make eye contact. There was no mercy in those gazes. Only hunger.

"Thank you, Grand Master. And thank you also for the rescue. That trap has taken much from me. But I will find the one responsible for it and make them suffer." He kept his tone neutral and as matter-of-fact as possible.

"Vengeance is admirable. But yours must wait. We have work for you and you have lost much ground. You have grown weaker. You have lost Antalia and all our servants there. You have failed in your mission to infiltrate Damerion. And the armies you sent into Elysia are no more."

The Dark One winced at the listing of his shortcomings. He suppressed the urge to argue or make excuses. Instead, he answered, "All you have said is true. But I can regain my strength the same way I gained it before. With your help. And I remain your loyal servant. I will find a way to take down Elysia and clear the way for our armies to destroy its allies."

"We shall see," the old wizard rasped. "You will be taken to one of the dungeons to regain your lost levels. Alexander is growing quickly as well and we believe he is already at level 70. When you have reached a comparable level, we will arrange for you to face him. Fail us again, and you will suffer unimaginable torment every moment you spend in our world for all eternity."

The ancient wizard looked down at him from his throne. His growing smile was the embodiment of pure evil. "In the meantime, we have prepared a lesson for the Elysians and their allies."

*****

Alexander and company were just crossing the courtyard after exiting the portal when the twin roars of two enraged dragons shook the earth. All eyes went instantly to the roost above them, just in time to see the winged forms of two gargoyles burst from the entrance. One was carrying a small form in its claws.

Sasha gasped, "Is that Fibble? Save him!"

The flying creatures were out of range for any spellcasting from the group. Lainey instantly leapt into the air, her wings straining to lift her quickly above the wall. She already had her bow and arrow equipped.

Kai burst from the roost in dragon form, immediately snatching up the nearest gargoyle in his jaws. The one carrying the small passenger dove toward the lake and forest below, likely trying to take cover in the trees. Kai's roar this time contained more anguish than anger as he turned toward the retreating monster. Braxis and his gryphons were already airborne and rushing toward the gargoyle as well, issuing challenging calls as they sped toward it.

Alexander focused on the thing's back and teleported himself. He appeared just above the monster and fell onto its back. Wrapping one arm around its neck, he held tight as he drew his sword. With a vicious swing, he severed the gargoyle's right wing near the first joint.

There were two screams of pain. The first from the gargoyle, the second from its passenger as the monster reflexively dug in with its claws. The small, high-pitched second scream tore at Alexander's heart. Looking down, expecting to see a bleeding Fibble, he was horrified to see one of the green hatchlings. Its head was drooping and blood ran from several deep claw wounds. Alexander frantically cast heals on the baby dragon as the three of them fell toward the ground. Even as he cast a second healing spell, he could tell it was doing no good. The wounds weren't closing.

Kai reached them first, his foreclaw sweeping Alexander off the monster's back just before his jaw clamped down on its head and torso. As Alexander continued to fall, he saw Kai grasp his child gently in his front claws and lift both the gargoyle's and his offspring's corpses higher into the air. That was all he had time to see before he hit the ground and died.

*****

Chapter 9

Consequences

When Alexander respawned after the longest limbo of his life, the keep was in a state of confusion. Dragons filled the sky and armed citizens rushed about in every direction. His UI was filled with notifications, but he waved them aside for a moment. In guild chat he said, *"Somebody give me an update!"*

The group knew that Sasha would answer, as their strategist, and left the channel silent so she could be heard. The sorrow in her voice was clear.

"Gargoyles attacked Kai's roost. Killed one of the babies." She came trotting up to him as she spoke. As soon as she reached him, she threw her arms around him and squeezed him harder than she ever could with his real-life body. She sobbed into his shoulder and he patted her back as he squeezed her back with his other arm. The others in the group began to assemble around them.

"I saw that much. I tried to save the little one, but the gargoyle's claws did so much damage. I... I think it was my fault. It squeezed harder when I cut its wing." His voice went hoarse and he couldn't continue.

Lainey and Jules joined in the hug while Brick shuffled his feet uncomfortably. Max came trotting over and, sensing the mood, put a hand on the dwarf's shoulder.

After a moment, Sasha pushed Alexander away. "No! This wasn't your fault. Those things came here to kill the babies. You tried to stop it."

Alexander shook his head. "If you had heard the scream... I thought-" he swallowed, his throat tight. "I thought it was Fibble." Jules hugged him tighter.

Alexander sent out another message in guild chat. *"Fibble? Can you hear me? Are you okay?"*

The only response was the sound of the little goblin crying. A moment later, Kai surprised them by answering. *"Fibble is unhurt. Two of our hatchlings were injured, and he helped to heal them."*

Alexander answered, *"Kai, I'm so sorry. Can I come up and join you?"*

There was a long hesitation before the dragon answered. *"That would be… unwise. Lia is not herself at the moment. She has gathered the remaining little ones to herself and might lash out at any intruders. Even I cannot approach. Give her time to come to her senses, please."*

"Of course. Whatever you need. We are here for you."

Kai's voice changed with his next message, a clear growl of anger mixed with heartbreak coming through. *"I do not know how they got so close. They smelled heavily of drow magic. The wizards must have discovered a way to mask their presence even from dragonkind. I have already sent one of my cousins to alert my father. You should do the same for our allies."* His voice went silent and Alexander left him to it.

"Jeeves, alert the other keeps that you can reach, please," he called out.

"Of course, Majesty."

Fitz appeared in the courtyard a moment later. He wasted no time with pleasantries. "I've been to the roost. The remaining little ones are fine. Fibble was deafened but has been healed. He's upset, but Lia has gathered him in with her own and is tending to him. I have set a ward across the entrance that will kill anything other than a dragon that tries to pass through. So do not attempt to visit until I tell you otherwise."

The wizard looked to the sky and one of the dragons dove toward the tower. It took humanoid form as it entered the upper room, then appeared next to Fitz. It was Del. Fitz ordered, "I want someone in the air over the keep and the roost at all times. Bring another wing if you need to. I want wings guarding the palaces in Stormforge, Broken Mountain, Antalia, Damerion, the elven kingdom, and every other nation or city that serves the light."

Del bowed to the elder dragon and disappeared. Fitz turned to Alexander. "Call your allies together. Now. Bring them all here, as this place is currently the most secure." Then he too was gone.

Alexander turned to Silverbeard and Lola, who were nearby. "We're going to have a bunch of royal guests. Please work with Jeeves and gather whomever you need from the crafters to make sure we have adequate quarters for them."

Silverbeard nodded. "Aye, lad. Won't be as fancy as they be used to, but we'll make 'em comfortable enough."

Alexander looked to his core group, who were standing nearby. "I'm going to send one of you to each city. Bring them back with you if you can, or get a commitment that they'll be here at sunrise. Tell them whatever you need to. No need to keep secrets." He lowered his voice. "Except about the Guardian."

He turned and activated the portal to the elven kingdom and Lorian dashed through. One by one, he sent his people to gather the rulers of the allied kingdoms.

*****

Matt logged out of the game to find that the house he was squatting in was pitch-black. Only the sound of the refrigerator running and a passing car outside reached his ears. He sat there in his chair, unmoving. The old drow wizard had sent an apprentice with him through a dungeon. The apprentice had healed him as he fought his way through but hadn't grouped with him, so he got all the experience for the kills. The single run had earned him five levels. It would get harder as he leveled up, but he estimated he could catch up to Alexander and friends in two weeks. Maybe three, if they continued to level at the pace they had been recently. He smiled to himself, already plotting his revenge in the game. But his reverie was interrupted by a question, which he mumbled out loud: "If the drow wizards didn't set that trap for me, who did?"

He set that question aside as he pulled out his burner phone. The odd message from earlier intrigued him. The only person with that number was his mole inside Olympus. And if she'd been caught, he would have surely heard about it by now. He had no illusions that she would hold out under interrogation of even medium intensity. No, if she'd been found out, the authorities or some Olympus goon squad would be at his door.

He turned the phone on. There were no new messages. He took a chance and sent a text.

"Missed your call. Problems?"

He waited five minutes, in case she was somewhere private enough to answer. She wasn't. Turning the phone back off, he set it on the arm of his chair and went to the fridge to get a beer.

Back in his recliner, he sipped his beer and munched on some teriyaki beef jerky. Turning his mind back to his in-game dilemma, he voiced his thoughts as he worked through the problem.

"It wouldn't have been another player. Nobody goes down there or even knows it's there. I don't even know how to get there from the surface. The drow portaled me down there and back each time. That leaves an NPC. Or, more likely, several of them. Did the prince somehow escape and tell the king where I was?" He hadn't thought to check on his prisoner before answering the old wizard's summons. But chances were that all his assigned drow were dead, if he'd been left in that room as long as he was and no one had reported to his master. By extension, he assumed that whomever killed his drow guards at the stronghold had also freed the prince.

"The old wizard said the armies I was going to use to take Damerion were wiped out in Elysia. I'll need to get them to trust me with more troops to take the city. It'll be harder now, if the prince has warned them." He took another sip as he mused, "I need something big. A way to wipe out a few thousand players at once, then spawn camp them back to level 1. Get them complaining on the forums. Maybe even do it in several cities at once. Get people to rage quit and badmouth the game and Jupiter Tech. Soften up the kingdoms for the drow to step in and kill every NPC and player everywhere. The game will go belly up. And as their stock drops, I'll destroy Olympus itself along with the Greystones."

*****

152

Richard and Michael were sitting in a small conference room in a tower basement level at Olympus. Sitting across from them was a team of devs, their leader speaking as he pulled up various holograms above the center of the table.

"As you know, we've been planning a world event around this content for over a year. But the plan wasn't to take it live for another year, maybe more. There is supposed to be a worldwide castle defense event where the drow wizards and their forces make their move on every major starting city for every playable race at the same time. Players would receive quests from their local ruler to help defend against the dark armies. If the players are successful in defending their city, they get access to the counteroffensive content, where they can raid the drow's underground strongholds. Or travel to help retake any cities that fall to the drow."

The hologram cycled through mocked-up battle scenes of dark forces attacking city walls, and of large player raid parties fighting underground.

"We've been building the new underground territories for two years now. Complete underground cities and networks of surrounding tunnels. Sentient races and monsters not seen in the game before. A whole world nearly as large as the surface world. A completely unique drow stronghold within a day's travel of each starter city. This has been our most ambitious undertaking since we created the world of Io itself."

Richard nodded. "Not that I don't appreciate the scale of the undertaking and the hard work that your teams have put in. But we know the history here. Why have you called this meeting?"

The lead developer looked uncomfortable. Clearing his throat, then taking a sip of water from a glass in front of him, he answered, "It seems Odin has pushed up our schedule. Or this Dark One has. But we believe it's Odin acting in response to the Dark One's attacks on Alexander and Elysia. And maybe the real-world attacks on Olympus, too. He's pushed up the time frame for the world event to get the players involved now instead of next year."

Michael chuckled. "We wanted him to have free rein to develop the details of Io as he saw fit. As long as he doesn't violate any of the basic directives we gave him, adjusting the timeline is within his parameters. Though I'm surprised he made such an extreme adjustment. Are the underground zones even finished enough to be playable?"

"That's the thing. They weren't. But they are. We had all the rough outlines and were filling it in on a schedule that would have had us ready for alpha testing in about six months. It seems Odin went ahead and finished it for us. Or at least, almost finished it. If my guys pick up where he's left off, we should be alpha test-ready in two weeks. Maybe less."

Richard shook his head. "A quantum computer is fast. Unimaginably fast. But it shouldn't be able to make creative decisions and invent quest lines and art."

The dev smiled. "We did that bit. The story arcs, the sketches, even the rough-ins were done. The next six months were going to be the grunt work. The details on the renderings, the algorithms for the fights, loot drops, experience awards. Odin's capable of all of that."

Richard was smiling to himself as he made notes on a paper pad in front of him. Though he and Michael ran one of the most successful tech-based companies on earth, they both liked to go old school during meetings and use paper and pencil.

He looked at the lead developer. "And you say this is all within the scope of the directives we gave him?"

The man nodded and looked sheepish. "It honestly never occurred to us that Odin might take it upon himself to speed up our timeline on something like a world event. He's taken care of a lot of the finish work. But we don't have any of the marketing material ready yet. We thought we'd have more time."

Richard snorted. "Don't worry about that. Marketing can throw something together and put it out on the forums. The players will spread the word for us. You guys focus on making sure the algorithms are good for the fights, the loot drops, XP awards, etc. And have the art team fine-tune the visuals. Let's make this event as glitch-free as we can, under the circumstances."

*****

In less than an hour, Alexander began to receive calls from his people who'd gone to retrieve the various rulers. As each one reached out, he opened the portal and welcomed his allies.

The first to arrive was Lorian with Ithaniel. Since his official coronation had not happened yet, Ithaniel brought two of the elders along. Alexander shook their hands. "Thank you for coming on such short notice. I expect the others will arrive shortly. If you'd like to look around, I can have someone escort you. Otherwise, we'll be meeting in the Great Hall as soon as everyone has arrived."

The elves were barely listening, their attention focused on the dragons circling above. Ithaniel, realizing Alexander had stopped speaking, shook his head. "Oh. Yes, of course. We'll take the tour later." He and the elders followed Lola, who gestured for them to accompany her to the Great Hall.

Thalgrin was next. He had barely stepped through the portal when Fitz appeared in the teleport zone with Charles next to him. The old wizard sent both kings to the Great Hall with a few terse words and a promise to answer questions inside. The two rulers didn't question him. Both shook Alexander's hand and murmured quiet greetings as they passed.

Prince Apollos and his father King Arand arrived next. The two looked tired, as if they'd not slept much. Alexander greeted them and asked about their city. The two of them spoke of siege preparations and the building of weapons until Alexander got the request to open the portal to Antalia. He asked the two men to join the others inside as he turned to open the gateway.

Queen Margaret brought Princess Kimberly with her. Alexander bowed to the ladies as he welcomed them to the keep. He offered the queen an arm and escorted them both into the Great Hall. Silverbeard had set up a long table and comfortable high-backed chairs to accommodate the visitors. There were platters of pastries and bowls of fresh fruit on the table, as well as pitchers of water, wine, and ale.

Alexander held out chairs for the queen and princess, then took one for himself. The others were all taking seats on either side of the table, with Fitz sitting at the head. He wasted no time on formalities.

"For purposes of this meeting, I am speaking on behalf of the dragon kingdom. And shall we all agree that Ithaniel speaks for the elves?" He looked to the elder elves first and they nodded in agreement. As did the others at the table, though most had never met him.

"Good!" Fitz pulled a pastry tray closer and snagged two with one hand. "You have all agreed to the proposed alliance to fight the drow wizards. That fight has come upon us sooner than expected. In case you have not been informed, the drow have attacked here in Elysia, Stormforge, Antalia, and Damerion."

He paused, and his face grew solemn. There was a catch in his voice when he continued. "Most recently, gargoyles serving the drow wizards attacked Prince Kaibonostrum's roost just above this keep. They murdered one of his new hatchlings and tried to take others." There were tears in the old dragon wizard's eyes.

He collected himself and pointed a pastry at Alexander. "Young Alexander there also managed to get himself killed attempting to save the little one." Thalgrin chuckled as the others looked unsure how to react to that.

Fitz looked to Thalgrin. "It is never easy to lose one of your people. But the loss of a child, as you know, strikes straight at the heart of the kingdom and its king, or queen. The dragon king will not tolerate this attack. The time for building strength and gathering allies has come to an end." Fitz thumped the table with his free hand. Platters and bowls jumped and spilled their contents. The old wizard *hmph*ed.

Alexander spoke up. "I'm all for attacking the drow wizards and their armies. But how do we find them? So far they've been working through this 'Dark One' in our kingdoms. And though I thought we had disposed of him, it seems he's still around. But I know of no way to locate him."

Fitz's smile sent chills through many of those seated at the table. "I found him. In Damerion. I and a dragon wing eliminated his underground base when we rescued the prince. I set traps that would kill him repeatedly. He may not have been reduced to level one before finding a way to escape, but I doubt he will be strong enough to attack you again soon."

Alexander's pulse raced. He clenched his teeth in an effort not to yell at the old wizard. Keeping his voice as calm as he could, he interrupted, "You had the Dark One and let him go?"

Fitz stood, his eyes blazing as he leaned over the table toward Alexander. "Do you think me a fool, boy!? I found his stronghold. He was not there when we arrived. You adventurers tend to disappear for long periods of time. So I set traps for him. Traps that would kill him time and again the moment he reappeared in our world." The growl that followed the wizard's speech left everyone at the table leaning back in their chairs.

Alexander shook his head. "Of course I don't think you're a fool, Fitz. I'm sorry. It's just that this man has killed friends of mine in both worlds and threatens to kill more. I did not think before I spoke. Please accept my most sincere apology." He bowed his head to the angry dragon wizard.

Fitz sat back down with a loud *harrumph* and took a couple bites of pastry as the others waited in silence. After washing the pastry down with some ale, he replied.

"I accept your apology, boy. I know you only mean well and that you were anxious because you care deeply for your people. Let us move on." Having finished his pastry, he quickly licked his fingers, then wiped them on his robe.

"Now, as I was saying… When we found the stronghold, I confiscated a few of the portal orbs he'd hidden under his throne. If I were to activate one or more of them, it *should* lead us to the domain of his masters. The drow wizards. I dare not test them before we are ready, in case they lead directly to one or more of the wizards themselves. That would tip our hand and take away any hope of surprising them."

The wizard looked at Charles and the other rulers in turn. "I have interrogated several captured drow over the past weeks. A few perished rather than speak, but those who broke all spoke of upcoming attacks. Damerion is currently under siege, though I believe the armies the Dark One intended to use for that attack were the same ones Alexander defeated here. But the drow do not think small. They plan to attack every major city on Io."

Queen Margaret spoke the question on everyone's mind. "When will these attacks happen?"

"Soon. Within days, I believe. Maybe a week or two. Their bold move against a dragon roost shows they believe themselves strong enough to attack. You should all prepare as best you can in that time. And the Mage's Guild is already putting the word out to all the other kingdoms. We are sharing information about ways to take away the drow's best weapon. Namely, consecrating their cities as Alexander, Charles, and yourself have done, Margaret. Take away the drow's ability to move through the cities and operate in stealth and you cripple their plans. Rather than quietly killing a few guards and opening gates, they will have to attack using more conventional plans."

Thalgrin was next with a question. "But if we each be defendin' our cities against the beasties, how can we hope ta succeed in attackin' their base? Most don't have so many soldiers to spare!" The other rulers nodded their heads. In peacetime, it was normal for a kingdom to reduce the size of its standing army in order to save on the cost of housing, feeding, and paying them.

Fitz's answer surprised all of them. "They likely will not attack here again. At least, not in force. Not after losing two armies here, and knowing that the keep is well guarded by dragons. And they are not foolish enough to attack the dragon's valley. Nor the dwarven cities, as they are too easily sealed and nearly impenetrable from outside. So while you defend your cities and hold their attention, we shall mount an attack from here. With a force of dragons, dwarves, and Elysians willing to go."

Alexander raised a hand, then lowered it again, feeling foolish. "The orcs and minotaurs may want to get in on the fighting as well."

Thalgrin grinned at that. "I'll be joinin' ye. Just ta see that!"

Charles added, "Edward will be joining you as well. To represent Stormforge."

Alexander shook his head. "Thank you, Majesty. But Edward is of more value on your own walls, making sure those light cannons are put to good use. Many of my Elysians are volunteers from Stormforge and will make you and your people proud."

Apollos spoke up. "I don't suppose you'll let me come along, either?" At which his father's visage tightened and the king's fists clenched. Alexander could see Arand's longing to deny his son the chance to join the battle.

Fitz saved him the trouble. "No, boy. Damerion has already given one son to this war. You'll be needed in the defense of the city."

Alexander added, "I'm going to make sure the first wave through the portals is made primarily of adventurers. We won't needlessly sacrifice the lives of citizens when there are fools like myself willing to throw ourselves into impossible situations without pause." He grinned at his allies around the table. "We will soften them up, at the very least. Let the dragons and our other allies finish them off."

Sounds of agreement and gratitude came to him from around the table.

"Alright, then. I'll go speak to the orcs and minotaurs to see if they'll join us. The rock trolls as well. Fitz, when do you want to launch the attack?"

"Two days. I want to make sure the cities have arranged proper defenses first. Thalgrin, advise all the dwarven cities to stock up on supplies today and tomorrow, then seal their gates. All of them. The rest of you, work with your priests and mages to prepare your cities. Evacuate nearby villages. The drow are not above taking hostages and using them to force your surrender. Or just killing them outright. Call up your reserves and arm them. And should attacks come, do as Alexander says and put the adventurers in your cities on the front lines. Promise them gold and experience for successful defense of the city. Add in bonuses for holding the enemy outside the walls."

The kings and queen began to discuss plans and ideas for defense, as well as ways to coordinate between themselves in case not all were attacked.

*****

The two days passed quickly as Alexander and company prepared for their attack. He sent parties of his citizens into the local dungeon one after the other, pushing his lower and mid-level people to get stronger.

The dragons continued to patrol overhead but there were no more gargoyle sightings. Sasha and Lydia recruited every available alchemist and burned through both Elysia's and Stormforge's supplies of ingredients to make health, mana, stamina, and cure potions, which were then distributed among the cities, with a generous supply given to the raid party.

Alexander spent much of his time enchanting weapons and armor for his people, starting with the players. His skill level was high enough now that he could add significant Strength, Stamina, Intelligence, and Agility buffs to items that weren't already enchanted. He infused armor pieces with Healing Light spells that could be triggered by the wearer in an emergency. The spell would provide a one-time three thousand-HP heal. At their current levels, that was ten percent or less of any of his players' health pool. But it might buy enough time for healers to get to a critically wounded raid member.

But before he began his enchanting work, he'd gone to visit his allies to the north. He gathered Molgo and Dawn along with the orc elders and explained their plan. Almost before he was done speaking, they were volunteering large forces of their fighters. Alexander held up his hands.

"We're taking a relatively small raid party to the drow strongholds. Almost all adventurers. And some dragons. But I would appreciate it if you'd send a few hundred of your best down to the keep to help defend it, in case there's an attack while we're away. And please keep watch on the forest up here as well. The dark forces attacked here once. They may try it again."

After sharing some of the fermented goat's milk with them, he'd returned to the keep.

The last half of the day before the raid, Alexander gathered all the players together. They sat in the Great Hall with Fitz and the dragons who would accompany them through the dark orb portal. Kai was still nowhere to be seen but Alexander didn't ask after him. Losing a child wasn't something anyone got over quickly. The dragon prince and his mate had been quietly huddled around their offspring, and Fibble, since the attack.

Fitz and Sasha outlined possible battle strategies for inside the drow stronghold. The dragons, all of whom had fought the drow wizards before, shared what they knew of old strategies used by the drow and the ways the dragons and their allies overcame them. Sasha and the players suggested some improvements, trying to think outside the box. They all moved as a group to the new dining area inside the mountain and practiced coordinated fighting techniques for hours, until they felt comfortable that they could respond quickly as a group to most situations. Before they all retired for the evening, Alexander gave each of the dragons a guild dragon pin with the Undying and Healing enchantment.

Up in their rooms preparing for bed, Jules asked, "How worried are you about tomorrow?"

Alexander paused, sitting on the bed and unequipping his gear almost without thought. "I'm not worried about us. I'm worried about losing. Losing the battle. Getting any of the dragons killed. Getting our people at the keep killed. I mean, if we wipe... what's to stop the drow from flooding through the portal while we're stuck in limbo? I don't know if our citizens can hold out long enough for us to return, even with the help of the orcs and minotaurs. And certainly they won't manage it without heavy losses." His shoulders slumped.

Jules crawled across the enormous bed and sat behind him. Wrapping both arms around his waist, she leaned into him as she spoke quietly near his ear. "I know you don't want to hear this, but get your head out of your ass." She squeezed him tighter as he straightened up and started to turn toward her. "Hush. Just listen. I know you take this seriously. But this is still a game. The citizens are just code. Yes, they are our friends. And they seem as real to me as any friend I've ever had in our world. But you cannot make yourself sick worrying about them. The game will kill some of them off. And there won't be anything you can do about it. Except mourn them afterward."

He opened his mouth to argue but she put a finger over his lips. "I'm not done. You and I, all of us players here, we have important things to do. One of them is to raise our sync levels and test the limits of this game, so that the information we help gather can be used to help people like you and me."

She let go of him and moved to sit beside him, taking his hand in hers and bumping shoulders with him. "Another is to find this Dark One asshole and shut him down so that he can't hurt anyone else in the real world. Or ruin the lives of more people he uses in-game. How many people have been arrested now? People who won't be able to provide for themselves or their families because they followed this dipshit?"

Alexander shook his head. "Too many."

"Right. So in the morning, we go on this raid. We give it our best shot. We hope that none of the dragons get killed. But if they do, you have to let it go. Focus on the fight. On the bigger picture. Get to the ones who can point us to this Dark One, or maybe even find him there. Point him out to Odin and take him down, both here and in the real world."

She leaned in and kissed him softly. "But also... maybe have some *fun*. This is still a game, after all. We're about to run a raid that nobody has ever done before. I'm betting Brick and Beatrix pass out from the legendary loot drops we're gonna get."

He pulled her close for another, longer kiss. "You're absolutely right. I'm too far into my own head. All the planning and building I've been doing for the kingdom, I sometimes forget I'm not really 'King of Elysia,' and you're not queen."

She smacked him lightly and gave him a pouty face. "Oh, I am *totally* a queen! My boyfriend is the richest kid on earth. We live in a castle atop a mountain with its own army and thousands of peasants just waiting to do our bidding." She gave him a wicked grin.

"Ha! Okay, Your Majesty. We need to get some sleep. Raid in T-minus ten hours. And take it easy with the 'peasants' talk. They can't hear you in here because of the privacy lock, but if you said that elsewhere, you might find your pod filled with itching powder or something."

He leaned back and placed his head on a pillow as Jules moved to lay at his side. They chatted for a few minutes more before Alexander heard a snore from Jules. He smiled and closed his eyes, sleep finding him much more slowly.

*****

Matt sat in his recliner, the only light in the house coming from the burner phone in his hand. A message had just come in from his operative inside Olympus.

"Got your message. Safe spot for now. Want to talk?"

Talking for any length of time was risky. If the Jupiter Tech people were onto him, they could trace the call within minutes. But the recent odd messages had him burning with both curiosity and fear. And all his plans for taking down the Greystones hinged upon the destruction of at least part of Olympus and the deaths of Richard, Michael, and most especially Alexander.

He dialed the number and initiated the call. The phone rang once before the voice on the other end said, "Hello."

Matt wasted no time. "What is your situation?"

"Stable, for now. Though security seems to be tightening. They've begun pulling people in for interviews, but as far as I can tell they are just fishing. The questions have been vague and don't seem to be targeted at you or me."

"And the explosives?" Matt's voice was tight, every second that passed being counted in his head.

"Buried still. They've had bomb-sniffing dogs going through the compound around the clock. Too dangerous to move the explosives inside right now." The voice on the other end of the phone was barely a loud whisper.

"How long till you can place the bombs?" Matt was beginning to sweat.

"Once it's clear to grab the stuff and bring it in, I can have them placed in a day. Maybe less. Depends on the security level at the time. But I need to know where you want them."

"Primary targets are the servers and the Greystones. Use what you need to make sure of them. Everything else… place them where they'll kill the most people. Use your best judgement." After a moment's thought, he said, "If you can bring down the tower and still accomplish the rest, do it."

The only response was the sound of the call disconnecting. Matt quickly shut off his phone and removed the battery. He thought about destroying it altogether, but replacing it was risky. He'd have to wait until one of his people stopped by and instruct them to get him another burner or two. With Jupiter Tech security, the police, the FBI, and who knew who else all looking for him, it wasn't safe for him to show his face anywhere any more.

After a quick trip to the bathroom to take care of necessities, he settled back into his recliner and reached for his headset.

*****

Richard's phone buzzed at him while he was watching Alexander's feed. Annoyed because he'd been told he didn't want to be disturbed, he glanced at his wrist. Seeing the call was from Talbott, the head of Jupiter Tech security, he immediately answered.

"What's wrong?" He knew Talbott wouldn't have interrupted him if it weren't important. And these days, important meant bad.

"Matt called his mole a few minutes ago. We got a lock on the location here in the compound. My guys are almost there. The FBI is closing in on the location the call originated from. It didn't last long enough for an exact pinpoint. But they've got plainclothes agents in unmarked cars searching the area."

Richard was already out of his chair and moving toward the elevator. "Where in the compound? I'm on my way."

Talbott's voice hesitated. "Richard, no. It may not be safe. They might have a weapon, or explosives. Or both. Let my guys get things under control. Please, just stay where you are for a few more minutes and let me do my job."

Richard kept walking and stepped into the elevator. He practically growled his response. "Fine. I'll wait in the lobby. But tell me where they are."

Again, there was a delay before Talbott answered. Richard was about to repeat the question when the man said, "Med labs. We think, specifically, the lab Jules' pod is in."

Richard's blood ran cold and his face turned ghostly white as the elevator doors closed and Heimdall began its descent toward the lobby. Images of the destroyed lab with body parts strewn about from the bomb that went off in Dayle's pod momentarily blinded him. He reached out and put a hand on the wall to steady himself. He could hear Talbott's voice, but the words had no meaning right then.

The elevator came to halt at the lobby level and Richard's knees nearly buckled. The doors opened and two security guards rushed in to prop him up and lead him to a seating area. The whole time, the concerned guards and Bethany were asking him if he was injured or unwell. The receptionist looked nearly panicked as he stared into her face, not really present in the moment. All he could think of was having to tell Alexander that Jules was dead.

He blinked a few times and took a deep breath. The sounds of the room around him came rushing back. He held up his hands to settle the people around him and managed to say, "I'm fine. I'm okay. Thank you." The guards straightened up and looked relieved, both speaking into their mics to update their boss.

But Talbott was still on the phone with Richard. He'd been listening, and he understood the man's reaction. "Richard, you back with me now?"

"Yes. Tell me." Richard took another deep breath. His inner voice kept telling him it was okay, he'd not heard an explosion yet.

"My men are there. They've taken and isolated six people in Jules' lab and those on either side. They're all med techs who are supposed to be there. My guys have moved them out of the labs into the corridor and are searching them now. Hold one moment."

Richard sat on the sofa in his lobby and stared out the window. Directly in his line of sight was the gate that Delbert Simms and his friends tried to penetrate with a car bomb. Repairs had been made and there was no physical sign of the incident. But his mind's eye showed him the twisted wreckage and the torn bodies from that night. He took a few more deep breaths. His body and soul wanted to get up, to run to the elevator to make sure Jules and his people were safe. But he gritted his teeth and squeezed the arm of the sofa until it creaked.

Talbott's voice came again. "We've got her. It was one of the techs. She had the burner phone on her. No weapon. My guys are searching the lab for any explosives now. I'll let you know when it's safe to come down."

Richard shook his head. "No. Bring her to my office. Have one of your female officers strip search her first. Check every stitch of her clothes. Throw some scrubs on her and bring her to me. Do what you can to scare the shit out of her. Her life is over. Make sure she knows it."

Richard didn't wait for a response. He ended the call and got to his feet. He paced back and forth for a few moments before looking up. He saw a look of astonishment on Bethany's face. Realizing she and the guards had heard what he'd said, he looked from Bethany to the two guards. Both gave him small nods of respect.

Bethany stammered, "Are... you going to kill someone?" She took an unconscious step backward as she asked.

Richard held up his hands. "No, of course not. But she doesn't need to know that. We just caught a mole working for Matt, the man who set off the bomb here and who has been sending people to attack us. When I said her life is over, I meant that she'll spend the rest of it in jail. Or she may be executed by the state for murder if they can tie her directly to the previous bomb."

Bethany's eyes grew wider and wider as Richard spoke. When he added, "They caught her in Jules' lab," the receptionist sat in a chair behind her and covered her mouth with her hands. Richard placed a comforting hand on her shoulder for a moment, then left her to step back into the elevator.

Michael was waiting for him when he reached his office. "I heard. Let's hope she's the only one. Do we know her name yet?"

Richard shook his head. He quickly dialed the HR office and asked who was on duty observing Jules' pod right then. He put the call on speaker so Michael could hear.

The HR director's voice came back a moment later. "Her name is Jenni. Been with us for six years. Promoted twice. Asked specifically to be put on Jules' team."

Richard cut her off. "Send her file to me. Now. She's just been detained by security. Found a phone on her she's been using to communicate with Matt."

The woman on the other end of the phone just said, "Oh, shit," and a moment later Richard's watch dinged at him, indicating he had email. He thanked the woman and hung up. A wave of his hand displayed the mole's file in hologram form above his desk. There was a photo of a young woman in her late twenties or very early thirties. Blonde hair, bright smile. Below the photo was a summary of her HR file, including her address, next of kin, and known associates. That last bit had been added when security had vetted all of the employees after the first attack.

The two men were silently reviewing the information when Heimdall informed them, *"Chief Talbott is bringing his prisoner up now. They will arrive in approximately one minute."*

"Thank you, Heimdall," Richard said absently as he took a seat behind his desk. Michael moved to stand behind him at his right shoulder, leaning back against a bookcase with his arms crossed. Both men adopted their most intimidating looks as the elevator doors opened.

*****

Chapter 10

Fight or Die

Alexander was awakened by a foot to the face. Not a kick, precisely. Just Jules' pink bunnymonster foot shoving at his jaw as she adjusted herself in her sleep. Somehow, she had managed to get turned head over heels in the giant bed and seemed to be dreaming. Like a dog chasing a dream squirrel, her feet were twitching.

Since she was also smiling, Alexander decided not to wake her. She deserved as many pleasant dreams as she could get. He rose and grabbed a quick shower before equipping all his gear. Today was raid day, and he could already feel the butterflies in his gut.

He reached out and gently nudged the still-sleeping Jules. She growled at him in her sleep and rolled away. Unfortunately, that roll took her over the edge of the bed to land with a thump on the floor. There was some soft cursing and grumpy complaints, and her head popped up above the bed. Seeing him grinning, Jules grumped, "What the hell?"

Alexander adopted his most innocent face. "Don't look at me. I just rubbed your shoulder a bit to wake you up. You rolled yourself off the bed."

She eyed him suspiciously as she got to her feet. He took a few steps around the bed, raising his arms in anticipation of a hug, but she stepped warily to the side and moved around him to the bathroom. He just chuckled and headed for breakfast.

Most of the other players were already there when he arrived. The anticipation of the raid, the chance to get a First Kill and the rewards that came with it had them all pumped and ready to go. Alexander grabbed some food and sat next to Helga. "You ready to kill stuff?"

She grinned at him, fire in her eyes. "I spent half the night polishing my baby here." She reached up and patted the enchanted sword on her back. Alexander couldn't help but remember she'd used that sword to remove his head not so long ago.

"I have a feeling you're going to get more than your share of mobs to kill today." He paused as he looked around. Jules had just arrived and it looked like all the players were present. Minus those who would be coming from the guild complex in Antalia. He walked over to the portal and opened it. Martin and a dozen or so of the players they'd recruited into the guild stepped through. They followed him back to the dining area and took seats. Several grabbed some food and drink for the buffs.

Standing up on the bench, he called out, "Listen up, folks. We're about to head out. Fitz says the portal will likely take us straight to one of the drow wizard's strongholds."

He paused as there were cheers and excited shouts. "Be on your toes. We might walk into an ambush. There will be lots of mobs to kill, and probably bosses, too. The loot's going to be *epic*!" He waited for the group to quiet down again.

"But I want you to remember, this isn't just a raid. We've got citizens to protect. Most especially those who are coming with us on this raid." The crowd grew silent. "If you have a choice between killing a mob and saving one of our citizens, you save them. Even if you have to sacrifice yourself to do it. We can worry about the mobs after. You are all expendable. Our citizens are not."

Everyone nodded agreement and Alexander stepped down. Helga grunted at him, her version of a respectful gesture. Lyra, who was sitting across from them, said, "Dayle would have loved this." All eyes went to her as a lone tear ran down her cheek.

Warren patted her back and said, "Yeah. He'd be the first one to dash forward and do something idiotic to grab aggro." He paused to remember, then chuckled, "He used to make these farting noises, then wave his hand in front of his nose and accuse the mobs. It was so stupid… but it worked!"

Helga raised her mug of coffee high into the air. "To Dayle!"

The other players all got to their feet and raised drinks and answered, "To Dayle!"

As they were all taking their seats again, their UIs lit up with a message.

Smiles appeared on everyone's faces as they mentally clicked the 'Yes' button. All except Alexander's. He was seeing only the countdown clock that was ticking down from 3:59 in the upper corner of his UI. When he began to curse and pace, the others turned their eyes toward him. Noticing the attention, he said, "This may change our plans. If this place is about to be attacked again, we can't very well leave it to the citizens to defend."

Sasha spoke up. "But we were about to do just that. I mean, you brought the orcs and minotaurs down, and the dragons are here as well."

Alexander shook his head. "That was when I thought an attack was unlikely. We've been assuming that the Dark One and his masters had given up on us after we beat their armies, at least for a little while, and moved on to cities like Damerion. But this world event says all capitol cities will be attacked. And now this keep is the capitol of Elysia."

Sasha still looked skeptical. She was about to speak when Melanie's avatar appeared behind Alexander. She poked him in the back with both hands and shouted, "Boo!" causing him to jump and spin with his hand on his sword.

"Ha! I got you good!" She beamed at him, clapping her hands together. When she saw he wasn't amused, she calmed down and dropped her hands. "I've got a message. Two, actually. The first is that security caught a mole in Olympus, and we think they're about to catch Matt, too." She waited for him to digest this.

Alexander asked, "Was anybody hurt?"

"Nope! Your pop and Michael are interrogating her now. But they caught her before she could do any damage. The cops are on their way to pick her up." She smiled again and this time Alexander smiled back. Jules stepped over and gave Melanie a hug.

"Oh! The second message. It seems Odin has decided to go ahead and start the planned world event *wayyyy* ahead of schedule. The drow wizards thingy wasn't supposed to happen yet. Your dad thinks you triggered Odin to start it early. Anyhow, none of us knows for sure what Odin's going to do, but we think you can expect bad beasties at your door just like everyone else."

Alexander sighed at the cheerful tone she used to deliver that news. He was reminded of when, as a child, he would listen to doctors try to be upbeat as they delivered bad news about his test results.

"Thank you, Melanie. We appreciate the heads-up. Please thank my father as well. And I'm glad everyone at Olympus is okay." He gave her the best smile he could manage as she waved and disappeared.

Sasha jumped up on a table and shouted, "Well, you all heard it! The raid's off! Time to defend this place against whatever they throw at us!"

The citizens, who had been frozen while Melanie was in-game, burst into action. Bodies rushed around the courtyard as they reacted to the alert message that they'd all seen. They knew from experience that defense quests could provide huge XP boosts and rewards.

Sasha quickly began to organize the players. "Max, Lainey, grab Lorian and bring all the hunters back in. Leave a couple up on the plateau as scouts. And one in the Dire Woods to warn us of approaching enemies."

She looked at Brick. "You've got four hours to repair any weapons or gear that needs it. You and Grumpy organize the smiths." The two dwarves were already moving toward the smithy.

"Lugs, please head over to the mine. Tell the miners and the rock trolls they're welcome to join us here in the keep. If they insist on staying out there, we'll need to figure out who to put with them to hold the line in case they need to retreat and seal the mine."

She turned to Alexander. "You should probably go get more of the orcs and minotaurs. If we're going to defend the outer wall, we'll need a lot more than the few hundred citizens we have here now."

Alexander agreed. He said, "Jeeves, loudspeaker please."

"Ready when you are, Majesty."

"Attention, all Elysians. You've all seen the alert. A dark army of unknown size and composition will attack our keep in less than four hours. I want all of you armed and armored immediately. Citizens already here in the keep, you know your stations. Begin preparations for battle. For all you citizens up on the plateau who are interested in participating in our kingdom's defense, please make your way to the garrison tower and teleport here to the keep."

Alexander looked around and spotted Beatrix. Motioning her closer, he said, "Please go and speak with the Duergar Council. Ask if their people are willing to help. Either on the wall, or carrying wounded to the healers, or delivering ammunition and supplies to the fighters. We'll take any help they're willing to give."

The diminutive mage adopted an earnest and determined look on her face and charged away toward the outer-wall dwelling where the portal mirror to the duergar city was kept.

With a few hours left before the start of the event, Alexander moved to the smithy. Every weapon or piece of armor that was crafted within the dragon forge was blessed by gods of light to do extra damage against the minions of the dark. But Alexander wanted his people to have every advantage, so he had one of the apprentices start bringing him items from the armory. He took a seat at one of the long tables in the dining area nearby and began to enchant.

For shields, he added a +3 Strength enchantment. For chain or plate armor pieces, he added +3 Stamina. To leather armor pieces, he added either Stamina or Agility. Every thirty or so items he had to stop to rest, eat a piece of fruit, and drink a mana potion. When he had worked through several piles of armor, he switched to weapons. Swords, hammers, and axes got +3 to Strength, while the crossbows got +3 to Agility.

After a couple of hours, orcs began to arrive through the mirror. The burly warriors were armed and armored, looking fierce with their faces and bodies painted. The average orc warrior stood seven feet tall, with shoulders too wide to fit through most doorways.

Alexander immediately had one of the guards stationed at the mirror to send all the arriving warriors to the smithy. Their weapons had not been forged at the keep and held no blessing, so Brick lined up three apprentices and had them begin a sort of assembly line to fix that. They took the swords and axes from the orcs three or four at a time and set the blades in the dragon forge. After a minute of being heated by the magical flame, they took each blade and hammered a stamp of the Elysian Dragon symbol into the metal of the blade. Then they quenched each one in a barrel filled with the blessed water from the underground stream.

In this manner, the magic of the dragon forge and the blessings of the light gods were imbued into each weapon. The orcs were each given a flask filled with the same water to drink, giving them the same buffs that the keep residents enjoyed on an everyday basis.

The orc warriors puffed out their chests and pounded on each other's shoulders as they felt the buffs take effect. They examined their newly-improved weapons with approval and practically vibrated with eagerness to test them on new enemies. Those few who wanted them were outfitted with shields from the pile Alexander had enchanted.

As each group was outfitted, they were sent to the outer wall, where one of the guard captains assigned them to a unit and a spot on the wall.

Behind the orcs came the minotaurs. Molgo and Dawn arrived first through the mirror, followed by four hundred of their people, appearing one at a time. They too were sent to the smithy, and two additional apprentices were assigned to update their weapons. With five of them working, there was a constant stream of blades going into and out of the forge.

Beatrix arrived with several of the Duergar Council. Gelag bowed his head to Alexander and said, "Our people are Elysians. We will do all we can to help. Most of our fighters were killed by our queen and the demons. But we can help in other ways."

Alexander replied, "Thank you. All of you. Please find Lola or Silverbeard and they will assign your people where they can be most helpful. And remind them to wear their dragon pins. I do not want to lose any citizens today."

As they left, he grabbed Beatrix. "What kind of enchantments can you do? Anything that'll help with weapons or armor?"

She thought for a moment. "I can add sharpness to blades with my water magic." She looked apologetic. "Most of what I know is intended for jewelry. Buffs to Intel, Wisdom, Mana Regen. Or spells for light, night vision, poison resistance."

Alexander patted her shoulder. "Sharpness is great! And if you can add Mana Regen to any of our caster's gear, that would be amazing."

The little gnome sat down across the table from him and began waving over minotaurs to add sharpness to their blades. Alexander took out half a dozen mana potions and set them on the table between them.

As the four-hour clock ran down, all of the orcs and most of the minotaurs had received their gear upgrades and moved out to their assigned positions on the outer wall. Alexander and Beatrix finished the last few enchantments with about ten minutes left to go. He sent her out to the gatehouse above the moat, where her water magic would be most effective.

Teleporting himself up to the control room, he sat on the control desk. "Jeeves, can I offer our people a 'Defend the Realm' quest like we have in previous battles?"

"I am afraid not, Majesty. Every citizen of Elysia has accepted the quest offered by the gods to defend the kingdom. You may not offer a second quest with the same goal. You could offer individual quests to kill a certain number of defenders. But that would take quite some time."

Alexander figured that was the case, but he had to ask. It never hurt to give his people bonus XP.

"Are all of our people inside the walls or the mine now?"

"Yes, Majesty. All but the hunter scouts that you requested remain outside. The miners and rock trolls have elected to stay with the mine and defend it. I heard them speaking to Lugs. They have closed and sealed the gate, and the rock trolls are gathering boulders to use as projectiles."

Alexander opened guild chat. *"Lugs, are you still at the mine?"*

"Yup. Figured I'd stay here in case they get attacked."

"I'm fine with that. But you might miss out on some sweet XP if they only attack here. If you want to fight here to start, I can always teleport you back to the mine to help defend there."

There were several seconds of silence before the big ogre replied, *"Good point. I'll head back."*

Alexander looked at the control table. Though he knew Jeeves wasn't physically in there, it was just in his nature to speak to an object. "Jeeves, how many stone golems do we have now?"

"Sixteen, Majesty. Four are up on the plateau patrolling and filling in any blank spaces on the map. Two are at the quarry assisting with moving stone blocks. Two others are in the corral near the quarry guarding the livestock. The rest are here in the keep performing various tasks for farmers and crafters."

"Please send four of them from the keep to the outer gatehouse. The other four should stay near the inner gate. They can help with moving wounded unless there is a breach in the gate."

"Yes, Majesty. They are moving now. Might I make a suggestion, Majesty?"

Alexander was taken aback. "A suggestion? Well, that is a surprise. Improved Interface?"

"Indeed, Majesty. As you know, I have the ability to repair the structures within the kingdom. And at the moment, I have significant stone resources available to me. Should you wish it, I could increase the height or thickness of the walls. The entire process would take several days, but I could begin now, before the battle starts."

Alexander considered it. As far as he was concerned, higher and thicker walls were never a bad thing. But those resources might be needed for repairs after the battle. And he didn't think an extra ten feet on the few sections of wall that Jeeves could improve before the battle would help much.

"Thank you, Jeeves, but I don't think that will be necessary. I would like you to focus on keeping us informed during the battle. Report the location of enemy forces as they move. Or let us know if you detect a breach anywhere. Especially up on the plateau."

"Of course, Majesty."

Alexander ported back down to the keep. The clock on his UI was winding down through the last minute. He looked around to see a few lower-level healers that Martin had brought from Antalia working with several duergar to fashion crude stretchers by tying sheets across pole frames. The Great Hall was designated as the hospital for the moment. If things got bad, they could transport the wounded up to the garrison tower as they abandoned the keep.

Silverbeard stood at the entrance to the donjon. Though he was a paladin and a trained fighter, his great age made it more practical for him to work with the healers. As well as organize things in the keep during the battle. He raised a hand in salute, which Alexander returned before teleporting himself to the drawbridge.

As soon as he arrived he called out to Rocky. "Hey, buddy! Are you down there?"

The moat monster stuck its head above the surface and blew a spray of water at him. He gave what Alexander considered to be a smile and bobbed his head. Chuckling at the prank, Alexander said, "Very funny. Now, listen. There's an army coming to attack us any minute now. I want you to be careful. You can eat your fill, but don't expose yourself. There might be hundreds or thousands of them and I don't want to lose you. So if you get hurt, or you hear me shout, you go hide in the cavern by the lake, okay?"

The moat monster growled indignantly and shook his head. Rocky had the heart of a dragon and he knew about the death of the hatchling. He wanted his share of the payback.

Alexander got on a knee at the edge of the bridge and reached out a hand. Rocky lifted his head higher so that Alexander could scratch his ear. "I know, buddy. I want to kill them all, too. And we will! But we have to be smart. And it would hurt all of us to lose you. Understand?"

Rocky whined, but nodded his head before slipping back under the surface. Alexander turned to face outward to look at the forest. The clock had long since run out, but he saw no enemies advancing. In guild chat he asked, *"Lorian? Any reported contact?"*

"Yes, I just decided to let them surprise you, Alexander." Lorian's dry and sarcastic reply came through. Alexander rolled his eyes and turned to walk through the gatehouse. As he moved, he said, "Jeeves, raise the drawbridge."

Just as he stepped off it, the bridge's chains began to clank and creak and the bridge section raised up slowly. Alexander passed through the gatehouse tunnel, nodding at the murder holes on either side, where he assumed some of his people were stationed. Once through the inner gate, he instructed Jeeves to close that, too. The massive stone doors moved nearly silently until they slammed together, causing the ground to shudder slightly.

Alexander took several more steps toward the inner keep before turning and looking both directions down the wall. He could see his people lined up, weapons ready. Some gazed down at him. Others looked nervously out toward the forest, anxious for some sign of the enemy. Two of the light cannons were mounted on either side of the gatehouse, one manned by a human guard, the other by a dwarf. There were a few duergar scattered amongst the orcs and minotaurs who had joined the human and dwarven forces.

The larger part of his forces were concentrated here, within a few hundred yards of either side of the gatehouse. This was where he expected enemies would try to breach the wall. Between the moat filled with blessed water and the high walls, that were enchanted to make them nearly impossible to scale, it was unlikely an attack would be attempted elsewhere. Still, he had small groups of fighters stationed every hundred yards or so along the entire length of the wall. They could call for help if an attack came to their section and Sasha would adjust their forces as necessary.

Several dragons circled the skies above and Alexander could see Braxis and two of his gryphons atop the inner wall keeping watch. He immediately thought of the gargoyles and their ability to evade detection by the dragons. A large force of them could drop on his people unseen until they attacked. But he didn't know what to do about it.

He said, "Jeeves, loudspeaker," and waited a moment before speaking.

"This is it, folks! Be sure to keep an eye on the sky. The gargoyles are invisible until they attack. So keep your ears sharp as well. Keep talk to a minimum. And watch your neighbor's back!"

Fitz appeared next to him. The old wizard was outwardly calm as he surveyed the wall, much as Alexander had just done. "I too am concerned about the gargoyles. They have always been rare, as they breed slowly and have a tendency to kill their young. But the damned drow wizards have had centuries to breed them." The wizard stroked his beard in thought.

Alexander thought back to all the old movies he'd seen that involved invisible enemies. With a grin, he asked, "I don't suppose you could summon a storm? Make it rain? That might expose any of them that are up there."

"Ha!" Fitz turned to look at him. "I may be the most powerful wizard on Io, but even I cannot just whip up a thunderstorm at will, boy..." His words trailed off as a thought occurred to him. "But I *can* do *this!*"

He slammed his staff down on the stone of the path and bursts of light shot upward, as if the weapon had just become a roman candle. Fitz tilted the staff this way and that, sending bursts in random directions all around them. Each light burst soared high into the sky before exploding in a rain of sparks.

"Fireworks!" Alexander shouted. "Fitz, you're a genius!" They watched together as the sky around them was filled with drifting motes of light that fell across the keep and out past the outer wall.

A roar from a dragon alerted them first. One of those patrolling the sky above suddenly altered course and dove toward the lake. Alexander's eyes followed its path and saw the outlines of several flying creatures. As more of the fireworks landed on them, their stealth was broken. The dragon wasted no time, breathing a long stream of fire that engulfed maybe a dozen of them.

Other dragons called out and dove in different directions. Gargoyles were appearing all around above the keep. Beams from the light cannons erupted into the sky, cutting at the exposed gargoyles while being careful not to strike the dragons. Players with ranged attacks were blasting at them with magic or arrows.

Alexander estimated more than a hundred of the flying monsters were still in the air above as he hit one after another with Wizard's Fire. Fitz was doing the same, only at a much faster pace. He growled from deep in his belly as with each wave of his hand a group of gargoyles lit up. After a few moments, he used his staff to send another volley of fireworks.

The gargoyles dove, screeching angrily at being exposed. Dragons incinerated them or grabbed hold of them to rend them with claw and jaws. Arrows and crossbow bolts streamed upward to strike at them. And though they did little physical damage against the tough stone skin of the monsters, each projectile was blessed with holy light. The monsters screamed in pain and rage with each impact.

Still, several made it to the level of the wall. Citizens were swept off the wall by wings as others were savaged by the creatures' talons. Those who were knocked off were the lucky ones. Some fell into the moat, while others fell the twenty feet or so to the ground inside the wall. They suffered a few broken bones and cuts, but none were killed.

Alexander witnessed one unlucky duergar get seized and lifted into the air by a wounded gargoyle. The monster's wings beat rapidly as it soared into the sky. When it reached a hundred feet or so, it turned back toward the wall and released its prey.

Gargoyle Infiltrator
Level 80
Health: 59,200/60,000

The screaming duergar fell upon a couple of orcs. The impact killed all three as it knocked the orcs from the wall. Even as they fell to the ground, the gargoyle was diving to grab another victim. A dwarf this time.

As the dwarf cursed and planted his axe in the thing's chest, it grabbed hold of his shoulders and began to lift. This time, a quick-thinking minotaur grabbed hold of the monster's leg and yanked downward. The weight and strength of the minotaur threw the gargoyle off balance and it foundered as one of its wings struck the wall.

Several nearby citizens leapt to the attack, driving swords and axes into the monster and using them to drag it downward. It screamed as it came in contact with the wall, as the very stone itself was consecrated by the gods of light. Half a minute later, it perished from dozens of wounds, but not without inflicting more than a few upon the defenders.

All along the wall, the warriors of Elysia were learning to pull the creatures downward as they attacked. The dragons continued to massacre the monsters in the air, getting payback for the death of the hatchling. The gargoyle's numbers were dwindling rapidly. Alexander could only see a couple dozen of them remaining, all of them attacking the walls. Too close to his citizens for the dragons to attack.

His people took another couple of minutes to finish off the attacking monsters one by one. But they were paying the price. He saw citizens ripped apart as the gargoyles struck the wall. The monsters had tough skin and plenty of health, and they dished out as much damage as they took. Blood ran freely down the interior of the wall in several places. Alexander saw the healers rushing toward the locations of each attack, casting even as they ran.

When the last of the enemy went down, Alexander called out, "Jeeves! Are any of our people still fighting?"

"No, Majesty. There are no attacks on the wall at this time."

Alexander didn't want to ask, but he had to. "How many did we lose, Jeeves?"

"Nineteen citizens have perished, Majesty. Forty more have been injured."

"Dammit!" Alexander kicked at a charbroiled gargoyle near his feet. He began to cast heals on any wounded that he could reach. His healers had things in hand, but he needed to do something to help.

Sasha's voice echoed through raid chat. *"Gather the dead and bring them to the inner courtyard. Priests and paladins, we need you there. Let's res as many as we can."*

Alexander heard a commotion atop the gatehouse and teleported himself up there. "What is it? Enemies in the woods?"

Molgo, who had stationed himself atop the gatehouse, chuckled. "No enemies. Look." He pointed down toward the moat. Alexander leaned over the crenellation and looked down. Rocky was swimming toward the bridge with a squirming dwarf gripped in his jaws. When he reached the bridge, he extended his neck upward and dropped the guard onto the stone section. The dwarf cursed and sputtered as he hit the ground. Half a dozen others were sitting on the bridge already, wet and slightly shaken. Healers were already taking care of any injuries from atop the wall.

Rocky looked up at Alexander, tongue hanging out to one side and looking pleased with himself.

Alexander laughed, along with several others on the wall. "Good boy, Rocky! Go fetch any of the others that might have fallen in!"

The moat monster disappeared without a splash. Alexander said, "Jeeves, open the gate and lower the drawbridge, please."

As soon as the bridge was down, Brick, Grumpy, Lugs, and two of the stone golems moved out beyond the nearly-drowned citizens and formed a shield wall. Those who had been pulled from the water made their way inside. Alexander heard the dwarf grumble as he cleared the inner doors, "Damned water beastie tried ta eat me!" The others just nodded in sympathy. Alexander imagined it wouldn't be a pleasant experience to be seized in a water dragon's jaws. Still, when this was over, he intended to reward Rocky handsomely.

Brick and the others held their position while Rocky rounded up a few more stragglers. The last he brought up was a dead dwarf. The warrior had been wearing plate armor when he fell in and had quickly sunk to the bottom and drowned. Rocky looked apologetic as he gently laid the fallen dwarf on the bridge. He made a sad whining noise and nudged the body.

Brick patted the water dragon on the head. "It be okay, Rocky. Ye did the best ye could!" He knelt down and laid a hand on the dwarf's head. The corpse was enveloped in holy light and a moment later the dwarf coughed out a lungful of water.

Rocky jerked back in surprise, his head lifting high above the bridge. He looked from Brick to the formerly-dead dwarf and back again. Trumpeting questioningly, he sought out Alexander up on the wall.

Alexander wasn't sure Rocky was intelligent enough to understand resurrection, so he just shouted, "Good boy, Rocky! You saved them all!"

Those gathered along the wall started to cheer and toss treats down to the water dragon. Still confused, Rocky was quickly distracted by the chunks of meat and pastries that were raining down upon him. He began to catch them in mid-air, earning him more cheers.

Brick and others brought the stragglers back inside as the water dragon scooped up his rewards. Jeeves raised the drawbridge once again. A moment later, Sasha's voice came across raid chat once again.

"This isn't over, people. We haven't received any notifications yet. This might be just the first wave. Get your shit together and keep an eye out!"

The mood atop the wall sobered quickly. Some looked toward the forest as others' gazes lifted toward the sky. Most had been thinking the battle was won, and Sasha's words had disheartened more than a few.

Alexander heard bursts from Fitz somewhere behind him and a moment later the sky lit up with more fireworks. His gaze lifted to the sky with everyone else's, but no gargoyles were seen.

Alexander reached out in guild chat. *"Grimble. How are things at the mine?"*

"All quiet here, Alexander. No beasties nor demons in sight."

"Alright, keep a close eye out. And stay close to the rock trolls. If a gargoyle appears, they can pull it down."

"Aye, will do."

Fitz shouted, "The roost!" just as twin roars from Kai and Lia shook the mountain above them. Alexander looked up to see three dead gargoyles falling and bouncing off the rocks below the roost. Seeing no wounds or burns on them, he realized they must have been killed by Fitz's ward.

Fitz disappeared, even as three of the airborne dragons sped upward. The roost was higher than the umbrella of fireworks that Fitz had spread over the keep, so at least a few of the gargoyles had gone undetected. They clearly intended to strike again at the hatchlings.

Gouts of flame erupted from the ledge outside the roost as Kai emerged and shot into the sky. Half a dozen more gargoyles appeared as they burned and fell screaming toward the ground. More flames erupted from the other dragons as they began to circle and execute a search pattern. The sky filled with dragonfire as more of the monsters were discovered and disposed of.

One of the dragons was badly injured when two gargoyles appeared on its back. They dug in with talons and teeth, tearing at the dragon's flesh. The dragon roared in pain and attempted to reach back and bite them. But they were too far up its neck and the dragon couldn't bend its neck enough to get at them. Instead, she rolled over and shook herself, trying to dislodge her attackers. Dragon's blood rained down as they held on and continued to savage her.

Kai passed beneath her, snatching one of the gargoyles in his jaws. He reached for the second with one of his foreclaws as he sped past, but missed. His jaws tightened and mangled the gargoyle before he spat it out.

Another of the dragons managed to snatch the final gargoyle from their wounded cousin's back. She righted herself but was too wounded to fly properly. She awkwardly spiraled down to the ground between the inner and outer walls of the keep, dripping blood in great quantities as she fell.

Several healers were already casting spells on her as soon as she got in range. As she landed, the bleeding began to slow, then stop. She laid her head down on the ground and closed her eyes.

When the last gargoyle died, players and citizens alike received an alert.

Quest Update: Hold What You Have
Stage One – Complete!
You have successfully repelled the first wave of invaders sent by the drow wizards.
Reward: 200 gold. 120,000 experience.

Quest Update: Stage Two will begin in one half hour.

At the same time, a message from Lorian came across raid chat. "*My scout has just reported an enemy force moving out of the dungeon south of the mine.*"

As Alexander was about to answer, a familiar gong rang out and fireworks erupted in the sky above the keep. Jeeves had just leveled up again.

"Congratulations, Jeeves."

"*Thank you, Majesty. It seems the points I received for the successful defense combined with the deaths of one hundred and twenty gargoyles were enough for me to reach level 23. Might I make an upgrade suggestion?*"

"Of course, Jeeves."

"*In light of the recent airborne attacks, I suggest selecting Aerial Defense for my next upgrade. It will allow me to form a magic barrier encompassing the entire keep, extending out to the outer wall in a dome. I am afraid it will not be strong enough to hold out long against a large number of high-level monsters like the gargoyles. But it will force them from stealth when they come in contact with it."*

Alexander didn't hesitate. "Jeeves, please activate Aerial Defense."

A moment later, an opaque bubble began to form over the keep. It rose up from the walls and out from the cliff face, growing into a bubble that enclosed them all. The dragons who were still circling above passed in and out of the magic field without any apparent difficulty.

"Aerial defense shield is in place, Majesty. With my current power reserves, I can maintain the shield for twenty hours. That period will decrease as the shield absorbs damage."

Alexander immediately teleported himself back to the control room. He removed two of his larger soul gems from his inventory and placed them on the control table. "How much time will these add to the shield, Jeeves?"

The two stones glowed briefly. *"Approximately thirty additional hours of normal use, Majesty. Again, damage absorbed by the shield will reduce the shield's available power."*

"Fifty hours. Just over four days. That should be long enough. Please alert me if your power reserves for the shield drop below twenty-five percent."

"Of course, Majesty."

With the shield up, Alexander felt a weight lifted from his shoulders. Even if it wouldn't kill the gargoyles, breaking their stealth would at least give his people a fighting chance. Having to deal with an enemy attacking from the ground while invisible monsters fell on them from above would be a nightmare.

He teleported himself back to the keep. Immediately, he went to the dining area and took a seat. Pulling chunks of obsidian from his bag, he began enchanting them with the Undying and Healing Light spells. He hadn't had time to make dragon pins for all of the orcs and minotaurs, and now some of them had paid the price. The pins weren't a guarantee of safety. The duergar he'd seen dropped on the orcs was wearing a pin. It would have saved him from the impact when he hit the orcs. But the subsequent fall from the wall took the one percent health that the pin maintained, killing him.

Still, he wanted as many of his citizens to have the protection the pins offered. As he cast the spell again and again, he called one of the apprentices from the forge over to add pins to the stones. He didn't waste time having them shaped into dragon form. They could take care of the aesthetics later. Ugly and functional was fine by him.

It took him about twenty seconds to enchant each stone. Having less than an hour, he was only able to create a hundred and fifty of the pins. He charged the apprentice with distributing them. The young dwarf grabbed the bag and ran off toward the outer wall.

As the clock ran down again, he moved to the top of the outer gatehouse. Molgo, Dawn, Brick, Sasha, Lorian, and an elder orc whose name he didn't know were standing there looking out toward the forest. Lorian spoke quietly.

"My scout says we should see them any minute."

"Is it a large force?" Sasha asked.

The half-elf got a wry grin on his face. "Well, yes. And no."

Sasha's face darkened and she balled her fists. Lorian didn't wait for the lashing she was about to unleash.

"The scout says there are… giants. Several of them. Along with orcs, hobgoblins, were-beasts, mountain trolls, and the drow commanders driving them. The force is only about six hundred strong, so not large in number. But… giants." He shrugged and tried a hesitant smile.

Sasha snorted at him. "You need to work on your jokes."

"Why would they send such a small number?" Alexander asked, thinking out loud.

This time it was Sasha who shrugged. "Maybe they assumed the gargoyles would still be softening us up?"

Dawn added, "They may not be aware that our people and the orcs have joined your forces. Without our warriors, the gargoyles and six hundred dark ones would have had you outnumbered."

Alexander nodded his head. "I suppose. But they had to know the dragons would be here. One dragon should be able to wipe out their entire force."

Sasha disagreed. "If they're coming from the dungeon, they may have been sent before the attack on the hatchlings. So they may not know about the dragons."

"Or they be havin' some nasty plan ta deal with our dragon friends," Brick added.

They were interrupted by the sound of cracking and splintering wood. The treetops about a hundred yards back from the forest's edge began to shake. A few moments later, the sound of hammering could be heard.

"Are they buildin' catapults?" Brick asked. "Mebbe siege towers? Be tough to make 'em big enough to reach across our moat."

Molgo spoke up. "If it were me, I would build a bridge. One that I could drop in place of the missing drawbridge section. With giants to carry it…" His voice trailed off as he let the others picture it.

"How big are these giants?" Sasha asked.

Lorian answered, "The scout says they're mountain giants. A dozen of them. They're about fifty feet tall. Strong, but stupid. They don't follow orders well. But if they see an enemy, they will attack without pause or mercy. Very hard to kill, with skin tougher than rhino hide. They are vulnerable in the same places as you or I – the eyes, ears, under the chin, armpits."

Sasha's eyes had gone wide as saucers. "Fifty feet? *Fifty*? C'mon, man… how are we supposed to kill something like that?"

Brick pointed upward. "Dragons."

Alexander shook his head. "This smells like a trap to me. It's too easy. The dragons could burn out the forest and all the monsters in it without breaking a sweat. There has to be something we're missing."

"Well, the drow have the dragon poison. The one that almost killed Kai. Maybe all their weapons are coated with it? I'm thinking a fifty-foot tall giant could throw a spear pretty high into the air. High enough to hit a dragon before it got close enough to flame them," Sasha mused.

"Shit! The poison. Please tell me you have some antidote?" Alexander pleaded.

Sasha nodded. "Fitz gave us the recipe. Lydia, the druids and I made a ton of it. All the healers have some vials in their bags."

"Don't forget that shit-weasel thing they shoot at us," Brick pointed out. "That be a horrible way to die. And it'll keep on eatin' whoever it hits, so the dragon pins won't save 'em."

Alexander grimaced. He'd felt first hand what it was like to be hit with those things.

"We need to destroy this force before they get in range of our citizens. It's too small to spread out and attack the wall in several places. We'll tempt them into grouping up here. Have our citizens fall back, or at least stay behind cover while we adventurers deal with them." He was already making plans for a stand at the drawbridge.

Chapter 11

The Bigger They Are...

The enemy wasn't waiting around for Alexander to execute their plans. A horn rang out from somewhere along the wall, followed quickly by several more. Alexander looked to the tree line as the treetops once again began to shake and sway. Only this time, the movement was coming toward the wall.

A moment later, Alexander and the citizens of Elysia saw the first giant. It stepped out of the shadows of the forest and into the sunlight, shading its eyes and blinking momentarily. The creature was massive. Built like one of the rock trolls, it had thick muscular arms and legs, with mottled skin that would provide perfect camouflage in rocky terrain. Its head was the size of a small car and a shower of thick saliva sprayed from its mouth as it roared a challenge. The fifty-foot giant held a stone club in its right hand that must have weighed at least a ton.

As the monster stepped forward, four others began to emerge from the forest. Giant after giant moved into the sunlight. Each carried what looked like an enormous makeshift shield made of logs from the forest. Five of them, fastened together side by side with crude spikes and vines. Each log was maybe three feet in diameter, making the shields about fifteen feet wide and taller than the giants themselves. The monsters could easily hide behind these as they approached the wall.

From out of the woods came a flood of smaller monsters that flowed around the feet of the giants. The smallest were hobgoblins. Half orc, half goblin, they were larger than their goblin ancestors, standing about four feet tall with muscular bodies gifted to them by their orc blood. They had the same big ears and feet as goblins and the same bloodshot eyes.

Scattered among them were were-beasts. Most were wolf-like creatures that walked upright like men. A few appeared to be of boar ancestry as well, with elongated snouts framed by sharp, curved tusks.

A force of maybe sixty orcs held the center of the of the line. Similar in size to the orcs on the wall, these had nearly black skin. Their bodies were pierced with dozens of bits of jagged metal and bone and each looked up at the wall with red glowing eyes. In fact, Alexander noticed that all of the enemy had the same glowing eyes, including the giants.

The last to arrive were slow-moving mountain trolls. These stood fifteen to twenty feet tall, with thick, slow-moving bodies. They had long arms that reached the ground as they walked and massive shoulders topped by boulder-like heads. Two of them carried a chair, upon which a drow in mage's robes sat. Alexander focused on the drow.

> **Drow Wizard's Apprentice**
> **Level 110**
> **Health: 65,000/65,000**

Alexander could sense his people beginning to panic. He quickly levitated himself so that all could see him. Then he told Jeeves to activate loudspeaker.

"*They look scary, don't they*?!" he shouted, pointing to the now-stationary giants. "*Big enough to swallow any one of us in one bite!*"

His people all looked at him like he was insane. Many of them were nodding their heads in agreement and looking skeptically at him.

"*Well, they're looking at all of you and thinking the same thing! They see the moat, and the walls, and all of you with weapons ready. They see your determination! Your courage!*"

"They see *lunch!*" A voice rose up from somewhere down the wall. Scattered laughter could be heard here and there.

"*Maybe so! But they're going to have to work hard for their meal! You are citizens of Elysia! Warriors, one and all! Trust in each other. Look out for each other. These big dumb brutes are no match for you!*"

Ragged cheers went up from the fighters on the wall. It wasn't the rousing roar he was hoping for, but then, he'd never been great at motivational speeches. He lowered himself back to the gatehouse roof and stepped to one of the light cannons.

The giants were out of his casting range. But the cannons emitted a beam that he already knew would reach to the tree line after Edward's 'testing' them by cutting down trees.

He took careful aim, then triggered the weapon. A beam of bright white light burst from the cannon and struck the lead giant in the face. Its skin began to smoke as it howled in pain. Dropping its club, it covered its wounded face with both hands and fell back against a tree as Alexander released the trigger. Cheers erupted from the wall as he Inspected the giant.

> **Mountain Giant**
> **Level 90**
> **Health: 98,400/100,000**

"Holy shit, these things have a massive health pool," he whispered. Still, they could be hurt. Just the short burst from the cannon had taken nearly two percent of its health.

The giant regained its feet and bent to pick up its club. With a pain-filled roar, it swung the club and obliterated the nearest tree. The stone weapon smashed right through the thick trunk and sent splinters flying halfway to the moat. The upper section tilted and fell upon one of the other giants, who just shrugged it off, letting it fall to the ground to crush several hobgoblins who were too slow moving out of the way.

In answer, the other three light cannons fired. Beams of light magic raked across the line of monsters facing the defenders. Creatures large and small screamed in pain as they were burned. Alexander moved aside so that the cannon he'd been using could be manned and fired as well. One of his guards gleefully stepped forward and went to work.

Unaffected by the raking beams, the four giants with shields stepped forward. Shields in front, they roared challenges at the puny defenders as they approached the moat. When they got in range, arrows, crossbow bolts, and spells bombarded their shields. A few managed to penetrate and do minor damage, but they kept coming.

Lainey managed to hit one in the foot with a stun arrow. When it began to convulse, the shield exposed its face for a few moments. Every ranged attacker on the wall took advantage of the open target and pummeled the giant's head and face with everything they had.

Its health bar plummeted as arrows penetrated its eyes, its open mouth. A huge spike of ice from Misty slammed into its face, rocking its head back slightly. When it recovered from the stun and managed to duck behind the shield again, it was down to ten percent health. Seeing this, the defenders took heart and increased their fire. They got smarter, aiming for exposed feet as the giants stepped forward.

Lugs followed that thinking and hurled one of his seven-foot-long spears at the closest giant. The air whistled as the projectile sped downward, gravity assisting Lugs' great strength. It penetrated the top of the giant's foot and continued down into the earth beneath, pinning the foot to the ground.

As the giant moved forward, the spear was ripped free of the ground. But the resistance unbalanced the thing and it stumbled forward. The weight of the shield pulled it down and it slammed face-first onto the ground. Immediately, every weapon within range on the wall was turned upon the prone monster. Spells exploded across its back and head as arrows and bolts slammed into it. Alexander cast Wizard's Fire on the shield underneath it, lighting both the wood and the giant on fire.

While his people peppered the downed giant, Alexander took a moment to cast Wizard's Fire on each of the other shields as well. The three giants that were still moving were nearing the moat and slowing down. They had reached the blessed ground, and were taking damage with every step. The fourth giant expired and several of the Elysians on the wall leveled up, bringing another round of cheers from his people.

A soft voice echoed across the battlefield. Alexander looked up to see the drow apprentice making a hand signal. As one, the three remaining shield giants stepped to the edge of the moat. Slamming the bottom edges of their shields into the earth, they pushed them forward so that they fell across the moat and onto the top of the wall!

"They're not shields! They be friggin' bridges!" Brick shouted the obvious as defenders who had ducked behind the wall to avoid being crushed by the logs crawled out from under them. Several orcs and minotaurs grabbed hold and tried to shove the bridges off, but to no avail. The giants had already placed their feet upon the improvised bridges and were attempting to climb to the wall.

Now unshielded, they were slammed with fire from the defenders on the wall. Beatrix used the moat water to pull massive globes up to surround the giant's heads, suffocating them. Misty quickly froze each one so that the giants couldn't see. One of them immediately stumbled off the side into the moat.

Rocky was there in an instant. He surged through the water, his jaws closing on the giant's neck just below the ice cube that was its head. With a vicious shaking motion, he ripped a sizeable chunk of the giants flesh from its neck. Blood fountained as the monster sank below the surface. Rocky moved underneath the closest wooden bridge. It was still burning with Wizard's Fire and the flames reflected in the moat monster's eyes as he waited for his next victim.

The giant that had previously been knocked down to ten percent health died quickly from the focused fire of the defenders. The remaining two stumbled around the field, trying to free their heads and get a breath. Fingers ripped at the ice to no avail. One of the giants fell to its knees, slamming its head against the ground and trying to break the ice. After a full minute of struggling, both of them collapsed and quit moving.

Another word from the drow and the entire mass of creatures surged forward. The were-beasts were fastest. They sped across the open field toward the smoking bridges. Alexander cast Wizard's Fire on all three of them again. But the beasts kept coming with no regard for their own well-being. They ignored the damage from the blessed ground, the arrows and bolts that skewered them as they ran. Hitting the bottom of the wooden ramps, they plunged right into the fires and used their claws to propel themselves upward.

"This isn't natural!" Sasha yelled. "It's like they're zombies. But still alive!"

The connection clicked in Alexander's head. "The drow! She's controlling them somehow. Maybe some kind of psychic power."

Sasha's voice echoed across raid chat. *"All light cannons! Focus on the drow! Burn her down!"*

Immediately, all four light cannons changed their focus. The four beams zeroed in on the drow apprentice and her robes began to smoke. She screamed a few words and the two trolls carrying her chair set it down gently before moving to stand in front of her. They didn't move an inch as the beams burned trails in their skin.

Alexander cursed and looked to the sky. The dragons had remained on patrol, warding against another wave of gargoyles. He wanted desperately to ask one of them to take out the drow. But the danger to them was high if they approached that closely.

He was distracted by screams from the defenders on the wall. The were-beasts had topped the wall, their bodies nothing more than flaming fur, melting skin, and sharp canine claws and teeth. They launched themselves onto the wall or down into the courtyard below, thrashing in pain and striking out in every direction. Elysians were savaged by both claw and flame as they tried to take down the maddened creatures.

"Push them off the wall! They're already dying. Just push them away from you!" Sasha's voice rang in everyone's ears through raid chat. The stronger defenders, the orcs and minotaurs, sacrificed their hands to grab the beasts and hurl them down, either into the moat or onto the ground below. One of the beasts that hit the ground ran off across a field of crops, burning a path as it went.

An earth-shaking roar from the across the battlefield turned every head back to the forest. The remaining seven giants were moving forward. The other monsters fled before them, charging toward the wall. The hobgoblins were the first to reach the burning ramps, and they too disregarded the flames and charged upward.

The orcs carried a pair of logs as they charged across the stone half of the bridge. They suffered terrible wounds as they copied the giants, planting one end of their logs at the end of the bridge and tilting it so that it fell across the moat. When both logs came to rest, they used their massive strength to shove them together. Then they began to charge across their makeshift bridge. Every single one of them was bleeding from multiple wounds as they reached the outer raised drawbridge and began to pound at it.

Alexander ignored them. There was no way they could penetrate the raised drawbridge anytime soon. And even if they did, they would be stopped by the inner gate and slaughtered inside the tunnel.

He looked back toward the ramps. Hobgoblins were pouring over the top of the wall, burned and bleeding, but swinging their weapons with all their might as they dropped down on the defenders. More Elysians fell. Alexander witnessed one of the hunters loose an arrow point blank into the face of a hobgoblin before a downward slash of the monster's axe severed his hand. His bow fell with the hand as the monster knocked him from the wall as it blindly barreled forward.

"Retreat!" Sasha's voice rang out across the wall. *"All citizens, retreat to the inner keep! Now! Adventurers, stay and cover them! Push these bastards into the moat!"*

Alexander levitated a were-beast that was causing havoc in its death throes, lashing at the legs of nearby defenders and hobgoblins alike. He tossed it onto a group of the monsters that were just reaching the top of the ramp, knocking them backward and sending all of them tumbling down the ramp into their own kind. Several fell from the ramp into the water. Others rolled downward in a flaming avalanche of bodies, clearing the ramp for a moment.

But only for a moment. The trolls, with their ponderous pace, had finally reached the ramps. The wood groaned and creaked as they stepped awkwardly onto the logs and into the roaring fire without hesitation. A couple of them leaned forward and used their hands and knees to crawl up the steep slope.

"We've got to kill that drow! No way these beasties would face that fire if'n she weren't in their wee brains!" Brick shouted. He pulled his shield from his back and leapt atop the pile of burning corpses stacked near the closest ramp. When he reached the top, he looked at Alexander and shouted, "Not a word!" before he tossed the shield onto the ramp and climbed onto it. Sitting on the fireproof shield like a sled, he pushed off with his hammer and began to slide down the ramp.

Alexander lost sight of him in the inferno, but wasn't particularly worried. Fire caused Brick's shield to heal him. He'd be fine. At least, until he reached the bottom and ran into one of those trolls.

A splash from his right drew his attention. He saw Rocky burst upward from the moat and throw his weight onto a burning ramp that was sagging in the center. The moat monster whined as the flames scorched his skin, but it only took a moment for the combined weight of the logs, the moat monster, and the two trolls climbing the ramp to overwhelm the weakened wood and send them all crashing down into the moat. Rocky fell backward, one of the troll's legs gripped in his jaws. They both disappeared under the water.

One ramp down, three more still blazing away. The giants were moving forward still, about halfway to the moat now. The wall was quickly clearing of defenders as the citizens either ran for the stairs or simply jumped the twenty feet to the ground below. A steady stream was moving toward the inner keep, those who were still healthy helping the wounded. Alexander took a moment to teleport some of the more heavily wounded still on the wall directly to the courtyard.

As he did so, he froze in horror. Laying atop the wall, not far away, was Taylor. His left eye was missing and his blood was pumping from a jagged wound that extended from his forehead down across his neck. Taylor's health bar was at ten percent and dropping. Alexander immediately began casting heals on his guard captain, uttering a prayer to Odin. The blood flow slowed and he teleported the man to the courtyard.

Not far away, Helga was using her massive sword to clear monsters from the wall. She muscled the blade back and forth like a scythe while Warren and Grumpy covered her back. Lugs was atop the gatehouse, hurling spears at the giants like a titan atop a mountain hurling thunderbolts. The big ogre shouted curses to follow each spear. "Here's one for *you,* ya massive pile o' troll dung!" He sent a spear whistling into the neck of a giant who had nearly reached the moat. The creature stumbled back and made a gurgling noise as the spear passed through its windpipe. The blow didn't kill it, but it was out of the fight for now.

Martin and his healers were still on the wall, doing all they could for the wounded as the DPS players dealt with the monsters who'd made it that far. Alexander saw Beatrix get bowled over by a screaming hobgoblin that didn't even see her. She was crushed under its burning feet as it stepped on her chest. Her health bar dropped below fifty percent and the flames caught on her robes. She tried to douse herself with water, but this was Wizard's Fire. Water had no effect.

Sasha threw heals on the little gnome, but it didn't matter. The hobgoblin fell backward, its head having been removed by one of the players. The burning body covered Beatrix and her health bar went grey.

Helga died a moment later. One of the trolls had managed to make it to the top of a ramp. She charged through a mass of burning mobs to stab the thing in the gut. Her Legendary weapon easily pierced its skin, and under normal circumstances the wound would have ended the fight. But the mind-controlled troll simply reached out and grabbed hold of Helga's head, then crushed her skull to pulp.

Grumpy charged up Helga's dead body and used Shield Rush to bash the monster backward down the ramp. He took fire damage before he managed to leap backward onto the wall. Sasha tossed him a quick heal.

Giants were hopping into the moat now. For most, the water only reached their armpits as they sank to the bottom. But the spikes Alexander and the mages had raised there punctured their feet as they tried to walk across. Though they screamed in pain loudly enough to vibrate the walls themselves, they kept moving, lifting their feet off of one spike only to step down upon another, and another. Rocky harassed them, taking large bites from their legs and torsos as he swam past. Clubs bashed at the water as the giants tried to crush him. But the water slowed their blows and Rocky managed to avoid them.

"Rocky! Stop that! Get away. There are too many!" Alexander yelled at him. He couldn't see the moat monster anymore through the frothing pink water. The giants' blood was flowing freely from their feet and whatever wounds Rocky inflicted. He hoped the water dragon had listened to him.

As they reached the wall, the giants were unable to scale it. Their arms weren't quite long enough to grab hold of the top. After a moment of useless scrabbling, they stopped trying to climb and began to pound at the walls with their stone clubs. The impacts thrummed through the stone walls and sparked off the magical enhancements Fitz and Kai had put in place.

The walls held up under the abuse, and Alexander returned his attention to the drow. He couldn't see Brick anywhere but a quick glance at his raid UI showed him that his friend was still alive and healthy. The two trolls who'd made themselves meat shields for the drow were dead, their bodies cut to pieces by the relentless light cannon beams. But their corpses still shielded the drow, who had stepped down from her chair and was crouching behind the trolls' thick bodies.

She shouted another command and the remaining giants stopped pounding on the walls. They gathered together in twos and threes and began to boost each other up so that they could reach the top of the wall!

"That's it! Everybody off the wall. Get inside the inner keep!" Sasha sounded the general retreat for the players. The citizens who could be evacuated had been and only players were left in the battle zone. They began to jump from the walls as giants pulled themselves up and over. There were only about fifteen players still alive, counting Alexander. The rest had sacrificed themselves to buy time for the citizens.

Alexander hit each of the giants in the face with Wizard's Fire as a parting gift. He took one last survey of the wall before leaving. The were-beasts and hobgoblins all lay still, either burned to death or killed by his people. Three giants had pulled themselves up onto the wall and were reaching down to help others up. Massive pools of blood were forming under them as it poured from the wounds on their feet.

The orcs were still pounding at the outer gate, trying to break through. A wicked smile grew on Alexander's face. He teleported himself to the gate room, where the mechanisms for raising and lowering the bridge were located. When the dwarves had built the drawbridge, he'd been given a cursory explanation of how it all worked.

He quickly moved to the lever that locked the gears in place, preventing the chains from moving up or down. Unlocking the gear, he pulled another lever that started to lower the gate slowly using a counterbalance weight system. He pictured the orcs massed together outside, pounding at the drawbridge. He gave it just a few seconds to gain some momentum, then pulled the pin that freed the counterweight.

The momentum and weight of the massive drawbridge was suddenly freed to succumb to gravity. The orcs tried to scramble away as it fell but only a few of them managed to escape. A couple moved to either side or fell into the moat before the bridge slammed down, crushing the rest. Alexander peered out a small window in time to see Rocky pick off the orcs that fell into the water. He also saw half a dozen of the survivors rush into the tunnel toward the inner gate. They would get nowhere, so he promptly disregarded them.

He was about to teleport back to the inner keep when he caught a flash of sunlight on plate armor near the tree line. Putting his head closer to the window, he focused on the spot. A moment later, he saw Brick disappear behind one of the troll corpses that the drow apprentice had taken refuge behind. Almost immediately, there was a flash of holy light.

Alexander thumped the wall, grinning. In raid chat, he said, *"Brick's taking on the drow! I'm going to go help."*

He teleported himself atop one of the troll corpses. Looking down, he saw Brick hunkered behind his shield as the drow bombarded him with magic attacks. She was mid-cast when Alexander drew his sword and leapt down at her, plunging the tip downward toward her neck. But the blade bounced off of a magic shield, half a second before Alexander himself bounced off of it.

"Shit!" was all he had time to say as he fell onto his back, off balance from the unexpected impact. He had managed to interrupt the spell she'd been casting at Brick, but now he had her full attention. He quickly cast his own magic shield as he scrambled backward and tried to regain his feet. The drow waved one hand and uttered a single harsh word, and one of the shit-weasel spells sped toward him.

His shield was nowhere near strong enough to stop the evil worm-thing that flew at him. He just hadn't used it enough since learning the spell. It was still at level one. But it *was* strong enough to deflect the thing just enough that it glanced off his Legendary dark mithril chest piece as he tried to dodge the thing by rolling to one side.

She growled in frustration and shouted, "My master has wasted enough resources on you, boy king! You will die here and now!"

She began to move her hands in an intricate pattern as she mumbled the phrasing of a major spell. Alexander managed to gain his feet and was about to try to dash behind the nearby troll when Brick slammed into the drow from behind.

She'd made the mistake of turning her back on the paladin and he took full advantage. Activating his Shield Rush ability, he shot forward and slammed full speed into the drow's back. Her shield burst and she screamed in rage as the force of the impact slammed her into the troll corpse. Brick pinned her there, shouldering his shield as he used his hammer to cast Holy Smite.

The drow's scream turned from rage to pain as the holy spell struck her face. Brick wasted no time, slamming his hammer into her right arm, using the stone skin of the dead troll as an anvil. The arm snapped, and the drow snarled, "Get *off* me, you stumpy worm!"

Drow Wizard's Apprentice
Level 110
Health: 54,100/65,000

Brick was a dwarf, with all the strength that came with his dwarven build. And the drow was slender and willowy, even for a drow female. But she was roughly forty levels higher than Brick and Alexander. As she struggled to push off and free herself, Brick's feet slid back as the soil gave way under him.

Alexander lunged forward, his sword piercing the drow's side as she struggled with Brick. The blade went deep, and he could feel it scraping against her ribs and deflecting off her spine before it stopped. He quickly tore the blade free as roughly as he could, twisting it as he pulled, trying to do as much damage as possible. At the same time, he cast Wizard's Fire on her face to distract her.

Her struggling increased as the pain sent her into a frenzy. She growled a three-word phrase and a burst of magical force sent dwarf and elf flying backward several feet. Alexander was stunned, the debuff timer appearing on his UI and counting down from ten seconds. Brick, being behind his shield, was able to avoid the stun and charge right back into the fray. This time when he got close to the drow, he used his Shield Bash ability to slam her back into the troll corpse and interrupt her casting. As a bonus, his shield struck her broken arm, inflicting more pain.

Bleeding, broken, half-blinded by fire and outnumbered, the drow wasn't giving up. She gritted her teeth and produced a wicked-looking dagger in her unbroken left hand. It was clear she wasn't used to wielding a weapon with that hand, but all drow were born knowing how to stab things. She slammed the dagger toward Brick's face even as he raised his shield to block it. The black blade scraped across the black scales of the shield and left a trail of poison behind.

Alexander warned his friend, "The blade is poisoned!" even as the dark elf struck again, and again, growling with each motion as her savaged torso objected to the movement. Brick managed to block each blow but the force behind them was pushing him backward, giving her space to move more freely.

Alexander swung his sword again, connecting with the drow's wrist. The blade bit deeply, lodging itself in the bone. She screamed and jerked her hand away. Even as she dropped her dagger, his sword was yanked from his hand. They stood staring at each other for a moment, both disarmed unexpectedly. She recovered first, uttering the shit-weasel spell again even as she shook her arm and the sword dislodged to fall to the ground.

Being just a couple feet away, Alexander had no hope of dodging the spell. It slammed into his chest with the force of a kick, knocking him back off his feet. The worm-thing didn't penetrate his chest piece, but as he hit the ground it began to crawl up toward his exposed neck and face.

A flash of light struck the thing as Brick cast Holy Smite on it. The spell didn't kill the thing, but did stop it long enough for Alexander to swat it off his chest. Jumping to his feet, he stomped on the thing, then cast Wizard's Fire on it. The nasty shit-weasel worm shrugged off both attacks and began to scurry after Brick, who had pissed it off with the holy attack.

The dwarf just laughed, watching it come at him, then stomped on the thing, pinning it beneath one of his iron-shod boots. "Ye don't scare me, ye-"

He never got to finish the sentence as the she-drow blasted his exposed face with a spray of dark magic bolts that looked much like barbed crossbow bolts. Brick took the full force of the attack directly in his face and was thrown backward. His face disappeared in a pink mist and he was dead before he hit the ground.

Alexander began to build up a Ray of Light spell. He poured mana into it as quickly as he could while the now-gloating drow turned toward him. She smiled cruelly at him.

"My master will reward me greatly when I bring him your head." Her voice was ragged, as she was clearly in great pain. "When I am done with you, I will slaughter each and every one of your people. When you return, you will find nothing but the corpses of those you swore to protect!"

She raised her badly bleeding left arm and began a spell. Alexander held his ground, building more mana in his own spell. At her level, he doubted even his best shot would kill her. But he had to try.

She finished the spell and a black cloud formed around him. His whole body erupted in pain as it ate at him. The spell was some kind of acid cloud. His UI showed a bleeding debuff and, for half a second, a poison debuff that instantly disappeared as his poison immunity negated it. He clenched his jaw against the pain and added even more mana to his spell.

When the spell reached two thousand mana, he felt himself begin to lose control of it. Still, he held it a moment, unable to see his target through the cloud. An idea struck him. He succumbed to the pain and let loose a scream.

"Yesss! Suffer! My poison rushes through your veins, boy king. The acid melts your skin. You will not die quickly. I'll make sure of it!"

That was all he needed. Focusing on the sound of her voice, he raised his hand and loosed the burst of light magic. There was no scream, no sound that his elven ears could detect. But the black cloud around him dissipated immediately.

Alexander heard a series of roars from the direction of the wall as he got his bearings and gazed upon the drow.

Most of her face was just gone. The blast of light magic he'd sent at her had struck her mouth and neck, incinerating everything below her eyes.

Level up! You are now level 71! ...

Level up! You are now level 72!
Your Wisdom has increased by +1.
Your Intelligence has increased by +1
You have 8 free attribute points available

Alexander cast a heal on himself, then another. The pain from the acid subsided as his skin knitted itself back together. He was glad he couldn't see what was going on there.

He bent and looted the drow and the two trolls, and was about to gather Brick's gear for him when another roar from the wall grabbed his attention.

"The giants! Shit! How could I forget?" He quickly grabbed Brick's gear and teleported himself back to the keep. As soon as he arrived, he turned and found a clear spot atop the wall and teleported himself there.

Looking out, he was immediately confused by what he saw. There were only four giants still standing in the area between his walls. All of them were badly wounded, sporting horrible gashes and broken bones. One was missing an arm, another had a half-crushed skull.

And they were fighting each other.

Alexander looked at his own people, a question on his face. Sasha was there and gave him a happy smile and a shrug. "Whatever you and Brick did to that drow, we think it must have cancelled her mind control over them."

"Okayyy…." he led her to finish her explanation. Fitz finished it for her.

"The giants are very territorial. In their mountain homes, they tend to range far apart. When they encounter another giant, there is almost always a fight to the death. Except when they mate." The wizard grinned and waggled his eyebrows at Sasha, who just rolled her eyes.

"So, as soon as they were free of the drow's influence, they went after each other instead of us?" Alexander's jaw dropped.

"Aye, lad." Silverbeard approached from further down the wall. He had a light cannon on his shoulder. "They be destroying our crops in their tussle but I advised Sasha to stop our own folk from firin' at 'em. No point in makin' 'em angry at us if we can just leave 'em alone 'n let 'em do our work for us!"

Alexander watched as the giant with the damaged skull tottered and fell, only to have his head stomped by another of his kind. Now there were only three.

"Fitz, are the giants servants of the dark? Like the drow?"

The old dragon wizard shook his head. "They worship no gods. Very simple creatures. They generally mind their own business, preferring to stick to their lands and avoid others. They'll fight like mad if you invade their territory. But otherwise they're mostly harmless." Fitz looked at him. "What're you thinking, boy?"

Alexander turned to face Fitz. "I was thinking it might be good to have a giant or three as allies."

"HA!" The wizard's grin stretched from ear to ear. "And how do you propose to stop them from killing each other first? And for that matter, how are you going to convince them you're friendly?"

Now it was Alexander's turn to grin. "I was thinking a certain crusty old dragon I know might have a way to stop them."

Fitz glared at him for a moment, then chuckled. "You know, boy. You've got me just curious enough to want to see what you do. I'll stop their fight. The rest is up to you."

A second later, Fitz ran forward and leapt off the wall. In a flash he morphed into his true form, growing in size as he gained altitude. All along the wall, the Elysians gasped.

When Kai had taken his true dragon form and flown over the keep, his shadow had blotted out the sun over a large portion of the keep's grounds.

Compared to Fitz, Kai was puny.

The ancient dragon was as white as fresh snow. As he beat his wings and gained some altitude, the true immensity of his size became apparent. The dragon's head alone was larger than any one of the giants still battling below. His shadow stretched out over the keep, the lake, and the entire battlefield. His wingspan was so wide that Alexander feared one wing would scrape against the cliff behind them.

Fitz let out a roar that shook the ground. The giants immediately stopped fighting and cowered on the ground. As did nearly all the Elysians. More than a few pissed themselves.

Lowering himself back toward the earth, Fitz began to shrink. When he was roughly twice the size of any of the giants, he settled in the fields nearby. His massive dragon voice growled out, *"ENOUGH!"*

When the giants made no move to resist or resume their battle, Fitz settled himself to the ground, tucking his front legs under himself like a housecat, and looked expectantly toward Alexander.

Alexander mumbled to himself, "Damn. How am I supposed to follow *that?"* making Sasha snort. Still, he had to try. He saw a lot of value in having the giants as allies. And even if he couldn't pull that off, he saw no reason to let them kill each other. They had been enslaved by the drow and had suffered enough.

Turning to Sasha, he said, "Spread the word. On my signal, I want every possible heal on those three."

Not waiting for her answer, he cast Levitate on himself. Shouting out, "HEY BIG FELLAS!" at the giants, he began to move himself in their direction. All three were still sitting on the ground, but he kept himself about sixty feet in the air. Just in case one of them decided to make a grab for him.

All three of the giants turned to look up at his voice. Their eyes grew wide to see an elf floating through the sky. Alexander spoke loudly enough for all to hear.

"I am Alexander. This is my kingdom! You have come here and killed my people!" He motioned toward the outer wall, blood-spattered and littered with corpses. Then he motioned to the ground the giants were sitting on. "You've ruined our crops! For this, I should kill you all!"

The giants cowered slightly, despite Alexander's small size. He tried to take credit for it in his own mind, but knew it was mainly because Fitz leaned his head forward to emphasize the threat.

"But I know you did not come here of your own will. The evil drow captured you and made you slaves!"

One of the giants nodded his head in vigorous agreement, blood from a head wound spraying in every direction. Alexander continued. "I think you have suffered enough. So rather than kill you all, I offer you healing, and friendship!"

All three giants lit up with several different shades of light as the healers poured on their magic. Green from the druids, gold and blue from the priests, white from the paladins. Alexander missed hearing Fibble's "Pew! Pew!" in the mix, and momentarily worried about his little green buddy.

The giants gasped in surprise and ran hands over their bodies as the heals mended bones, closed wounds, and stopped bleeds. Likely none of them had ever experienced healing magic before. Alexander took advantage of the moment.

"You see! The drow enslave you. Force you from your homes against your will. Make you fight and die for them. I offer you healing! Protection from the evil drow. And food!" He waved at the wall and several of the hunters began tossing down bear and wolf carcasses. The giants looked to Fitz, who nodded his head. Each of them rushed toward the wall and began scooping up meat and shoving it into their mouths.

Alexander grimaced. He'd made a big mistake and lost their attention. Looking at Fitz, he whispered, "I should have held back the food until the end, right?"

The dragon just snorted at him, blue flames leaking from his nostrils. They all waited as the giants greedily finished off the offered meal. At their size, each bear carcass was no more than a mouthful. Alexander began to reconsider any long term offer of food. Just these three could eat more than the citizens living in the keep each day.

When the food was gone, Alexander lowered himself to the giants' eye level. Fitz cleared his throat, and Alexander had their full attention again.

"You have been healed. And fed. Look around you! We could have easily taken your lives, as we took those of your fellow giants." He motioned to the dead giants, then to the dragon behind him. Then he pointed to the wing of dragons circling above. The giants shrank back upon seeing them, not having noticed them before.

"Instead, I will spare your lives. And offer to make you Elysians, if you like. You can join our clan. Live on our lands in peace. Hunt as you like, as long as you don't harm each other or any of our people."

The giants looked slightly confused. Fitz coughed quietly and said, "Use small words."

Alexander rolled his eyes, but followed the suggestion. "Safe place to live. Plenty of food. But no fighting unless I ask you to!"

The smallest of the three giants had heard enough. He took a step toward Alexander, smiling and nodding his head. The others watched to see what would happen.

Alexander asked, "You wish to become one of us? You will swear to behave?"

The giant nodded again. His booming voice said, "Swear! Friend! Name is Dag!"

Fitz spoke behind Alexander, his voice less growly and more friendly this time. "Dag, you swear by the gods to obey Alexander and protect the citizens of Elysia? If you break this oath, it will end your life."

Dag's eyes widened a bit and he got a thoughtful look on his face. After a tense ten seconds or so, he nodded again. "Dag swear!"

A blue light enveloped the giant and a black dragon symbol appeared over his head. Alexander smiled. "Welcome to Elysia, Dag!"

"Thank you, boss elf!" Dag grinned at him. He looked around for a moment, then raised one hand. "What do now?"

Sounds of laughter echoed down from the wall as Alexander smiled at the giant. "Just take a seat for now. I must speak to these other two."

Dag sat, crushing a significant section of corn stalks, shaking his head. "No need them. Stupid giants. Dag only one you need. Kill them."

The other two began to move toward Dag with dark intent in their eyes. That is until Fitz growled at them, freezing them in place. Both put their hands behind their backs and tried to look innocent.

Alexander tried to hold a stern look as he addressed the two. "What are your names?"

"Grud," said the first, thumping his chest.

"Moog." The second giant pointed to himself. "No kill Moog. Moog not want to hurt little shrimps." He looked fearfully at Fitz.

"No, no kill Moog. Or Grud," Alexander assured them. "If you do not wish to stay, we will send you away. I'm afraid I do not know where your homes are."

"Mountains!" Grud said with assurance. As if that explained everything.

"There are many mountains. And I have no way to know which ones are yours. We can send you far away to new mountains. Or you can stay here, become our friends. And live in our mountains." Alexander waved to the forest on the other side of the wall. "Or you can live in this forest. One of you, anyway."

Moog got back to his feet. He looked up at the wall, at the people there. And then up at the dragons above. Facing back toward Alexander, he whispered so loudly that everyone could hear anyway. "Any girl giants here?"

This time, Alexander couldn't help but laugh. "No, no girls. But maybe the dragons will help you find one after the fighting is through?"

Fitz snorted at him again but said nothing. Alexander thought he detected a dragonish smile trying to break free.

Moog nodded his head. "Moog stay. But not in forest here. Up in mountains."

Grud shook his head. "No stay. Grud be friend. Not hurt little ones. But want to go home. Find place and live alone. Is giant way."

"Fair enough!" Alexander looked to Fitz. The dragon administered the oath to Moog, who smiled and very carefully reached out to Alexander, who was still floating in the air. He patted Alexander's head gently – for a giant – causing him to drop about ten feet before he recovered.

Moog yanked back his hand. "Sorry."

Fitz looked to the air, and Del ceased his circling to land next to him. Fitz indicated Grud. "Please escort Grud here to a secluded mountain someplace."

Del nodded his head and motioned for Grud to approach. The wary giant stepped closer, then cringed as Del took hold of him by the shoulders. The dragon lifted the giant with a little effort, then took several steps forward and leapt as he beat his mighty wings. The two of them rose slowly into the sky, then turned and disappeared over the top of the cliff above.

Alexander looked at his two newest and largest Elysians. "Again, welcome to Elysia! We will find a good place for each of you on the mountain above. But we are still fighting a battle against the drow."

Moog growled. "Hate drow!" Dag nodded in agreement.

"Yes. Me too, Moog," Alexander agreed. "I was wondering if you two would stay here for a day or two and help us defend the keep? You can say no. It's okay. The drow are dangerous."

Moog agreed immediately. "Stay. Kill drow. Eat more?" He looked longingly at the burned corpses of the were-beasts and hobgoblins that had yet to be looted. Dag followed his gaze and licked his lips.

Alexander wasn't about to refuse such an easy favor. "Let my people loot the corpses, then you can eat all you want. But ONLY the were-beasts and hobgoblins. None of our people."

Both giants agreed. Alexander looked to the wall and the gates opened. Several of the players exited onto the battlefield. Some who had died trotted over to recover their gear, then helped with the looting. Alexander called to Brick and handed him his gear as he lowered himself to the ground.

Sasha walked up. "We didn't get a quest completion or wave completion notification."

Alexander looked at his UI, scrolling through his notifications. She was right. He looked around, mentally counting the giant corpses. "Is there still a giant out in the moat or something?"

Just then Beatrix, who had gone up onto the wall where she'd been killed, called out in raid chat, *"Something's banging on the doors down below."*

"The orcs!" Alexander felt like an idiot. "I killed most of the orcs with the drawbridge. Rocky got some, but there were five or six who made it into the tunnel."

He turned to the two giants. "I'm going to let some orcs in the gate. I want you guys to stand behind me." Moog and Dag stepped toward the gate and waited for Alexander to catch up. "Close enough," he mumbled, making Brick chuckle.

When Alexander was maybe fifty yards from the gate, he shouted, "Jeeves, please open the gates!"

The two doors instantly began to swing inward. Six orcs raised a battle cry and charged through as soon as the opening was wide enough. Alexander held up and hand and shouted, "Stop!"

The orcs ignored him.

Until they saw the giants standing behind him. And the dragon behind them. And a dozen or so players with weapons drawn advancing in a half-circle around them.

The lead orc skidded to a halt maybe twenty yards from Alexander. Without the mind control, they had the good sense not to commit suicide in a hopeless fight. The other orcs halted as well, all of them panting and gripping their weapons tightly.

Alexander called out, "You don't have to die. We know the drow forced you to come here. You paid a heavy price. Throw down your weapons and we will let you live!"

As they were thinking it over, three of the orc elders from the plateau tribe stepped forward. One of them grunted out something in the orc's language. From the tone of it, it was half challenge, half explanation.

The lead orc snorted in disgust at the elder's words. He hefted a war axe onto his shoulder and looked as if he was considering a charge. Alexander looked to the elder.

"Dark ones," the elder explained. "Follow dark gods. Only know how to kill. Surrender is a sin for them. They will attack soon."

Alexander decided to force the issue. He needed to see to his own people. "Drop your weapons now! Or die where you stand!" Both giants growled their agreement.

The lead orc pulled the axe from his shoulder and laid the blade flat on his off hand, as if presenting the weapon to Alexander. He took several steps forward, not saying a word. When he was within reach of Alexander, he said, "Die first!" and used both hands to shove the weapon at Alexander. The sharp blade rang out as it struck his chest piece. It didn't penetrate the armor, but the force of it knocked him back.

Which was a good thing. Because two seconds later, Dag's fist swept across and grabbed the orc. Lifting him up, he bit the creature's head off even as he grabbed another with his left hand. Moog was more efficient, simply stomping the remaining orcs to pulp. The moment the last one died, golden light showered nearly every player and citizen as they leveled up.

Quest Complete! Hold What You Have
You and your people have successfully defended the Elysian capitol against attacks from the forces of darkness.
Reward: 500 gold. 250,000 experience. Title: Defender of Light!
You may now further the cause of light by entering the nearby lands of the drow wizards and taking control of their stronghold.

New Quest: The Heart of Darkness
Attack and defeat the drow in their own stronghold. Capture or kill the drow wizard in control of the dark forces there. Use the portal orb received from the defeated apprentice to gain access to the drow lands.
Reward: Variable
Bonus Reward: Experience doubled for capture of the drow wizard.

Alexander got to his feet. "Thank you Dag, Moog. You have earned a reward!" Looking at Brick, he said, "Please give each one of them a keg of spirits? I'll pay you for them."

Brick shook his head. "No need. That were fun to watch! HA!"

Sasha tapped Alexander on the shoulder. "Any chance you could move the giants outside and save whatever crops haven't been squished?"

Alexander looked at the two giants. "Umm… Fitz? That might be too much weight for me. Would you mind?"

A blink later, the two giants found themselves standing on the other side of the moat. They immediately began picking up burned and mutilated monster corpses and munching on them. They sat contentedly and focused on the meal.

Beatrix started to object that those mobs hadn't been looted yet. Alexander laughed. "Feel free to go argue with them about it!" He laughed even harder as she ran out the gate and started yelling at them.

His laughter subsided abruptly as he saw the bodies of too many of his citizens still littering the wall and the ground below. "Jeeves, how many did we lose?"

"Eleven of the citizens who perished in the first stage were resurrected, leaving eight killed. In the second stage, we lost an additional fifty-three citizens, Majesty."

The blow hit Alexander like a truck. He'd seen the carnage with his own eyes, but somehow had expected the number to be smaller. He fought back the urge to cry for his dead, telling himself over and over that they weren't real.

Jules appeared at his side, taking his hand in her own. She pulled him toward the inner keep. "Let's go. You're not needed out here. Come with me." He numbly followed her lead as he listened to Silverbeard and Lola calling out orders to take the looted bodies out across the bridge and gather up their own dead for burial.

Chapter 12

Recovery

Despite their victory and the massive gains in both experience and wealth that most of the citizens received, the keep was a somber place. The healers had resurrected as many as they could from the first wave, but they were limited to one resurrection per day, leaving more than threescore citizens of Elysia who were lost to them in the battle to defend their homes.

The vast majority of those killed were orcs. They charged at their enemies in a battle-induced rage that was both deadly and dangerous. To themselves as much as their enemies. Alexander had seen the first two killed when the duergar had been dropped by a gargoyle on their heads. But in all, thirty-five of the sixty-one dead were orcs.

Alexander sought out the surviving elders to give his apologies, but when he located them, they were celebrating. They'd 'liberated' a few dozen barrels of ale from the Ogre II and were toasting the heroic deaths of their comrades. As Alexander observed, listening to the outrageous claims of courage and lethality being heaped upon the dead, one of the elders approached.

"You do not share in our joy," the elder stated.

Alexander shook his head. "It is difficult. I feel responsible for their deaths. If I had prepared them better…" He was thinking of his failure to provide dragon pins to the newly recruited orcs and minotaurs.

The elder grunted. "You have given them a great gift. They died with honor, as warriors in a glorious battle! They died protecting our lands, our people. It has been many generations since our warriors have achieved such deaths. We have been reduced to clan fights and raids against the minotaur settlements. Honorless fights driven by greed or pride."

The elder waved an arm toward the battlefield, hidden behind the high walls of the keep. "We are proud of our dead. They will be remembered. You have given them this honor. We thank you." He bowed his head to Alexander.

Alexander bowed his head slightly in return. "I am glad their deaths have earned them honor. Still, I would prefer they had lived to fight on to greater glory."

The elder clapped Alexander on the back. "Yes! Greater glory. Let us continue this fight. Now we have dead to avenge!"

Shaking his head at the bloodlust of the orcs, Alexander answered, "We may well have to assist our allies in the defense of their cities. But for now, let us mourn our dead. Or celebrate them. And prepare for another attack, should it come."

Leaving the orcs to their rituals, he went to find Molgo and Dawn. They were seated on hay bales in the stables, several of their people scattered around them. All had been healed. Save the fourteen who had been killed in the battle.

"Molgo, Dawn. I want to thank you and your people for coming to defend the keep. And to say that I am sorry for your losses."

Dawn got to her feet, towering over Alexander. "We are honored to have been able to fight at your side, Alexander. As for our dead, they were warriors. Each of us goes into battle knowing we may die. We accept the deaths of our brothers and sisters as gifts to us, and honor them in return. Their sacrifice has allowed us to remain in our new homes, with our families, and theirs." She looked over to where the orcs were once again loudly celebrating and smiled. "Though we do not crave battle as the orcs do, we are a warrior race. Few of us die of old age. Thus it has ever been, and shall always be."

Molgo simply grunted in agreement, along with the others gathered around them.

Alexander asked, "Can I get you anything? The orcs have put a dent in the ale supply, but there is plenty left. Or we can bring you food…"

"We are content. Unless you would be willing to allow some of us to accompany you when you seek out the dark ones in their stronghold?" Molgo pressed.

Alexander opened his mouth to deny them. But he hesitated. He owed these people a great debt. And it might dishonor them to refuse. He still didn't want to risk the lives of any citizens in the drow lands. Enough of them had died already that day. But their attitude toward honorable death and the echo of Jules' voice in his head reminding him that they were in fact NPCs made him rethink his earlier position.

"As you know, I did not intend to bring any citizens with me, other than a wing of dragons. But after the sacrifice your people have made for Elysia today, I must reconsider. Choose ten of your people. If possible, I would prefer it be those without families to leave behind should they be killed."

There was a roar of approval from the gathered minotaurs that shook the stables. Alexander left them to their choosing and moved on.

The remainder of the dead were three duergar, six dwarves, and three humans. Alexander looked around for Gelag, but didn't see him. In fact, he didn't see any duergar anywhere.

"Jeeves, can you tell me Gelag's location please?"

"Gelag has returned to the duergar city below. Along with all of his people. They are conducting burial rites."

Alexander hoped that the duergar were simply very private when it came to their death rituals and that their losses had not caused a rift between them and the other races of Elysia. Or resentment toward him directly. But he'd honor their desire for privacy.

Moving to the dining area, he found several of the players who'd been killed sitting around bragging about their epic deaths, or the loot they received. His lips twitched into a smile as he listened. They didn't sound that much different from the orcs.

Many of the players, especially the healers who had come from Antalia, were lower-level. They had gained as much as five levels worth of XP from the battle and the quests. And since the were-beasts and hobgoblins were, for the most part, higher-level than they were, they picked up some usable weapons and armor as well.

Alexander took a seat among them, enjoying the banter and decompressing after the battle. As he listened, he realized he hadn't checked the loot drop from the drow in his rush to get back to the keep.

Opening his inventory log, he began to read. There was the portal orb. No different than the others, except that it had a purple halo around it, indicating that it was a quest item. And that solved Fitz's concern about using one of the other captured orbs and ending up directly in some wizard's throne room surrounded by guards. A quest item like this would almost certainly send them to a safe zone where they could organize their pre-battle buffs and make other raid preparations.

He noticed that the drow had also been carrying more than ten thousand gold, as well as a collection of spell components. He tucked those away to give to Sasha for analysis. And her inventory bag had two hundred slots. That would be a major upgrade for most of his players. Next on the list was a staff.

> ### Ironwood Staff of Culling
> ### Item Quality: Rare
> ### Stats: Wisdom +10, Intelligence +15, Mana Regen +10
> *This staff was given by a drow wizard to his apprentice as a reward for murdering every man, woman, and child in a human village single-handedly. The staff can generate a protective shield around its bearer that will absorb damage equal to the bearer's health pool. Cooldown: One hour.*

"No wonder the drow was so hard to kill," he mumbled. The weapon effectively doubled the health of a player, while at the same time protecting them from hits that might interrupt spell casting. In addition to the attribute buffs. For those whose builds made them glass cannons, this would be a huge improvement. They'd have to make those who were interested in the staff roll to see who would win it.

> ### Apprentice Mantle
> ### Item Quality: Epic
> ### Stats: Wisdom +20, Intelligence +10, Armor +10, Magic Resistance +20

This item can only be worn by those with Dark alignment.

Not of any use for his people. But he'd give it to Max to sell at the auction house and each of the players would get a share. Several of them, including Max and Brick, used the funds they could raise in-game to pay their real-world bills. Though since signing up with Jupiter Tech, his core group and the other testers were earning solid salaries. Still, Max loved selling items at auction.

The last item was more interesting.

Tyrolean Hat of Death
Item Quality: Epic
Stats: Agility +5, Dexterity +10
This hat, taken from the corpse of an elven lothario after a run-in with several jealous husbands, grants its user the ability to become invisible for one minute. Cooldown – twenty-four hours. In addition, the hat's pins can be thrown at enemies, each with a different effect, such as poison, silence, stun, petrification, exsanguination, or discombobulation. Pins will regenerate twelve hours after use.

This one he thought they'd probably keep. If Max or Jules didn't want it, he was sure one of the casters would jump at the chance to be invisible.

With their battle won, Alexander decided to see if the Elysian players could assist the other cities in their battles. He walked across the courtyard and waved his hand to activate the portal to Stormforge first.

Nothing happened.

He tried it again, thinking he'd simply been distracted and messed up the spell. But again, nothing. He quickly tried to open portals to Broken Mountain and Antalia with the same result.

Looking up at the sky, he asked, "Allfather, have you shut down the portals for the event?"

A moment later, thunder rolled across the forest and echoed off the mountain. Alexander took it as a 'yes.'

"Interesting," he mumbled to himself. He had been given reports on the development of a drow-world expansion way back when the development first started. But he hadn't really paid much attention. The world event had taken him by surprise. And now this isolation of the cities during the event. Though he supposed it made sense. Otherwise, massive groups of players from cities who completed their defense could portal around and zerg the drow still attacking other cities, making the event less challenging for the players.

He considered taking all of his players with mounts and making a run for Stormforge. But again, he figured it violated the intent of the event. For all he knew, Odin would somehow punish the NPCs in Stormforge to balance his interference.

So he began to move about the keep, checking on his people. He congratulated some for leveling and sympathized with others who'd lost friends in the battle. As per their new tradition, they would hold a ceremony at sunset to honor the dead. Brick and another shaper were already working on adding the names to the monument by the druid's grove.

Before the immersion pods, after an event like this Alexander would have spent some time offline looking at the forums. He'd watch some of the trending videos and the commentary from the several networks that had sprung up just to cover the various games out there.

Since logging out wasn't an option, he decided to fill his time by making more of the dragon pins. He took a seat at one of the dining tables and got to work. For nearly two hours, he sat there working, only interrupted occasionally by Silverbeard or Lola wanting his input or approval on something. Citizens and players came and went, sitting to consume a meal or work on some craft, much as Alexander was doing.

The spells were so familiar and easy for him now that his mind wandered while he worked. He thought about Fibble, still trapped up in the roost with a paranoid mama dragon and the hatchlings. Since he hadn't seen Kai during the battle, Alexander assumed his friend was still trying to calm his mate. Or just sharing their grief at the loss of their dragonling.

Alexander knew about grief. Especially the kind caused by the sudden and senseless loss of a loved one. Even now, more than a decade later, the attack that took his mother from him was still haunting him.

*****

Matt looked around through the eyes of his Dark One avatar. His drow muscles complained as he knelt before the throne of the ancient drow wizard who was his mentor and master. The wizard ignored him, as he'd been doing for the last few hours. Matt knew it was purely a power trip, but he needed to play along. To stay on this drow's good side. He was, after all, the source of Matt's power within the game. It was the wizard's gold, intelligence network, and portal system that had allowed Matt to level quickly as he gathered power to himself. And it was the wizard's army of demons and dark creatures that Matt was hoping would destroy the game world and make it unplayable, or at least undesirable, for the average person.

The world event that had been announced fit perfectly into his desires. He just had to make sure the drow armies won their battles for the major cities. That would take away the infrastructure that the players had come to count on. Safe zones for new players would no longer be safe. Auction houses, healing temples, class trainers, even guild houses would become inaccessible. The millions of players who visited the cities to repair or replace their gear would have to stand in line to visit the rare blacksmiths and merchants in the small villages outside the cities. At least, until those were destroyed too.

Jupiter Tech could create new cities, of course. Or simply grow the remaining villages to accommodate the players' needs. But all of that would take time, and players were not patient people. Those who played for fun would get bored and move on. Those who played to earn a living would quickly find they couldn't pay their bills without access to auction houses and a dwindling number of buyers. Millions would abandon the game. The company's stock would plummet. Real-world economies would take significant hits, causing even more blowback against Jupiter Tech.

And that was when Matt would strike.

The combined financial losses and destruction of their infrastructure at Olympus would be the end of Jupiter Tech and the Greystones. They would finally pay for the needless death of his mother. For the pain she suffered in the hours it took her to die. They would learn that their choices had consequences!

Turning his attention from his thoughts of conquest, he cleared his throat for maybe the twentieth time, hoping the old drow would finally respond. Matt himself, even in his powerful Dark One avatar, couldn't directly impact each of the dozens of battles taking place across the continent of Io on multiple servers. Even if he'd had time to plan this campaign himself, he was still only one person.

But what he *could* do was teach the old drow wizards how to beat an army of players. Because that would be their primary obstacle. None of the cities maintained armies large or powerful enough to hold off the attacks of the dark forces. If they were to survive the invasions, it would be by using players to defend them.

So Matt was trying to educate this wizard. The problem was, the NPC's programming seemed to be interfering. He'd tried a few hours ago to convince his master that his troops should stop and loot every player they killed before moving on. This would mean that as the players respawned, they would find at least some of their best gear missing. And maybe the gold they needed to pay for repairs or potions. Players were an effective tool because of two main factors: they threw themselves into battle without much concern for their lives, and they generally had better gear than the NPCs and monsters they faced.

But if that gear disappeared when they died, they would become a less effective - and less motivated - fighting force almost immediately. The forums would spread news of the gear losses like lightning. And fewer players would be willing to risk getting involved. Those who died and lost their best gear might stay in the fight. But again, they would be less effective, rejoining the fight with inferior gear and at a lower level than before.

He'd wanted to share all this with the wizard. But he'd only gotten two sentences into his explanation when the drow had held up a hand to silence him. Matt had remained on his knees, the position his master demanded he maintain whenever they spoke, waiting for permission to

222

continue. Having plenty of time to think, Matt had almost decided that he'd run up against some kind of NPC block. That talk of the players respawning and losing gear and levels after being looted by NPCs and losing their desire to return to this world seemed to break some kind of interactive algorithm or something.

This time when he cleared his throat, the wizard turned his head and stared straight at Matt, who went from feeling invisible to feeling like a squirrel being eyed by a hawk. Though he knew in his logical mind that this was just an NPC, a bunch of code, the old wizard was still intimidating as hell. He'd seen his master destroy servants and soldiers on a whim. And in the most painful and bloody ways. With the pain settings for the game as high as they were, Matt would just as soon avoid that type of reaction.

He took a chance as he lowered his eyes to avoid the wizard's gaze. "I can help you and your fellow wizards defeat your foes." He focused on the only thing he had to offer that would interest the drow. "I know how the adventurers think. How they operate. I can help you win!"

The wizard made a face that suggested he'd just sucked on a rotten lemon. "Fool! What could you know that we have not learned in the thousands of years we have battled against mankind?!" The drow thumped his fist down on the arm of his throne. Somewhere behind him, servants whimpered in fear. When their master got angry, someone usually died.

"Adventurers are new to Io. We arrived after your last war with the light races. Though your spies and scouts have had some interaction with them, you cannot claim to understand them. Being an adventurer myself, I can tell you how they think. What motivates them, and what they fear. I can predict how they'll act in battle and help you prepare countermeasures, Master." Matt tried his best to sound subservient but confident at the same time.

The drow on the throne looked down at him with a scowl. But his voice held a hint of curiosity. "And in return for this information, you want… what?"

Matt's smile was cruel and filled with malice. "I want only to ensure that you succeed, Master. If your armies are victorious, I will return to my world and continue the battle there. You won't see my face again."

The wizard leaned forward in his chair, his face coming within a few inches of Matt's. "And if we follow your advice and lose… you will suffer beyond anything you can comprehend."

Matt lowered his head to floor in obeisance, hiding his smirk. If the dark armies failed, he'd simply abandon his avatar and let the old wizard have his way with it. He was betting everything on this event and he needed to roll a proverbial natural twenty to pull it off. He found that the long odds against him made it more exciting.

"Come, then. We shall meet with my colleagues and you can share this information with all of us. Our armies are already moving to attack. Let us be quick about it!"

With a wave of his hand, a portal at the end of the throne room opened. On the other side, Matt could see a dimly-lit room with a long table and high-backed chairs, all made of some blood-red wood. The wizard got to his feet and stepped past Matt as he moved toward the portal. Matt straightened his stiff legs and rose to his feet to follow.

*****

Special Agent McCoy and his partner rounded the block, each of them laser-focused on the houses they passed. The neighborhood was a quiet one, in an older suburb of the city. The kind where kids still rode bicycles or skateboards in the street.

They'd been assigned a quarter-mile square section of the area that his counterparts had traced the cell leader's call to. The man who was responsible for so many deaths was somewhere within a mile radius. Or at least, he had been a few hours ago.

McCoy and his partner were one of twelve teams in plainclothes and unmarked cars who worked a grid in search of some hint of the man's location. They had his photo and a profile that included everything that was known about him. Now they just needed a location.

An overweight woman in her fifties huffed and puffed her way toward them as they cruised slowly down the block. She was walking one of those tiny ankle-biter dogs that were back in fashion. The little thing looked like a hairball with legs and a nose. Just as they drew even with her, the mutt stopped to take a dump on somebody's driveway.

The woman looked briefly at McCoy, then turned away and pretended not to notice the little shitbomb her precious pookie was dropping. McCoy stopped the car and leaned out.

"Excuse me, ma'am. I was hoping you could help us. We're investigating a series of petty crimes in the neighborhood. Have you seen anything unusual or suspicious in the last few days?"

The woman took a step toward the curb and peered at him. "Who are you? You don't look like police."

He gave her his best smile. "That's sort of the point, ma'am. We don't want the bad guys to go into hiding because they see police cars cruising up and down."

She looked thoughtful for a moment, then tugged on the leash as she stepped closer to the car. The little dog nearly flew across the sidewalk after her. She leaned in close to the car window and spoke in a loud whisper.

"Now that you mention it, there have been some things going on. I think Linda that lives two houses down from me is smoking the wacky weed on her back porch at night. I swear I can smell it! I think she's growing it in her back yard. And I *know* for *sure* she's banging the pool boy while Cliff's at work."

She paused to take a deep breath and look over each shoulder to make sure nobody was listening in. "We have a private security company under contract. Our homeowners' dues pay for a guard to be patrolling 24/7. But I haven't seen them in a week! I think they just sit in their little booth down the street and watch porn or something!"

McCoy tried not to let her see him roll his eyes.

"Thank you, ma'am. I'm afraid there's nothing we can do about your security patrol. But I'll be sure to have somebody look into your neighbor's growing habits." He produced the photo of their suspect. "Have you seen this guy walking around, by any chance?"

She leaned even closer to stare at the photo. After a moment, she shook her head. "I don't believe so. He's a handsome young man. Shame he's turned to a life of crime. I'll keep an eye out for him."

McCoy handed her a card with his cell number on it. "If you do spot him, call us right away. Don't approach him, or even let him see you staring. We don't want to spook him."

She nodded enthusiastically as she reached into her sweatsuit and stuffed the card into her bra. "Very hush hush. I understand completely." She tried to act casual as she stepped back and resumed her walk. Every couple steps she turned and looked over one shoulder or the other, looking like a kid who just stole from the cookie jar.

McCoy's partner chuckled and handed him a slice of cold pizza as they continued down the block.

*****

Richard and Michael stared grimly at the young woman as she was escorted by Talbott from the elevator to stand in front of them. For her part, she looked scared, but unrepentant. As if to prove this, when Talbott brought her to a stop a few feet from Richard's desk, she spat at him. The glob of saliva didn't reach him, landing on his desk instead. He ignored it.

Richard spoke first. "Let's save us all some time here. We know you've been working for Howard and Matt. We have your phone and have used it to track his. We'll have him shortly, too. You're done. You've failed. You're going to spend the rest of your life in jail, or, if we can prove that you had something to do with the bombings, you'll be put to death. It's that simple." He waited for her to react in some way. She just stared defiantly at him.

"What I want to know… is why? Why would you do this? Why would you help murder innocent people?"

Jenni continued to glare at him. Her eyes burned with hatred. No one spoke a word for a full minute or more. Finally, she screamed at him, "And *you* haven't killed people?! What a hypocrite!"

Richard leaned back at the force of her outburst. Composing himself before speaking, he looked more carefully at her face. "I don't think we've met before, outside of Olympus, I mean. And I've never killed anyone in my life. In what way have I wronged you?"

"Matt told me what you did! You murdered his mother! Sent her into a war zone because you were too cowardly to go yourself! Even though you KNEW an attack was likely!"

All three men in room looked shocked. Michael recovered first. "And you believed him?"

"Of course I believed him! Why would he lie about such a thing? And the pain in his eyes. There was no way he was faking that. You rich people, you think you control the world. You sacrifice us like we're peasants, then pay for the best lawyers and buy off judges and politicians so you never pay for your actions!"

"*ENOUGH!!*" Richard's voice thundered through the room as he slammed both hands down on his desk and rose to his feet. He leaned forward, his face growing red and his expression deadly.

"You stupid little bitch! A cute boy told you a sob story, one that he made up, by the way, and you agree to help him kill people who've never done anything to anyone?" He looked as if he were about to crawl over the desk and strangle her. She tried to step back, but Talbott held her in place.

"Matthew's mother was indeed killed. She was a great lady, and beloved by all of us. One of our original crew. She was family." Richard's voice grew ragged, grief warring with his anger. "There was no war zone. She attended a tech conference with my wife, here in the US. A simple industry conference to discuss trends in VR tech, among other things. My wife was a speaker. There was no threat, no reason to suspect any danger whatsoever." He stopped leaning over the desk and sat back in his chair.

"Seshat… Miriam. Matthew's mother. She was upstairs in the hotel while my wife was speaking in one of the ballrooms. A crazy man with a bomb walked in, shouted something about technology being evil, and set off the bomb. My wife was among the first killed. Matthew's mother was trapped in the rubble for a while before she died as well. He blames us for her death, because like the rest of us, he can't wrap his mind around the senseless nature of it."

Jenni growled and tried to lunge at him. Again, Talbott easily restrained her. "Lies!! You'd say anything to save your own skin!"

Michael snorted. "Save it from what? From you? A foolish little girl who's thrown her life away for nothing? An angry boy who thinks killing innocents will somehow erase his pain? Or that vengeance will bring back our loved ones?"

He motioned for Richard to get up from his chair, then for Talbott to put Jenni into it. When she was in position, he activated Richard's desk interface. Pulling up a search engine, he said, "Go ahead. Type in her name. Miriam's. Read for yourself."

Jenni sulkily typed in the information and hit 'SEARCH.' Immediately, several holographic windows appeared in front of her. News stories about Jupiter Tech that featured Miriam in some way. Stories about awards she received from women's and business associations. And several stories about the bombing. The young woman read them, one after another, shaking her head. "This can't be right. You've done this! You've paid for fake news articles!" She swiped her hand to the left and cleared all the windows away.

Richard, still fuming, took a step toward her. Talbott held him back with one hand. "Easy, boss."

Michael answered, "Why? Why in the world would we do that? The bombing was carried out by an anti-tech terrorist organization called Light of Truth. We were not suspects. Were not involved in any way, other than losing our family members in the blast. You think we'd go to all the trouble and expense to create fake news stories just to convince a stupid little girl like you?"

He was interrupted by Richard. The man's voice growled out his rage. "You are only here because I wanted to know why you would help a psycho like Matthew. And because we want to know his plans. Other than that, you are meaningless. I don't care what you believe or don't believe. It's clear you're just another of the morons that Howard and Matthew have conned into doing their dirty work. I've no need to convince you of anything. This is what's going to happen. You're going to sit there and tell us everything you know. Write it down. Draw us pictures if you have to. And in return, I'll recommend that you only receive a life sentence. Refuse to help us, and I'll become exactly the rich asshole you've accused me of being. I'll pay the best investigators, the best lawyers, the most prestigious professional witnesses to make *damned sure* you get the death penalty. Then I'll attend your execution. Do you have family? I'll bring them to watch you die, and *laugh* as they push the drugs into your arm. My laughter and the shocked tears of your family will be the last thing you hear."

Jenni leaned back in the chair as his face inched closer and closer. Her eyes were wide and tears rolled down her face. Michael and Talbott both looked shocked as well. The two men glanced at each other, both wondering if they should interfere. After a moment, Michael shook his head.

Jenni looked up at Michael and Talbott, avoiding Richard's accusing gaze and hoping for some help. Both men just gave her hard looks and remained silent. Her gaze dropped to her hands as she removed them from the desk and clasped them together in her lap. Her shoulders began to shake as she broke down and cried quietly.

Richard showed no mercy. "You can cry later. Start talking. What did Matthew want you to do for him? How are you helping?"

Jenni didn't speak for a while. Talbott reached down and touched a button on the desk's interface to start recording what she had to say.

After a few deep, ragged breaths, she began to speak. "I'm… I'm sorry. I believed him. I believed you were killers. He was just so…" She trailed off, not bothering to finish the sentence.

"He plans to blow up Olympus. He's been smuggling explosives into the compound for months. Stashed here on the grounds. He used some of it in the lab where Dayle was killed. But only a little bit. He's got twenty times that much still. I hid it for him in the woods near the lake. He just told me to plant bombs that would take out the servers and this tower, and a few other places, making sure to kill you and Alexander. And to take out as many others as possible."

She actually sounded ashamed as she finished the last part. "I was going to do it, too. For him. For Matt. I'm not even sure why."

Talbott stepped in, interrogation being part of his job. He began by asking, "Where exactly are the explosives?"

He pulled up an aerial map of the compound and zoomed in a bit on the lake region. "And how is he getting in and out of Olympus?"

*****

Chapter 13

Into the Belly of the Beast

Alexander put all his unshaped dragon pins into a cloth bag and dropped it off at the smithy. The apprentices there knew what to do with them by now. He left instructions for them to be finished as quickly as possible and given to Lola for distribution.

The sun was nearing its drop behind the forest treetops and the evening meal would be served soon. After dinner, they would hold a memorial for the friends and fellow citizens they lost in battle.

Alexander was surprised to find Blix sitting alone at a dining table. The little gnome banker was looking glum. "Blix. What is wrong, my friend? You look like somebody just cleaned out your bank."

Blix looked up and gave Alexander a half smile. "No, no. Everything is fine with the bank. In fact, many of our citizens just deposited significant sums of gold they received for defending the keep." Blix passed a log book over for Alexander to inspect.

Alexander took a quick look, not really interested. He did see that something like a hundred Elysians had each deposited several hundred gold that day.

"It looks like business is good, Blix! Why the long face?"

"During the battle, I sat in the bank. Safe and secure while so many of my fellow Elysians gave their lives. I wasn't always a banker, you know. I used to be an adventurer, like you. Until I took an arrow to the knee. After that, I became a banker because it runs in my family." The little gnome produced a pair of daggers out of nowhere, showing them to Alexander before making them disappear again. "But I still know how to fight. I should have been out there today."

Alexander had to strain not to laugh at the phrasing. He looked up into the sky, winking at whatever devs might be watching. He quietly whispered, "Well played, working that in!"

Turning back to Blix, he tried to offer some solace. "We all have our jobs to do here, Blix. Yours is to run the bank. To protect the financial health of our kingdom and its people. And yes, sometimes that may mean physically protecting the bank. You did the right thing, staying there. If the enemy had broken through the inner wall, it would have been up to you to defend the bank building and the gold inside."

He patted the grieving gnome on the shoulder gently. "We lost good people today. And that is hard to accept. Each of us will blame ourselves in some way. That's only natural. But none of this is your fault, Blix. You bear no responsibility. If you wish to help, then work with Lola to make sure that the families of the dead are taken care of."

Blix brightened up at that. "I can do that! You have funds set aside for death benefits? Bah! Of course you do." The gnome jumped up, happy to be given a chance to be useful. "We'll set up accounts for the families who don't have them. Transfer the funds immediately! Give them some gold now for immediate needs. Maybe loan them funds and help them to start new businesses…" His voice faded as he hurried off to find Lola.

Alexander watched the gnome until he disappeared inside the donjon, his heart lightening a bit to see the once-businesslike and standoffish banker embracing his new life as an Elysian.

Jules appeared at his side, seemingly out of nowhere. Alexander barely flinched, growing used to his girlfriend sneaking up on him. "Well, hello there." He smiled at her, pulling her into a hug. He held here there until she began to squirm. The moment he let her go, she stepped back a half step and held up a bundle.

"I… thought maybe we could put this up somewhere? Near the grove, I mean. If you don't think they'd mind…" She sounded unsure of herself as she handed over the item.

Alexander took the cloth and began to unfold it. Seeing that it was quite large, he moved to a table and unfurled it across the surface.

It was another banner, with a light grey background and bordered with black and red scrollwork. In the center, a vibrant green hatchling surrounded by a faint golden halo. The dragonling had a faint dragon smile on its rounded snout and eyes that seemed to gaze directly into Alexander's soul.

"Jules! This is… this is beautiful! I mean, I know you've been practicing your tailoring with your dresses and banners and… wow!" He reached out to touch the dragonling. The stitching was amazingly compact, making it look almost as if the image had been drawn onto the banner instead of sewn.

Jules smiled softly at him. "Thank you. And yeah. This actually leveled my skill up to Journeyman. It… gives a buff. I'm not even sure how I did it."

Alexander used Analyze on the cloth.

Tribute Banner: Green Dragonling
Item Quality: Unique
Stats: Morale +10, Keep Defense +10
This beautiful tribute to a life cut short will serve as a reminder to all Elysians of their victory over the forces of darkness. And the evil deeds of those who serve the dark. In times of battle, the banner will boost the morale of Elysia's defenders, making them more effective and increasing the keep's overall defense rating.

Alexander put an arm around Jules and pulled her close as he admired her work. Remembering what she'd said a moment earlier, he reassured her. "I'm sure Kai and Lia won't mind a bit. Thank you, Jules. This is wonderful."

She gave him a peck on the cheek and disentangled herself before disappearing. He gently folded the banner and went to find Silverbeard. The old dwarf was in his office, dealing with the inevitable reports and paperwork that followed a battle.

Alexander handed him the banner. When the chancellor had opened it and nodded in approval, Alexander asked, "Can you make sure this gets properly displayed somewhere near the memorial obelisk?"

"O'course, lad. This be a fitting tribute to the young one. I'd be proud ta help."

"Anything you need me to take care of right now?"

"Aye. Two things. First, ye need to figure a plan to replace the citizens we lost today. Elysia be growin' fast, and her population be growin' along with her. But we ain't so big as to be able to shrug off the loss o' so many at once. A dozen or so o' those killed today were guards here at the keep. Both human and dwarf."

Alexander sat in one of the chairs in front of the desk. "I know. And I have no idea where to find them. The other cities will all have lost people too. And trained fighters are hard enough to find among the citizens without those kinds of losses. I'll think about it. If you have any ideas, please speak up." Silverbeard stroked his beard and nodded thoughtfully.

"You said two things. What was the second?"

"What? Oh! Ye need to be gettin' yer raid party ready. Ye should go tomorrow, first thing."

"We're ready. In fact, the party will be bigger than I originally planned. We're going to take some minotaurs with us. And orcs, if they wish to join us." Alexander frowned as he continued, "But shouldn't we wait until we're sure our allies survived their fights? I mean, I can't activate any of the portals right now. But they might need some aid from us when the portals do open."

"Aye lad, they just might. But they don't need yerself or yer fighters to deliver aid. Lola and meself can handle that. We need you lot ta put an end ta them drow once 'n for all. Before they have time to organize another attack."

Seeing that the old dwarf was right, Alexander didn't argue. Instead, he opened up guild chat. "*Alright, folks. We're gonna hit the drow stronghold in the morning. So get yourselves ready. We'll be taking some minotaur fighters with us. Maybe orcs, too. Probably orcs, too. Doubt I could stop them from coming at this point. As well as the dragons.*"

With that settled, he went up to his chambers. He wanted a little alone time before dinner. His people would be looking to him to set an example. To be strong and kingly. Whatever that meant.

There was an itch in the back of his brain. He was worried about Stormforge and the other allied cities. The ring he wore allowed King Charles or Captain Redmond to speak to him, but not for him to reach out to them.

The RING! Alexander smacked himself on the forehead. *The Ring of Communication you made and gave to the captain. You never tested it. Now's as good a time as any!*

Alexander pulled out the last of the three rings he'd made. Putting it on his finger, he said, "Captain? Can you hear me?"

There was no response. He tried channeling some mana into the ring and spoke again. "Captain? Are you there?"

Still nothing. Alexander shook his head. This was the disadvantage of experimenting with skills and spells. One doesn't get the mental instruction manual that comes with the spell when it's taught by a mentor or trainer. He'd figured out how to *make* the rings, but didn't have a clue how to *use* them.

"Ah, well. Guess it's time for more experiments." He took the ring off and placed it in the palm of his hand. Closing his eyes, he channeled mana into the ring. At the same time, he pictured the ring he wanted to reach. He focused on the memory of handing the ring to the captain. Then he tried to picture a sort of thread connecting the two rings.

For a long while, nothing happened. He began to worry that channeling too much mana into the ring would cause it to explode. Just as he was about to quit, he felt a sort of *give* in the pressure of the built-up mana.

Skill Level Up! Enchanting +5!

You have managed to connect two enchanted items that were created by you. Normally a difficult task for beginners in itself, you managed to connect items physically separated by ten miles or more.

Alexander pumped a fist in the air as he felt the connection between the two rings take hold. When the flow of mana equalized, he spoke again.

"Captain! Can you hear me?"

This time there was an answer! He heard the captain's voice, along with the sounds of battle in the background.

"Alexander? Is that you? Where are you?"

"I'm at my keep. Just figured out how to make these rings work. We have defeated the drow here, but the portals don't work. I think Odin wants us each to fend for ourselves."

There was a long pause, filled only with screams and grunting and the sounds of metal on metal. Finally, the captain spoke again. *"Things are rough here, but we're holding. We held off one wave, barely. A second wave has hit us. Many of the adventurers were killed in the first wave, and are only now returning. My men are holding the wall with the help of the mages. It will be a close thing."*

"Please let me know the moment it's over. We'll send every healer we have." Alexander began to pace. Stormforge was like a second home to him. He and his original guildmates had started the game there, established their guild house, and become friends of the realm. Now its citizens were being killed and there was nothing he could do. And at this point, even if he and his players rode for the city, he doubted they'd get there in time to be useful.

"AAAAARGH!" Alexander shouted at the room around him. He kept trying to tell himself the citizens who were dying in these battles were just bits of code. But it wasn't working. His mind treated this world as being just as real as the world outside the pods. His adrenaline was pumping, his brain telling him to get into the fight!

Looking up at the ceiling, he said, "GM1, we need to talk about this immersion. Or, I guess, the sync level. Maybe put some kind of governor on it. I don't think whatever level I'm at is healthy."

Sitting at the desk in his study, he tried to think about anything other than the battle happening at the walls of Stormforge. When that failed, he imagined ways that he might help. A nuke would be good. Or at the very least some grenades.

A thought struck him. He removed a few of the larger diamonds from inventory. Holding one in his hand, he filled it with Wizard's Fire. But not the standard spell. As he poured mana into the gem, he imagined the fire being so hot that it would melt stone. Turn flesh to ash. He focused on that heat, fanning it until it glowed white-hot. When he felt the gem push back against the flow of mana, he stopped. Opening his eyes, he found the diamond glowing with a flickering purple light.

Here was his grenade. Just like the stone he'd used to kill the abomination under the garrison tower. He could send it into the enemy force, push that last bit of mana into the gem, and loot the larger bits of whatever was left after the explosion.

But again, he couldn't go help. Growling in frustration, he shoved the stone into his inventory and got up from his chair. His thoughts were on the captain, who was clearly seeing action on the wall. And Prince Edward, who was likely on that same wall with his light cannon crews.

Not able to get out of his own head without some distraction, he went back downstairs. The orcs and minotaurs were joining the other citizens of the keep for the evening meal. There were too many to be fed in the usual dining area, so the larger kitchen and dining hall inside the mountain had been put to use as well. Alexander spotted one of the orc elders and approached him. "Good evening. You may have heard from Molgo and his people already. But I'm going to allow a small group of citizens to join us in the drow stronghold. We'll be leaving tomorrow. If you'd like to choose ten-"

He stopped talking as the elder chuckled at him and ten orc warriors got to their feet in unison. The elder said, "We heard. Warriors already chosen. They will serve you well, king."

Alexander nodded respectfully at the orcs. He wasn't surprised. "Then I will see you in the courtyard at sunrise. Be sure to get one of the dragon pins if you don't already have one."

When the meal was through, citizens began to drift from the dining areas out to the courtyard and gather 'round the obelisk. Alexander smiled to see the dragonling's banner hanging from a nearby tree branch, fluttering in the slight breeze. He took his place close to the monument, the face of which was now much more crowded with the names of sixty-one additional heroes.

He laid a hand on the monument and channeled his Light spell into the stone until it glowed slightly in the darkening evening. Not sure he had the right words, he took a few deep breaths, keeping his hand on the stone and his eyes on the ground. One last breath, and he began.

"We've been gathered here too often lately. Though we all knew this would be a dangerous place when we came here, and knew that some of us would perish, still, it is a hard price to pay. These heroes gave their lives for all of us. They were friends, brothers, cousins, neighbors. Elysians, one and all!"

The gathered crowd cheered or roared, fists and weapons thrust to the sky.

"I promised each of you I would do my best to keep you alive. And every day I strive to keep that promise. But I am not all-powerful. And I failed these Elysians today." He paused for a moment, his voice threatening to crack as tears formed in his eyes. "So I... we... will remember these people. These Elysian heroes! We mark these names in stone today, not because there is any danger of us forgetting. No, we mark these names for the grandchildren of our grandchildren! So that they might know the courage and the sacrifices of those who helped us create this nation!"

The roar of the crowd was louder, more fervent. Alexander shouted over them. "Tomorrow, we take the fight to those responsible for stealing these warriors from us! *WE* will invade *THEIR* home and teach them the price owed for these lives!"

He waited as the crowd shouted agreement and encouragement. He waited even longer for them to grow quiet in anticipation of his next words.

"But for tonight, we remember. Let us drink and share our memories of the fallen. Then drink some more!"

The crowd didn't need to be told twice. They quickly dispersed back to the outdoor dining area, where kegs were already set up. Mattie and the staff from the Ogre II were manning the taps, passing out mugs of ale and spirits.

Alone with the obelisk, his hand still resting on the glowing stone, Alexander felt a gentle shift in the breeze. Kai and Lia stepped out of the darkness of the grove. Lia placed a hand on Jules' banner and sobbed once. Kai put an arm around her for support. He bowed his head slightly to Alexander.

"This is lovely," Lia whispered. "Please, thank Lady Jules for me." She didn't take her eyes from the little green dragon in the center of the banner. Kai smiled slightly as he too gazed at the hatchling. Tears streamed down the human faces of both dragons.

Alexander felt a tug on his leg. Looking down, he was thrilled to find Fibble gazing up at him. The little goblin was crying as well. He looked from Alexander to the banner and back again. "Baby dragon is gone. Was Fibble's friend. Bad monsters took him, killed him. Worse than demons."

The pathetic little goblin's voice trembled as he spoke. Alexander couldn't resist. Dropping to his knees, he gathered their tiniest guild member into a hug. "Very bad monsters, yes. And tomorrow we're going to go and kill them. We could use a good protector." His guts twisted as he made the offer and he prayed that Fibble would decline. But he couldn't exclude the valiant little goblin without breaking his heart.

Fibble nodded his head slightly, his ears barely making one flap. "Fibble heard. Not sure what to do. Sasha and other pretty ladies need protector! But sad dragon mama and dragonlings need protector too." His face fell as he watched Lia cry softly nearby. Alexander could feel his own eyes welling up.

"You do what you think best, Fibble. You are right, the dragons need you just as much as we do. Whichever you choose, I will be proud of you." He patted Fibble's shoulder and stood back up. Pointing to the crowd, he said, "Lugs is over there. He has dwarven spirits. And he's been worried about you. You should go let him know you're okay!"

Alexander expected the easily distracted goblin to tear across the courtyard and launch himself at Lugs. The two of them were usually the life of any party. Especially when they'd been drinking.

But the little goblin healer just nodded his head and gave Alexander a half-hearted smile. "Okay. Not want Lugs to be sad too. I go help," was all he said as he walked slowly toward the celebration.

Alexander was still watching him when Kai's hand came to rest on his shoulder. He turned to find both dragons standing in front of him. Lia reached out and gathered Alexander into a hug. "We want to thank you. For trying to save our little one. Kai told me what you did. And that you gave your life trying to free him."

Alexander shook his head, the tears that had been forming earlier now falling freely. "I fear my actions may have caused his death. When I hurt the gargoyle, it squeezed harder, and..." He couldn't finish the sentence. His soul ached as he admitted to the prince and princess that he was the reason their hatchling died.

Lia sobbed once, then took a deep breath. Kai answered, "No. I saw the wounds when the gargoyle snatched him. He would have bled to death slowly. Your attack on that monster only ended his pain quickly. I will be forever grateful to you, Alexander."

The anguish eased a bit at Kai's words. Still, the guilt pushed him to ask, "I tried my best to heal the little one even as I rode the thing's back. My spells didn't work."

Kai nodded. His voice was strained as he said, "Their claws were coated with the dragon poison. Your spells had no hope of defeating that. In one so small, even if given the antidote immediately, the poison would have taken him. Damned drow and their invisible assassins!"

Alexander didn't know what to say to that, so he stood there in silence and shared their grief. After several minutes, Kai spoke again. "I cannot go with you tomorrow." He looked at Lia, and Alexander understood. Kai was needed in his roost to keep her from acting rashly in her grief. "But our very best warriors will join you. Each of them fought the drow wizards the last time they emerged from their holes."

Alexander bowed deeply to the prince and princess. "Thank you. As a king, and as a friend, if there is anything I can do for you, please. You need only ask."

"I ask that you bring me the head of the drow wizard who sent those gargoyles," Kai growled.

"And I want his heart!" Lia's voice was flat and icy cold. "I will feed it to my offspring to make them stronger."

Alexander mentally waved away the quest notifications that popped up on his UI. This wasn't the time. "Of course. We will do our best." He caught Kai's gaze and looked at him meaningfully. "And this will only be the first battle. The first stronghold. There will be many more battles before we're done."

Kai nodded his head, understanding and accepting the offer. When Lia was more stable, he would join Alexander and the others in slaughtering the drow. Alexander did not envy any enemy that faced an enraged Kai.

Lia hugged Alexander again and the two dragons disappeared from the grove. Alexander turned to head toward the dining area, only to find Jules walking toward him with a tankard in each hand. When she reached him, he accepted one of them, saying, "Lia and Kai were just here. She asked me to thank you for the banner. It made her cry, but it made her happy as well."

Jules gave him a soft smile, then leaned forward and kissed his cheek. "Good speech tonight. Better than normal. Still not great, but you're improving."

He rolled his eyes and took a drink. "The women in my life. Never let me get too full of myself," he sighed dramatically.

She took his free hand in hers and led him deeper into the grove. They found a comfortable spot at the base of one of the trees and sat down with their backs to the trunk. It smelled faintly of apple blossoms.

"You okay?" she asked, squeezing his hand.

"Nope. But I will be."

*****

Alexander was awake well before sunrise. Miraculously, so was Jules. He hadn't even had to wake her. The moment he rolled out of bed, so did she. In just a few minutes, they were geared up and headed downstairs.

They found several of the players as well as both groups of minotaurs and orcs already in the dining area. Sasha was there passing out potions and Lola was making sure every citizen had a dragon pin. Kitchen staff were passing around bowls of scrambled eggs, bacon, fruit, and biscuits. Several of them never made it past Fitz and had to return to the kitchen to reload.

Fibble was there as well, absentmindedly munching on a handful of bacon strips. He wasn't at the tables with the others. He'd moved off to sit alone against the wall near the kitchen door. His face was scrunched up in concentration, and Alexander assumed he was trying to decide whether to join the raid. He left the little guy to his musings as he made the rounds of the tables. He spoke a few words at each table, asking after his peoples' readiness.

More and more of the players filtered in over the next ten minutes. Even a few who were too low-level to join the raid showed up to see the others off.

Alexander felt as if he should make some kind of rousing speech, but after the memorial service, he didn't have it in him. Sasha solved his dilemma for him.

"Alright! As soon as the dragons join us, we're outta here! This is a raid, people! Against an enemy that wants to destroy us completely. An enemy that killed our friends yesterday! You know what that means!" She paused and looked around. Everyone was silent. The minotaurs and orcs looked confused. A few of the players snickered. Finally, Max helped her out.

"It means we kill everything that moves?" he asked in a quiet voice.

"IT MEANS WE KILL EVERYTHING THAT MOVES!" Sasha shouted back, grinning her most evil grin. There was a roar of approval from the orcs and minotaurs, and a few of the players. A small voice from the back shouted, "Gnomes rule!"

Alexander took a seat as Sasha began to break the raid members into small groups, in case they needed to split up for some reason. Each group of ten included two tanks - or a tank and a shield-bearer, at least - two healers, and various forms of damage dealers. Every group had a mixture of ranged and melee.

The dragons appeared as she was nearing the end of the assignments. One moment, they were just there. Del lead the wing of six dragons, all of whom bowed their heads in greeting. Sasha paused in her assignments and moved to speak with Del.

"How do you and your wing want to participate? I mean, I'm breaking the raid into groups. Would you like to be mixed into the groups, or a be a group of your own?"

"In the tight spaces, we would be most effective as scouts and ranged attackers. Though each of us can heal at need." Del hesitated for a moment and a smile crept across his face. "In larger open areas where we can assume our natural forms... well, each of us will be a group of our own!"

"Ha! Then in that case, we will act as support if you get all big and snarly," Sasha replied.

Alexander cautioned, "I don't want any of you killed, Del. My adventurers should take the front line in any fight. Let us absorb the damage while you and your cousins devastate from a distance."

Del growled in objection, the sound an unconscious reaction. "We shall see," was his only response. There was a deep hatred between the dragons and the drow wizards. Even more so since the murder of the royal hatchling.

Fitz crammed a plateful of breakfast into a pocket of his robe and got to his feet. "I'll be joining you. When we reach the wizard, he is mine. I will question him, then we will kill him. It won't take long. I only have three questions."

The ominous tone of Fitz's voice made more than a few of those gathered nearby shiver.

Alexander fished the portal globe tied to the stronghold quest from his bag. He handed it to Fitz, then looked around at those gathered. He had ten orcs, ten minotaurs. Six dragons – seven including Fitz. There were twenty-two players altogether, counting Alexander himself. That added up to forty-nine. Alexander looked to Fibble. All the eyes in the dining area followed his gaze.

Feeling the attention on him, Fibble looked up. Seeing everyone waiting, he pulled out his 'stick' and held it up. "Fibble help kill bad monsters!"

Sasha invited him to the raid group, now a nice round fifty members strong, as a cheer of encouragement for Fibble rang out. He puffed out his chest and waved his wand about like a rapier. Several of the players laughed and applauded.

With everyone ready, Fitz stepped to the center of the courtyard and set the portal orb down. Alexander motioned to Taylor, who was, as ever, close by. "Protect this keep. If there's an attack, call us in guild chat. Do your best to hold the fort until we return." The captain saluted with fist to chest before stepping away.

Fitz finished a long and complicated series of hand movements accompanied by a phrase, and the orb began to vibrate. A moment later, a murky purple gateway materialized above it.

Wasting no time, Brick and Lugs dove through, shields held high. Right behind them were Grumpy, Warren, Benny, and two tanks from the Antalia group. Alexander followed next, with Sasha, Lyra, Martin, and one of his healers. The others would wait for an all-clear before following.

The group found themselves in a tunnel. The feel of a great weight of stone above them pressing down suggested they were deep underground. The tunnel was pitch-black and people were stumbling into each other as they exited the portal. Alexander quickly cast a light globe to float above them.

It was a wide passage, easily twenty feet in diameter. The stone walls were nearly smooth, as was the floor. It stretched in both directions beyond the range of the globe's light. But for a few hundred feet in either direction, there were no enemies in sight. Sasha spoke into raid chat. *"Clear enough. Come on through. Scouts first. We need eyes out ahead and behind."*

Almost instantly, the dragons emerged from the portal. Del took one look in either direction and made two hand motions. A single dragon moved forward, becoming invisible as she moved. Another went the opposite direction. They waited as the rest of the players moved through, followed by the orcs and minotaurs. No one spoke. Only the occasional rattle of armor or creak of leather broke the silence.

Based on game mechanics, Alexander assumed that the direction the portal was facing when they came through was 'forward' – meaning it led toward the stronghold. He said as much in raid chat. Several of the others nodded in agreement.

The dragon who had gone out 'behind' them was the first to return. He reported nothing but empty tunnel going back a quarter mile. Alexander, not taking any chances, faced the tunnel in that direction and used his Earth Mover skill to raise a wall that blocked the tunnel. He made it two feet thick. Something large could break through, but he and his people would hear it coming.

As he finished the wall, the other dragon scout reported in. *"There is a chamber approximately one half-mile up the corridor. Looks like a way station. There were two drow. They did not have an opportunity to report my presence."*

Brick chuckled at that last bit. "Remind me not ta piss off our dragon friends here."

With no reason to split up yet, the entire raid formed up and moved down the tunnel. The tanks were all up front, except Grumpy, who volunteered to bring up the rear, just in case. Melee fighters followed the tanks, then healers. Behind the healers were archers and casters, including Fitz. Helga had elected to walk with Grumpy at the rear.

The noise increased as the group moved, ironclad shoes striking stone, weapons shifting with the movement, but no one spoke. Each of them was preparing themselves in their own way. Psyching themselves up for the fight to come. All except Fibble, who walked next to Jules, holding her hand as he nibbled on a cookie. He didn't seem to be thinking about much of anything.

It only took them a few minutes to cover the half-mile and reach the chamber where the scout had left two drow bodies. She was gone, having already moved ahead to scout further. Max and Beatrix each looted a body, shaking their heads to say there was nothing interesting.

Alexander looked around the room. The light from the globe illuminated the whole space. It was roughly circular, with alcoves cut into the walls all the way around. A rolled blanket was placed in each alcove, obviously meant as beds. There was an indentation in the center of the floor, burn marks around it suggesting it was a fire pit. The ceiling was only about ten feet high, and flat.

Sasha spoke up, her voice causing some folks to jump as it echoed around the room. "This suggests that the stronghold is a long way away. Why would you provide a way station within even a few miles of your home?"

"Mebbe it's a guard barracks. The dragon did find two drow here. Outpost guards?" Brick offered.

After Fitz and the other dragons assured them that there were no secret doors or hidden caches, the tanks led the way further down the tunnel. Alexander kept the light globe floating above the center of the group. The light extended far enough ahead of the tanks for them to react to any oncoming foes, while still allowing those who had it to use their dark vision.

They were maybe another quarter mile down the tunnel when the scout reported in again. "*Branch in the tunnel. Natural chamber with three other exits. One directly across is the same size as this tunnel. Two smaller ones to the left.*"

Sasha called, "Let's pick up the pace! Everybody up for a jog?"

The tanks began to trot forward, their shields on their backs so as not to tire their arms. The rest of the group followed at pace, quickly eating up the ground on their way to the chamber. The scout met them at the mouth of the tunnel. As soon as they came to a halt, she said, "Nothing living in the chamber. No sounds, except you lot crashing down the tunnel." She grinned at the tanks, whose plate gear made most of the noise.

Sasha looked to Alexander. "Ignore the side tunnels and keep going?"

He shook his head. "Let's check them out, just in case. Break off a group for each and the rest of us will wait here."

Sasha quickly organized everyone. "Group two, left side tunnel. Group three, the other one. Follow them for ten minutes. If you find nothing, turn around. We'll seal it off here and worry about it later. If you come in contact with enemy you can't handle, call out and retreat as quickly as you can without exposing your backs."

The two groups split off and moved out. Group two consisted of Lugs, Warren, Lyra, Beatrix, two orcs - one of whom was a tank - two minotaurs, as well as a healer and an archer from Antalia. They made their way at a slow walk toward the leftmost of the smaller exits and disappeared. A light globe created by Fitz followed above them.

Group three included Grumpy, Helga, Pollock and his guys, Misty, a minotaur tank, Benny, and Martin. They were just a second or two behind the other group, and quickly faded into the darkness of their tunnel. Alexander used Earth Mover to raise several long stone benches from the ground and the rest of the group relaxed. All except the dragon scout, who winked at Alexander before exiting into the large tunnel ahead.

Less than two minutes passed before the sounds of battle echoed from group two's tunnel. Lugs' voice came through raid chat seconds later. *"Bunch of goblins. Maybe a hundred of them. Low-level, in their 30's, but the little buggers are quick!"*

Sasha ordered, "*Retreat back here. We'll trap them and wipe them out.*" She looked down at Fibble, standing nearby. "Are you going to be okay with fighting other goblins?"

Fibble nodded his head. "Not my clan. Greystone my clan."

The main group all moved toward the tunnel as the sounds of fighting grew closer. They formed a semicircle around the entrance, leaving space in the middle for group two to join the line. A few goblin arrows came whistling out of the entrance, shots that had gone high over even Lugs' head. Half a minute later, the group started to emerge, backing out of the tunnel. Lugs was last, bashing his shield against a tide of the small green monsters.

As soon as he was clear of the entrance, Sasha cast her aoe Thorn Trap. With her recent level increases and near-constant use of the spell in battle, her skill level had increased greatly. The spell now covered an area thirty feet wide, and the thickness and strength of the vines had nearly doubled from what they'd been when she first learned the spell. The thorns were now each three inches long.

The first thirty or so goblins charged right into the trap, the vines snagging their legs, then working their way upward to wrap their bodies and penetrate their skin with thorns. The screaming and whimpering alerted those behind, who managed to stop inside the tunnel. Alexander cast Wizard's Fire on the thorns, and the pitch of the little monsters' screams rose as they burned. The archers in the group sent arrows into burning goblin bodies, quieting several of the screams. The casters finished off the rest. It wasn't much of a battle. As they saw their brethren die so easily, the remaining goblins turned and fled.

As the bodies were looted, Alexander raised a wall to block off the tunnel. He didn't think the goblins would dare return, but they might. When he completed the wall, he turned to find Fibble standing among the bodies. He nudged one with his fuzzy slipper-covered toe.

"You okay, buddy?" He knelt down next to the little goblin healer.

"Goblins stupid. Attack strong clan. Dragons. Lots die for nothing."

Alexander thought it over for a minute. Fibble had been growing in leaps and bounds as he leveled from the various dungeons and battles that they'd dragged him into. While he was never going to be a genius, he had certainly grown smarter in their time together.

"I know, buddy. But most goblins are not as smart as you. Or as strong. They hide in caves and fight and eat, and that's all. You've had adventures and learned many things."

Fibble blinked a few times, then nodded slightly. Only one ear slapped him in the face. "Fibble do big magic! Learn tricks from Hermsey! Learn to dance from Lugs!"

Alexander chuckled at the suddenly-enthusiastic little goblin. "That's right. You are the *best* goblin on Io!"

Fibble stuck his chest out again. Turning from Alexander, he marched over to Sasha and Lainey. "Fibble *best* goblin!"

The two ladies both knelt to hug him. "You certainly are!" Sasha agreed. "Our protector! We would be lost without you!"

Jules looped her arm through Alexander's as he stood up. "That was sweet. We were worried this fight would bother him. You're a good daddy." She squeezed his arm as he stammered.

"I… I am *not* his daddy. Sasha and Lainey adopted him. Let them be – I'm not." He saw the grin on her face and the twinkle in her eyes. "Very funny." His look of surprise turned to mischief. "You're getting a tickling for that when we get back!"

"Nooo!" Just as quickly as she'd appeared, she disappeared. A moment later, he spotted her behind Lainey, smiling down at Fibble.

The other group returned from their tunnel, having found nothing. A few empty rooms, but no monsters of any kind. Alexander sealed off that tunnel as well and they moved on. Following the dragon scout into the much larger main tunnel, they moved at a brisk pace.

The tunnel sloped down, and even seemed to curve in a very gradual spiral to the left. Alexander used his Earth Sense to try to get a picture of what was around them. But the spell had a limited range and he was able to see nothing but the tunnel itself and surrounding rock.

It was a good ten minutes before the scout reported in. *"I have reached the stronghold. Single structure cut into a cavern wall. Stone gates. It's smaller than the Elysian keep."*

The group attempted to move more quietly now that they knew the enemy location was close by. Sound echoed through the tunnel and they wanted to give as little warning of their presence as possible.

Alexander, Fitz, and Brick cast Mage Sight on everyone in the group except the dragons, who didn't need it. Then Alexander extinguished the light globe. They moved forward at a walk, tanks in the front as usual. The dragons moved out to form a sort of ring around the group. Alexander didn't like it, but didn't argue.

When they finally caught up to the scout, she whispered, "I counted six patrols roaming the cavern. All drow. There are four trolls chained up not far from the entrance. They appear to be trying to break the trolls' will and subjugate them."

Del added, "There are likely to be more drow we can't see. We'll smell them when we get close enough. But be prepared."

The tunnel began to glow with a dull red light as they approached the stronghold's cavern. It grew slightly brighter the closer they got, though the low light couldn't be considered bright in surface terms. Barely enough to see by for a normal humanoid, Fitz explained.

"The drow use slaves. Lower races like orcs and goblins with limited dark vision. The light is to keep them from crashing into things all the time."

They reached the end of the tunnel and crouched low to the ground. Ahead, they could see open ground that stretched maybe a hundred yards to the stronghold gates. Drow walked the perimeter, the patrols spaced out so that one was always in sight as they made their way around.

Sasha used raid chat rather than whisper. *"The patrols are far enough apart that we can take them one at a time. The question is whether those at the gate will notice them go missing."*

The scout waved a hand and grinned at her. She pointed toward the gate. *"I have been considering this while I waited for you. I believe I can distract the guards at the gate and get the gates open without anyone realizing we're here."*

"Then let us spread out," Del answered. *"The rest of our wing will move around the perimeter. When your distraction begins, each of us will remove one of the patrols. The main group here will take the last patrol, then charge the gate. We'll meet there."*

Sasha wasn't about to argue with the dragons' plan. She just shrugged and nodded her agreement. All six dragons faded into stealth mode and spread out. Alexander and company simply sat and waited.

Less than two minutes later, the scout appeared behind the trolls who were chained near the gate. Alexander could see her bend down, then heard the squeal of rending metal. In seconds, the dragon had snapped the chains, freeing the trolls. She growled something to them and pointed at the gate, then faded from sight again.

Happy to get some revenge against the drow who had tortured and imprisoned them, the massive trolls plodded their way toward the stone doors that blocked entry into the stronghold. The drow guards had already sounded an alarm and were moving to intercept the trolls. One of them cast a light spell that burst directly in the trolls' faces, temporarily blinding them.

The gates opened and a score of drow warriors rushed out to surround the trolls. They carried long pikes and ranged weapons, as well as several heavy ropes. As one, they began to bombard the trolls with spells and physical attacks.

Alexander and company rushed forward. There we no battle cries – they wanted to remain unseen as long as possible. The trolls and their drow captors stood right between the raid group and the gates. The two drow on patrol directly in front of them had both turned to view the action at the gate. They were cut down instantly, every member of the group with ranged abilities attacking at once. Beatrix paused to loot the bodies as they passed, her tiny legs pumping to catch up when she was done.

Sasha called out, "Take out the drow. Avoid the trolls. Let's help them get inside the gates. Cause some trouble for us!" She was grinning as she ran, imagining the havoc the angry trolls would inflict.

The drow were focused enough on the now-enraged trolls that the raid's tanks were nearly upon them before they were spotted. Brick, Lugs, and Grumpy all activated Shield Rush at the same moment. The three of them flew forward, shields high, and smashed into the drow. Six of the enemy were knocked off their feet and tossed into the center of the circle with the trolls.

The monsters, surprised by the attack, recovered quickly and gleefully stomped the stunned drow into paste. They roared in defiance and charged toward the gates.

With nearly a third of their number dead in seconds and an enemy force twice their size charging toward them, the remaining drow attempted to retreat. Turning their backs on the fight, they dashed toward the gate.

Six dragons in humanoid form appeared in front of the stone doors. The drow skidded to a halt. One of them produced a horn and managed a single note before a blast of magic from one of the dragons caused his head to explode. Alexander and the other ranged players all hit them with spells as they continued to charge forward. The orcs and minotaurs picked up speed, moving ahead of the casters and even the tanks. Swords and axes drawn, they mowed through the overwhelmed drow with little effort.

Behind the dragons, chaos had erupted. Defenders were scrambling toward the gate, trying to push the massive stone doors closed. The scout dragon roared and began to transform. Alexander immediately recognized her as the one who had been injured and knocked from the sky by the gargoyles during the battle.

She grew to maybe half her natural size, then plunged through the gates. One foreclaw ripped a stone door from its hinges and flung it across the courtyard inside. The multi-ton door bounced and skidded, crushing drow, orcs, and hobgoblins in its path. A blast of blue fire burned more of them to curled, crispy husks as they fled.

In moments, the area immediately inside the gate was clear of all but the dead. Several of the party members leveled up as the dragon reverted to her humanoid form.

The trolls, frightened by the appearance of the dragon, had frozen in place. A word from her, and they roared in unison. She stepped aside and bowed slightly, sweeping her hand ahead of them as if inviting them inside. They trundled past her, picking up discarded weapons from among the dead. Alexander and company watched as they burst through the inner doors of the keep and began to slaughter everything in their path.

Each troll stood at least ten feet tall, with wide shoulders and long arms. Their skin was tougher than leather, but not quite stone. They jabbed spears and swung swords with abandon even as defenders bombarded them with spells and projectiles of their own.

For nearly half a minute, the natural tanks shrugged off the damage. Moving forward, they cut down their tormentors left and right. They threw spears that passed through two and three defenders before stopping. As they discarded one weapon, they simply stooped and picked up another from a corpse. In some instances, they picked up entire corpses and flung them forward.

Eventually though, the massed attacks from the drow and their servants inside overcame the monsters. One by one, they dropped, taking as many of their enemies with them as they could.

Sasha didn't give the defenders a chance to recover. "Inside!" she shouted. The tanks rushed forward, right up to the back of the last troll as it died. Lugs shoved it forward with his shield, giving it a little extra momentum to fall on a couple of orcs who'd gotten too close.

The tanks leapt over their fallen allies and formed up, interlocking their shields and creating a semicircular wall. The rest of the party grouped up behind the wall and began killing. The melee players and orcs bunched up behind the tanks, stabbing and slashing over top of the shields at any enemy who was within reach. The minotaurs stood behind, each of them having picked up a spear. They waited for openings and jabbed at hobgoblins, or picked out a caster target and hurled their weapons to impale them. The tall warriors each held a shield as well and made an effective screen for the ranged attackers.

Alexander and the casters targeted the enemy casters first. Healers were rare; Alexander only spotted two. They died quickly and Sasha directed attacks at the enemy mages.

One of the minotaurs went down, a dark missile having struck him in the face. It was one of the shit-weasel spells. The worm tore at the minotaur's face, trying to penetrate his thick skull to get to the brain.

A dragon stepped forward and grabbed hold of the worm with his bare hand. Squeezing tightly, he caused the thing to burst. Sasha and the healers hit the minotaur en masse, bringing him back to full health. He shook off the shock of the attack and took up his place in the line.

Two of the orcs had fallen, but were still alive. The healers worked on them as two other orcs pulled them back off the line. Brick was singing a song and the tanks were shoving their shields forward and swinging their weapons to the rhythm. There was too much noise for Alexander to hear the song, but he was sure it was something classic and wholly inappropriate.

He looked around the courtyard as the tanks pushed in and filled the inner doorway. "This is too easy," he said out loud. Looking up at the windows above, he expected archers or mages to appear and rain down hell upon them. What he saw instead made his gut clench.

Gargoyles.

Chapter 14

Shit Happens

All around the perimeter, set on ledges above or to the sides of the windows, sat stone gargoyles. Not one of them had moved, and Alexander almost convinced himself they were just stone carvings. Until one of them blinked.

"Del!" Alexander shouted above the noise of the battle. "Gargoyles! Above us!"

Every dragon in the group stopped what they were doing and turned to face Alexander. Following his gaze, they took in the thirty or so statues, whose eyes began to glow. Almost in unison, the monsters began to move as they faded from sight.

Del and his wing moved to the back of the group, facing outward toward the new threat. Alexander quickly cast Wizard's Fire on the last one he could see, just as it was about to disappear completely. The damage from the fire interrupted its stealth ability and the thing screamed at them.

Three dragons immediately raised a hand and shot the thing with bolts of blue magic. Everywhere the bolts hit the gargoyle's body, chunks of it burst into sprays of blood and bone. The spray from that one partially coated two more who had been behind it and the dragons began blasting at those as well.

Del grunted and fell onto his back as one of the invisible monsters dove into him. It became visible as it dug into the dragon's chest with its talons. The dragon calmly reached up and grabbed its arms with his hands. A twist of his elbows snapped both the gargoyle's arms. Releasing the broken left arm, Del reached up and ripped the throat from the creature crouching over him as if it were nothing more than tissue paper.

Holding the dead thing by the throat, he got back to his feet and tossed it into the air. It collided with another gargoyle who had been hovering there. Magic blasts immediately struck that one as well.

Two more dragons went down, the weight of at least one gargoyle slamming into them. Blood flew as more of the creatures ripped into them while they were down.

Fitz struck the butt end of his staff on the stone and a bubble of force rippled outward from him in all directions. As it passed through the gargoyles, it negated their stealth ability. The twenty-plus remaining monsters were now visible, and taken by surprise. The dragons and a few of the players took shots at each of them to prevent them from recovering their stealth. Lainey shot Shock Arrows into several of the ones atop the dragons in rapid succession, causing them to seize up and drop to the stone floor.

Alexander held out his enchanted ring and called out, "Stone Golem!" The golem that arose this time was a true monster. Fifteen feet tall with hands the size of wagon wheels, it turned and bowed its head to him, awaiting instructions.

"Kill the gargoyles!" He pointed at the ones on the ground who were just recovering from Lainey's stuns. Without hesitation, the golem turned and moved past the dragons, who made room. It reached the grounded gargoyles as they began to leap back into the air. Grabbing two by their legs, it began to thrash them around. First, the golem slammed them back to the ground, then into each other. Wings and long bones cracked with each impact. The golem advanced, slamming first one and then the other into a nearby wall. That finished both of them.

Hurling the corpses into the air one at a time, it knocked another down, its wing broken from the impact. The golem stomped on its chest, killing it instantly. This one too, it hurled into the air, but the other gargoyles had gotten wise and dodged away.

Del shouted, "Knock them down, let the golem finish them!"

The six dragons began to operate in pairs. One would call out a target and both would hit it with magic. They focused on crippling the wings, which were the biggest targets anyway. As each of the monsters fell to the ground or dropped within its reach, the golem finished them. Limbs were torn from the bodies. Wings were pulled off and used to swat others hovering in range.

More than two dozen of the creatures perished before the rest lost heart and fled through the outer gate. The dragon scout, the one who'd been so badly injured by the gargoyles at the keep, began to give chase. But Del called her back. "We can find them later. When we have finished off the wizard."

She nodded and turned back to the battle still raging inside the structure. Sasha cast her biggest heals on the dragons, all of whom had taken some damage during the fight. But even those only returned a small fraction of the dragons' health. Del smiled at her. "We appreciate the thought, but we are capable of healing ourselves. Preserve your mana for your fellow citizens."

As if to prove his point, he cast a heal on himself that raised his health bar from about eighty percent to a hundred percent. Sasha's eyes widened. "That had to have been… thirty thousand HP? At least! You have *got* to teach me that!"

The leader of the dragon wing smiled at her. "When you are ready, child. When you are ready."

The rest of the raid party had pushed further into the interior of the building. Past the doorway, the room opened up to a considerable size. The far wall was maybe thirty yards distant and the walls to either side were lined with columns, behind which enemies were hiding, popping out to prosecute ranged attacks here and there.

A force of at least a hundred dark orcs and hobgoblins were pressing at the tanks, who were having to spread out as they advanced further into the room. Sasha saw this and moved to correct it.

"Tanks! Hold. Six steps back toward the doors. Let's use the walls while we can. I don't want them to be able to surround us!"

The line of tanks obediently began to step backwards, still bashing and slashing at the enemy as they closed ranks in a smaller half-circle. Shields locked together as they came to a stop. Lugs was in the center, his massive tower shield anchoring the wall. The others spread out on either side in a line that curved back toward the walls on either side of the door.

"Ranged! Focus on the assholes who keep popping out from behind the columns. Melee, keep doing what you're doing. Grind them down!"

The tanks were all taking damage, but the healers were keeping up. A quick survey showed Alexander that they were all still above sixty percent mana. He knew Sasha had packed plenty of mana potions, so he wasn't worried.

Helga went down as a dark spell enveloped her. Alexander moved in her direction but Benny beat him to it. The light of a holy spell fell from the ceiling and dispersed the darkness. It also healed Helga, who was squirming in pain on the ground. The dark cloud had been made of acid, and it had eaten at her exposed flesh. Two orc citizens who had been too close to her suffered as well.

The healers went to work, cleansing the poison, then healing the damage. In less than a minute, all three were back in the fight. Though their armor and weapons were pitted from the acid. All except Helga's Legendary sword, which seemed unaffected as she stabbed over top of the tanks' shields into a particularly large hobgoblin's face. With a primal scream, she levered her long arms and lifted the blade. It temporarily lifted her victim as well before its skull gave way and a spray of blood and brain covered everyone nearby.

She shouted, "Lugs! Make some room!" and triggered some barbarian berserker rage ability Alexander hadn't seen before.

Lugs looked behind him and his eyes got wide. "Oh, shit!" he shouted. "Shield Bash! Now!"

Brick and Grumpy, on either side of Lugs, triggered their abilities at the same time he did. Lugs alone was over a thousand pounds of ogre flesh, armor, and shield smashing into the enemy line. Every foe in an eight-foot swathe in front of the tanks went ass over teakettle, knocked backward several feet. Immediately, Lugs stepped back and turned sideways, pulling his shield close to his body and dropping to one knee. Then he tilted the shield like a ramp.

Helga took two steps. The first foot landed on stone, the second on Lugs' shield. She propelled herself up and over the ogre, screaming in rage as her sword swung in a wide arc in front of her.

The orcs and hobgoblins in front saw a giant woman with blood-red eyes covered in blood and brains flying toward them. Her sword glinted in the red ambient light as it carved off pieces of their comrades. She was unstoppable. Landing amidst the still-recovering enemy, she slashed and stabbed in a frenzy. Completely disregarding any kind of defense, she took multiple wounds herself as she used her incredible strength to power her blade through body after body.

In ten seconds, not a single living creature remained in a six-foot wide radius in front of her. The terrified enemy fighters still standing closest to her had pushed back against those behind them, getting clear of her blade's reach or dying in the attempt. She snarled at them, breathing heavily as her own blood dripped from multiple wounds. Three separate heals struck her at the same time and the wounds began to close.

"Cowards!! I am but one barbarian! There are scores of you! Come taste my blade!" She jumped over the pile of bodies in front of her, taking out three hobgoblins as she landed. Again, the enemy retreated from the blood-soaked madwoman. She spat blood onto the floor in front of them. "Bah!" As her ability's time wore off, she came to her senses. Lugs beckoned to her and she turned and strode purposefully back through the line of tanks.

Not one enemy tried to take advantage when she turned her back.

Using the space that Helga had created, Sasha cast her Thorn Trap on the center of the enemy force. Dozens of the dark soldiers were caught in the thorns as Alexander lit them up with Wizard's Fire. The smell of roasted meat accompanied the screams of the trapped fighters. Others moved around them and charged into the line of tanks again.

Brick smiled. "Let's use the fire!" He counted loudly to three and the tanks all shoved forward two steps. The mass of enemies was pushed back and the ones at the back got knocked into the burning thorns, catching fire themselves.

The tanks all stepped back to their previous positions and waited for more monsters to fill in the gap. They hacked with sword and axe, smashed with shield and hammer for a full minute, then Brick began to count again.

"Huah!" the tanks shouted as Brick hit three and they all shoved. Again, the strength of the tanks pushing in unison moved the monsters back and caused more of them to catch fire.

Sasha didn't re-cast the Thorn Trap, as her mana was getting low and she needed to focus on heals. The Wizard's Fire burned down the thorns and the monsters trapped in them before Brick and the tanks could take advantage for a third time.

Grumpy screamed and fell backward, a shit-weasel spell having struck him in the face. The nose guard on his helmet had stopped the thing from burrowing directly into his face on impact. But now it was trying to crawl down his throat.

The dwarf abruptly stopped screaming and clamped his jaw shut on the thing. He bit down hard, blood erupting from his mouth as the front end of the worm dug at his flesh. Grumpy began to choke on chunks of his own gums and tongue.

Heals erupted over his head as he growled with pain and effort. He squeezed his jaw shut with all his might, trying to bite the evil thing in half. But its skin was tough, and the worm was made of mostly muscle and teeth.

Just as he was tiring and about to lose his battle, Lugs grabbed hold of the section that still stuck out beyond Grumpy's teeth. When he had a firm hold, he shouted, "Let go!" and pulled.

Grumpy unclenched his jaw as Lugs yanked the nasty thing out. His hand bled from the spikes along its spine, but he held on. Grumpy's tongue erupted from his mouth as the worm came free. Lugs nearly puked at the sight but managed to slam the thing to the ground, stunning it. A stomp from his massive ogre foot ended the threat.

The momentary distraction of the two tanks opened a hole and a squad of orcs charged through. They formed a sort of wedge, pushing Brick and another tank farther aside as they came at Grumpy and Lugs from behind. Grumpy took a wickedly-barbed spear to the back, its point erupting from the joint between his breastplate and spaulder. The orc on the other end of the spear yanked it back and the barb caught on the edge of the dwarf's breastplate, preventing it from doing even more extensive damage on its way out.

Grumpy calmly put his axe away and took hold of the spear tip in his gauntleted hand. When he had a firm grip, he spun his body, his shield smashing into the orc as the spear's shaft was ripped from its hands. Grumpy roared in pain but managed to pull the spear tip forward several inches. Then he snapped the shaft against the edge of his breastplate.

One of the Elysian orcs behind the tank observed all of this, and with a nod of respect he took hold of the shaft and quickly withdrew it from Grumpy's back. The dwarf nearly lost consciousness from the pain.

Heals rained down on him as he used his shield to prop himself up. He was dizzy from blood loss. Heals could close wounds and stop bleeding, but they could not replenish lost blood. The only ways to do that were to sit and wait for time to take care of it, or eat and drink. Grumpy pulled a health potion from his bag and chugged it down as he walked toward the rear of their party. Then he removed some of Sasha's roasted boar meat. It would replenish him as well as give him regen buffs. Five minutes or so, and he'd be back in the fight.

Lugs and the other tanks closed ranks, taking a step backward to shorten the line they had to cover. They were all taking damage, the sheer number of the enemy troops hacking and stabbing at them taking its toll. The healers behind them were already gulping their first round of mana potions as the ranged damage dealers poured it on.

Del approached Alexander at his position among the casters, busily casting Wizard's Fire at locations where the enemy was thickest, other than right in front of the tanks. The flames quickly spread from one victim to the next. The fire alone wouldn't kill any of them. But it would weaken them.

"We have dealt with the gargoyles," Del reported. "Let us seal the doors behind us and take the lead. We can clear this room of the wizard's servants in just moments."

Alexander said, "Yes, please seal the door. But I don't want you out front. A lucky hit might kill one of you. And since this is just the front door, I have a feeling we're going to need every dragon we have later on."

Beatrix must have found a source of water somewhere, because a series of waves rose up and engulfed the monsters in the room. Immediately, Misty began to freeze the now-soaked enemy fighters. The layers of ice that formed on the monsters didn't hold them still. But it did slow their movements enough that the players on the front lines were able to work their way forward across about a fourth of the room. They killed everything in sight, the enemy fighters too slow to defend themselves, then retreated back to the door and reformed their arc of a shield wall.

The room was hushed, the din of battle dying down as the defenders saw a quarter of their number slaughtered in moments. As they hesitated to rush forward into the meat grinder, a group of drow mages appeared at the opposite end of the room. Alexander Inspected the closest of them.

Drow Wizard's Acolyte
Level 90
Health: 50,000/50,000

There were seven of them in total. The monsters at the back of the room gave them space as they moved forward. As they reached spellcasting range, they spread out in a line. Each of them made an identical series of hand gestures. Alexander could see their mouths moving, but couldn't hear the words.

Apparently, the dragons could. Several of them growled out spells of their own, trying to beat the drow to the completion of their spells.

They weren't fast enough.

The drow finished their spell in unison, thrusting their hands out toward the invading raid party. A nasty black cloud descended upon the entire line of tanks. It smelled of infection and decay. In seconds, the tanks were screaming, then coughing. With each cough, they inhaled more of the cloud's substance.

Sasha was screaming at the healers to target the tanks via their UIs since they couldn't see the darkness. Heals began to land on the tanks, but not fast enough. Their health bars were steadily dropping.

The dragons finished their spells and a blue mist rose up around the group of mages, as well as a large number of the monsters surrounding them. A moment later, the mist turned to a blue flame. The same flame that heated the dragon forges.

The drow didn't even have time to scream as their bodies were consumed and rendered down to ash. A score or more of the orcs who'd been protecting them disappeared into ash clouds as well.

With the death of the acolytes, the dark cloud faded quickly. But the damage was done. The tanks all lay on the floor. Pools of vomit and blood surrounded them as they continued to cough out their insides.

The healers began casting Cleanse on them as quickly as possible, followed by focused heals. A few of the tanks staggered to their feet, but the enemy force was now pressing across the corpse-covered gap in a wave of spears and swords.

Fitz and Alexander began casting Wizard's Fire on the corpses. A semicircle of fire rose up in front of the tanks as the flames spread from body to body. The enemy was halted, at least temporarily.

Two of the player tanks had been sent to respawn. The healers had done their best, but the damage from the cloud was severe, and it had hit too many too fast. Another two citizen tanks had been killed as well. One orc, one minotaur. Sasha made the decision not to resurrect them. They had a long way to go, and among their group only Brick, Benny, and Martin could rez. They might need those three chances for a healer during a battle, or some other key member.

The dead tanks left gaping holes in the line as the remainder of their comrades regained their feet and hefted their shields. Once again, they all took a few steps back toward the wall. Defending a smaller piece of floor, they could tighten up their lines and close the gaps.

As the Wizard's Fire consumed the corpses and began to run out of fuel, a battle-enraged orc attempted to jump through the flames. He was too early and his armor and skin were set ablaze as he passed through.

Screaming, he fell and rolled forward, lighting more corpses on fire in the process. His allies smartly held back after observing his fate. His screaming continued until Max used his Multi-Shot skill to blast him in the face with five arrows at once. The impact didn't leave much of the orc's head intact.

Grumpy rejoined the line of remaining tanks, who were now all back on their feet. Several of them had leveled after the deaths of the acolytes, their bodies brought back to peak condition and full health. One of those being Lugs, who roared out a challenge to the forces facing him.

A deep, resonating sound vibrated its way through the stronghold. A horn of some kind, blown deep in the depths. Immediately, every orc and hobgoblin in the room went silent. A moment later, they fled. Turning their backs on the raid party, they sprinted for the nearest exit. The last of them didn't bother closing the doors behind them, just disappeared as the raid members listened to the sounds of their running steps fade into the darkness.

"Ha!" Brick slapped Lugs' belly. "Ye scared 'em right outta the room with yer hollerin'!"

There was muted laughter among the group at the dwarf's quick-thinking quip. At the same time, most of the tanks just dropped where they stood, sitting on the floor and trying to catch their breath. A few of the melee fighters and healers did the same. Many pulled out food of one kind or another and began to eat.

"Any chance they'll just keep running and we won't have to fight them later?" Max asked hopefully.

Sasha shook her head. "They were told to retreat. Somebody down there will throw them back at us later. Probably when we're most vulnerable. Use them to surround us or something."

"Well, thank ye fer that!" Brick laid down on the stone floor, one hand up in the air to wave at Sasha. "Ye couldn't just let Lugs have his minute o' glory? That were a damn scary growl he cut loose there."

Lugs, who was sitting nearby, rolled over onto one butt-cheek and released a tremendous fart in Brick's direction. "I got yer cut loose right here!"

"Bah! Agh! Ye giant stink-bomber! What the hell 'ave ye been eatin'?" the dwarf blustered as he tried to roll away from the pollution. Lugs just chuckled and patted his belly. Most of the orcs began to roll around on the floor, finding much humor in the exchange. Followed up quickly by several 'pull my finger' mimes around the group.

Jules moved to stand behind Alexander, as if he could somehow protect her from the cloud of smell that was surely headed their way.

After a ten minute rest, during which Beatrix, Max, and the others looted the monster corpses, Sasha called everyone back to their feet. "They know we're here. They know this place, and we don't. They outnumber us by a *lot*. The smart thing would be to stop now and regroup. Maybe come back with a larger group."

Her comment was greeted with silence. Until Max said, "We hardly ever do the smart thing." When he got some nods and grunts of agreement, he shouted, "Are we gonna be smart!?"

"NO!!!" came the resounding answer. Lainey snorted.

Sasha couldn't help but grin a bit herself. "Okay, idiots. We'll keep going. The doors behind us are sealed. I see three exits from this room. Anybody notice any more as our enemies fled?"

There was a general round of head-shaking. Del spoke up. "There are just the three exits."

Sasha took the dragon's word for it. "Okay, so we have door number one…"

Max moved toward the left-hand door and stuck his head through. "Long straight hallway. Can't see the other end."

Lainey was already moving to the second door. When she'd peered inside, she said, "Another room. Much smaller. Door on the other side leads out to a hall, but all I can see is the wall on the other side."

Jules took the third door. "Stairs. Going down. I hear… something. Thumping."

"Ooh! I vote for the thumping!" Lugs leaned toward the right hand door without quite taking a step.

Shaking her head again, Sasha said, "Alright, thumping it is. Alexander? Can you seal off the other two?"

Alexander began to seal off the left-hand door and Fitz took care of the middle one. In just a few seconds, both doors were blocked by a thick stone wall. Sasha pointed to the right-hand door and Lugs very nearly skipped in that direction, his enormous ogre belly wobbling as he moved. Fibble, with a very similarly-shaped pot belly on a much smaller scale, jogged after him.

As the group moved toward the stairs, several of the orcs lifted hobgoblin bodies and carried them along. Sasha and several of the players looked askance at their comrades, whispering queries to each other. Finally, Fibble stopped and looked behind him. When he saw the orcs carrying the bodies, he nodded his head once in approval.

"Good idea. Bring food. Could be long, long way down."

Jules' eyes grew wide as she whispered to Alexander, "They're not really going to…"

He shook his head. "I don't think so."

One of the orcs in front laughed at Fibble. "Har! Not food. We go down stairs. Old trick our masters teach us when fighting inside. Need to go down? Already know enemies down there? Throw bodies down first. Surprise them, maybe hurt them. Then you follow!"

"That's friggin' genius!" Max grinned at the orcs. Molgo agreed and, with a grunt, lifted a body of his own. Each of the minotaurs did the same. Max laughed. "Awww yeah. We're gonna make it rain!"

Sasha motioned for them to proceed to the stairway, where Lugs was already sticking his head through the door and looking down the stairs. "It's getting louder. The thumping!" He sounded like a kid shaking a gift to guess what was inside.

Alexander, inspired by the orcs, had an idea. "Hang on, guys. Is it a curved stair? Or straight?"

Jules answered first. "Straight."

Alexander grinned. "Let's give them more than bodies to worry about." Using his Earth Mover, he pulled up a block of stone from the ground. It stood about five feet high and wide. "Brick, if you don't mind?" He looked at the stone, then at the stair, and waggled his eyebrows at the dwarf.

"Bwahaha! I get what yer layin' down!" The dwarf laid hands on the block and began to smooth the corners. In two minutes, he had turned the block into a five-foot high, nearly-round boulder.

One of the dragons said, "Allow me," and placed his hands on it. He gave what looked like a gentle shove and the stone ball began to roll toward the stair.

Lugs moved out of the way, a smile on his face. "I remember this movie!"

The others stood by and listened as the stone rolled across the landing and down onto the stairs. It rolled gently at first. Then it bounced once. Then again, higher. It hit the ceiling of the stairwell and crashed back down. Off-center now, it began to bounce off the walls as it picked up speed. They could no longer hear the thumping as the crashing stone drowned it out.

As the stone continued down and the crashing sounds became quieter, screams were mixed in. A loud roar was cut short, presumably as the stone projectile silenced whatever beast was challenging it. A second later, Alexander and nearly everyone else in the room leveled up.

Fibble was the lowest-level among them. He received several new levels at once, moaning and holding his tummy, falling on his butt as his eyes rolled up in his head. Alexander was reminded that he needed to work with the tiny goblin so that he could choose what attributes to raise with all the points he was accumulating.

Sasha gave them all a few moments to work with their character sheets, then prodded them along. They began to descend the stairs. Brick took the lead, with Lugs and Grumpy right behind. The others followed in roughly their same formation. The stairs were wide enough for two people, or one Lugs, to stand next to each other. As they moved downward, they came across several broken steps, as well as chips in the walls and ceilings where the boulder had impacted.

Nearing the end of the stairs, they began to find crushed and broken bodies. Orcs, goblins, hobgoblins, were-beasts, all of them smashed by the juggernaut of a boulder.

"This might not be sportin'," Brick said, "but it be damned effective!" He stepped over the corpses as he picked his path down the steps, leaving it to Max or Beatrix to loot them. At the bottom of the stairs was a bloodbath. Marks on the walls smeared with blood and flesh told the tale. The boulder had reached the bottom at a high rate of speed and crushed everything in its path. Then bounced off walls at three more points, effectively pulping everything in the room.

Including the source of the short-lived roar they had all heard.

The boulder was lodged in the body of a much larger beast. It was hard to tell exactly what the monster had looked like before the stone projectile had crushed most of it. But Alexander's best guess was a massive dog. It most closely compared to Cerberus, the three-headed dog from Greek legends. It would have stood eight feet high on all fours, with a thickly-muscled body and legs. Its claws were each six inches long and razor sharp. Two of its heads had been pulped by the impact of the boulder, along with its right front leg, shoulder, and most of its ribs on that side. The third head hung limply, blood dripping from its maw. Its corpse blocked most of the double doorway that led out of the stairwell. Alexander tried to Identify it, but since it was dead, nothing came up. Max provided better information when he looted it.

"This thing was called a Mongrel Sentinel. I just got its heart, which is a purple crafting item! Along with claws, teeth, and hide." Max held up the heart, which wasn't the bloody pulsating organ Alexander expected. It was in the form of a large crimson gem about the size of a softball.

Brick stepped up and held out his hands. Max obligingly handed him the heart. "This be... purple items be used in Legendary crafting recipes. The kind o' thing Masters make usin' resources o' the crown or an entire guild." He voice was reverent as he brought it closer to his face. "We could sell this fer... well, it could pay off me new house."

He handed the heart back to Max, who stowed it in his bag with the rest of the loot.

Alexander looked over the corpse to the chamber beyond. "We can talk about the loot later. Let's get through this place and get back. I don't like leaving our home so lightly defended."

They quickly finished looting the rest of the bodies, then two at a time climbed over the corpse of the sentinel. The room beyond was circular, with a hole in the center about twenty feet in diameter. There was a vibration in the room, barely felt but definitely there. As if someone had struck a giant tuning fork and touched it to the floor.

As they group began to make their way across toward the center, the vibration became audible. An almost mechanical humming tickled at Alexander's auditory limits. The dragons heard it even before he did and were warily scanning the chamber.

Alexander's elven hearing allowed him to pinpoint the direction of the sound. "Get ready. Something's coming up through that hole."

Every member of the raid party took weapons in hand and moved back into their battle formation. The tanks formed their line about ten feet from the hole. Brick used raid chat to instruct his comrades.

"Whatever it is, as soon as it steps forward, we Shield Rush it and knock it back into its hole."

The others grunted in agreement. Shields up and legs braced, they awaited the arrival of their next foe.

Which turned out to be an empty disc. What could only be described as an elevator platform rose up from the hole and stopped just as its surface became flush with the rest of the floor. Had they not seen it arrive, none of them would have been able to distinguish it from the surrounding floor.

"It's a trap!" Pollock cried in mock horror, getting laughs from several of the players.

Sasha quieted them down. "It might well be. Or just an invitation. The drow want us dead. And vice versa. My guess is that they're down there." She pointed to the floor. "And that thing goes down." She looked up at the flat ceiling above the platform. "At least, I hope it does. If we get on and it goes up…"

Fibble finished her thought for her. "Squish!"

Alexander looked to Del. "I don't see any obvious exits, other than the platform. Any hidden doors?"

The dragons all simultaneously shook their heads no.

Sasha offered, "Seems we have two choices. We can go back up and choose one of the other doors. Or we can keep going down. I vote down." When nobody spoke up to disagree, she continued. "Right! Down it is. Next question… do we all get on at once? Or send some poor sucker out there as a guinea pig?"

Jules shoved Alexander toward the platform. "One of us here can levitate if the thing is a trap."

He turned to see her smiling innocently at him, as if she'd just suggested he have another helping of pancakes. Giving her a 'quit trying to kill me' glare, he was about to agree that he should be the one to go. But as he turned back toward the lift, it dropped out of sight.

"Err…" Brick began. "Anybody think ta count how long it were up here? Like mebbe it just goes up 'n down every minute?"

"Or somebody at the bottom called it down and plans to come up here and say hello!" Max offered.

Alexander was counting seconds this time. The time it took for the platform to drop and then return might give him some idea of the depth of the shaft. He used his Earth Sense to look downward into the stone as he continued to count out loud. He could see the shaft clearly, stretching deep into the stone below. It continued beyond the range of his spell.

"That thing's deep. I can't see the bottom."

Del nodded his head. "More than a mile down. It makes sense. The drow are creatures of the underground. Masters of the dark and the creatures that dwell in it. When they lost the last war, they would have retreated deep into the earth to avoid detection while they rebuilt their armies."

Alexander, still counting and using his Earth Sense, caught the platform returning. His ability didn't allow him to detect whether there were any life forms on it. "It's coming back. Maybe twenty seconds."

Grips tightened on weapons and shields were raised. This time, another sound accompanied the hum of the rising lift. A low growl grew louder as the platform drew closer. When it reached the top, everyone took an involuntary step back.

Purebred Sentinel
Level 120
Health: 110,000/110,000

If they'd thought the doggy in the stairwell was imposing, this one was simply terrifying. While the mongrel had stood less than ten feet high at the shoulder, this purebred was double that. It nearly filled the platform as it stopped flush with the floor. Not even Lugs, the tallest of the raid party at nine feet, could have reached the monster's shoulders. And its head rose up another several feet at the end of a thick neck.

The sentinel had only one head, but that head was plenty imposing. Its canines stretched at least two feet long from the bloody gums to their needle sharp points. Spikes rose up from the back of its head and stretched in a line down its spine to a long tail that bristled with thick, sharp hairs like stilettos.

When it growled at the assembled intruders, the floor trembled. It took a short hop off the platform when it began to descend again like clockwork. Alexander had, unfortunately, lost count upon seeing the giant bulldog from hell appear.

Tilting its head from side to side, the giant sentinel studied its prey. Its jaw hung open, and a tongue large enough to cover Alexander's bed lolled to one side, dripping saliva that hissed when it hit the floor.

"Looks like it has poison, or acid," Sasha warned needlessly. Nobody had failed to notice.

A deep growl resonated from the thing's gut, erupting from its maw as a sharp bark that had a physical force behind it. The tanks all staggered slightly as the sound passed over them. The melee behind them leaned into it but still, most were forced to take a step back. Several of the healers and casters were knocked off their feet.

The entire party received a debuff called 'Sentinel's Crawl' that slowed their movement speed by ten percent for thirty seconds. Not wasting any time, the monster bounded toward the tanks. Even with their shields already raised, the slowed reaction time left a few of them vulnerable as the massive body slammed into them. It didn't strike the center of the line, where the obviously-strong ogre anchored it. It crashed into the left side, crushing Wayne and one of Pollock's guys as well as an orc. The other tanks quickly pivoted left and rushed to put themselves in between the monster and their people.

Sasha's eyes went to her UI instantly. None of the tanks had been killed, though the orc was down to under ten percent health. The two human tanks had been somewhat protected by their plate gear and shields. She cast an AOE heal over all the tanks, then cast her biggest heal spell on the orc first, quickly hitting the other two as well. Martin, who was just returning to his feet after being knocked down, did the same.

Lugs bellowed a challenge at the dog, raising a spear he'd lifted from the bodies above. The moment the dog turned its head in his direction, he hurled the spear. He'd aimed for an eye, but the head movement caused the fast-moving spear to strike its snout, just above the nose. It gouged a long line along the snout before sinking deep into the flesh between its eyes. The sentinel snorted in pain and shook its head, one paw rising to swipe away the spear, which looked more like a toothpick next to the monster.

"Archers! Casters! Focus on its face! Blind it if you can! Melee, get behind it and work on its legs! Tanks, don't forget about the acid!"

A swipe of its front paw tore rents in the shields of the remaining tanks, deep gouges forming in the steel as the metal screeched in complaint. Grumpy and Brick were pushed back a step from the impact, while Lugs managed to hold in place. Benny stepped forward with his shield, casting Holy Smite into the monster's face as he took a place in the line. The creature howled in pain and shook its head in response.

Helga and the melee dashed around to their right side, the sentinel's left. Orcs with spears and minotaurs with massive axes began to stab and hack at the two left legs as Lugs produced another spear and hurled it up at the thing's face to keep it distracted.

Brick used his Serpent's Screech, scraping his hammer across the surface of his Legendary shield. The high-pitched sound was particularly irritating to the dog, which lunged down and seized Brick, shield and all, in its maw. The sound of metal creaking under the pressure of the massive hound's bite was accompanied by Brick's 'love poetry.'

"Yer mama's a chihuahua and yer daddy's a rock troll!" he shouted as the thing shook him like a ragdoll. "Put me down! I ain't no chew toy!" He managed to smash his hammer against one of the sentinel's canines, causing the tooth to crack and the dog to whine in pain. It opened its mouth and dropped the dwarf tank nearly twenty feet to the stone floor. Brick's health, already reduced by the biting and whipping about, plunged to zero on impact.

Sasha shouted, "Benny! Get Brick back, now!"

The young paladin was already moving, holding his shield high as he dashed for his friend's corpse. Lugs shouted at the sentinel to get its attention while Benny dropped to his knees as he slid to a stop next to Brick and laid his hands on him. A golden glow surrounded the dwarf and he coughed. His armor was punctured in several places and crushed in to squeeze him uncomfortably in others. Three healers hit Brick at once and he was quickly back to full health. He and Benny hopped up and rejoined the fight.

Purebred Sentinel
Level 120
Health: 92,000/110,000

Alexander looked at the health bar of what had to be a mini-boss monster. They were making a dent, but it was too slow. He cast Wizard's Fire on the sentinel's face. The flames leapt from hair to hair, engulfing the thing's head in fire. The DPS poured on the damage, banking on the distraction to keep them safe for a moment or two.

Panicked by the flame, the sentinel spun around in a circle, as if chasing its own tail. The movement of its feet knocked several of the orcs and minotaurs off of theirs. Several took significant blunt force damage from being knocked back. Two were injured badly when an orc got kicked into one of Pollock's guys, both of them knocked senseless at the feet of the rampaging mutt.

Helga, having managed to avoid a shifting paw and stay on her feet, shouted at Alexander, "Lift me up! Get me on its back!"

Alexander obligingly cast Levitate on her, raising her up twenty feet in seconds. Then with a twitch of his hand, he sent her flying leftward over top of the sentinel's back. When he thought she was positioned to miss the spikes along its spine, he let her down as gently as he could. Which, as limited as his experience with the spell was so far, wasn't all that gentle.

The monster didn't register the weight of the angry barbarian on its back as it continued to thrash and paw at the flames on its face. To add to the distraction, Del and three of the dragons began casting blue magic missiles into its face, attempting to blind it. The other dragons had taken up healing to assist Sasha and the others in counteracting the massive damage that the hound was inflicting.

Wayne and the other two tanks who'd been crushed were recovering their feet and moving toward the line when the tail whipped around and smashed into their backs. The three of them flew forward over the line of tanks and skidded into the healers and casters. Sasha was knocked flat, her leg split open by the edge of Wayne's shield.

After casting a heal on herself through gritted teeth, she tried casting Thorn Trap on the dog. Huge, thorn-covered vines shot up through cracks in the stone. They wrapped themselves around the sentinel's legs, the thorns piercing its flesh and muscle to dig in and grip the limbs. The dog stopped spinning, the resistance holding it still for a moment. But a lunge toward its enemies snapped most of the vines. Still, the melee moved back in and resumed stabbing and slashing at the legs.

Helga, who had been gripping the tough hairs of the dog's back with both fists, trying to hold on as it spun, took advantage of the relative stillness. Drawing her sword, she activated her Berserker skill. Running up its back just to the left of its spine, she reached its neck and drove her enchanted sword downward into the flesh.

The sentinel let out a howl that caused nearly everyone in the raid to drop their weapons and clutch at their ears. All except Helga, who was immune due to the buff she received from her weapon. She planted a foot on either side of the sword and jerked the weapon free, levering it back and forth as she did so to open the wound and do as much damage as possible. As soon as the sword was clear, she stepped forward and slammed it in again, this time angling it toward the monster's spine. She could feel the tip of the weapon grind against its vertebrae. But it didn't penetrate.

Worse, the attack caused the dog to roll over in an attempt to dislodge her from its back. The melee, who were grouped at its left feet, had no warning. Some were alert and fast enough to dodge forward under its belly, the rolling hound passing harmlessly over them. But the majority were caught beneath its body as it slammed to the floor and rolled.

Sasha shouted and cast an AOE heal as Martin and the others did the best they could. One of Pollock's guys perished under the crushing weight along with two other players, three orcs, and a minotaur. Helga was able to throw herself from the sentinel's back, taking her sword with her and widening the wound she'd made as she dragged the weapon free.

Sasha cursed loudly at the loss of more citizens. She watched as their health bars dropped to zero, then back up to just a sliver. But as the sentinel rolled, it had the same effect as a DoT, causing additional damage that finished them off. The large number of party members trapped under the monster meant that the aoe heals were spread thin, and not strong enough to save everyone. She gritted her teeth and cast as quickly as she could to heal those who had survived the attack.

Alexander had gotten an agreement from Fitz and the dragons that they'd stay out of the fight until it was absolutely necessary for them to step in. Mostly because it somehow seemed worse to him for an eternal and noble creature like a dragon to perish than for an orc or minotaur. And the gamer side of him didn't want them to disturb the XP distribution algorithms.

But they were losing people too quickly and this mini-boss sentinel was still over half health. With a nod toward Del, the dragons entered the fight. Almost in unison, they each held up a hand and sent a sustained ray of blue light streaming into the beast. Its fur and skin smoked and crackled where the light moved across it. It howled again, a simple howl of pain this time, rather than the previous stun spell.

The mostly-healed melee fighters jumped back into the fray, more wary now of the sentinel's movements. The casters, who had never stopped attacking, redoubled their efforts, draining their mana at an alarming rate. Several already had mana potions in hand ready to reload. Fibble, who had fallen to the floor screaming, his sensitive ears bleeding from the sentinel's aoe attack, got back to his feet. He deafly shouted, "PEW! PEW!" much louder than normal as he shot heals at the melee fighters. Alexander couldn't help but smile when the little goblin finally realized he needed a heal for his hearing and shot himself in the face.

With the channeled attacks from the dragons added to the group's DPS, the sentinel's health dropped rapidly.

Purebred Sentinel
Level 120
Health: 58,400/110,000

Sasha shouted in raid chat, *"Fifty percent! Back off and be ready!"*

The melee raiders ceased what they were doing and fled from the beast as its health dropped down to the halfway point. They stopped about twenty feet away and turned with weapons ready. There was no cover to hide behind, so they were going to have to try to dodge whatever attack came their way. Several of the players, expecting another stun howl, covered their ears.

When the sentinel's health dropped to the fifty percent mark, it froze. The casters and ranged DPS continued to blast away as the thing's hindquarters began to lower as if it were going to sit. A moment later, it froze again and a steaming pile of excrement dropped to the floor. A stench filled the chamber as the pile grew to over six feet in height. The odor was a mixture of what Alexander imagined toxic waste would smell like, combined with rotting meat, intestinal gas, and death.

"Aagh! Durin's hairy bunghole, that stinks!" Brick groaned as he fell backward several steps, trying to use his shield hand to cover his nose. Instantly, the closest raid members were overwhelmed with the toxic fumes. Their eyes watered and several vomited up their stomach contents. The minotaurs, with more sensitive noses, were forced back, half blinded and unable to withstand the olfactory assault.

The sentinel took immediate advantage of the temporary incapacitation of the melee group and lunged their direction. Its jaws snapped down on Pollock, quickly severing his torso from his legs. Several others were bowled over and took impact damage as the sentinel savagely shook its head left and right. Blood and internal organs sprayed the area, causing a few more players to vomit. Even the casters, far removed from the shit pile, were having trouble casting spells that required them to speak, preferring to hold their breath.

Fitz cast Wizard's Fire on the pile of shit, instantly creating a column of smoke just as toxic as the original odor. He immediately followed up with a wind spell that pushed the smoke away from the group.

As everyone began to recover, they resumed their attacks. Lugs and the tanks began to shout and cast taunts as they crouched behind their shields, which were raised overhead to protect them from the sentinel's acidic saliva.

The sentinel moved back to its original position, right next to the burning pile of shit, driven by some game mechanic meant to inflict more misery on melee players. This forced the tanks to follow in order to keep aggro. Each of them held their breath as long as they could, but it wasn't long before they had to suck in more air.

After an experimental breath, Brick called out, "Fitz, ye bloody genius! Ye cleared most o' the stench fer us!" He hit the dog with a Holy Smite and pounded his shield. "C'mon, ye big shitmonster!"

Hearing this, the melee DPS charged back in. The minotaurs were especially motivated, angry bulls wanting revenge for the assault on their senses. Huge axes cleaved recklessly into the feet and legs of the sentinel. Molgo managed to sever a claw and a chunk of toe with one mighty swing.

Max got a critical hit with one of his Multi-Shots, the single arrow bursting into five arrows right in front of the hound's left eye. The arrows blasted into the eye in unison, pulping the orb and blinding the eye. It shook its head as it whined in pain, sitting down and using a forepaw to try to remove the shafts. But it quickly shot back up, having sat upon its own pile of flaming shit. The Wizard's Fire spread to the hair and skin around its ass, causing even more pain. The massive beast tucked its tail between its legs and fled.

Lugs and the tanks were knocked down as the mini-boss rushed through them, fleeing the flames on its ass and tail. The ranged and casters scattered and fled as it blindly bounded in their direction. Between the flames on its face and its blinded left eye, the sentinel's sight was extremely limited. It crashed head-first into a wall behind the spot where Sasha and the healers had been standing.

Momentarily stunned, the hound wobbled on its feet. The casters and archers, now scattered on both sides of the beast, resumed their attacks even as they backed away. Fibble shot the thing in its face a few times, fearlessly standing his ground. The dragons continued their channeled attacks as its legs gave out and the creature leaned against the wall. With a shout from Del, they all focused their streams on the underside of its belly. Like a laser scalpel, the concentrated beam cut deeply into the skin, opening a widening cut from which intestines and internal organs began to drop.

The entire raid was struck again by the stench and fled. Only the dragons managed to keep up their attack for several more seconds. By the time they quit and retreated, a ten-foot long gash in the sentinel's belly poured out blood and bile onto the floor. It whined again and Sasha almost felt pity for it. The thing had to be in immense pain.

Its legs buckling completely, the hound slid to the floor with its back against the wall. It lay there, legs twitching as it tried to rise, its strength gone. Sasha quickly cast Trap Soul on it.

Purebred Sentinel
Level 120
Health: 19,100/110,000

"Finish it!" Sasha shouted at the group. She wanted this miserable fight over, and for the dog's pain to end. This was more intense than any fight she'd experienced, and not in a good way. She stopped healing, as none of her party were taking any damage just then, and cast her own meager damage spells on the mini-boss.

The melee were unwilling to approach. Even the tanks stayed back, the monster clearly not going anywhere. Orcs and minotaurs began throwing their weapons at the thing, trying to do what little ranged damage they could. Lugs pulled one of the seven-foot spears from his bag and dropped his shield. He raised the spear above his shoulder and trotted forward like an Olympic javelin thrower. When he'd built some momentum, he hurled the spear. It flew fast and straight to penetrate the dog's neck and drive up into its skull.

The sentinel's legs twitched again briefly, then went still. Its health bar dropped to zero and everyone but the dragons leveled up.

Level up! You are now level 74!
Your Wisdom has increased by +1
Your Intelligence has increased by +1
You have 8 free attribute points available

Max took a deep breath before dashing forward to loot the corpse. He laid a hand on it, took everything without looking, then turned and sprinted away. The rest of the group retreated back to the stairwell entry, where the game mechanics had left the air clear. They sat and recovered as they waited for the corpse and the burning dung pile to disappear.

As they rested, Pollock's voice came across raid chat. *"Hey guys! Respawned back here at the spot we teleported into. The others are here, too. They tried to get back to the group, but the doors are sealed. So we're just kind of sitting here twiddlin' our thumbs..."*

Alexander laughed. They had assumed any of the dead players would respawn back at the keep. *"Hold on, I'll come get you. Clear some space around the entry point."*

He waited several seconds, then closed his eyes and focused on his memory of the room they had stepped into when they entered the portal. He pictured the center of the room and activated Teleport.

There was a golf clap from the respawned players when he appeared. Pollock grinned at him. "Glad you could come fetch us. As nasty as that was, I'd rather be in the fight than just sitting here."

Alexander looked around. "Did you guys get XP from that mini-boss?"

"Yup!" Pollock looked pleased with himself. "Seems as long as we're in the raid and physically still on this side of the portal, we get to share in the XP. These fellas..." he jerked at thumb at the first two players to have died, "tried to get back but couldn't get past the doors. So they came back here for a nap, content to let the XP pile up."

Alexander chuckled at the guilty looks on the player's faces. "Don't sweat it. I'd have done the same thing. Not your fault we sealed the path behind us. Can I assume everybody's up for jumping back in? This is looking like it's gonna be a long day."

They all answered in the affirmative. Alexander had them gather close and teleported them to the chamber where they'd just fought the sentinel. Immediately, all but Alexander began to cough and gag at the stench, which still hadn't faded. One of the players who'd died first asked, "What the *hell* did you guys do? That's just rank!"

Grinning at them, Alexander simply turned and walked back into the stairwell to join the others. The respawned players quickly followed. Brick caught sight of Pollock and laughed. "So... what were the view like inside tha' beastie? Did ye see its tonsils?"

Chapter 15

Orcs, Hobgoblins, and Drow, Oh My!

Richard sat in his office, watching a feed on his holo. Michael sat next to him, along with Talbott the security chief. The FBI had come to claim Jenni and she seemed to be cooperating completely. They were watching the interrogation live as it was happening in a room down below.

"Where exactly is the cache of explosives?" the agent asked. The two of them were seated across a conference table from each other. They were alone in the room, but two armed guards stood just outside. There was a half-full glass of water in front of Jenni, which she paused to drink from before answering.

"Northeast side of the lake. About fifty yards beyond the tree line. There's an old oak with a triple-forked trunk. Knot on the trunk just below the split looks like a face. The stuff is buried in a plastic box between the two biggest roots."

The agent looked significantly at the camera and Richard knew that a team had just been dispatched to retrieve the explosives.

"What about inside the buildings? Have you planted any explosives anywhere? Like the bomb that went off in the pod?"

Jenni shook her head. "Not that I know of…"

The agent slammed his fist down on the table, causing the water in the glass to ripple. "Don't bullshit me! You've had weeks to plant more bombs! Tell me where they are!"

Jenni glared at him. "Stop yelling at me! I didn't plant any more. I was about to… but you found me. I just don't know if Matt planted any more before he left. He didn't tell me he did…" Her voice turned bitter. "But clearly he didn't tell me lots of things."

"Yeah, so you say." The agent smirked at her. "Just poor, innocent Jenni, duped by the mastermind, right? Except this kid's no mastermind. His father is the smart one. Matt was barely smart enough to get into college. You expect me to believe he outwitted a smart girl like yourself?"

Jenni sniffed. "He didn't *outwit* me, asshole. There wasn't a contest. He just fooled me. He was cute. Charming. And when he told me about his mom, I felt sorry for him…"

The agent cut her off. "Don't really care how he got into your pants. Where is he now?"

"I don't know! How many times do I have to say it? We've been here for hours. I need to pee. I'm hungry. I'm scared. And no matter how many times you ask me, I can't tell you what I don't know!" she screamed across the table at him.

Richard turned off the feed. He looked at the ceiling. "Heimdall, please ask the kitchen to prepare some sandwiches and send them down to the interrogation room. Tell them to leave them with the guards."

"*Of course, sir,*" Heimdall replied as Talbott spoke softly into a microphone on his throat. He was informing the agent in the room that food would be available shortly if he chose to change gears and play nice. A slight nod of his head told Richard that the message had been understood.

Michael leaned back on the sofa, letting out a long breath. "So. We'll have the hidden explosives in a few minutes. Assuming she's telling the truth and that's all there are. She claims there isn't another mole, at least not that she knows of. I think I believe her there." He looked at Richard and Talbott, both of whom nodded in agreement.

Talbott added, "She said he was outside the walls before the last bomb went off. He knew we'd go into lockdown. So that's one mystery solved. It was really pissing me off, not knowing how he got past our guys."

Richard gave him a sidelong glance. "You still don't know how he got out. There's no video of him going out through the gate. So he had to have gone over the wall somewhere. And gotten past all the men and sensors in the woods."

Talbott inhaled sharply. He didn't enjoy being reminded of his failure. "Our best guess is that he stowed away in the back of a vehicle that was exiting. Before the second bomb, we were only searching incoming vehicles and personnel. We had no real suspicion of any 'inside man' at that point. As soon as Dayle's pod exploded, we went into full lockdown and searched everything going both ways every time. Half a dozen delivery trucks and eighteen personal vehicles left the compound in the hour before that bomb went off. But again, that's just our current theory. We just don't know for certain."

Michael asked, "Do you believe what she says about him having a way to get back in?"

Talbott shook his head. "I believe he told her that. And that he *thinks* he can get back in. But I don't see how. This place is possibly the most secure private compound on Earth right now. You two have spent a ridiculous amount of money on every conceivable security measure. Besides the small army of armed guards and dogs patrolling inside and out, you have cameras placed throughout the woods for a mile in every direction. There are microphones, motion, and heat sensors everywhere. We have our own radar system monitoring the skies in a ten-mile radius. There are automated surveillance drones moving in random patterns across the entire top of the mountain, equipped with every type of sensor available. I know where everything is and I couldn't sneak in here myself. If you wanted, we could probably tell you how many rabbits, squirrels, and bears live here on the mountain. Two, by the way. Two bears."

Richard nodded thoughtfully. "So maybe we'll get lucky and catch him sneaking in. He'll have to try something when he figures out we've caught Jenni."

Talbott grimaced. "I'm praying the agents find him before he figures that out. If he does have other bombs planted, he may set them off the moment he learns she's lost to him."

*****

Agent McCoy's phone buzzed on the dashboard in front of him. They'd just resumed searching their sector after catching four hours' sleep and a shower in a nearby hotel. The local number on the phone wasn't one he recognized.

"Hello?" he answered the call.

"Hi. Hello. Um, this is Martha. We spoke yesterday?"

McCoy rolled his eyes and put the call on speaker so his partner could hear. He mouthed *dog lady* before speaking aloud. "Yes ma'am. I remember you. How can we help you?"

"I think there's a meth lab in the neighborhood! In a vacant house one block over from mine."

"What makes you think that?" he asked, trying to keep his voice friendly and interested. He was already regretting giving the woman his card.

"No one is supposed to be there. But there was a light on last night. And I saw a shadow. Someone was pacing back and forth. I couldn't see inside because someone put something on the windows." She paused and took a deep breath before continuing. *"I watch the news! I know those meth labs explode all the time. A big cloud of drugs getting everyone in the neighborhood addicted to meth, just like that! You need to get in there and stop them!"*

Both men in the car had perked up at the mention of somebody in a vacant house. McCoy barely heard the rest of her hysterics. "Martha, can you tell me the address?"

"What? Oh, no. I'm afraid I didn't look at the house number. It's two doors down from James and Jeanette's house. On the right side. Oh, my. You don't know James and Jeanette, do you? Okay. Go to the corner of Henry and Naylor. Face... east. I think it's east. Third house on the right." She paused again. *"I... I could show you. If you stop by my place and pick me up."*

"Thank you Martha, but that won't be necessary. We can find it. We appreciate you letting us know. Now please, stay in your house and keep this to yourself. You can't say anything to anyone. Never know which of your neighbors might be in cahoots with the bad guys."

McCoy's partner had to cover his mouth with both hands to stifle the laugh that threatened to escape. McCoy winked at him, making it worse.

"Oh, okay. Of course. I'll stay right here. Thank you. You be sure and let me know what you-" McCoy ended the call before she finished her sentence.

He immediately picked up a radio and informed his command of the report. It was the best lead they'd found so far. The agent in charge listened, then began to reassign nearby units to positions surrounding the house. When everyone was in place, they'd begin to close a net around it.

*****

Matt paced back and forth across the living room. He was juggling a lot of concerns and he found that pacing cleared his mind and helped him think.

"A fucking world event! Just when I'm launching my attacks to massacre the players and NPCs in every city, the assholes at Jupiter somehow turn it into an event! Getting all the players together and ready to defend against my armies." He spat on the carpeted floor. "How did they *know?"*

He'd just exited the game after hearing reports from the drow that several of the cities had successfully fought off their attacks. Alexander and his people had frustratingly massacred the small army sent after them and even turned around and attacked a drow stronghold. The one belonging to his 'master.' The old drow wizard was furious that the Elysians were coming for him and Matt had deemed it wisest to be offline for a while. The wizard couldn't torture or kill an avatar that wasn't online.

"Goddamned Greystones! I spent more than a year building up that avatar, making deals with the dark forces and eventually the drow. Building my influence as the Dark One. Recruiting morons to do what I told them. Wasted time!!" He kicked a nearby wall, his foot smashing through the drywall.

He picked up his phone and turned it on. As soon as the screen was loaded, he sent a message to his mole. *"In-game plans a bust. Proceed with instructions. Take the tower down."*

*****

Alexander and the raid party got to their feet as the corpse, and the stench, faded from the chamber. As they formed up, he noted the absence of several orcs and minotaurs. His gut clenched a bit and he shook his head. It was growing more difficult for him to think of them as just NPCs and shake off the guilt for getting them killed.

Jules poked him from behind, causing him to jump slightly. "Get out of your head. We're doing just fine."

He gave her a half smile. "I know. Thanks. Let's get this over with."

The replenished line of tanks moved forward across the chamber to the hole in the center. The raid party gathered around in a half-circle at the edge. A few of them braved looking down into the darkness of the shaft.

"We'll have about ten seconds to step on once it gets here. Don't get left behind," Sasha warned everyone.

When the platform arrived, every raid member stepped forward onto the disc. They had to push close to the center to make sure there was room for everyone. A moment later, the disc began to drop.

There were exclamations from several of the NPCs, who had never been on an elevator. The sensation of their stomachs rising into their chests as the platform dropped was new to them. Even some of the players reached out to others to steady themselves. The fall was much faster than a normal elevator, and the platform had no walls. The stone of the shaft rushed past them as they fell. Most of the party instinctively pushed closer together in the center, avoiding the walls.

After nearly a minute, their rate of descent began to slow. "Get ready. They're probably waiting for us," Sasha called out. A moment later, they burst from the ceiling of a huge cavern and began to fall through open air. The sensation and the visuals were disconcerting, to say

286

the least. A few of the raiders dropped to one knee and placed a hand on the disc to steady themselves.

Brick shouted, "Wheeeeee!"

Within seconds of emerging into the cavern, the ground below lit up with spells. Defenders formed a thick ring around the spot where the platform would come to rest. Spells and projectiles rushed upward at the raiders even as the platform dropped. Fortunately for them, many of their attackers didn't allow for the drop, and most of the attacks soared over their heads as they fell. One of the minotaurs was struck by a shit-weasel and fell backward, grunting as the thing ate its way into his gut. A dragon quickly steadied him, then reached in and seized the thing, crushing the life from it.

Sasha healed the minotaur even as she called out, "They have us surrounded! We need to break free and group them up! On my mark, we're all going to rush to my side. Tanks, get in front of me. Blast us a path through! We're not going to wait for this thing to stop. So be ready to jump!"

The platform continued to slow as it approached ground level, meaning more and more of the attackers' spells were hitting home. A moment later, with the platform maybe ten feet above the floor, Sasha shouted, "Now!"

Lugs and the tanks activated their Shield Rush abilities, shooting forward into the crowd of casters and archers in front of them. The others leapt off right behind them, following in a tight group as the tanks blasted through several ranks of the enemy. The moment they were through, the tanks turned and formed a shield wall with a gap in the middle. Their people dashed through, some of them staggering from wounds taken as they descended. The moment Helga, who brought up the rear, was past the tanks, they closed ranks. The entire raid began to backstep as the mass of enemies that had surrounded the elevator tried to move to flank them.

The commander of this particular force had made a mistake. They chose almost all ranged attackers with very few melee, thinking that the crossfire they established by surrounding the platform would allow them to annihilate the invaders before they even reached the ground. And now, with the sheer volume of spells and projectiles flying toward the tanks, any melee who tried to approach would be committing suicide. Unlike the armies of the light, the ranged DPS of the dark forces wouldn't blink at killing their own.

The raiders continued to back up slowly, the tanks in a near half-circle to protect their people from the casters who were hurrying toward the left and right sides. Sasha looked behind them, seeing that the nearest wall was still a hundred yards away.

"Alexander! Fitz! We need some walls! We won't make it that far!" She pointed to the wall behind them.

The mages both obliged, raising a fifteen-foot high wall to their left and to their right. Then Alexander began making a back wall to connect the two while Fitz created a shorter waist-high wall along the front side. The tanks immediately moved behind the protection and set their shields atop the wall, creating a barrier tall enough to protect all those behind it.

In half a minute, they had a mini-stronghold inside which they could take a breather. The space was about ten yards square. Room enough for the forty-odd remaining raiders. The healers brought the wounded back up to full health, then took a seat to recover as much mana and stamina as they could.

Spells and bolts impacted the stone walls and the tank's shields as more than a hundred ranged attackers threw all they had against the defenses. A few lobbed fireballs in an arc over top of the tanks' shields, but their aim was off. The spells continued beyond the back wall to splash down harmlessly on the stone floor.

Sasha stuck her head out and cast Thorn Trap on a tightly grouped bunch of about twenty casters. Alexander quickly hit it with Wizard's Fire and the casters began to scream and thrash, causing the thorns to push deep into their flesh. They were nearly all drow, as hobgoblin and orc mages were rare. Nimble and nearly immortal, the drow focused on their mental attributes rather than physical. As a result, their health bars were short compared to humans. As the DoT from the flames kept them from casting, it also reduced their health considerably.

The core group, minus Brick, who was manning the shield wall, gathered in the center of the space along with Molgo, Del, Fitz, and the most senior of the remaining orcs.

Sasha spoke loud enough to be heard over the crashing impacts on their shelter. "We need a way to wipe these guys out. With minimal risk to ourselves."

"I could liquefy the stone under some of them, trap them in the stone," Alexander volunteered.

Sasha nodded once at him. "That *has* worked well in the past. But how big an area can you cover?"

"Not large enough to get them all. Not unless they were bunched up tight."

Fitz added, "And the drow are not stupid. Those may be just novices or acolytes out there. But it won't take them long to realize what you've done and do the same to us in here."

Max volunteered, "We could just snipe at them from in here until they're all dead. I didn't see a lot of healers out there. Open us some slots in the walls and let us do our thing."

Sasha shook her head. "We'll do that, but it's not fast enough by itself. Can you feel that? It's already getting warm in here from the spells heating the stone."

Brick shouted, "Errr... guys? Whatever ye're plannin', ye might want ta get to it! We got more beasties comin'!"

He motioned toward the stronghold, far on the other side of the elevator platform. It was built of stone, with high walls and a massive double-doored gate that looked large enough for a giant to step through. The gates were open now and a short column of trolls were shuffling out. There were eight of them, walking two by two almost in step. Each of them carried a club larger than Lugs in one hand and a spear in the other.

"They be slow, but they'll not be stopped easy. We got mebbe three minutes 'til they arrive."

"Alexander, if they stay in formation, or even just grouped that close, save your earth magic for them. Wait 'til they're within spitting distance, then sink them. They might disrupt the casters some," Sasha ordered.

Beatrix, who was small enough to stand on the wall behind the shields and peek between them to attack, was using her water magic to create a water globe around the heads of one caster at a time, suffocating them. She called from her position. "If you can get us access to a water source, Misty and I can murder these fools!" she shouted enthusiastically. "Get that sweet, sweet XP!"

Sasha looked at Alexander, who sent his Earth Sense below them. He found a stream about twenty feet down. Just a small water flow, not really enough to qualify as a stream. Still, he used Earth Mover to open a shaft about a foot wide so that Beatrix would have access.

She closed her eyes and pushed her hands out toward the shaft. Water began to gurgle down below, then rise up. As soon as it cleared the shaft, she turned and pushed the stream toward the enemy directly in front of them. Misty moved forward and prepared to cast.

Beatrix wielded the stream like one of her arms, slapping across the line of casters, soaking them all. She used her other hand, wiggling her fingers at the enemy, to create globes of water around half a dozen heads. Misty popped her head up long enough to cast Arctic Blast in a cone that reached out and froze the water on the enemies' bodies. For the six that had water around their heads, it became a solid chunk of ice. The others were simply encased in a thin layer of ice that slowed or interrupted their casting.

Max and Lainey and the other ranged DPS took their chance. They popped out from behind the tanks and fired as rapidly as they could at the disabled line in front of them. As they whittled down the casters' health, Beatrix splashed the exterior of their shelter with water, cooling the heated stone and easing things a bit for those inside.

Sasha recast her Thorn Trap on the group she'd hit initially. The new vines caught fire, increasing the damage being done to the casters trapped there. Alexander joined in with the DPS, casting Magic Bolts at the faces of as many casters as possible, interrupting their spells and forcing them to take precious seconds to recover. The dragons grouped near the back of the shelter, waiting to be asked for help.

Alexander looked around his limited range of view. A score of the casters were soon going to burn to death inside Sasha's thorns. Their health bars were already nearly empty. The frozen group directly in front was another dozen or so. The DPS was focused on them and they would be dead in half a minute or less. That was nearly a third of the force arrayed against them, not counting the trolls. Which were still approaching, but too far away yet.

He smiled when he saw that Fibble had hopped up on the wall next to Beatrix and was shouting, "Pew!" with each shot he flung toward the enemy. He walked up to Beatrix and tapped her shoulder. When she turned, he handed her a soul gem from his bag. "Recharge Fibble when he runs out." She nodded and went back to suffocating drow.

He turned back to the trolls, which were nearing his casting range. Which meant they were also nearing the group of frozen drow. Alexander had an idea. "Stop firing on the front group. Shift fire to the left!"

His people all reacted quickly, shifting fire to a group of thirty or more casters to the left of the icy drow mages. Alexander waited until the first of the troll ranks reached the back of that group. They clearly had no intention of stopping and simply stomped right over the helpless drow. Alexander quickly cast Wizard's Fire on the one on the left, causing it to scream in a surprisingly high pitch as its face began to boil. He quickly cast Levitate on the other of the front-rank trolls, lifting it just a few inches from the ground. With a movement of his hand, he pushed the floating troll to one side, using it to crush more of the frozen drow. When he'd mowed down the last of them, he reversed his hand motion and tossed the troll into the second rank of the column.

As soon as it struck, he released the spell and let it drop to the stone. Then he used his Earth Mover to turn the stone under the front several trolls to soft mud. The heavy creatures immediately began to sink. Alexander let them go until they were nearly waist-high, then solidified the stone.

Roars of frustration and fear erupted from the front four trolls. The one with the burning face had lost its eyes and was laying about with its club. It crushed every drow within reach and did some damage to its brethren as well. Confused and annoyed, the other three who were trapped quickly got tired of the abuse and teamed up to beat the blinded troll to a pulp.

Meanwhile, the rest of the column, having seen those ahead of them sink into the stone, had split up and moved left and right to go around them. Two in each direction. One of the back-rank trolls paused to try to pull a comrade free from the stone. He gave up after dislocating the arm he held. Picking up his club, he moved after his still-upright cousin.

Alexander grinned. He'd managed to disable four of the trolls, then get one killed and another injured. But he had four more to go.

The trolls who had moved to his right were once again advancing. After seeing their fellow casters get crushed, the mages in their way wisely moved aside. But Alexander wasn't going to let it be that easy. He cast Levitate on one of the drow and flung it into the face of the lead troll. It swatted away the attack, then lifted the offending drow and crushed it between massive hands.

The other drow took offense and began to attack the troll. Chaos ensued as the brutes turned on the mages. The two trolls were dying quickly, but taking several drow with them.

Leaving them to it, Alexander turned to confront the remaining two on his left. He was about to cast Wizard's Fire on the nearest of them when it sprouted an arrow from its eye and began to convulse. Looking around, Alexander saw Lainey grinning at him. "I channeled the Shock spell into it for like, six seconds. Wasn't sure it would work!"

"Ha! It worked!" He gave her a little salute before turning back to the fight. The stunned troll was being pummeled with bolts and arrows from the ranged players. Its second eye exploded in a spray of blood and brain matter. The dying troll flailed about with its club as it fell to the side, taking out four drow who had been working together on some kind of combined spell.

The final mob, after it sunk in that its companions on the march across the cavern were all dead or disabled, turned and ran.

Helga, Pollock, and his men dashed out from the shelter and set upon the trapped trolls. Unable to turn, they were vulnerable from behind. So, the raiders hacked and slashed at the stone-skinned monsters, getting critical hits one after another because the trolls were incapacitated and they were attacking from behind. It took less than a minute to finish them off. The melee players took some damage, exposing themselves to get the kills. Sasha and healers struggled to keep them alive until they returned to the shield wall and protection.

"That was stupid!" Sasha snarled at Helga. The barbarian woman looked down at her boots. "Sorry, I saw the easy kills and... well, half the bad guys are dead. I figured we could use the trolls for cover as we killed them and we'd make it okay."

"Don't ever do it again." Sasha's tone allowed for no argument. The melee group moved back behind the tanks and sat down.

Alexander estimated the enemy force was down to just over thirty drow. The ones who had been on the flanks had realized they no longer had the numbers to penetrate the walls, so they moved around toward the front to pound on the tanks. The ranged raiders were punishing them, as only a few had put up magic shields and the only physical cover was the bodies of the trolls. As he scanned the battlefield, Alexander didn't see a single drow with more than fifty percent health. The assault on the walls slackened as some of the smarter drow decided to save their mana for a clear shot at something.

He cupped his hands on either side of his mouth and shouted, "Surrender now! We don't need your lives! Surrender and we'll send you to safety!"

The only result of that offer was a renewed assault on the shelter. A fireball lobbed over top of the tanks actually managed to splash down inside the walls, burning and knocking back several of the raiders. Molgo took the blast full force and suffered hideous burns. His health bar down to fifteen percent, he clamped his jaw shut against the pain and didn't utter a sound as the healers converged and brought him back to a safe level. Though his skin healed, the hair that had burned off did not regrow. He was left looking splotchy and rough.

Alexander looked to Beatrix and Misty again. The two of them had been picking off individual drow one after another. They worked well together. He decided to try something stupid, with their help.

The first thing he did was cut four large blocks of stone from the floor behind the casters. He raised them up and set them to either side and in back of the hole. Then he softened the stone at the bottom of the hole. This gave him a pit about ten yards wide and three yards deep behind the largest concentration of drow.

With that done, he called Beatrix and Misty to him. A quick explanation of what he wanted had them laughing and nodding. Beatrix went first.

Climbing back atop the wall and standing behind Brick's shield, she waved a hand in a circular motion as she gathered water from the stream. It spun in a sort of whirlpool disc behind her as she gathered more and more. Finally, when it was nearly too large for her to control, she sent it surging in a wave over top of the tanks' heads and out toward the enemy. The wave was only maybe four feet high, but it had the speed and power of magic behind it. Most of the enemy were knocked off their feet and pushed back. A few were washed into Alexander's pit.

Beatrix immediately started gathering more water as Misty stepped up and cast her Cone of Frost spell as widely as she could. The wet floor and wet drow became encrusted in ice. The ranged attackers hit the drow with everything they had, knocking some of them back. Beatrix held her next wave while the other raiders whittled away at their targets. When nearly all of the drow had broken loose of the ice on the floor, she launched her next wave.

This time, the drow were pushed back as a group. The slick ice at their feet left them no purchase as the force of the water sent them sliding into the pit. Only six of the drow mages managed to stay at surface level, still casting spells at the raiders. Six of the tanks each chose a target and charged forward, knocking the drow off their feet. The melee group were right behind the tanks, quickly finishing off the stragglers. Misty jogged forward and cast down into the pit, freezing the waist-deep water down there. With the drow trapped, Lugs and the dragons shoved the stone blocks back into the pit, crushing the drow and ending the fight.

Once again, several of the NPCs and lower-level players leveled up. Fibble sat down and rubbed his tummy, smiling down at it like a pregnant mother admiring her child. Max and Beatrix immediately began looting the bodies as the others sat down to rest.

Alexander, not wanting Max to complain about lost loot, liquefied the stone above the crushed corpses in the pit and raised them up. There were several sounds of disgust from the raiders when what was effectively drow paste broke the surface.

A distant roar caught everyone's attention. Alexander scanned the cavern and his eyes found the last remaining troll. The beast was waving its arms and plodding directly toward them. At the same time, Sasha called out, "Jules is hurt, but I can't heal her. She's out of range."

Alexander's eyes immediately went to the raid UI and Jules' icon. Her health was down to eighty percent, but not dropping. Some chuckles from the raiders made him focus back on the cavern. He saw Molgo first, smiling as he watched the troll approach. Alexander followed his gaze.

The troll had turned slightly, revealing Jules perched on its back. She was hanging from her daggers, each one plunged into a shoulder just behind the troll's collarbone. The troll was frantically trying to reach back and remove her, but its arms just didn't bend that way. As they watched, Jules shifted her weight, causing the troll to turn back in their direction. She shouted at the monster and it roared back in anger.

Sasha shouted, "Shoot it! But make sure you don't hit Jules."

Max, Lainey, and the other ranged obliged, sending arrows at the thing as it walked closer. Every time it tried to turn away, they quit firing and waited for Jules to turn it again.

Finally, Lugs moved forward and slammed into the thing with his shield. Jules took advantage of the two-second stun to remove her daggers and plunge them both into the troll's kidneys for critical hits before dropping off and stepping back. The melee group moved in to assist, but Jules didn't appear to need it. She activated an ability of hers and leapt back up at the troll's head. The beautiful rogue became a whirlwind of blades, black leather, and blood as her daggers stabbed and sliced several times per second. She stabbed her victim in the face, the neck, under its chin. A slash across its belly opened it like an overstuffed sausage.

The troll tried to defend itself but moved too slowly to catch the elf. When the six seconds of speed her ability granted her expired, she planted her feet on the troll's chest and pushed off, executing a flip as she passed over Lugs' head and landing gracefully on her feet. A few of the raiders, including Alexander, applauded. The blood-covered elf gave a little curtsy, daggers spinning in each hand.

Lugs smashed his shield into the troll's face again to get its attention, but it wasn't necessary. The big monster wobbled a bit, then fell backwards. It struggled briefly as it bled out from the multiple wounds Jules had inflicted. A moment later, it was dead.

Fibble ran over and shot Jules directly in the face, "Pew! Pew!" healing her back to full. She bent down to hug the little goblin but he made a face and backed up a step. "Lady Jules smell like troll doody."

As Jules looked down at her blood-and-guts-soaked gear and smiled, the others had a good laugh. Lainey came over and whispered, "First time I've heard Fibble accuse somebody *else* of being the stinky one." Jules sought out Beatrix and gave her a pleading look. The little gnome sent a spray of water into the rogue, effectively hosing her down. As soon as she was clean, Fibble took a running leap and wrapped himself around Jules neck.

"Lady Jules kill big troll all alone! Now you are protector like Fibble!" he beamed at her. She gave him a squeeze before setting him down.

"I'm glad you approve, Minister Fibble. Did I maybe earn a cookie as a reward?"

Fibble nodded his head vigorously, producing a cookie from his bag and handing it over. He watched a bit jealously as she thanked him and took a big bite. Seeing the look on his face, she said, "This is a big cookie. I'm all full. Would you eat the rest for me?"

Again the nodding and the flapping ears as Fibble reclaimed the prize and quickly made it disappear.

Beatrix looted the troll as Sasha gathered the group back together. They looked across the cavern to the stronghold that sat beyond the elevator platform.

The walls were thirty feet high and seamless, with blocky-yet-smooth-and-perfect construction that gave it the appearance of having been built by dwarves. Surrounding the gates was a massive structure that rose fifty feet and must have contained the mechanisms for moving the heavy doors. Alexander's elven sight showed him dozens of enemies with crossbows manning the top of the wall. Beyond the wall, he could see several rooftops and narrow windows. A single tower rose up in the center.

Brick spoke up. "That gate be a death trap. Much like our own keep. There'll be beasties waitin' ta murder us as we try 'n pass through. Arrows, fire, mebbe hot oil or acid."

The doors stood open, as if inviting them in. Alexander looked to Sasha. "How do you want to handle this?"

"We can't hang around outside all day waiting for more of them to come out. For all we know, they have a portal in there and can just summon a never-ending supply of reinforcements," she thought out loud. "Rushing the gate will get some of us killed. We've already lost too many orcs and minotaurs." She looked over at the two diminished groups. They had weapons in hand and appeared eager to fight.

She looked again at the open gate and the courtyard beyond. "You know there's going to be some kind of inner portcullis or something. As soon as we step through the doors, they'll drop it and trap us. Then wipe us out."

Alexander looked to Fitz, who was already smiling back at him. "Fitz and I can get us through the gate. The question is, where do you want to start? In the courtyard? Up on the wall?"

Sasha looked at Fitz. "Tell me, you old goat. If you were a drow wizard, where in there would you be? Top of the tower? Lowest level of the dungeon? Great hall somewhere in the middle?"

Fitz thought about it for a moment. "Well, right now I'd be in the tower, watching you." They all looked up at the tower. It was wider than the gatehouse and comparatively squat, only rising two stories above the level of the wall. The roof was flat and probably had a short wall around it. There were windows dotting it here and there, narrow slots too small for a humanoid to squeeze through.

Sasha nodded once as she made her decision. "Right. We'll start with the tower. Work our way down from the roof."

Brick was stroking his beard. "That be grand if we catch the dark wizard in his tower. But if he ain't there and we have ta search through that place, we'll be leavin' lots o' baddies behind us." He pointed to the figures on the wall.

Del spoke up. "Please, allow us to take care of that. Nothing we see there is any real threat to us. Likely the strongest of the wizard's casters and fighters will be inside with him. We can attack the gate, distract the enemy while you insert yourselves into the tower. We'll join you inside."

Alexander's stomach clenched. He wanted to say no. He wanted to offer to send healers with them. But he knew the dragons were in fact more powerful than anyone he could send and were perfectly capable of healing themselves or each other.

Jules gave him a discreet nudge with her elbow. "Get out of your head."

"Thank you, Del." He turned to address all the dragons. "Thank all of you. A distraction would be much appreciated." A vision of six angry dragons tearing down the walls came to him and he grinned. "And who could make a more spectacular distraction than dragons?" The group returned wicked smiles as he added, "But please, try to stay safe."

Without a word, Del and the rest of his wing turned and trotted toward the gate. As soon as they began their approach, the activity on the wall increased. Drow filled in the spaces between orcs and hobgoblins along the wall. Two more trolls appeared just inside the courtyard. These two were heavily armored, their bodies covered in spiked plates. Each wore a helmet with wicked-looking horns. One carried a two-bladed battle axe that must have weighed two hundred pounds. The other wielded a flail. The ball at the end of the chain was the size of a beach ball and covered in sharp spikes.

The dragons began casting as they jogged. Balls of blue fire shot upward in arcs before falling atop the defenders on the wall. The screams could be heard echoing across the cavern.

Alexander looked to Fitz. The wizard nodded and disappeared, along with all of the orcs and minotaurs. Alexander quickly grouped the players closer together and looked to see where Fitz had landed. Choosing a clear spot atop the roof, he teleported himself and the players up to join the others.

The screams and sounds of battle were suddenly much louder. Alexander looked around the roof and found three drow corpses with sword and axe wounds. Molgo looked at him and shrugged. "There were guards. They were not very alert."

A short stair led down to a door that gave access to the tower. Brick led the way. Lugs took up the rear this time, as he was going to have to duck through and might even have to crouch in the stairs and corridors below. Dwarven-built structures were not often ogre-friendly.

The dragons outside roared and the whole keep shuddered as something impacted the wall. Alexander mentally chided himself for worrying about the ancient dragons as he stepped through the door into the top room of the keep, where another battle had started.

It was a single round room, large enough to hold a concert for a hundred people or more, with room left over for a bar and dance floor. Six drow were hiding behind furniture in one corner, casting spells at Brick and the tanks. There was only one door that Alexander could see, and Brick had wisely moved between that door and their enemy, cutting off their escape route. The tanks and melee were advancing on the drow, while ranged DPS were keeping them pinned down. The fight didn't take long.

Max and Fitz quickly searched the room for anything interesting. They found some ancient-looking tomes on a table on one side of the room. But no secret caches. Brick cleaned out a weapons rack near the door that held crossbows, spears, and thin curved swords that resembled katanas with jet-black blades. He gave the spears to Lugs.

Once again, Brick led the way through the door and down the stairs. They moved as quietly as possible, not wishing to alert their enemies of their presence. The battle noise outside helped mask any creaking of leather or scraping metal.

Jules volunteered to scout ahead and faded from view. The group kept moving as she hurried ahead. Alexander resisted an itch to remind her that drow were experts in stealth, and to be careful not to expose herself.

A minute later, she reported in. *"Next floor is offices and labs. Haven't seen anyone. Heading farther down."*

The group quickly reached the next level and entered a hallway. There were three rooms on either side. Sasha quietly broke them into small groups with a tank and healer in each. They moved to their assigned rooms and opened the doors on the count of three. As Jules had reported, the rooms were empty. They grabbed anything that looked interesting and moved on.

In this manner they worked their way down the five floors of the tower to the main level. Jules had assassinated the only two drow she'd encountered as she scouted. Alexander assumed the rest of the normal inhabitants had either joined the battle outside or been called to defend the wizard.

Upon reaching the ground level, they found they had a choice. There were two doors, and a stairwell that continued down to underground levels. One door led out to the courtyard, where dark soldiers were rushing about. The other led into the main part of the keep.

Fitz quickly sealed the courtyard door. "No need to go out there, or let them in here."

Sasha looked around at the gathered raiders. "Let's have a vote. Down, or in? Raise your hand for down."

Nearly every hand in the group went up. Grumpy commented, "If I had half a dozen angry dragons tryin' to eat my face, I'd hide in small spaces underground. Make them stay in human form. Set a bunch of traps and ambushes on my way down."

Fitz nodded in agreement. With a wave of his hand, he sealed the second doorway. That was good enough for Sasha. "Down we go! Brick, sweetie… try not to set off any traps, K?" The dwarf just snorted and raised his shield, stepping down gingerly onto the first step.

They proceeded downward for more than a minute. The long, straight stair had no landings or curves. Brick gradually moved faster as step after step failed to trigger any traps. He reached the bottom without incident and approached an open archway. There was no light of any kind inside the chamber beyond. Not even the dull red glow that had been prevalent since they entered the raid zone.

Alexander was about to cast a light globe when Sasha stopped him. She smiled sweetly at Brick as she said, "How 'bout we make our friend here a shining target for whatever's in there?"

Brick's eyebrows shot up and he looked a little nervous. "What're ye thinkin'?"

"We're going to light up your shield. Just think how handsome and brave you'll look to the ladies watching the feed." She continued to smile, making him more nervous. Sasha only smiled at him that way when she was about to send him to his death in some horrible way.

Alexander laughed as the dwarf took a wary step back from Sasha. He put a hand on the tank's shield and concentrated on modifying the Light Globe spell. He channeled the spell into the shield, watching it glow slightly, then get brighter. When he thought it was bright enough to light their way, he stopped channeling.

Brick gave them a dirty look before stepping through the archway. The light from his shield illuminated an area about fifty feet ahead of him in an arc. Behind the shield, he was standing in shadow. Seconds after he stepped into the chamber, a roar that shook the walls echoed around them.

"Oh, sure. Make the dwarf the bit o' tasty bait. Ye know I be too sexy fer any beastie to resist."

Brick moved farther out into the dark space. The light from his shield illuminated a rough stone floor, small rocks scattered here and there in shattered pieces. Likely having fallen from the ceiling. As the others moved into the room behind him, the tanks fanned out in their usual half-circle. The others maintained their battle formation, keeping pace.

Another roar echoed around them and chunks of stone could be heard bouncing off walls or striking the floor. Brick slowed a bit as he walked, turning his body slightly left and right to shine the light in a wider arc. He called back quietly, "I be thinkin' this weren't the best idea. I dunno-"

He was interrupted as something swooped into the light from his right side, roaring in irritation as it grabbed hold of the tank and lifted him into the air. Brick and the light sped up and away. The raiders could hear him yelling and cursing as whatever it was flew off with him. The light from the shield gave them flashes of a leathery wing and a horned head, but most of the creature was in the shadow behind the shield with Brick.

Alexander checked his buddy's health bar on his UI. Brick was still at ninety percent health. His armor mostly protecting him from the claws of whatever grabbed him. He could hear the dwarf cursing.

"Ye big featherless canary! I ain't no snack fer ye! I'm gonna roast yer scrawny wings 'n eat 'em fer dinner with some hot sauce and-"

There was a familiar flash as Brick hit the creature with Holy Smite. It was briefly revealed to them in full as the holy light illuminated it.

Gargoyle Matron
Level 110
Health: 80,000/80,000

The creature screamed and dropped the dwarf.

"Aaaaaahhh dammit!" Brick hollered as he fell maybe sixty feet. There was a resounding crash of metal mixed with breaking bones when he struck the floor. The impact killed him instantly.

Despite the fact that a giant mama gargoyle was flying around somewhere above them, Alexander could hear Max laughing in the dark.

"Hahaha! That was classic! I'm…He…" He gasped for breath. "He just shot *himself* out of the sky! That's gotta be worth some kind of achievement or something!"

Fitz cast several light globes up into the sky, then began casting Mage Sight on every member of the raid. Alexander assisted, beginning with the healers and ranged DPS. As soon as Max was able to see the mini-boss, he began firing arrows at it. Lainey started channeling Shock into an arrow, letting it build up as she'd done with the troll. After several seconds, she loosed the arrow at the matron.

It struck true! Blasting into the matron's face just below her eye as she'd been diving toward the group, the Shock spell caused her muscles to seize. She dropped from the sky, her forward momentum carrying her closer as she bounced, then skidded, on the stone. The stun wore off almost immediately and she began to flap her wings.

More and more of the raiders began inflicting damage as Mage Sight or the light globes allowed them to see their target. Her skin was jet-black and nearly as hard as stone. Crossbow bolts bounced off her torso and legs but managed to penetrate her wings, tearing rents as they passed through. Alexander hit her with Wizard's Fire, then cast rapid-fire Mage Bolts at her damaged left wing. The holes in the wing grew larger and several of the muscles and tendons were severed as the damage was poured on. The wing was disabled before she could regain flight.

Letting loose the now-familiar, but no less intimidating roar, she charged the tanks. Her claws dug into the stone floor as she propelled herself toward the line. At the last minute, she spread her wings and beat them once as she leapt over the tanks and landed amongst the casters and archers. Her hands shot forward and snatched Sasha. Talons ripped into her shoulder and arm as the matron pulled her close to her chest. Jagged teeth clamped down on Sasha's other shoulder as she screamed in pain.

The matron spun about, causing several attacks that had been aimed at her back to strike Sasha instead. Her wings swept raiders off their feet as she turned and kicked Pollock so hard that he flew back, crushed ribs complaining as he hit the floor.

She continued to spin every few seconds, forcing attackers to duck her powerful wings or leap back out of range. The whole time she tightened her jaws on Sasha's shoulder, trying to tear out a large chunk of the healer. Sasha was casting heals on herself, as were Martin and the others. But the gargoyle matron kept squeezing with jaw and claw, doing more damage every second.

Lugs caught up to the matron, managing to get behind her and grab hold of her wings. He used his ogre strength and the bulk of his belly to lift her off the floor. Her back legs immediately began to shred his legs as he held her there. He pulled harder on her wings, trying to rip them from her shoulders at the joints.

With a roar of pain and determination, Lugs flexed his arms. One of the wings dislocated out of its socket with an audible pop. The gargoyle let go of Sasha with her jaws and screamed. Her eyes flashed blood-red and her whole body seemed to grow larger.

Gargoyle Matron
Level 110
Health: 39,000/80,000

Moving her arms in opposite directions, she tore Sasha's arm off and dropped both pieces of her to the floor. Pushing off with her feet and flinging herself backward, she tipped Lugs off balance and they both fell to the floor. She tried to roll off the ogre to regain her feet, but he determinedly held on. His weight was sufficient to keep her pinned.

Helga jumped forward and swung her Legendary weapon. The sword sliced through a waving arm, severing it just above the wrist. Alexander, seeing her health dropping, cast Trap Soul on her. Pollock and his guys were right behind her, leaping atop the monster's torso and hacking away with no regard for their own safety. Pollock jammed his sword into the matron's mouth as she screamed at them and swiped at his neck with her remaining hand. The sound cut off with a gurgle, and she lay still. Pollock collapsed atop her, his health bar at ten percent and blood pumping from his wound.

Martin healed Pollock and Lugs as the others focused on Sasha. She was barely conscious and bleeding badly, moaning in pain. Alexander was inclined to let her die. They could heal her, but couldn't reattach her arm. She'd have to finish the dungeon with one arm.

"Stop! Don't heal her. Let her die. She'll respawn with both arms."

The healers backed off and Sasha used her remaining hand to make a rude gesture at Alexander before passing out. A few moments later, her health bar went grey.

Max went to loot the mini-boss. Beatrix walked over to Brick's corpse and retrieved his gear for him, then did the same for Sasha. The others took seats against the wall and rested. Some ate rations or drank some of the keep's water that gave buffs.

Jules asked Alexander for a light globe so she could explore the room better. Mage sight revealed many things, but not everything. He conjured a globe and assigned it to float above her head. She began to walk the perimeter of the cavern they were in. Alexander chuckled as he watched her go – she looked like a wandering NPC with a quest to give from the old turn-of-the-century MMORPGs.

As they waited for Brick and Sasha, Alexander pulled up his stats. He'd leveled again with the death of the gargoyle boss.

Mage: Alexander	Level 75	Build: Ranged Magic/Melee DPS	
Heath: 46,000	Experience:	1588,000/1,600,000	Atrrib Pts Avail: 13
Mana: 43,000			Skill Pts Avail: 5
Stamina: 18 (31)	Dexterity: 10	Armor: 240	Heath Regen: 250
Strength: 16 (32)	Wisdom 85 (114)	Defense: 150	Mana Regen: 500
Agility: 12 (24)	Intelligence 85 (114)	Phys Attack: 110	Magic Attack: 240
Luck: 15 (23)	Charisma: 14	Stamina Regen: 35	Race: Elf

He decided to wait and assign his available points later. Still a glass cannon, the thirteen points he had weren't going to make a huge different in his Stamina or Strength, Agility or Dexterity. He briefly considered just dropping them all into Charisma to make himself a more effective leader and public speaker. He was distracted as Fitz approached him.

"You've grown again, boy. I have more magic for you, if you're ready."

"We have some time before Brick and Sasha respawn. So, yes, please. Take your best shot." He grinned at the old wizard, who'd nearly killed him with new spells last time.

Alexander closed his eyes and felt Fitz's hand on his forehead. A moment later, the familiar pain of new knowledge made itself known. This time it started as a vague itch somewhere in the back of his brain. He suspected Fitz was being gentle with him out of guilt. But soon enough, the itch turned into a burning sensation, which quickly increased to a searing pain that felt like a white hot needle being pushed through his brain.

He gritted his teeth, telling himself that it was almost over, he could endure *any* amount of pain for a few more seconds.

Five seconds later, he wasn't so sure. His legs felt weak and he couldn't seem to open his eyes. The pain had increased by an order of magnitude, and he could feel sweat trickling down his back. His fists were clenched so tightly he could hear his knuckles creaking. It was all he could do not to wet himself.

When Fitz finally removed his hand, Alexander simply let his legs fold and his body fall to the floor. His eyes still closed, he heard a few surprised exclamations. Molgo had to be restrained from attacking the wizard, whom he thought had just attacked Alexander. He could hear Max's voice saying, "It's okay. That's just how Alexander learns new ways to get us into trouble."

Chapter 16

No Time Like the Present

Alexander woke to the sound of Sasha's voice. "Dammit, Fitz! We're in the middle of a raid and you broke his brain!"

He blinked his eyes a few times, taking in his surroundings. The first thing he saw was the floor, a few inches in front of his nose. Followed by Sasha's boot not much further away. He inhaled deeply, taking in the scent of stone and blood, which made him cough.

"Oh! He's awake." Lainey bent down and rolled him onto his back. "How are you feeling?" she asked with a concerned look on her face. Ever his nurse and trainer, even in the game, he'd rarely seen her this worried.

"I'm good. Fitz offered to train me. Hurt more than usual. I might have passed out for a minute."

Sasha snorted. "A minute? Brick and I respawned. Fitz came to get us cuz your happy ass was snoring on the floor there. We've been here fifteen minutes or so."

As Sasha spoke, Lainey was looking into Alexander's eyes and checking his pulse. He smiled at her as she fussed over him. "You realize that my pupils here may have zero correlation to my pupils back home, right?"

Lainey smacked him lightly on the head. "Shut up and humor me."

He relaxed and set his head down on the stone. In no hurry to get up, he was fine with letting Lainey check him out. He knew it would make her feel better. And probably Sasha too, though she'd never admit it.

His eyes found Jules standing next to Sasha. She gave him a half-smile and a wave, seeming much less worried about him than the others. Feeling a little hurt that she wasn't more worried, he decided to mess with her.

"Hi there. I'm Alexander." He looked into her eyes and tried his best to look innocent. "You're very pretty. What's your name?" He smiled warmly at her, doing his best to be charming.

Her eyes widened as Lainey gasped and put a hand to his forehead. "I didn't see him fall. Did he hit his head when he fell?" She began looking around frantically for someone to answer her. Alexander immediately felt guilty.

Jules saw the guilt cross his face and her mouth dropped open. "You big ol' FAKER!" She pointed at him.

Alexander blushed and looked at Lainey. "I'm sorry. I was trying to trick Jules. I didn't realize…" He let his voice tail off. When he looked back at Jules, she held a dagger in one hand and was using a stone to sharpen it as she gave him a look filled with promise.

Lainey stood up and kicked him gently in the leg. "You idiot!" She turned and walked away to sit by Lugs and Fibble.

Sasha kicked him too. Not as gently.

"Nice going, dork. Lainey is already afraid this immersion stuff is messing with your brain. And you go and pull a stunt like that?" She and Jules both gave him dirty looks and moved away to join Lainey.

Alexander was left staring up at Fitz, who was doing his best to look innocent.

He slowly got to his feet. The wizard watched him, waiting for him to speak. Finally, he said, "Well, that was an experience."

Fitz nodded his head. "I am sorry, boy. I felt it was appropriate to give you some knowledge that may help in the battle ahead."

The wizard paused as Alexander rubbed his eyes and tried to shake off the past two minutes.

"When we reach the wizard, he is mine." Fitz held up a hand to forestall Alexander's response. "Do not argue, boy. The war between these wizards and the dragons is an old one. It is my right to claim his life. Do not presume to get between me and my prey." The wizard's voice took on the growling echo of his dragon form. The tone and threat behind that last statement caused several of the raiders to get to their feet, weapons in hand.

Fitz continued, "The apprentice you faced outside your keep? There will be more like her. Maybe dozens more, guarding the wizard. You must be prepared to face them. Which is why I've given you what I have. You've neglected some of your spells, boy. Not used them enough to increase your skill levels. So I was forced to advance them for you."

"Aaaand that's why the pain was different this time." Alexander took a moment to pull up the Spells tab in his UI and seek out the new spells. It wasn't difficult; they were helpfully highlighted for him.

Mage Shield: Level 5 *Cost: 1,000 mana. Cast time: Instant*
Caster can create a single shield over themselves or others that will absorb up to five times the caster's HP in physical or magical damage. Alternately, caster can create up to five smaller shields on multiple targets that will each absorb the caster's HP in physical or magical damage. Once cast, shields can be maintained or recharged with the infusion of additional mana.

Alexander grimaced. Fitz was right. He'd neglected his shield spell. Thinking back over the past weeks, he could only recall using it maybe half a dozen times. As opposed to his teleport spell, which had become second nature. He returned to the list.

Mage Bolt: Level 5 *Cost: 50 mana. Cast time: Instant*
Casts a bolt of magic at a target, dealing 2,000 damage per bolt. Critical hit multiplier: 2.5

Wizard's Fire: Level 6 *Cost: 200 mana. Cast time: Instant*
Sets target ablaze with Wizard's Fire. Deals 200 burn damage per second. DoT has 60% chance of interrupting target's spell casting. Can be applied to multiple targets at once. Wizard's Fire cannot be extinguished by physical means.

Reclaim Soul: Level 1 *Cost: 2,000 mana. Cast time: 5 seconds*
This light magic spell can return a target's soul to their body after death. Must be cast within ten minutes of target's expiration. Cannot be cast during combat. Target will be restored with 20%

Health, Stamina, and Mana. Reclaimed souls will not suffer experience loss from death. Cooldown: 24 hours. Cooldown will reduce by 2 hours per skill level.

"Holy shit, Fitz!" Alexander looked at the grinning wizard as he finished reading. "These are totally worth getting my brain squeezed!" The res spell alone was huge. Not only did it mean no loss of XP when his people died, but if he used it enough he could level the spell to where he could resurrect multiple people per day. Level twelve would eliminate the cooldown altogether. Then again, he'd never heard of a player achieving a skill level of twelve in anything.

Turning toward the group, he said, "I just got a rez spell. Anybody wanna take one for the team so I can test it?" He grinned, looking at Max specifically. His friend sidestepped to hide behind Lugs.

"Thank you, Fitz." Alexander bowed to the dragon wizard. "And thanks for not warning me ahead of time." The wizard winked at him. Then he turned to the other players.

"As I'm the only one here able to do so, I will instruct the rest of you as well. All of you have new levels and qualify for training of new skills."

Lainey was first on her feet and moving toward the wizard. She threw Alexander a dirty look as she passed by and turned her back on him. Fitz laid a hand on her and her body locked up as if she'd been struck with her own Shock spell. When he was done, she dropped to her knees, breathing hard. Tears flowed down her cheeks. Alexander moved to assist her but Jules hip-checked him and stepped in herself to comfort Lainey.

One by one, the players all accepted new knowledge from Fitz. Then, much to Alexander's surprise, the wizard called the NPCs forward as well. The orcs and minotaurs had no magic that Alexander had been aware of. When he threw a questioning look at Fitz the wizard just chuckled. "You'll see, boy."

Sasha had a different question. "Hey, ummm, Fitz? How come you can train everybody here? I mean, you're a wizard. But you're giving skills to warriors and archers."

"Ha! I have lived for eons, child. Do you think I spent all that time fighting with Rufus over tasty treats?" As if summoned, Rufus appeared atop the wizard's hat and waved. "I have traveled many worlds and fought in more battles than I can count. I have mastered languages and crafts. And yes, I learned to wield sword and hammer, shield and spear. Come here, and I'll teach you something that might surprise you."

Though Sasha had already received her training, she stepped toward the wizard. He placed a hand on her head and a moment later she began to laugh. As the wizard waggled his eyebrows at her, she said, "The old goat just raised my cooking skill to ten! And gave me a dozen new recipes."

Lainey's eyes widened. "All those times you've demanded one of us cook for you and you could easily have done better yourself?"

Fitz shrugged. "What would be the fun in that? I'm an old man. It's only fitting you young ones should pamper me. As payment for the pleasure of my company." Rufus rolled onto his back atop the wizards hat, holding his belly and emitting a chittering laugh. Fitz's eyes rolled up, as if looking at the little familiar, and he snorted.

"Yes, well." Fitz cleared his throat as he waved a hand at Rufus in a shooing motion. "I think it's about time we continued on."

Sasha agreed, and soon had everyone back in formation. Brick and his still-shining shield led the way across the cavern. On the other side was a thick ironwood door with deep gouges in it. Brick tried to pull it open, but found it locked. Max stepped forward and produced his lock picks. Moments later, the lock clicked and the door opened slightly on its own. He stepped back and let it swing open fully.

Brick shouted, "Look out!" and shoved Max through into the darkness beyond. The ranger, caught by surprise, stumbled and fell on his butt. He looked around frantically for whatever danger Brick had spotted, scrambling to his feet and nocking an arrow.

A quiet chuckle from Brick grew into a full-belly laugh. "Bwahaha! Ye should see yer face!"

"What the…? Dammit! There could have been a monster in here. Or a dozen drow!" Max shot looks over both shoulders as he yelled at his friend.

Brick put on his best innocent face. "Aye. If ye'd been killed ta death, our king woulda got a chance ta test his new magic!"

The indignant look left Max's face as he began to chuckle along with his friend. "Well played, sir."

Brick stepped into the room, the light from his shield illuminating a small chamber with a stairwell leading down. He proceeded down the stairs, which only took them maybe thirty feet lower than the level they'd just left. Just as he reached the bottom step, a grinding sound could be heard. The step underneath him settled about six inches, stopping with a click. Ten steps above him, spikes shot out from the walls in a wide swathe. Players and NPCs were skewered, pinned to the opposite side of the stairwell. Most of those who'd been standing in that area were casters. Martin and one of the other healers, Misty, and one of the minotaurs were impaled in various places. Worst of all, Fibble let out a squeal as one of the spikes drove through his shoulder and pinned him to the wall.

Max immediately went to work on the trap, pushing Brick off the step and lifting the top cover to examine the mechanism. After some tinkering, the spikes withdrew back into the wall, peeling off their victims as they did. None of them had been killed outright, though Misty had a nasty gut wound from the spike driving through her side and out her back. The healers went to work, but their comrades' health bars weren't rising.

Fitz lifted Fibble and took a sniff of his wound. "Poison. Drow poison."

Sasha and Lydia had prepared for this. They'd concocted and distributed large quantities of the poison's antidote to the various allied cities. She reached into her bag and withdrew several vials, handing one to each of the stricken.

Fitz poured Fibble's vial down his throat. The little goblin had lost consciousness and was down to twenty percent health. As soon as the potion reached his gut, the little guy coughed and opened his eyes. His health bar stopped draining and Fitz cast a heal on him that immediately brought him back to one hundred percent.

Fibble hugged the wizard, causing him to sputter and blush. Fitz set Fibble down quickly and turned away, pretending to check on the others.

While the injured recovered, Max inspected the only door that led out of the room. "No traps here that I can see. Though I won't promise there isn't one on the other side."

Brick had the others stand back and took his spot in front of the door. Max pulled it open and jumped back, readying his bow.

Brick's shield illuminated… a stone wall.

Outside the door, a corridor ran left and right, the opposite wall about six feet from the door. Brick stuck his head out, then quickly jerked it back. Spells and arrows blasted past the door in both directions.

"Well shit." Brick scratched his helm with his hammer. "There be baddies in both directions, just waitin' fer us to stick our beards out there."

"Could you tell how many?" Sasha asked.

Brick shook his head. "Ye saw me, right? I did no' take time to look, but…" He grinned at her and stuck his head out again, this time looking the other way. As he pulled it back once again, attacks passed by the door in both directions. "Based on tha… I'd say a LOT."

Sasha thought for a moment. "Okay, we have enough tanks for two rows. They step out and push apart so that the rest of us can take cover between them. Then we move to the…" She looked at Alexander.

He shrugged. "Left."

"We move to the left and take out that group. When they're dead, we reverse and finish off the others."

Brick and Grumpy looked at each other and laughed. They were both huge J.R.R Tolkien fans, and exactly in unison they quoted a famous line from Gimli in a favorite movie.

"Certainty of death. Small chance o' success. What're we waitin' for!"

They both had a good chuckle when the remaining orcs roared their agreement.

Sasha was not amused. Alexander tried to help. "How 'bout I just build a wall on one side? Then we don't have to worry about the crossfire."

Sasha felt like smacking her own forehead. "Or, yeah. We could do that."

Brick stepped back and Alexander hugged the wall to one side of the doorway. The angle of his view through the door allowed him to see part of the corridor without being seen - or shot - by the enemy. He used Earth Mover to raise stone from the floor and block the corridor in that direction. There were loud shouts of surprise and anger from both sides.

The moment he stepped back, Brick, Lugs, and Grumpy leapt out into the hallway in that order. They put their backs to the wall and the three of them locked shields. Immediately, spells began to impact their shields. The onslaught was fierce, but the ogre and two dwarves had the strength to hold.

As they stepped forward, three more tanks rushed out and got behind them, adding their strength to the front row. With each step the tanks took forward, more and more of the raiders stepped into the hallway, three and four at a time. Alexander brought up the rear in case he needed to make repairs to the wall. Even over the noise of the battle, he could hear impacts on the stone.

The raiders advanced, the tanks taunting and holding the attention of the enemy as the ranged DPS groups fired all they had. There were a few melee NPCs at the front of the enemy force, trying their best to stay alive as deadly missiles both mundane and magical passed over their heads in both directions.

"Focus on the healers!" Sasha heard herself shout.

"What healers?" Max smirked at her as he fired another arrow. "I haven't seen one of them get healed yet."

Sasha scanned the enemy health bars. Max was right. Not one of them was recovering health after taking wounds.

"They don't have healers!" She rolled her eyes when Max snorted. "Forget the melee. Focus on the drow casters!"

Alexander decided to test one of his newly-improved spells. He cast Magic Shield on the front line of tanks. A shimmering wall appeared in front of the tanks, just inches from their shields. Immediately, the wall began to pulse as spells impacted it. A bar appeared on his UI showing the remaining strength of the shield.

Magic Shield
Level 5
Capacity: 214,500/230,000

In just a few seconds, the combined attacks from the drow down the corridor had dropped the shield's 'health' by more than fifteen thousand HP, or about six percent. But with five times his health as a starting point, the shield might last as much as a full minute. In combat time, that was huge. A full minute to heal, drink potions, or prepare spells while your enemy wasted their mana or ammo was an eternity.

Looking back at the front line, he saw a shit-weasel strike the shield and stop dead before dropping to the floor. It tried to crawl forward, but couldn't penetrate the magic barrier that apparently extended all the way to the floor. A moment later, Lugs stepped forward and crushed it beneath his iron boot. Alexander noted that the shield moved forward with him.

On a whim, he shouted, "Brick! Lugs! Grumpy! The shield in front of you moves when you do. Try running right at the enemy. See if it pushes them back!"

With a wicked grin on his face, Lugs roared and stepped forward, moving into a fast walk, then a jog. Grumpy and Brick kept pace. The second line followed behind.

The shield proceeded in front of them as they sped down the corridor, magic attacks and crossbow bolts exploding in front of them. The shield's strength was dropping fast, but they still had close to fifty percent.

The few melee fighters among the enemy stepped forward and drew their weapons as the tanks approached. Lugs and the others didn't hesitate. They bowled into the front of the enemy force, the shield knocking them back with a flash of light. Lugs and the dwarves pushed, the second line adding their strength from behind. The enemy were shoved back, falling into a tangled mess. The three tanks began lashing out with weapons, which passed through the shield easily, while the blows from the enemy just bounced off the magic shield.

"Bwahaha! This be fun!" Brick smashed in the head of a dark orc, then leapt atop its fallen body to smash his hammer into the face of a drow. Lugs had switched to a spear and was impaling mob after mob from behind the shield. In seconds, the back row of drow broke and retreated down the corridor. The raiders stepped over the fallen and continued to massacre everything within reach. Spells and arrows flew over their heads to take down the fleeing drow.

Not quite a full minute after he cast it, the shield failed.

The raiders finished off the last of the defenders that were still in range. The rest had fled down the corridor and around a corner. Brick led the way as they followed at a jog, the entire raid behind them.

Once again, still grinning like a madman, Brick poked his head around the corner. This time, no spells or other attacks tried to harsh his melon. There was no sign of any foe. A short corridor led to an arched doorway with dual ironwood doors.

Lugs volunteered this time. Taking a deep breath, he stood ten feet from the doors. "This is gonna leave a mark," he said, before activating Shield Rush. His massive ogre frame sped toward the doors, impacting right at the seam in the center. The doors burst open and Lugs tumbled face-first into the room beyond.

"Damned things weren't even locked!" he complained from the floor. A moment later, a dozen hobgoblins swarmed over him, stabbing and slashing with short swords.

Brick and the other tanks rushed in, slamming into the mobs and knocking them back from a badly injured Lugs. The healers focused on him as the tanks herded the hobgoblins toward the back of the room. An open door stood behind them and a few turned to run.

Alexander cast his shield again. Only this time, he focused on the doorway. Not sure if he could cast the spell on an inanimate target, he closed his eyes and concentrated. A moment later, he felt the shield spring into place. Opening his eyes, he was just in time to see a fleeing hobgoblin bounce face-first off the shield. The tanks and melee raiders moved in and made short work of the mobs, pressing them against the shield and mauling them.

Alexander dropped the shield and the group proceeded into the next room. They found the remainder of the drow who had attacked them in the corridor. No surrender in them, the wizard's acolytes attacked with everything they had. Lyra, still standing in the previous room, took a random stray shit-weasel hit. It struck her face and began to burrow into her even as she fell. Fitz was there almost instantly but the nasty thing was too fast. It disappeared into an eye socket as she screamed. A moment later, she was dead as it ate through her brain.

With an apologetic look to Sasha, Fitz drew a dagger with a sparkling blade and rammed it into Lyra's skull. The worm inside screamed and died, smoke rising up from the wound.

Off to the side, Fibble looked horrified. He stared at the wizard, eyes wide and lower lip trembling as tears rolled down his face. "Fitz?" The goblin protector hadn't seen the worm kill the healer, just Fitz slamming a dagger into her head.

Sasha stopped healing to crouch in front of the little goblin. "Its okay, Fibble. Lyra was already gone, sweetie. Fitz just killed the nasty worm that killed her."

The goblin's terrified eyes looked up at her. "Fitz not hurt nice lady?"

"Not even a little bit. Fitz is one of us. Family."

Fibble nodded his head, then cast a still-suspicious look at the wizard. Fitz gave the little guy his most friendly smile. "I would not hurt one of our own, Minister Fibble. I promise."

Fibble looked more convinced, and when Sasha reminded him that the tanks needed healing, he turned and rushed into the room where the battle was happening, already shooting Lugs with his stick as he went through the door. "Pew!"

When the fight was through, Sasha called Alexander over. "Okay dorkboy, here's your chance to test that new res spell." She pointed at Lyra.

He held up a hand, then hesitated. "If I res her with that thing in her head…?"

Sasha shrugged. "Only one way to find out!"

He pointed at Lyra and cast the Reclaim Soul. A golden glow enveloped her body for three seconds, then she opened her eyes. Both of them. The eye lost to the worm had been restored. She lifted a hand to her face and groaned.

"That was… a little too real. No, a *lot* too real. I… I felt it eat into me. I don't ever want to go through that again." She accepted her brother's hand to help her get to her feet. Sasha handed her some food and drink to restore her stats.

Lainey commiserated. "Yeah those nasty worm things are no joke."

Beatrix looted as Max and Jules explored both rooms, finding nothing interesting. The raiders made their way back to the wall Alexander had erected and made themselves ready.

"On the count of three," Alexander called out. "One… two…"

Max interrupted him.

"Wait, is it one, two, shoot? Or one, two, three, shoot!"

Alexander rolled his eyes. Max pulled this particular prank about once a month. "You know damn well it's one, two, shoot."

Max adopted an innocent face. "Sure, I mean, I know. But all these new folks might not have known."

Molgo put a giant hand on the ranger's shoulder. "Everyone knows its it's one, two, shoot."

Alexander chuckled and began again. "Get ready. One... two... three!"

The wall liquefied, much to the surprise of the defenders behind it. The moment the air was clear, the ranged DPS bombarded the drow and their servants. Then the tanks raised their shields and stepped forward. There were fewer enemies on this side of the corridor and the fight took less than two minutes. The raid's only casualty was a minotaur who took a crossbow bolt to the throat. Sasha was able to save him before the bleed effect emptied his health bar.

Brick led them down the corridor in that direction, finding another T-intersection at the end. The new passage was much shorter to the right, leading to another set of double doors. These were engraved stone. The artwork on the doors showed a drow on a high throne overlooking a sea of kneeling supplicants.

Brick said, "Call it a hunch, but I be thinkin' this'll be where we find the boss."

Misty snorted. "Thank you, Captain Obvious." Brick gave her a graceful bow.

Lugs stood in front of the doors and once again raised his shield. "I got this."

But instead of activating Shield Rush, he simply took a couple steps forward and used his weapon hand to push on the right-side door. It swung open without a sound. He turned and grinned at the group, earning him chuckles from many of the raiders behind him.

Lugs swept his arm across his body, motioning politely for Brick to go first. The dwarf obligingly stepped through, shield and weapon at the ready. The others followed behind in their now-familiar formation.

The room beyond the door was impressive. Maybe fifty yards long and wide, its ceiling rose up three stories into the darkness. Wide stone columns lined a cultured marble walkway that led the length of the room to a dais where the drow wizard sat on the same throne pictured in the engraving outside.

Scanning left and right, Alexander saw no other occupants in the room. But with the size and number of columns, a veritable army could be hiding behind them unseen.

The old wizard spoke. "Ah! Do come in. I must say it was kind of you to deliver yourselves to me here in my home. I've been waiting for this day for quite some time."

Fitz growled from the middle of the crowd, stepping to the side into plain view. "Your time is ended, drow. I have come down to your little hole in the ground to make certain of it."

The wizard's eyes widened briefly, then narrowed in pure hatred. "You are mistaken, dragon! Our time is just beginning. We will reclaim the surface world and destroy you and your pathetic allies. We-"

He was interrupted as twin daggers slammed into his back. Jules appeared briefly, standing behind his throne. She gave a smile and a wave, then disappeared. Fitz roared with laughter, pointing his staff at the drow and firing a beam of blue light into his chest. "The girl's right! Too much talking, not enough killing!"

The ancient drow cast a heal on himself, replacing the miniscule amount of HP that Jules' attack had taken from him, and the more significant loss from Fitz's attack. Then with a shout, he flung both hands forward. A shield bubble appeared around him, stopping a second blast from Fitz and several attacks from the other raiders. Alexander took a good look at him as the raid group advanced toward the throne.

Veldizar
Drow Wizard
Level 140
Health: 180,000/180,000

Fitz took a few steps forward, switching to Magic Bolts and firing them using his staff as a focus. The shield rang with each impact, as if a wooden mallet was being used to strike a large bell. The bolts didn't dissipate on contact, but rather ricocheted upward or off to the sides.

The drow completed a long casting of his own and a wall of flame shot forth, running along the walkway and expanding as it traveled. Alexander quickly threw up a shield on the front line of tanks, now six wide. "Get behind the tanks!" he shouted, needlessly. Everyone could see for themselves where to be.

The wave hit his shield and parted, the flames pushing off to either side. The barrier created a sort of cone of safety behind it. But the damage from the flames reduced the shield's strength by eighty percent.

Sasha shouted, "This isn't going to be a melee fight! Take cover behind the columns! Tanks and melee watch for adds! Everybody else, kill this asshole!"

Fibble, standing right next to Sasha as usual, squeaked out his version of a battle '*rawr*!' and shot forward. His fuzzy slippers were a blur as he used the speed gifted to him by Hermes. Running straight at the drow, he fired with his stick. "Pew! Pew!"

The drow smirked at the little goblin as the light attacks were deflected by his shield. He returned fire, casting a dark bolt that missed the speedy goblin by inches as he dodged to one side. Just as he'd done with the demon when they'd first adopted him, Fibble began to harass the drow, running here and there and firing again and again, shouting, "Pew!" with each shot.

The raiders roared their approval, redoubling their attacks as they cheered their little buddy. Alexander drew his sword and focused his Ray of Light spell through the weapon. The beam's heat caused the air around it to waver as it burned through the room and into the shield. The light spread out in ripples across the shield's surface as Alexander tried to bore a hole in it or destroy the shield altogether.

The drow shouted again and a door to one side of the room burst open. Two enormous trolls in full plate armor stepped into the room. These were nearly identical to those who'd stood at the gate above, only much larger. Each carried a shield and a spiked flail.

Sasha shouted, "Tanks! Do your thing! Melee, back them up! Martin, Lyra, Benny, you're on that group. Shout if you need help."

The tanks left the cover of the columns and rushed toward the trolls with the orcs and minotaurs, as well as Warren, Helga, Pollock and his guys right behind them.

Alexander broke off his attack for a moment and cast Levitate on one of the trolls. Lifting the massive thing with the heavy armor was nearly too much for him. He had flashbacks of lifting the stone that had wrenched his magic from him not so long ago.

Barely lifting the thing off the ground, he shoved it sideways into its ally, knocking them both to the ground. Breathing hard and feeling drained, he left it to his people to take advantage of the opportunity.

Turning back to the drow, he cast Wizard's Fire on the shield. The flame quickly spread to engulf the top half of the bubble, obscuring the view of the drow inside. Reverting back to his Ray of Light, he resumed his efforts to break through.

Fifteen seconds later, he glanced to the side, checking up on the group fighting the trolls. He saw one of the beasts was still on its back, Lugs stomping on its chest every time it tried to rise. The other one was back on its feet and Alexander watched as it whipped the flail around. The spikes of the ball embedded themselves into Warren's back as he tried to dodge. The ball was nearly as large as the warrior himself and two of the longer spikes erupted from his chest as he was flung forward, stuck to the weapon. His health dropped to zero and he dropped his weapon. The troll swung the weapon back, then slammed it to the ground, trying to dislodge Warren's corpse. Molgo and the others took advantage and rushed in, pounding with axe and sword at joints in the beast's armor.

Troll Juggernaut
Level 90
Health: 192,400/220,000

"Damn, each of the trolls is a boss all on its own!" Alexander said to nobody in particular. His group was doing well, managing to separate the upright troll from the one still on the ground, not allowing their people to get trapped between them.

Fitz shouted something Alexander couldn't quite make out. A second later, Rufus appeared through a hole in the wizard's hat. The adorable little squirrel-thing leapt to the floor and dashed toward the trolls. As he went, he grew and transformed. His front legs got longer and stronger. His bushy tail thinned and grew scales. His head elongated, as did his teeth and claws.

By the time Rufus reached the closest troll, he stood eight feet tall and weighed easily eight hundred pounds. He was all teeth, claws and muscle, resembling a raptor more than the furry pet he'd been just moments before.

Rufus darted in behind the battling troll and latched onto its armor with his foreclaws. Pulling the troll back toward him and unbalancing the monster, he clamped his jaw down on the monster's weapon arm bicep and began to gnaw at the metal armor. The sound of bone on metal screeched through the battle.

The drow, still safe in his bubble, cast another wave of fire while Alexander was distracted. This one impacted the melee and tanks, and Rufus, before he had time to react and throw up a shield. It blasted through the group, burning the raiders and heating up the armor of the trolls. Two minotaurs right in the center of the wave died, along with two of the players from Antalia. The group's healers were far enough away to have been unharmed, and were working frantically to do their jobs. Alexander cast heals on those who were most badly injured, then turned back to the drow.

As long as the evil wizard was safe in his bubble, the raiders were at his mercy. Desperate to end the fight before more citizens were killed, Alexander pulled up his nuke. He focused on the shield and cast the Divine spell gifted to him by Odin and the pantheon of Light.

The blast of divine magic crashed down through the ceiling, nearly blinding everyone in the room. There was a resounding boom as the spell impacted the shield, then a sound like shattering glass as it failed and burst into millions of shards.

The drow screamed as some portion of the divine spell reached him. His skin smoked and his long white hair melted on his head and shoulders.

Fitz took immediate advantage, blasting the drow with attack after attack of blue magic as he stalked forward toward the throne. Alexander hit him with Wizard's Fire, hoping to further interrupt any casting he attempted.

When Fitz reached the throne, he slammed the butt of his staff into the drow's face, breaking his jaw and several teeth. The drow spat the fragments out, along with a nasty-sounding spell that knocked Fitz back and surrounded him in a dark cloud.

A shout from the direction of the trolls caught Alexander's attention. The second troll had regained its feet and was wildly swinging its flail in an arc. Two minotaurs lay bleeding at its feet and Lugs was limping out of range of the attacks, his left leg mangled.

Sasha redirected all the healers to cover the tanks and melee as Lainey and Max peppered the drow with arrow after arrow as rapidly as they could. Fitz was still within the dark cloud, and Alexander could hear him cursing.

Pointing toward the troll that was swinging its weapon, Alexander raised the stone underneath. With no time to be precise, he flung the his hand upward. A column of stone rose under the troll's feet, lifting it high into the air. Surprised and off balance, it stumbled. Alexander kept channeling the spell until the platform was thirty feet in the air. Which was when the now-frightened troll fell off.

Alexander liquefied the stone as the armored troll plummeted thirty feet to the floor. Its armor deformed as it impacted, a loud clang sounding through the room. It lay there stunned and partly broken as Lugs and the others closed in and began to hack at it.

Alexander turned back to Veldizar. Channeling his Ray of Light, he built up the mana for a burst. Putting more than a thousand mana into it, he blasted the wizard in the face. The spell peeled the flesh off of half the drow's face and knocked him backward in his chair.

Veldizar
Drow Wizard
Level 140
Health: 110,050/180,000

Fitz shouted something that echoed through the room and the dark cloud around him exploded, shredding into wisps that floated to the floor and dissipated. His clothes and skin burned with acid, the dragon wizard looking a bit worse for wear. Ignoring his physical condition, Fitz leapt back into the fight. He began an incantation that ended with him slamming his staff into Veldizar's chest.

The drow went stiff, his body rigid. Hatred boiled from his eyes as he strained against Fitz's spell. The ranged damage-dealers once again poured on their attacks, using the fastest and strongest they had available.

Veldizar's health dropped to fifty percent and a wind began to howl through the room. A whirlwind formed around the throne, spinning faster and faster. A moment later, the millions of shards from the shattered shield were lifted into the air and the whirlwind became deadly. Fitz tried to retreat, but the vortex moved with him. He quickly cast a shield around himself, followed by a heal.

Alexander frantically tried to interrupt the spell. He hit the drow with magic bolts, bursts of light, even a healing spell. Nothing broke the focus of the drow wizard, intent as he was on killing the dragon. Even at the cost of his own life.

Alexander was about to try surrounding Fitz with stone to stop the wind when the spell just stopped. Looking to the throne, Alexander saw Jules once again standing behind the throne. Her right-hand dagger was jammed through the side of the drow's throat and the left protruded from his chest. She yanked out both daggers, then activated the ability she'd used on the runaway troll.

Her daggers stabbed into the drow's chest, face, and neck over and over. She slit his throat and gouged out one of his eyes. When it was over, she stood panting in front of him, covered in his blood. It ran down her arms and dripped from her blades.

The drow managed to cast a heal that closed his throat wounds and gasped in a ragged breath. He pointed a finger at Jules and croaked, "DIE!"

Jules was blasted backward, her limp body sliding across the marble. A black ooze coated her front side and ate away at skin and armor alike. Her health bar dropped to zero in seconds, and she was gone.

Alexander and Fitz shouted challenges in unison. Fitz held out both hands and blasted Veldizar with blue flame. The drow lifted his cloak to ward off the blaze, hiding behind it. Alexander charged forward, ignoring the danger. He lifted his sword in front of him and impaled the drow, the blade plunging through his chest and pinning him to the chair. He channeled a burst of light magic through the weapon, causing the drow to scream as the light illuminated its body from the inside. Gritting his teeth, he levered the sword upward, the razor sharp blade snapping ribs and slicing flesh as he poured more mana into the channeled light spell. Light began to pour from the drow's eyes and open mouth as he continued to scream.

Veldizar
Drow Wizard
Level 140
Health: 31,900/180,000

Veldizar's hands shot forward, blasting out the same spell he'd killed Jules with. Alexander and Fitz both flew backward, with Alexander taking the brunt of the force. His chest was protected by his Legendary armor piece, but his left arm snapped as he impacted the floor. His brain felt like jelly as a 'Stunned' debuff appeared on his UI. Twenty seconds. An eternity.

The drow was about to cast another heal on himself when a Shock arrow from Lainey interrupted him. The stun lasted less than a second, but it forced him to start again. Immediately, a burst of five arrows struck his face as Max jumped in. A second later, a Silence arrow struck the drow in the face as well.

Fitz managed to sit up and begin casting bolts at Veldizar. Each one took about a thousand points off the drow's health. Alexander could only sit, helpless, as the clock on his stun ticked down.

Veldizar
Drow Wizard
Level 140

Health: 2,900/180,000

Fitz himself wasn't looking too healthy. He'd absorbed a lot of damage from the drow wizard. Alexander saw him begin to change to dragon form even as he pounded Veldizar with magic once more.

"I have waited millennia to take your head, Fitzbindulum! Oldest and wisest of the dragons. He who wastes his time playing among the insect humans!" Veldizar blasted Fitz again, this time with one of the shit-weasel spells. The worm impacted Fitz in the face as he transformed. Veldizar had timed the attack perfectly. With his hands on the floor and changing into forepaws, Fitz couldn't react quickly enough. All he could do was bite down on the worm trying to dig its way down his throat.

Alexander rushed toward Fitz and grabbed hold of the nasty thing with his one good hand, trying to pull it free.

As he struggled, he heard a high-pitched scream. Looking over his shoulder, he saw Fibble leap up over the arm of the throne to the drow's right side. Tiny sword in hand, the furious little goblin soared through the air. "No hurt Fitz! Die!" he screamed, driving the sword into Veldizar's remaining eye as he landed on the wizard's chest. With his other hand, Fibble shoved his stick into Veldizar's open mouth and shouted, "Pew! Pew! Pew!" as he fired light bursts over and over. The combined critical hit with the light-blessed sword and the light magic delivered straight into the wizard's mouth were enough to drain his last sliver of health.

The worm that Fitz and Alexander struggled against went limp when Veldizar died. Fitz unclenched his jaw and allowed Alexander to yank it free as both of them fell backward. Alexander heard Max shout.

"Holy shit! Fibble just killed the boss!!"

Everyone in the raid except Fitz leveled up. Which was good, because the two trolls, now freed from whatever control was exerted over them by the drow, went berserk. They began tearing pieces of armor off of themselves and hurling them at nearby raiders.

The tanks did their job, grabbing the attention of the enraged monsters and absorbing damage as the rest of the raid burned down first one troll, then the other.

Quest Complete! The Heart of Darkness
You and your raid party have successfully infiltrated the drow stronghold
and killed the drow wizard Veldizar. Reward: Experience – 350,000, Gold – 650
Bonus reward for capture: None

Alert! You have captured a drow stronghold!
Would you like to claim ownership of this stronghold?
Yes/No?

Alexander looked around at the faces of his core group. Max and Brick nodded their heads, grinning. Lainey and Sasha just shrugged. Jules was, of course, in limbo.

Fitz stepped forward, a back-to-normal Rufus sitting atop the brim of his hat. "If you do not claim the stronghold, others might. There are many more drow out there. Do not let them regain a foothold so easily."

Alexander didn't need a better reason than that. He mentally selected 'Yes' on his UI.

>>>System Alert!<<<

World Event Update

King Alexander of Elysia and his raid party have captured the stronghold belonging to the drow wizard Veldizar! They are the first to both successfully defend against the drow invasion of their capitol and take the fight to the aggressors to destroy the enemy.

Alexander's UI lit up with system messages again. With a sigh, he scrolled through them.

First Kill!
Congratulations! You and your group are the first to defeat Veldizar's Stronghold.
Reward: Experience – 800,000; 1,000 gold; Reputation with all citizens of Io: +50

World First!

Congratulations! You and your group are the first to complete the World at War event.

Reward: Experience: 500,000; 500 gold; Reputation with all citizens of Io: +100

Level up! You are now level 78!
Your Wisdom has increased by +1
Your Intelligence has increased by +1
You have 13 free attribute points available

The raiders were celebrating like madmen. The massive experience boosts leveled all of them at least once. And fifteen hundred gold on top of everything else they'd earned on this raid was huge for some of the players, and all of the NPCs. Alexander noted a flashing light in the shape of a money bag along the left side of his UI and focused on it. After reading the message that popped up, he smiled and called Molgo over.

"I just got a message. Those of your people and the orcs who have fallen in this place have each been awarded a full share of the gold. To be given to their families or designated heirs."

Molgo bowed his head briefly. "Thank you, Alexander. The families of the fallen will be greatly pleased. Not only have our fallen earned great glory, they have provided well for the tribe."

"Don't thank me, I'm just the messenger. Thank Odin and the light gods."

Molgo grunted and moved away to inform the orcs and minotaurs.

Max looted the wizard and whistled. "There's some seriously sweet loot here, boss!" he called out.

Alexander, tired of being underground and concerned for his people, was ready to leave. "Grab it all, we'll go through it later. Also, get Jules, Warren's and everyone else's gear to take with us."

The moment Max looted the old wizard, a portal appeared behind the throne. The group of dragons that had been providing the distraction up top joined them, arriving through the same door the raiders had. Del reported in.

"We left nothing alive from the gates to this room." He looked around at the dead trolls and the drow wizard. "It seems you were quite busy yourselves."

Alexander offered Del his hand. "Thank you, Del. Without your distraction, we might never have made it this far."

"No need for thanks, Majesty." Del bowed his head. "This was our war long before your people arrived on Io. It is we who offer you thanks for the death of the wizard."

The dragons helped Max search the throne room for any secret caches. Fitz pointed them toward the throne, as he'd found a stash of the orbs under the throne in the Dark One's stronghold. Sure enough, there was a panel there that, when pressed, opened a section of floor behind the throne and revealed a ramp leading downward.

At the bottom, they found a treasure vault filled with items. Weapons, gems, gold and silver, magical trinkets, and the like. Beatrix squeaked with joy, then growled at Alexander when he closed the passage. "What are you doing?"

"We can go through and divide all this up later. Jeeves, please make an accounting of all these items and their value if possible," Alexander said. "We need to get back to the keep."

Jules voice came through raid chat just then. *"Well, that sucked. I'm guessing from the portal in front of me and the way my UI has lit up that we won?"*

"Yup! Tons of XP, lots of loot. We ROCK!" Beatrix answered.

Alexander added, *"You and the others, take the portal. It should drop you back at the keep. Let us know if it doesn't and we'll come find you."*

He waited a few moments before she answered. *"Back at the keep. There's a party going on here already."*

Alexander looked to the raiders around him. "Well done, my friends! This has been our hardest fight to date. We lost some of our best along the way. Their sacrifice will not be forgotten." He took a moment to catch the eye of each of the remaining orcs and minotaurs.

"Unless anyone else has business here, I say we go back to the keep. There is food, drink, and comfort!" A ragged cheer went up from the raiders.

Fitz broke off from the group. He walked over to Veldizar's corpse, drawing a sword as he went. One quick blow removed the head from the body. It was gruesome looking. Both eyes gouged out, the flesh and hair burnt and melted. His mouth still formed his death-scream.

Walking back as he produced a box and stuffed the head in it, he noticed everyone watching him. Brick asked, "Gonna mount it above yer mantle?"

Fitz chuckled at him. "No, master dwarf. I plan to use one of our captured orbs and send a message to whichever wizard it leads to. I imagine it will ruin their day." He waggled his eyebrows as the others laughed.

"That reminds me." Alexander held up a finger. "Who wants to remove his heart for Lady Lia?" Molgo obliged, stepping over the corpse and reaching into the wound Alexander had made with his sword. A moment later he retrieved the black heart of the drow and handed it to Alexander with a bow of his head.

Leading the way, Fitz stepped through the portal. The others followed in ones and twos.

Chapter 17

Close Call

Matt waited as patiently as he could for a message from his mole. She'd need time to safely retrieve the stash of explosives and distribute them through the Olympus compound. It might even take her several days. He knew security was beefed up well beyond normal measures.

He'd lain down on the mattress that was set on the floor of the living room and gotten a solid six hours of sleep. He'd made himself some hot oatmeal with honey for breakfast, then spent some time scanning news feeds for any news on the manhunt by the various agencies pursuing him. All he'd found was an update on his father, who was still being held in solitary and who was still refusing to cooperate with authorities.

Matt spent some time thinking that over. He didn't trust the news feeds. Could that story be meant to put him at ease, when in truth his father had given him up? Not that it mattered much. Most of their network had been destroyed as people were arrested and questioned. The FBI was good at tracing financial transactions, phone records, travel, etc. His people were probably dropping like flies.

Which was fine by him. This was the endgame. Except for the few who still provided him with food and arranged for the next safe house, he didn't need the others. And many of the fools had been arrested before being paid, so the FBI was saving him money.

After a few hours of pacing and thinking, he decided to get back into the game. If nothing else, he was curious about the old wizard's response to his failures.

Taking a deep breath to prepare himself for the pain his avatar was likely experiencing, he closed his eyes and logged in.

>>> *System Message*<<<
Your last bind point is no longer valid.
You will be transferred to the nearest available faction bind point.

"What is this?" he asked himself aloud as he appeared in an unfamiliar room. Even before he was through speaking, he was seized by rough hands. "A human! How did he get here? Take him to the wizard!" A drow guard standing in front of him spoke to the two who were now holding him captive.

"Yes, take me to the wizard, fools!" Matt nearly spat at them. "And take your hands off me. Do you not know who I am?"

"A dead man. That is who you are." The lead guard looked at him with disdain. "The wizard will want to know how you managed access to this stronghold before you die. I suggest you save yourself some pain and tell him quickly. Or don't. All the same to me, really." He motioned with his hand and Matt was dragged out of the room.

Two long corridors and a set of doors later, he was dragged into a throne room. This one was smaller than his master's home, but it held all the ominous feelings of threat and fear he was used to.

The guards dragged him forward and tossed him to the ground in front of a throne. This one was set at ground level rather than atop a dais. When Matt lifted his eyes, he saw a drow wizard, but not *his* wizard. This one appeared much younger and had a cruel smile on his face.

"A human in my home. Of his own volition. I don't believe that's ever happened. Who are you?"

Matt looked around. There were a dozen or so drow gathered around, watching. None of them looked familiar.

"On this world I am known as the Dark One." He puffed out his chest and held his chin high.

"Ahhh… Veldizar's adventurer. That explains much." The drow tapped a finger to his chin as he considered this information.

"Why am I here? I should have arrived in Veldizar's stronghold," Matt demanded.

"Ha! Have you not heard?" He leaned forward in his throne and sneered at Matt. "Veldizar is dead! The boy king, the one that *YOU* failed repeatedly to eliminate, captured his stronghold and ended him."

Matt absorbed that. This new drow was right. That did explain a lot. His bind point had been in Veldizar's stronghold. If Alexander held it now, the game would have automatically moved his bind point so that he didn't appear in enemy territory and get killed immediately.

"And where am I now? May I ask your name?" he ventured to the wizard in front of him.

"You may ask, worm. But I will not answer. I will not make the mistake my colleague did. Your grand plan to attack all the light capitols has been a failure. All but two cities repelled our invasions. Even now, my stronghold and others are being attacked by groups of adventurers like yourself."

The drow rose from his seat. "We have learned much about you adventurers in recent months. Including the fact that you can retreat to your world at will, leaving your bodies here."

He took a step forward, his hands clasped together. "Unless, of course, you are in combat." Too fast for Matt to follow, he drew a slim dagger from a wrist sheath and stabbed it into Matt's shoulder. "Which you are, as of now."

Matt grunted in pain and placed a hand over the wound. He instinctively reached for his bag to retrieve a health potion before remembering that he no longer had a bag. He cursed under his breath and tried not to make eye contact.

The drow didn't care one way or the other. With a wave of his hand, he told the guards, "Feed him to the dogs. One small bit at a time. Keep him alive as long as possible to enjoy it."

Matt screamed obscenities at the wizard as he was dragged away. He knew as long as he was in combat, he couldn't log out. Meaning he'd have to endure all the pain they were about to inflict upon him. As they reached the door, he changed to pleas for mercy. The drow just turned his back and stepped back to his throne.

*****

Back in the safehouse, Matt was screaming as he ripped the headgear off and fell out of his recliner. His nerves screamed with echoes of the pain the drow had inflicted upon him.

"God dammit!" He was breathing heavily, his face on the carpet, spittle adding to the various stains there. "If I wasn't hiding from Odin, I'd report that shit to the devs. That was way overboard! Leave it to fucking Jupiter Tech to allow such a broken mechanic in their game."

But not for much longer. He quickly regained his feet, though his legs were wobbly. Opening his phone and turning it on, he waited for the powerup sequence to finish, then checked for messages.

Nothing.

A quick look at the time showed him he'd been in the game for about thirty minutes. It seemed much longer than that. As he used one hand on the back of his recliner to support himself, he happened to glance at the window. The light from a pair of headlights was barely penetrating the paper his people had used to cover the widows.

Light itself was no big deal, but this light was moving very, very slowly. And now stopping outside near the house.

That was all Matt needed. He grabbed his headgear and his bag and dashed for the back door. He didn't take time to sanitize the place and remove any fingerprints or DNA that might be found by the cops. If they were here now, they already knew who he was. If it wasn't cops outside, his people would clean up the house later.

Slamming open the back door, he flew across the yard. A few spare cement blocks gave him steps to get up and over the eight-foot high wall. Once on the ground on the other side, he ran down the alley and cut left across a yard. Roughly a minute and four blocks later he was in his truck.

Starting the engine, he cut off the headlights. A quick check for anything suspicious, and he made a U-turn. As soon as he was moving away from the safe house, he turned the headlights back on and drove the speed limit for two blocks. He carefully came to a complete stop at a stop sign, then turned right and went another few blocks. He tossed his phone into an alley as he passed it, thinking they may have used it to track him.

He continued this pattern for nearly a mile before taking a main road and leaving the area entirely. After holding it together for half an hour, he pulled over in an airport strip club parking lot. Putting the truck in park and turning off the engine, he sat there, breathing deeply and trying to think.

"Shit! Shit shit shit shit!" He pounded on the steering wheel. Now he was second-guessing himself. Maybe the headlights were just someone stopping at a neighbor's house. Maybe he just bailed for no reason.

A moment later, a helicopter passed overhead, moving in the direction of the safehouse. That settled it. He hit the steering wheel again. "They must have caught Jenni. Which means they know everything." He sat and seethed for a while.

After an hour of alternating between being pissed and feeling sorry for himself, he got out of the truck. He'd parked behind the building and away from any lights. Pacing back and forth, he mumbled to himself. The sound was drowned out by the *thump thump thump* of the music from inside the club. But it didn't matter, he knew what he said.

"It has to be me. I'm the only one left I can count on. Have to assume everyone else is compromised. I need to get inside and find those explosives. If she hasn't told them yet. They'll never expect me. They'll think I'll run."

The adrenaline rush of his flight from the safe house was gone and he was crashing. He needed to rest. As with many strip clubs near airports, there was a motel right next door. He left the truck where it was, making sure to lock it before he left. Walking over to the motel office, he paid cash for a room for three hours. The kid at the desk smirked at him. "Three hours? Right on, stud," he said as he looked around for Matt's companion.

Matt ignored him, leaving the office and walking calmly as his heart pounded in his chest. He felt exposed. Constantly looking for the video cameras that were everywhere these days. He tried to keep his head down and his face hidden as he located his room and unlocked the door. Not bothering to turn on a light, he closed and bolted the door and sat on the bed.

A few minutes of deep breaths and he was sufficiently calmed. He'd brought nothing in with him, leaving it all in the truck. It was safer there.

He went to the bathroom and unwrapped one of the plastic cups. Two cupfuls of water later, he set the cheap alarm clock next to the bed and laid himself down. It took him nearly an hour to calm his mind enough to sleep, but eventually exhaustion won out.

*****

McCoy cursed as one of the local PD undercovers rolled right up in front of the house and parked. "What the hell?" he hissed into the radio. "What are you doing?"

There was no answer from the police vehicle, but it didn't matter. There was a fast-moving shadow inside the house, then the bang of the back door slamming shut. McCoy and his partner leapt from their car and ran towards the house. By the time they'd leapt the fence into the backyard, no one was there. They followed Matt's route up the concrete blocks and over, stopping to look and listen when they were on the other side. There was no sign of their suspect.

They split up, each going opposite directions down the alley. McCoy went at a jog, talking into this radio as he went. "Suspect fled out the back when fucking local PD spooked him. We're searching the alley. We could use some eyes in the sky."

He listened to the radio chatter. The units they'd had coming in to surround the house were adjusting into a search pattern. He cursed the cops again. Ten more minutes and they'd have closed a net, and it wouldn't have mattered if the kid ran. He was too old for this running around shit.

Five minutes later, they gave up the foot search. There was no sign, no trail to follow. He was walking down a block of mostly-lit houses. A man sitting on his porch smoking a cigar called out a greeting. McCoy turned with a start. The guy'd been sitting in the dark and McCoy hadn't even seen him.

"Good evening, sir. Have you been out here long? Did you happen to see anyone suspicious run by?"

The man leaned forward to get a better look at McCoy. "You a cop?"

"Something like that. I'm a federal agent. We're looking for a suspect who fled on foot from a house about four blocks that way." He jerked a thumb over his shoulder.

The man nodded. "Guy in a hurry got in a pickup truck. He wasn't running, but he acted weird. As soon as he started the truck, he turned the headlights off. Made a u-ey and went off that way." The man pointed down the block.

"Did you get a good look at the truck?" McCoy was already on the radio as the man gave him a description of the vehicle. It was an old Chevy pickup truck. An antique. The kind built in the late 20th century when they still made them out of metal and they came with 8-track players and AM radio. It wouldn't have any electronics that could be tracked, unless the kid had been stupid enough to add a GPS. And based on his vehicle choice, McCoy doubted that.

The good news was, trucks like that were not that common anymore. He put the description out over the radio and thanked the man before turning to head back to his own vehicle.

When he reached the car, his partner was waiting for him. The first of the helicopters arrived overhead as the two of them walked to the unmarked cop car that had spooked their suspect.

The two officers were still sitting in the car. They hadn't even gotten out to assist with the chase or the search. McCoy tapped on the window. The officer in the driver's seat rolled down the window. "Yeah?"

"Yeah? YEAH!? That's what you have to say to me? Are you shitting me? What's your name, officer?"

"Cheek. What's yours."

"Cheek. Oh, that's perfect. Cheek. What the actual fuck did you think you were doing here?"

"Screw you, pal. I don't answer to you. You got a problem with me, call my sergeant."

Just then McCoy's partner shouted, "GUN!" and the passenger side window exploded. McCoy ducked down and moved back by the rear door of the vehicle as he drew his own weapon. He saw through the windows that his partner was hit and falling backward. McCoy didn't hesitate. Shouting for assistance into his radio, he fired through the back door window toward the front passenger seat. Three rounds, just to be sure. Then he stuck his hand through the shattered window and put three more rounds through the driver's seat headrest.

Other agents and officers were arriving, some by foot and others screeching to a halt in vehicles. McCoy shouted that the cops in the car had fired on his partner. As he did, he moved up slowly toward the driver's window. Gun first, ready to fire.

He relaxed slightly when he saw the brains splattered across the windshield. Another officer who had approached from the other side of the vehicle shouted, "This side clear!" and bent down to check on McCoy's partner.

McCoy sheathed his weapon and ran around the back of the car to do the same. He found his partner laying in the grass, groaning. The cop looked up and said, "His vest stopped the round. He's fine."

"Screw you! I feel like a damn elephant just kicked me in the chest!"

McCoy laughed, shaking with a combination of relief and adrenaline.

His partner looked up and said, "What the hell, man? Those were cops? Why'd they fire on us?"

McCoy looked at the cop standing next to them. "Good question. And why'd they pull right up here and spook our guy? Did you know these guys?"

The cop bent to look in the passenger window. "This one's Clinton. Not much left of the other one's face, but I'm guessing it was his partner, Cheek."

"Yeah, Cheek told me his name before his partner tried to kill mine. Any hint they might have been crooked?"

The cop shrugged. "Don't know them well. But we'll find out."

Another helicopter arrived as McCoy was dealing with the procedure involved when an agent fires his weapon and splatters brains around. As it turned out, Clinton was also wearing a vest and had survived. He was cuffed to a medic's gurney nearby and was being questioned. McCoy's SAIC had arrived on site to take charge of his weapon and get his initial report. He'd also found out from the local police captain at the scene that Clinton and Cheek had taken money from their suspect to keep him informed of any hint that authorities were closing in.

"Apparently they'd heard the call on the radio and volunteered to be part of the net. They knew if he happened to be captured and questioned, he could and probably would give them up. Since they didn't have any way to contact Matt to warn him, they did the next best thing by pulling up in front of the house and springing the trap before it was ready. Their genius plan was to plead an honest mistake afterward, thinking the house was half a block down."

"Damn." McCoy shook his head, sitting on the bumper of the ambulance they were using to check out his partner. "This kid's either an evil mastermind or the luckiest idiot who ever lived. How many other officers or agents are on his payroll?"

The SAIC just shrugged. "They've had years to plan this. We're playing catch-up for sure. But we'll get him. We're bringing in agents from two other offices and the state troopers and county sheriffs are in on the hunt."

McCoy was left to himself as he waited for permission to leave. Forensics was scouring the house looking for any clue that would tell them where Matt might go next. He watched the coroner remove the mostly-headless Cheek from the car and place him in a body bag. "Screw that asshole." McCoy didn't feel the least bit guilty for killing the man.

*****

Matt was startled awake by the sound of someone pounding on the door. "Hey man! Your three hours are up! You need to go, or buy more time!!"

He looked at the crappy alarm clock, which was bathing the room in a sickly green glow. It hadn't gone off when he'd set it to. Piece of shit. He got up and opened the door. "Your alarm clock doesn't work for shit," he said as he passed the desk clerk on his way out. He walked across the parking lot in the opposite direction from his truck. If the kid remembered him at all, he didn't want him to be able to point the cops in the right direction.

Instead, he went to the strip club. The flashing sign out front said they had a 24-hour buffet. Normally he'd never eat the food in such a place, but it was late and he was hungry. And he fully expected to be dead or eating prison food after tomorrow.

Walking inside, he ignored the small herd of dancers at the bar near the door and went straight to a table in the darkest corner he could find. A scantily-clad blonde waitress came to take his order. "What's your pleasure, sugar?"

"Captain and Coke. In a big boy glass. And the sign out front says you have a buffet?"

She snorted. "Used to. Health department shut it down cuz they never cleaned the trays. But the kitchen's okay, and its open. What would you like?"

"How 'bout a bacon cheeseburger? No lettuce. I hear that shit's dangerous these days. Maybe some onion rings?"

"Comin' right up, darlin'. And… if ya want some company after…" She winked at him and turned to give him a close-up view of her thong-clad assets before walking away with a little extra sway to her hips.

Matt shook his head. "Maybe I should take her up on it. Might be my last time…" He thought it over as he stared at his hands and waited for his food. The girl on stage was gyrating frantically, trying too hard. She didn't do anything for him.

The club wasn't busy, maybe half the tables occupied. It wasn't long before his waitress returned with his drink. "Here you go, lover. My name's Heather. What's yours?" She took the seat next to his at the small table. Her knee rubbed up against his outer thigh as she leaned forward and presented him a view of her breasts in a push-up bra.

"I'm Matt." He didn't see any reason to make up a name at this point.

"Nice to meet you, Matt. Your food will be ready in a few. Are you in town for the convention?"

And there it was. Any possibility that she might have been interested in him for his looks faded to nothing as she uttered the universal code phrase. She'd be happy to spend time with him after her shift, as long as he was paying.

He shook his head. "Running from the cops. I figure they'd never think to look for me in here."

She laughed, thinking he was joking. "Oh, so you're a bad boy, then. Let me guess, bank robber? Maybe a hit man?" She reached forward and squeezed his knee. "I like bad boys."

"I'm on the Ten Most Wanted list. I'm a bad, bad man. You can't hear them in here, but there are helicopters above us circling around trying to find me." He winked at her. It felt good to open up, even if she didn't believe him.

Her eyes narrowed and she looked sideways at him. "You don't look like a badass to me. I mean, you're cute enough. Look like you used to play ball. But you don't have the look of a killer."

He shook his head. "I'm just a misunderstood boy far from home who misses his mama."

Sure he was joking this time, she let go of his knee and playfully slapped his shoulder. "I'll go check on your food, hon. Don't go anywhere."

She got up slowly, displaying herself as best she could as she turned and headed to the bar. Matt watched with a little more interest this time. Maybe another hour at the motel wouldn't hurt. When she returned with his food, she set it down, then sat herself down in her previous spot. "Hope you like it." She smiled as she stole an onion ring from his plate.

He checked the burger to make sure there was no lettuce, then took a bite. It actually tasted quite good. He chewed slowly, then swallowed. "So… what time does your shift end, Heather?"

She beamed at him, a reward for remembering her name. "'Bout thirty minutes. But I don't have a lot of time. Gotta go to my other job. Workin' girl's gotta hustle if she wants to make the rent and tuition payments…"

Matt shook his head. "C'mon. There's no need for all that." He took another bite of the tasty burger and looked into her eyes as he chewed. He could see her calculating the odds of him being a cop. He swallowed and took a drink. "I'm not a cop."

She let out the breath she'd been holding. "Two hundred for an hour. And trust me, I'm worth it!" She twirled her hair as she smiled at him, then placed her hand back on his knee and squeezed.

"I believe you are." He picked up an onion ring and popped it into his mouth. It had been a while since he'd had food that wasn't microwaveable or some kind of cold-cut sandwich. He was starting to enjoy himself and relax a little. She abandoned him for a while when another of her tables became occupied by a couple of obvious business travelers. But she looked over and winked at him as she took their orders.

Matt finished his burger and a few more of the onion rings. His drink was badly watered down and didn't taste right. He waved at Heather as she passed by with a couple plates and mouthed the word 'water' as he made a drinking motion. She nodded and winked at him again.

He picked at another onion ring, but they were starting to get cold. She brought him a glass of water on her way over to another table, running her fingers through his hair as she passed behind him. He felt a little tingle of pleasure at that.

That tingle turned into a sinking feeling as he noticed a cop walking in the door. He turned his back and pretended to be interested in the girl onstage as his heart began to race. His grip tightened on the water glass until he had to focus on loosening it before it shattered. Heather returned and, seeing the look on his face, frowned.

"Somethin' wrong with the burger, darlin'?" She caught his furtive sideways glance toward the bar, where the cop was talking to the bartender. Sitting down next to him again, she whispered, "Holy shit, you were serious when you said you were hiding from the cops!"

He hissed at her, "Hush!"

She giggled, then covered her mouth. "That's just Jake. He comes in here every week to collect for the policeman's retirement fund, or whatever they call it. He'll pick a girl and go in the back for a free lap dance in a minute. Guy's all clumsy hands and drool." She made a disgusted face and shook her head slightly.

Matt kept his head down, pretending to focus on his meal. Sure enough, a minute later the cop passed by him, his gaze focused on the redhead who was spinning around the pole just then. Heather put her hand over his. "Relax, sweetie. Soon as he goes in the back, we can leave. Just let me give my last table over there the check and cash out."

Matt gripped her hand to keep her seated. "I'm sorry, Heather. I would have enjoyed spending some time with you. But I think its best I move on." He pulled out two hundred dollars plus another twenty for the burger. "How 'bout you just forget you ever saw me?"

She gave him a momentary pouty face, then took the money. "I'd have done that for free, hun. I'm no big fan of the cops myself. But thank you for this. And good luck." She got up and went directly over to talk to Jake the cop. Matt was about to make a run for it when she walked around to Jake's other side and took hold of his arm, turning him so that his back was to Matt. She motioned to the redhead on stage, then shook her head and said something that made Jake laugh.

Then, with a wink in Matt's direction, she took Jake's hand and led him behind the curtain into the VIP room.

With a sigh of relief, Matt casually got up from his table and headed for the door. He dropped a ten dollar bill on the bar in front of the bartender and thanked her on his way past. The moment he was out the door, he moved around to the back of the building and got into his truck. Thirty seconds later, he was back on the road, headed in the direction of the mountains and Olympus.

Chapter 18

Endings and Beginnings

Alexander and Jules attended the brief memorial for the NPCs lost in the raid and the celebration that came after. Jules was celebrated by several of the players for her badass takedown of the troll and her unexpected start of the boss fight. A few of them seemed quite smitten with her. But she discouraged them by clinging to Alexander's arm all evening.

Fibble and Lugs were a huge hit as usual, the two of them being handed drink after drink. Lugs sported his robot dance moves again, to the howling approval of everyone. A few of the players and one of the dwarves began to try to copy the moves, and Fibble played along as he perched on Lugs' shoulder. Even the normally-reserved dragons couldn't resist the cuteness, chuckling at the little goblin's antics.

When Alexander and Jules said their goodbyes and retired for the night, they found Richard's avatar waiting for them in their sitting room.

"Something happen, Dad?" Alexander was half drunk, but still sober enough to know that his father wouldn't visit without a serious reason.

"Matt had a mole at Olympus. We caught her earlier today and questioned her. They had more bombs stashed in the compound, and she had orders to destroy the tower and kill as many people as possible."

Jules gasped and sat down on a sofa. Alexander joined her, taking her hand in his and squeezing. "Anybody hurt?"

"Everyone is fine. She eventually cooperated. We used her phone to track Matt. The FBI was closing in on him, but some cops on his payroll managed to interfere and he got away seconds before they'd have nailed him."

"Dammit! I'm sick of this. Why is he so willing to kill innocent people?" Alexander thumped his fist on a coffee table. "Is Talbott sure that there aren't more bombs already set?"

"No. But he's got people checking right now. They're sweeping every inch of every building. If there's anything, they'll find it. I had them start with all the labs with pods in them. You and the others are safe."

Alexander nodded and took a few deep breaths. He couldn't do anything to help apprehend Matt out there in the real world. He needed to just accept that fact and move on.

"While you're here... just a couple things. We maybe need to discuss dialing down the realism for immersion players. It's getting a little... intense."

Richard nodded. "Your sync levels, you and Jules, are the highest of any of our testers. Others may reach your levels eventually, but we think its unlikely. The system was designed around your brain, Alexander, so it makes sense you'd sync so well. And Jules has spent more time in the game than anyone, ever. She literally lived in the game nonstop for months. So, two pretty unique cases. But yes, we can discuss some kind of restriction."

Alexander asked, "And what's the deal with the world event all of a sudden? I hadn't heard anything about that."

Richard grinned at him. "We think it's your fault. You got into this war with the Dark One and Odin sped up the event. It wasn't going to launch until next year."

Jules patted his leg. "That's my guy. Dragging a few million people into his own little private war." She smiled at him.

"I... it wasn't me..." Alexander stammered for a moment before realizing she was teasing. Richard tried to ease his burden.

"Howard and Matt targeted us years ago. This was all planned out and executed before we were even aware of a problem. There was nothing you could have done to avoid being in Matt's crosshairs eventually. I think you actually forced their hand ahead of schedule by picking a fight with PWP when you did. Things might have been much worse."

Jules squeezed his hand. "None of this is your fault. Don't take the blame for the actions of disturbed assholes. They put all this in motion. All the people who followed them? They made that choice for themselves." She paused, squeezing his hand tighter. "When my ex started to get abusive... I thought it was my fault. I thought maybe if I behaved differently, or tried harder to make him happy, things would get better. But the harder I tried, the worse it got. I mean, I know it wasn't my fault. But in the moment... it was easy to convince myself it was. Don't go down that road."

Alexander put an arm around her and hugged her close. "I'm sorry all that happened to you. But he's gone, and I'm here now. And even when..." He looked at his father and changed his phrasing. "Even *if* the time comes when I'm not here anymore, Pop and Lainey and Sasha will look out for you. You'll never suffer like that again."

Richard nodded and smiled at Jules as tears rolled down her cheeks. Then he cleared his throat. "Well, I think I've taken enough of your time. Congrats on the raid, and the tasty, tasty loot you haven't even bothered to look at yet!" He gave them a small wave and disappeared.

The two of them sat there on the sofa for a while, just holding each other. Eventually, Jules got to her feet and pulled him into the bedroom.

*****

The next morning, Alexander and Jules were up well before dawn. When they went downstairs, they found the dining area was littered with hungover or still-drunken citizens. Only the immersion players were present, and most of them didn't look well. Lugs was curled up in front of the auction house, his immense bulk blocking the door. Fibble, Beatrix, and Bacon were leaned up against him, and all of them were snoring.

Helga was passed out on top of a table, a smiling dwarf asleep under her arm. His black eye and swollen nose suggested she'd resisted his advances, at least at first. Grumpy and Brick were in the smithy, drinking coffee and talking quietly as apprentices bustled about slowly.

Alexander, curious how his allies were faring, walked over to the portal. First, he tried Stormforge, and the portal opened. He stepped through quickly, Taylor and his squad magically right behind him. Taylor didn't ask why they were there, just quietly followed Alexander to the

Redmond's home. The sun still wasn't up and Alexander could see lamps lit inside. He tried the shop door and found it open.

Stepping inside, he called out, "Lydia?"

She stepped out of the back room and rushed to gather Alexander into a hug. "Oh, Alexander! It's so good to see you!"

He stiffened as her voice wavered. "I see you defeated the drow's army. Was it bad?"

Lydia released him and stepped back. There were tears in her eyes. "Yes, we held. But we lost… many." She looked down at the floor as she began to weep.

Alexander opened guild chat. *"Sasha, get your ass to Lydia's. She needs a friend."*

Sasha answered immediately. *"I'll be there in five. Silverbeard, can you please open the portal?"*

Alexander patted Lydia on the shoulder and led her to the back room where they could take a seat. "The captain?"

"He's fine. He was badly wounded more than once as they defended the walls. But I was there to heal him. I healed as many as I could. We passed out potions and bandages… but there were just *so* many wounded…" She trailed off, her eyes unfocused as she relived the battle.

Alexander felt guilty. "We tried to come to your aid, but the gods prevented it."

She nodded her head. "I know. My husband told me. And I saw the message that you took the fight to the enemy and killed one of the wizards." She smiled and patted his leg. "I'm proud of you. That could not have been easy."

They spoke quietly for a few more minutes until Sasha, Lainey, and Jules arrived. Alexander quietly took his leave. Jules followed him out and walked hand in hand with him to the palace. They found Captain Redmond in the inner courtyard.

"Alexander! Good to see you. And good morning, Lady Jules." The captain's smile was forced, but friendly.

"Good morning, Captain. We just spoke to Lydia. She said it was rough here yesterday."

"We were fighting until very early this morning. Most of my men haven't slept yet." The captain rubbed his face with both hands. He took a water flask from his bag and poured some over his head. "Ahhh. That helps a bit." He led them into the palace and to the great room where they took a seat at one of the long tables. The room was a mess, with bandages and bloody clothes scattered around. The captain grimaced. "My apologies. We used this as our hospital. I'm afraid everyone was too tired to clean up."

Alexander offered, "I can have Silverbeard send some people. We'd be happy to help."

The captain considered it for a moment. "We'd appreciate it. But wait and see what the situation is in Broken Mountain, Damerion, and Antalia. They may have a need for more than just cleanup."

Alexander didn't want to ask, but he had to. "Your losses?"

The captain put his elbows on the table and rested his head in his hands. He didn't lift his head when he spoke. "I lost nearly a third of my guards. And another thirty or so citizens perished, either up on the walls with us or from attacks that flew over the walls into the city. We had a couple of fires. But overall, the city fares well. The adventurers saved us, without question. They dove into battle, giving their lives again and again to protect us. It was… remarkable."

Alexander was at a loss for words. More than a hundred citizens lost in the defense of Stormforge. He wondered if any of those killed were people that he knew. But he didn't have the heart to ask. As he sat there, trying to find some words that might express his sorrow, the captain spoke again.

"We appreciate your coming here to check on us. I know the king would have liked to see you. But I just convinced him to go and rest. He was on the wall with us, never stopped fighting until it was done. Then he helped with the wounded. I'll let him know you were here. But you should go check on the others now."

Alexander nodded and shook the captain's hand. "I'll send some people. You look like you could use some rest yourself. Go sleep. Your city is safe for now."

Alexander and Jules returned to Greystone Manor and he activated the portal to Broken Mountain. The moment he stepped through, he was surrounded by shields and bristling weaponry. It took several seconds for the guards to recognize him and relax. He asked about the battle.

"Aye, them nasty drow and their beasties came at us!" An elder guard captain informed them. "They dinna' try to break through our gates. Instead, they came up from the depths below the city. But me king expected exactly that and we were ready. The lower tunnels be runnin' with darkling blood!"

"And your people?" Jules asked.

The dwarf lowered his gaze. "We sent ten o' our own ta Durin this mornin'. Could ha' been much worse. But thanks to ye and yer dragon forges, our weapons cut them down like paper dolls." He grinned as he held up a battle axe that glowed slightly with enchantment.

"I'm glad to hear it. The losses in Stormforge were much greater. Please pass on to King Thalgrin that Charles and his people could use any aid you can provide. And give him my regards. I must go and check on the others."

The old dwarf nodded, placing hand to chest. "Aye, we'll do all we can. That's what friends be for. I know me king will be sorry ta miss ye."

Alexander tried to open the portal to Antalia, but it wouldn't work. "It seems the fighting continues in Antalia," he said aloud for everyone's benefit. The dwarf captain sent a runner to update Thalgrin and the elders.

Next, Alexander tried Damerion. The portal opened and he nodded to the dwarves as he stepped through.

He and Jules found themselves in the palace courtyard, surrounded by guards. They instantly came to attention and saluted as they recognized their visitors. A lieutenant stepped forward and bowed. "King Alexander. Lady Jules. I'd be happy to escort you to King Arand."

With a nod from Alexander, the young soldier spun on a heel and led them inside. Arand was in the throne room with his queen and his two remaining sons. He rose and clasped hands with Alexander.

"I'm happy to see you and your family are well, Majesty," Alexander offered.

"We're all still alive, though I don't know about well. It was a hard battle. The adventurers fought bravely and with abandon. And thanks to you, we were well prepared for the attack. Still, we lost four dozen of our guards and twenty civilians. And four of our mages were lost to some kind of combined spell the drow attacked with."

Alexander was growing numb to the numbers of lost citizens in these reports. Which bothered him a little bit. He had to remind himself once again that these were simply NPCs.

"I'm sorry for your losses, Majesty." He took a few minutes to fill the royal family in on the situations in the other kingdoms, finishing with, "And it seems Antalia is still fighting."

King Arand shook his head sadly. "That does not bode well. Could the city have been overrun?"

Alexander thought of Queen Margaret and Princess Kimberly dead in their throne room. "I don't believe so. I think they still fight." When he took a moment to think about it, he smacked himself in the forehead. "In fact, I know they still fight. Otherwise my guildmates in Antalia would have been killed and returned to their bodies at my keep."

He excused himself for a moment and opened guild chat. "*Michael? Tiny Sam? You guys alright?*"

Michael's voice came back almost instantly, the sound of battle in the background. "*Still alive, but barely!*"

"*Is the city still secure?*"

"*Yes, for now. We're holding well enough. But in the beginning, it was close. Several adventurers elected to take the side of the wizards and murdered some of our people in an attempt to open the gate. We almost weren't able to stop them. Our guildmates who are too low-level*" *to fight on the walls have been gathered at the cemetery to make sure those players don't get another chance to do harm."*

Alexander nodded to himself. Those players would be spawn-camped back down to level one. And they deserved no less. The consequences of one's choices.

"We can't send aid until the battle is over, Michael. But as soon as it is, let me know and we'll get people there to help."

Michael didn't answer and Alexander assumed he was busy fighting. He took a minute to update the royal family with the new information. As he rose to take his leave, he said "Elysia and Broken Mountain can offer assistance if it's needed."

Apollos shook his head. "It sounds like Antalia will have a greater need. We'll manage well enough. Send your people there when you can." The king nodded in agreement.

They said their goodbyes and Alexander took Jules back through the portal to Elysia. He called together the players who were online, as well as Silverbeard and Lola. After updating them all, a party of thirty players and citizens went through the portal to Stormforge. They were to report to Lydia for instructions on how best to assist.

Fitz appeared in the courtyard not long after. Del and the female scout dragon whose name Alexander couldn't remember appeared with him. The old wizard was smiling.

Jules asked, "What kind of shenanigans have you three been up to that makes you smile like that?"

Fitz produced one of the drow's portal orbs. "We've been having a bit of fun."

Del explained as Fitz waggled his eyebrows. "We took the orbs up onto the mountain, where we had some room. Taking our natural forms, we used each of the orbs to open a portal. The moment it was open, we all three breathed dragonfire through the portal before closing it."

Fitz added, "I tossed the head of the dead wizard through the last one afterward." Rufus nodded and laughed, holding his belly with both tiny paws as he leaned against the peak of the wizard's hat.

Alexander grinned at the squirrel that had so recently taken down a troll. "Good! Maybe that will make it easier for the adventurers who will be attacking the strongholds." He quickly updated them on the various other cities. Fitz frowned when he heard the news of Antalia.

He looked at Del, who nodded. Then he turned to Alexander. "You adventurers may not be able to assist. But this is a dragon war. Odin would not prevent us from killing the dark forces wherever and whenever we find them!" A second later, all three were gone. Alexander was glad. He hoped Fitz was right that Odin wouldn't interfere.

*****

Matt pushed the old truck to its limit as he sped up the nearly-deserted back road that would take him up Olympus Mountain. His thoughts raced as he became more and more sure that his time was running out. He pictured Heather whispering in Jake's ear and the cop racing out of the building just seconds behind him as he left the parking lot. He watched the skies constantly for helicopters and even pulled off the road into the trees a couple of times when he thought he heard one. Sure that his people had been captured and questioned, he assumed they had a description of the truck. He warred with himself over whether to try to steal another vehicle or just keep the truck and move as fast as possible.

In the end, he decided that since he had no idea how to hotwire a car, and thus would have to either carjack somebody or get extremely lucky and find a car with keys in it, he would stick with the truck.

All of this spun through his mind as he blasted through an intersection of two county roads. He never saw the stop sign, nor the deputy sheriff's car parked in the bushes nearby. Twenty seconds later, lights and sirens blazing, the deputy's vehicle came rushing up behind him on the road.

Matt panicked. His initial response was to punch the accelerator. But the old truck was already giving all it had, and there was no way he was going to outrun the cop. So he pulled over and did his best to look innocent.

He watched the deputy approach in his driver's side mirror, his heart thudding in his chest. With his right hand, he removed his revolver from the bag on the passenger seat and tucked it under his leg, where the deputy wouldn't be able to spot it.

He heard the tap on the glass followed by, "License and registration, please."

Matt couldn't produce either. He rolled down the window using the old-style manual crank. No power locks or windows in this classic. The deputy placed a wary hand on his weapon.

"I'm… I'm sorry, officer, I'm afraid I don't have them on me. I just popped out for a quick cigarette run and didn't grab my wallet."

"Do you know why I pulled you over, sir?"

"Was I speeding? I'm sorry. It's late and I'm in a hurry to get home. There's never anybody on this road this time of night…"

"Yes, you were speeding. But you also blasted through a four-way stop back there. Interrupted my breakfast." The deputy gave him a stern look. A moment later, a lightbulb seemed to go off, and the look on his face turned to one of surprise.

"You. You're… the guy. The one everyone's looking for." He reached again for his weapon, but was too slow. Matt already had his weapon in hand. Raising it up, he pointed it out the window and pulled the trigger twice. The deputy was knocked back and fell to the ground in the middle of the road.

Matt was about to drive away when a thought struck him. The deputy probably called in the plate number before getting out of his vehicle. The authorities would quickly realize the deputy was dead when he didn't report back in or answer his radio. So the truck would be a big fat target.

And he still needed to get into Olympus. He looked in his rearview at the deputy's car with its lights still twirling. "If I put on his uniform and take his car, it might get me past the roadblock at Olympus."

Decision made, he moved fast. He opened the truck's door and leaped out. Bending down, he reached for the deputy's jacket and began to try to pull it off. He felt a little squeamish about wearing a dead man's clothes, and would have to figure out how to hide the blood stains...

He froze. "Where are the blood stains?"

Just as he started to wonder about this, the deputy rolled over with a grunt. Gun still in hand, he pointed it at Matt.

Matt saw the impossibly large barrel of the deputy's weapon pointed right at his face. He heard the gun fire the bullet that slammed into his neck, severing an artery and smashing vertebrae on its way out. Pain seared through him as he coughed up blood. His body went limp, falling to the ground and causing his head to bounce off the pavement. He lay there in disbelief, choking on his own blood as the light faded.

The deputy reached for the radio hooked to his shoulder as he dropped his weapon and felt around frantically with that hand, searching his torso. "Officer needs assistance. Suspect shot me! I... I think the vest caught both rounds. Shit, this hurts!" His fingers found first one, then another slug embedded in his vest. He looked at his hand and saw no blood. With a sigh of relief, he added, "It was the guy. The terrorist one the FBI's hunting. I got him. Shot that fucker in the face." He scooted himself off the road, leaned back against a tire, and listened as dispatch sent backup and an ambulance to his location.

*****

Alexander and Jules were sitting down to a late breakfast as Lugs woke up. His movement woke Fibble and Bacon as well. Beatrix was already up and sitting at a table, drinking coffee and holding her head.

Lugs, carrying a still-sleepy Fibble in his palm, ambled unsteadily over to take a seat with Alexander and Jules. He set the little goblin on the table and reached for the nearest pitcher. Not even checking to see what it held, he gulped down the contents.

"Ahhhh! Good party last night," he mumbled. Fibble tried to nod his head, then groaned and changed his mind. Jules took pity on them and got up to fetch them some food.

A short while later, as Fibble was 'stealing' several strips of bacon and putting them in his bag, Brick and Grumpy came walking over. Grumpy carried an object covered in cloth. When Alexander saw the familiar shape, he grinned. Brick had completed the surprise project for Fibble.

He nodded to the dwarf, who addressed their goblin minister. "Fibble. We talked it over, and decided ye needed a mount o' yer own. Besides Lugs here, we mean." He stuck a thumb at Lugs, who smiled in between shoving mouthfuls of eggs into his maw.

Fibble's eyes grew wide and he stood up on the table, bringing him nearly eye to eye with Brick. "You mean… like Tigger?"

Brick laughed and shook his head. "Not quite. This one you don't ever have to feed."

He turned to Grumpy and nodded. The dwarf grabbed hold of the cloth and whisked it off the item underneath. Then he held it up for Fibble to examine.

It was a tricycle! Fashioned after the Big Wheel that inspired it, it had a large front wheel with a chain that ran back to a gear attached to pedals. A post rose up from the front wheel to a set of wide handlebars. There was a small seat with a high back mounted just in front of two small rear wheels. The two dwarves had somehow found neon green paint and drawn flames along the side. The metal wheels were all covered in dragon hide recovered from Daginalistros, the undead dragon the demons had sent against them. The handlebar grips were wrapped in leather and had green streamers extending out both ends.

Jules clapped her hands and squealed in amusement as Lugs and several of the others chuckled. They all got to their feet to watch Fibble's reaction.

The little cookie thief stared at the contraption, tilting his head from one side to the other. Noticing everyone watching him, he tried his best to look excited. "What… what is it?"

"D'oh!" Max laughed. "He won't have ever seen a bike of any kind before."

Brick took the trike and set it down on the ground. "It's a special mount just for you. It's like a small cart, but you don't need a horse to pull it," he explained patiently. Lifting Fibble from the table, he set him on the seat. The goblin looked almost afraid to touch the thing until Jules crouched next to him.

"Here Fibble, like this." She placed his hands on the handlebars, then moved his feet to the pedals one at a time. When he was all set, she pointed to his right foot. "Okay, hold tight to the handles and push with the foot. Start it slow."

Fibble did as instructed and began to push with his foot. The pedal moved, the gear turned the chain, and the trike began to move forward. Fibble immediately screamed and leapt off the contraption. It crawled to a halt as he clung to Jules.

"It can't hurt you, sweetie!" Jules patted his head. "Come on, let's try it again. When you push the pedals, it will move. Just like if you were riding Tigger."

Fibble reluctantly got himself back on the machine. Gripping tight to the handlebars, he pushed forward with his foot. The trike moved forward a few feet and stopped. Fibble looked back to Jules, and she said, "Push with your other foot next. One… two. One… two. Just keep going. And turn the handle when you want to turn."

Fibble pushed with his other foot, then jerkily again with the first. He moved slowly toward the wall, getting the hang of it. Brick called out, "Turn!" and the little goblin obediently turned the handles to the left. He shouted "Wheeee!" when the machine obeyed his command and began to pedal faster.

As the trike picked up speed and people were having to dodge out of the way of the speeding goblin racer, Brick muttered, "Huh. We might have a problem."

Everyone looked toward the dwarf, who was looking sheepish. "I… I dinna think to put any brakes on it."

They all turned back to watch Fibble, who was now zooming toward the stables across the courtyard. His little feet were pumping hard and he was shouting something Alexander couldn't quite make out.

A moment later, Bacon stuck his head out of the stable doors as if by a summons. The war pig's eyes grew wide as he saw the goblin contraption flying toward him. Fibble, for his part, tried to turn to avoid a collision. Instead of turning smoothly at that speed, the sharp angle caused the bike to tip up and flip over. Goblin and machine bowled into Bacon, who just grunted at the impact.

A moment later, Fibble was up on his feet and jumping around. "Again!" he shouted, grabbing the tricycle and setting it upright before jumping on. He didn't go as fast this time and weaved around the courtyard, seemingly practicing his turning.

Max patted Brick on the back. "I think he's fine without brakes. As long as he doesn't get pointed downhill!"

A guild chat message appeared on all of their UIs. It was Michael.

"*It's finished. The battle is won. We... lost some people. Too many. And there is still much work to do. Anyone you could send would be appreciated.*"

The man sounded exhausted. The fight in Antalia had gone on a full day longer than Elysia's. Alexander turned to find Silverbeard but saw that his chancellor was already organizing teams. Lucas, one of the Antalia healers and new immersion players who'd been stranded in Elysia during the battle, asked, "*How's my little Sprite?*"

Tiny Sam answered. "*Pop's already asleep. Annabelle is fine. She's here at the guild house. She's been putting bandages on people with minor wounds.*" They could all hear the amusement in the young girl's voice.

Lucas looked at Alexander, who nodded and opened the portal. Before Lucas could step through, Brick shouted, "Wait!"

He ran back to the smithy and returned carrying another tricycle. "We thought mebbe yer lil Sprite might want one too. But erhmm... this one do no' have brakes either."

Lucas took it from him, thanking the dwarf. Then he winked and said, "Anybody who rode one of these as a kid knows you can just lock up the pedals and it'll go into a slide. I'll teach Annabelle what to do. And I'll bring her back here to teach Fibble!"

With that, he dashed through the portal to see his daughter. The relief teams streamed through as well, carrying loads of potions and rations. Silverbeard went with them to help organize things.

The portal closed behind them and a roll of thunder echoed across the forest. Alexander looked up at the sky just as Richard's avatar appeared. He said, "Get everyone to your quarters," then blinked out again.

Alexander used guild chat. *"All guild officers to my quarters. Now. Pop has something to tell us."* He opened the portal to Stormforge so Sasha and Lainey could return.

Five minutes later, they were all gathered in his sitting room, Sasha and Lainey having just walked in.

Richard, sitting in a padded chair near the fireplace, got right to the point. "A little while ago, I got confirmation from the FBI. Matt is dead. Killed early this morning by a deputy sheriff, apparently on his way to Olympus."

There was an assortment of cheers, sighs of relief, and fist-bumps as they celebrated the news. Alexander asked, "And you just now got confirmation?"

Richard tried not smile. "DNA confirmed it's him. Shot in the throat. Choked on his own blood."

"Couldn't happen to a nicer guy!" Max did a little touchdown dance by the fireplace.

Richard let them celebrate for a while... then cleared his throat.

"The FBI will finish cleaning up his organization. We're sure there are more of them out there, but without Howard and Matt to provide funds or leadership, they shouldn't be much of a threat. We'll stay in turtle mode for a bit longer, just to be sure."

He paused as they all nodded along. Then he changed topics. "Since we have you all here, Alexander and I would like to take this opportunity to discuss something with you." He looked to Alexander, who nodded and stood.

"You all know that my dad built the immersion pods to help me. To try to extend my life by making my brain create new connections to move my muscles. So far, the pod – along with medication – has helped me quite a bit. Maybe added several years to my life. You've all seen how much it helped Jules during her recovery." He looked around the room. Everyone there was an immersion player now and had been filled in on all the details.

"And we want to do that for others, so we've formed this Foundation. We're going to give away a lot of these pods, and use them to help people…"

When he was done explaining, every single player in the room volunteered to help.

End

Greystone Chronicles Series.

Acknowledgements

As always, I would like to the thank my family first and foremost. They are my alpha readers, co-conspirators, monster generators, (also responsible for the Tyrolean Hat of Death) and the people who tell me to stop and get some sleep when I'm exhausted, or get off my ass and work when I'm procrastinating.

I'd like to thank those among my beta readers who are willing to be publicly associated with me. Bobby Bjurstrom, Taj El McCoy, Jake Goodrich, J.D. Williams. And to those who wish to remain anonymous, I don't blame you!

My thanks to Richard Sashigane for the inventing the chick-magnet that is Fibble from a few rough sketches, and for providing the epic cuteness that is this book's cover. Also thank you L.E. Sherrard for editing the many mistakes m' fingers makes.

Most Importantly* PLEASE LEAVE A REVIEW !!*

Reviews are vitally important to indie authors like me. The quantity of reviews in part dictate whether Amazon pays any attention to the book, and helps me market it. As well as helping others decide whether the book is worth reading.

You can always find my books, art, and random interesting things at my website: www.davewillmarth.com or on twitter @davewillmarth (Yeah, I know. Twitter. I tweet now. Sort of).

Or find my other series here https://www.amazon.com/Dave-Willmarth/e/B076G12KCL/

Please check out my Greystone Guild facebook page for information on upcoming books, to hang out and chat, or ask me questions. https://www.facebook.com/greystone.guild.7

You can also get great information and reviews from Ramon Mejia's LITRPG Podcast at https://www.facebook.com/litrpgpodcast/

If you enjoyed this book, or even if you didn't, but you DO enjoy the LitRPG and GameLit genre, then I recommend you check out the following Facebook pages (you might find some authors loitering there):

https://www.facebook.com/groups/RPGGamelitSociety/

https://www.facebook.com/groups/GameLitSociety/

https://www.facebook.com/groups/LitRPGBooks/

https://www.facebook.com/groups/GameLit/